Eye of the Storm

Book 2 in the Caddo Bend Series

Mary Dan Eades

This book is a work of fiction. While certain people, place names, and historical current events of the time are real, all characters and events in this work, other than those clearly in the public domain, are fictitious, and any resemblance to situations or actual persons, living or dead, is purely coincidental. Caddo Bend exists only in the world of fiction.

ISBN: 979-8-9857878-2-5 paperback; 979-8-9857878-3-2 e-book

For the grandchildren
—Thomas, Will, Emma, Charlie, Ben, Kent, and Robbie—
who I hope will always love reading, writing, and storytelling!

ACKNOWLEDGEMENTS

I wish to gratefully acknowledge the help of a number of people, who contributed expertise in their fields to the greater accuracy of the final storyline and/or helped guide my head and hand toward a more interesting and fulfilling experience for the reader. Thanks to Deputy (ret'd) Judy Wehunt Daniell for graciously answering all my questions about how a deputy in a county sheriff's department in Arkansas would behave and what an illicit pot and drug syndicate's activities might be like. Any errors that remain in that storyline, I can assure you, are entirely mine. To Brent Peterson, for his help with Spanish translations. To my darling husband for reminding me to interject a little humor (his strong suit) as I went along and for offering some very specific suggestions about how to do it, most of which I took. To my friend Mikki Capparelli-Lally for her spot-on suggestions about starting with a bang and keeping the bang going and going. Mikki, you were right! And to my Sistas, Linda Curll Padgham and Becky Hughes, for always and ever being my tireless beta readers and suggestion givers, my most ardent fans, and my best buds. Thanks for taking this unexpected journey with me! And last, thank you to all my family and friends for supporting the series out of the gate and being willing to read it in its evolution.

Table of Contents

CHAPTER 1
Trials and Blessings

Maggie sat alone at her desk, feet propped up, reading. They'd had a light schedule today at the clinic and finished all the appointments by noon, so she'd let her staff go early to do some early Christmas shopping. She'd begged off joining them and had been enjoying solitude and soft music in the quiet of her office when her peace was shattered by the sounds of pounding and shouting out front. She sprinted to the front door before whoever it was broke it down.

"I'm coming!" She unbolted the door and threw it open. Three men stood outside. Well two men stood, one very tall and the other much shorter and squat, awkwardly supporting between them a third, who was pale, sweating, and writhing and raving like a mad man.

"Help me." The man they carried could barely breathe out the words between pants, "Help me... Please don't let me die!"

"Bring him in!" Maggie stepped back and motioned the men inside. "What's happened?

"Snake bite," the taller of the two men said, tossing his head to get the stringy blonde hair out of his face as he and his buddy struggled to carry the man inside and follow Maggie down the hallway to the treatment room. The signature smell of green marijuana rolled off them and polluted the close air of the back hallway. Skunkweed they called it, for a reason.

"Put him on the table here," she said.

"Where's the doctor at?" the shorter man asked.

"I am the doctor," Maggie said, shaking off the irritation that always welled up in her when she encountered that medieval mindset. She wrapped a blood pressure cuff around the man's left arm and took a quick reading. *155/95. High for a thin, young man.* She put her stethoscope to his chest. *Heart sounds normal, but rate well over 100 beats a minute. And he's panting like a lizard. And pale and sweating profusely.* She needed to calm him down. "Where's the bite?"

"On his right hand," the tall man said, grabbing the man's bitten hand and holding it still; the fingers, she noticed, were drawing toward his wrist in spasm. A belt was strapped tightly around his right forearm, and she immediately released it.

"What are you doing?" The tall man reached out his hand to stop her.

"Helping him," Maggie responded calmly, but firmly, evading the restraining hand. "A tourniquet doesn't really help." She glanced down at the two discreet punctures. "And neither does cutting and sucking, so thank God you didn't do that."

Maggie snapped on the bright exam light and focused it on the hand. The two small punctures were distinctly visible on his index finger, but there was minimal redness around them and no discoloration or swelling of either the finger or the rest of the very sweaty hand.

"What's your name?" she said to the victim. In response he muttered something unintelligible, and Maggie looked to his companions.

"Dak," the taller one said, then clarified, "Dakota."

"How long ago did this happen?" She looked to Dakota, but he didn't seem to even hear.

"About 30 minutes or a little more," the tall friend answered. "We drove him here quick as we could."

Maggie's training had been in the city, in an uptown urban hospital in Manhattan. Plenty of stabbings, gunshot wounds, and overdoses, but she'd never seen a snake bite let alone treated one firsthand. To be fair, there probably weren't a lot of venomous snakes on the upper West Side. She closed her eyes to dredge deeply into her memory banks, all the way back to med school classes, to parasitology lectures, which at the time she thought an odd place to learn about venomous bites. She dimly recalled that most snake bites were dry, defensive not offensive—meaning the viper didn't choose to waste its venom when it didn't need to—and that serious envenomation was rare, but that when it did occur, it often resulted in the rapid onset of discoloration, swelling, and necrosis—tissue death—at the site. Or systemic cardiovascular or neurologic symptoms—body wide heart and nerve issues—depending on the toxin in question, which of course meant depending on the species of snake.

"Did you see the snake?"

"Yeah, we did," the tall man responded. "Dak leaned over and dropped his smokes out of his shirt pocket, and they fell in a bush by the porch. When he reached down to get them, it nailed him. Late in the year for it; musta been keeping warm under the porch. Fang got hooked on his finger! He had to bang it on the fuckin' porch post to get it off him for Christ's sake. I cut its damn head off. It was a cottonmouth; it's in the bed of the truck if you wanta see."

"No. No need." Maggie had a deep, abiding, nothing-short-of-primal fear of snakes and had no intention of meeting this culprit face to fang. She'd get the patient stabilized and then go look up that specific snake online. And even that digital encounter would probably give her the creeps. She cleaned the punctures, then took a roll of self-adhering bandage tape from the drawer and wrapped it around the finger and hand, past his wrist and up his forearm to put even, dry pressure on the entire area. He twisted and rolled his head from side to side. "Dakota?" Maggie shook his shoulders. "Dakota? Can you hear me?"

Wild eyed and between pants he responded, "Uh huh... I hear ya." His body was quivering from head to toe. "I'm t-t-tingling all over." He clamped his sweaty, free hand around her wrist. "Please don't let me die."

"Listen to me. I know you're frightened, but I think this was a dry bite. Do you understand what that is?" Maggie brought her face closer to his, trying to focus his attention.

He closed his eyes and shook his head rapidly back and forth. "Please don't let me die. Please don't let me die! My brother died of a snake bite."

Aha! There's the cause of his panic. Maggie disengaged from his hand, opened a crash cart drawer, and pulled out a brown paper lunch sack. Low tech equipment but extremely effective. She shook it open, put it over his mouth and nose, and held it in place, ignoring the skeptical looks from his cohorts. "Here we go. Breathe deeply now. Slowly...slowly...in and out. That's it." His panic was the issue, she realized, not the bite. Though a snake bite could cause some of the symptoms he displayed, she suspected he was experiencing *hypocarbia*—his blood levels of carbon dioxide had gotten too low from his rapid panicked breathing. Rebreathing his exhaled air would raise the levels back to normal. That alone would drop his rapid heart rate, slow his anxious breathing, lower his elevated blood pressure, stop the tingling, and relax the spasmodic drawing of his wrists and fingers. "Just breathe. In and out. Deeply and slowly."

In a few minutes, once he was a bit more relaxed and stable, Maggie explained the situation. "Most snake bites don't result in the snake injecting venom. They're called *dry bites*. It's terrifying, of course, especially if someone you know died from a snake bite. But I'm pretty sure there was no venom here, or at least no more than the tiniest trace amount. I feel confident that you're going to be fine, but you really ought to be monitored for a while to be sure. I'd like to send you over to the hospital where if you needed it, they could administer the appropriate antivenin; I don't have that here. The closest place is Mercy General at Hot Springs."

"I... I... don't really want to go to a hospital," Dakota said.

"Why not?" Maggie replied.

"Can't afford it; lost my job and don't have insurance no more." He looked away from her gaze and cocked his head toward his buddies. "That's why they brought me here."

"I understand. I can start an IV and watch you here for a little while, but if the situation changes for the worse, you'll need to go to the hospital. OK?"

"IV? That's a needle. Do you have to?" He was still slightly agitated, as evidenced by the thin film of sweat on his upper lip, but he'd settled down considerably from his previously overwrought state.

Maggie persuaded him to let her start the IV drip, as a precaution, just to keep a vein open in case she might need it. And stuck cardiac leads to his chest and limbs to monitor his heart, relieved at the very normal if still slightly rapid heart rhythm that appeared on the display. She felt confident that if all his vitals held stable over the next couple of hours, there would be little risk to sending him home with his friends and following him up in a day or two.

"I'm going to give you a prescription for an antibiotic to take for a few days," she said. "It's generic and shouldn't cost you too much, but we don't want it to get infected. I think I've got a couple of sample capsules of it I can start you on before you go. And for the record, when was your last tetanus shot?"

He shrugged. "I dunno. Long while ago, I expect."

"More than ten years?"

"Yeah, probably. Junior high, maybe."

"OK. Then we need to get that up to date."

"Do I have to? I really ain't much of a fan of needles." He pushed his sweaty bangs out of his face with his free hand.

"You wouldn't be much of a fan of tetanus, either. It can be fatal, and even when it's not recovery can come at the end of a very long and expensive hospital stay. Besides, the shot's not as bad as the IV." She patted his shoulder and turned to his companions. "You guys stay here with him. I'll just step into the lab to draw up his tetanus booster and be right back."

She stepped first, however, into her office and thought about calling Tee and Donna back. *No real reason to*, she reasoned. *I can handle this without them.* She laid the phone back down, noting as she did that her battery strength was in the red; she plugged the phone into its charger and sat down at her desk to do a quick online search for journal information on cottonmouth bites. She found an article and read:

"Also known as the Water Moccasin, the Western Cottonmouth is among the deadliest species on the planet."

Then farther down the article she found the bits she was specifically looking for:

"Typically, there is immense swelling and discoloration with envenomation, usually starting within five minutes; infection from the bites is common."

And perhaps the most important bit:

"Fortunately, there is antivenin for these bites."

The article recommended observation for six to eight hours post bite, even if it looked to have been dry. If he was adamant about not going to the hospital, she'd need to keep him around for a few more hours anyway to be safe.

She went to the lab and loaded a syringe with a dose of tetanus vaccine and returned to the trio to give him the shot, which she was relieved he accepted without much objection. She snapped off the used needle and tossed it into the sharps jug and the syringe into the biohazard can, then warned him the shot could make his shoulder muscle sore tomorrow. Warm compresses and some ibuprofen would help if needed. Then she imparted the welcome news that if it were necessary—and she stressed, yet again, that she didn't think it would be—there was antivenin to counteract the venom of this snake species.

"Dakota, I'd like to keep you here for a few more hours, then barring anything new turning up, I think you'll be OK to go."

"Hours? Dude," said the short friend, hitching up his drooping jeans. "Marty's gonna kill us. And besides I could eat the ass out of a-" he stopped short, eying Maggie. "Uh, I mean…uh, sorry, ma'am." Then with a more reserved demeanor he turned back to his friend. "OK if we run over to that diner we saw and grab a burger?"

"Sure," Dakota said. "Can you bring me one, too? With cheese. And some fries. And a coke?"

"What kinda coke?"

"Dr. Pepper, if they got it."

It had struck Maggie as odd when she'd first arrived in Arkansas to hear people refer to all soft drinks as 'a coke' whether they meant a Fanta Grape soda, a Dr. Pepper, or a Mountain Dew it was still 'let's go get a coke'. *Strange.* But then, she supposed, no stranger than calling them *pop* or the word she'd grown up with *soda*. Around here like kleenex was the generic name for all tissues, coke was universal for fuzzy, sweetened beverages.

She noted that Dakota's color had improved markedly and, clearly, his appetite was back. She'd be babysitting him for a couple of hours but felt confident he was going to be fine. And, indeed, by 4:30 nothing untoward had developed with her patient. The bite site looked fine; there was no discoloration or damage visible to the surrounding tissues. He was duly boosted against tetanus. His blood pressure, pulse, and respirations had all returned to normal and remained stable. And he'd been well fed, courtesy of his skunky-smelling friends. She'd given him his sample antibiotic dose and a prescription for more, then signed him off to the care of his compatriots and locked the door behind them. And left a note for Donna explaining it all. She hoped.

Maggie, though a dedicated and capable doctor, hadn't a clue about how to generate a computer bill for service or take a payment, so she'd just jotted down everything she'd used and the services performed for Donna to sort out later. She'd told Dakota she'd have Donna mail or email the bill to him, but he'd said he didn't really have an address where he could get mail and no email account. So, she'd told him he could pay when he returned to have her check the bite again. Skepticism and experience told her he might not show, but so be it. She'd taken an oath to help those who needed help if she could, and so she had. She couldn't in good conscience have done otherwise, paid or not. But the interlude had unsettled her a little, and it troubled her some that she had been alone and had opened the door to three rather unsavory-looking characters who might have done her harm. They hadn't, of course, which was a good thing, but she realized she was too trusting of the good intentions of others. She made a mental note to consider upgrading the security of the clinic somehow then turned off the lights and headed home.

Thursday had dawned bright and clear and significantly colder than it had been in the last week or so. Maggie's breath came in visible puffs as she jogged easily along the country road in the early morning chill. Four or five mornings a week, after yoga, she'd do her cross-training workout of the day, or WOD as it was called; today she had scheduled as a rest day as far as workouts were concerned, and her plan had been to do zip, but she'd opted for a run after her yoga salutation. The morning had been simply too gorgeous to ignore, and the surprise of waking to near-freezing Arkansas temperatures reminded her of autumns in New York. So, she twisted her long blonde hair up under a fleece cap, donned a light-weight thermal jacket over a long-sleeved t-shirt and running tights, and headed out. She made a loop that took her from McSwain's Boarding House—the comfy Victorian lodging in town where she had boarded since her arrival—along the road that ran past her clinic and down to the low water bridge over the Caddo River and back, about a four-mile circuit. When she got to the bridge, she ran to the middle and stopped to look down into the water, now as placid and clear as it had been the day that she'd first driven across it into Caddo Bend last summer. Yet it was right here not so many days ago that she'd come precariously close to dying young, as her still bruised and aching shoulder reminded her. Here, where a sociopath had tried to kill her and two others in the raging torrent of the flooded river. But today was Thanksgiving Day, and despite all that had happened, she had a lot to be thankful for. It was here where she'd first realized that after so many lonely years adrift, she might have finally found a place that felt like home. And JD.

She'd promised Miz Hendri, the grandmotherly proprietrix of the boarding house, that she'd be back by mid-afternoon to help her with the last-minute chores for their Thanksgiving dinner, something she was very much looking forward to. But first she wanted to drive over to the hospital in nearby Hot Springs to look in on the two other victims who had been in the car with her on the river that night: Rose Ellen Prescott, the young girl who had nearly drowned and the girl's father, Waylon, who'd been shot. With one last look at the bridge, she whispered a prayer of thanks for her good fortune and jogged back home. After a long, hot shower, she made the 45-minute drive in her loaner, pulling up in the Mercy General Hospital parking lot a hair after 9 am.

Maggie had stopped at a grocery store on the way to pick up a helium-filled mylar balloon—a Tom Turkey, complete with jaunty Pilgrim's hat—to take to Rose Ellen. The little girl was recovering nicely; her doctors at Mercy felt she would be in the hospital for only a few days longer, but the greater issue was what would happen then? She wasn't quite eight years old and currently without either parent, because the awful truth they'd all learned that harrowing night on the river was that Rose Ellen's mother had not simply walked away from her family two years ago, as had been thought, but had been killed by the same sociopath who had tried to kill them all that night on the bridge. And sadder still that her father had been at least complicit in covering up the death, which was why a police officer now sat outside his hospital room.

Maggie stopped and checked in at the surgical ward nurse's station to get her clearance to visit him then walked down to the door. The uniformed officer stood as she approached.

"May I see your identification, ma'am?" the officer said.

Maggie handed him her driver's license, which he took and compared to the Approved Visitor's List on his clipboard. Finding her name, he handed her back the ID. "I'll need you to leave your bag and the balloon out here, Dr. McKinley." Maggie handed him her purse and the floating turkey and waited as he looped the ribbon of the helium balloon around the arm of his chair and gave her a quick pat down. "You're not allowed to give the prisoner anything, not even food or drink, or use a mobile phone inside. The room is video monitored."

"Yes," Maggie said, "I understand. Thank you."

"Ten minutes," he said. "I'll be out here if you need me."

Maggie stepped inside the room to find Waylon Prescott lying in the hospital bed, propped up slightly on a couple of pillows. The curtains were drawn, and the room was quiet, somber, and dark except for the flashing light of an IV infusion pump and the blipping trace of a heart monitor. She crossed to the window and opened the curtains a little, letting some soft morning light into the room, then moved back to stand beside the bed. She was surprised to see that his dark brown hair was cut and combed and had a distinguished touch of silver she'd never noticed before at the temples. And he'd been recently shaved, revealing a chiseled face with a lot of character. It occurred to her that she'd never seen him that way. In the few months she'd known him—since her first day as the new doc at Caddo Bend, when she'd been called on to sew up his daughter's bleeding scalp laceration—he'd been reliably unkempt, unpleasant, and usually hung over.

"Mr. Prescott? Waylon? It's Maggie McKinley," she said gently, touching his arm. He was a big man, but lying in the bed, connected to monitors and infusion lines, he seemed frail and vulnerable.

He opened his eyes and said hoarsely, "How's Rosie?"

"I haven't been up to see her yet, but I spoke to Dr. Hill, the pediatrician in charge of her case, last night, and he assured me she's doing very well. How about you?"

"Guess, I'll live," he said softly. "Got a few tubes I didn't have before. For a while at least." He closed his eyes and lapsed into silence, and she thought he might have fallen back to sleep, but then he looked up at her, his earnest eyes searching her face, "Think they'll let me see her before they take me outta here?"

"I think so. Dr. Hill seemed to think it would be very good for her to see you. You were amazingly lucky that shotgun blast didn't do too much permanent damage to anything vital in your gut, but your surgery wasn't a small thing, and you've still got some recuperative work ahead of you. She'll probably get discharged before you do."

An anxious, pained expression crossed his face. "Aw hell. What's she gonna do? She can't go back to the farm all by herself."

"No, of course she can't," she reassured him, glancing up at the monitor and noting that his heart rate had ticked up to 90 beats per minute. "Don't worry; I'll personally make sure she's well cared for. I've been working hand in hand with Child Protective Services, and they think they've found a qualified foster couple in the county willing to take her until you're back on your feet and all your legal issues are resolved."

"Why the hell'd I ever listen to the bastard?" He looked positively miserable, then quietly added, "Sorry."

"That's a pretty accurate description, as far as I'm concerned. We were all taken in by him. Every one of us, except maybe JD. The guy's a true sociopath, and they can be extremely charming and persuasive. And, unfortunately, often dangerous. Miz Hendri's beside herself over it. He lived at her boarding house for 3 years. She'd treated him like family."

"Shoulda turned the sumbitch in right when it happened," Waylon whispered harshly, bunching the sheets in his hands and, Maggie noted, sending the heart monitor to 100. "Shouldn't've let him talk me into keeping quiet. Just too damn wasted that night to think straight," he shook his head sadly. "Then too scared later that if I told they'd take Rosie. She's all I have left. And now…" he trailed off.

"She's going to be fine. You'll see," she said, giving his hand a reassuring squeeze. "And before I forget, Mr. Purifoy offered to check on the hens, make sure they're fed and watered, gather the eggs and winterize the vegetable garden. If you've got a list somewhere of your customers, he says he'll arrange to keep the egg deliveries going while you're away."

Waylon, if anything, looked even more miserable than before. Finally, he looked up and met her gaze. "There's a ledger book in the Hoosier cabinet in the kitchen. Tell him I don't know how to repay his kindness. But tell him when I can I'm gonna try."

The officer rapped on the door as he stuck his head in. "Time's up, ma'am."

"OK," Maggie replied. She turned back to Waylon. "I'm going to go up now and check on Rose Ellen, OK?"

"Yeah. Will you tell her I … tell her-" His voice broke, and he clenched his eyes shut, pressing his thumb and fingers over his lids.

"I'll tell her that you're okay and getting stronger, that you're thinking of her and that you love her. And that you'll see her as soon as you can."

Waylon nodded and swallowed hard then gave her a tight, sad smile. "Thanks," he whispered. "Tell her I'm so sorry."

"You can tell her that when you see her," Maggie said and quietly closed the door.

The pediatric ward was a couple of floors up, and Maggie took the stairs rather than brave a crowded elevator again with Tom Turkey in tow; her floating friend had nearly gotten itself trapped between the closing doors as she got off before. She walked up the two flights and down the hall to Rose Ellen's door, which was slightly ajar, and tapped lightly, letting the balloon squeeze through the gap and float into the room.

"Can we come in?" Maggie said from the corridor.

Rose Ellen's joyful squeal greeted the turkey's appearance. "Yes!"

Maggie followed the balloon inside, thrilled to hear the happiness in the child's voice. Actually, she was overjoyed to hear her voice at all, since when Maggie had come to Caddo Bend and first encountered the girl in the clinic, she suffered from traumatic aphasia and hadn't spoken a word in the couple of years after her mother had disappeared. Or rather, as they now sadly understood, after she'd been murdered. Rose Ellen's psychiatrist had briefed Maggie on her case last night by phone, relating that the girl had confided to her that she'd witnessed the event. Maggie could only imagine how traumatic that had been for a 5-year-old child. She'd been present herself, at 13, when her own parents had been killed in a car crash that she'd survived. She'd seen their mangled bodies and sobbed, alone and afraid on that desolate river bridge. But even that, awful as it had been, was nothing like seeing your mother bludgeoned to death before your eyes.

"Hey, sweetie. How are you feeling?" Maggie laid a hand softly on Rosie's knee.

"Good," she said simply and brushed a strand of her honey-brown hair out of her eyes.

"What are you doing there?" Maggie indicated the picture Rose Ellen was busily coloring. It was a turkey she'd made by outlining the shape of her hand, with each tail feather colored a different vibrant hue. "That's beautiful. Your Tom Turkey balloon will have a friend."

"Uh huh," she said. "But this one's for my daddy. I can make another one."

Maggie's swallowed to try to relax the lump that formed in her throat. This poor, sweet child, her mother forever gone and her father facing probable jail time or worse, and here she is coloring beautiful pictures. "He's going to love it," she said softly; it was all she could manage for a moment. She cleared her throat and went on, "I stopped in to see him on the way up. He's doing well and getting stronger, and he told me to tell you that he loves you and can't wait to see you."

"I love him, too," she said softly. "Can I go see him?"

"Not just yet, but soon, I think," Maggie said, then searching to redirect the conversation she added, "Hey, would you like to watch the Macy's Thanksgiving Day parade with me? I think it should be on now."

"What is it?" Rose Ellen asked.

"It's a huge parade they have every year on Thanksgiving in New York City, where I used to live," Maggie said, incredulous that a 7-year-old child had never seen the annual spectacle. "You've never watched it on tv?"

"No, ma'am. We don't have one at our house."

"Well, let's do it now!" Maggie said.

Tuning the television in the room to the local NBC affiliate station, they settled in to watch together. The marching bands and enormous floats with singers and dancers stretched for miles down Central Park West headed toward Sixth Avenue and finally down to Herald Square in front of Macy's department store, cheered on by the massive crowds that had braved the cold very early on Thanksgiving morning to get a ring-side spot for viewing. Rose Ellen declared the huge Hello Kitty and Kermit the Frog balloons were her favorites, though Pikachu was a close runner up. Maggie agreed they were pretty wonderful, but said her heart still belonged to Good Ol' Charlie Brown.

Seeing New York again on such a beautiful autumn day, the state she'd grown up in, the city where she'd spent the last seven years in med school and residency, made Maggie's heart ache. It brought back a flood of happy memories of her time there, especially the past three years with Jeff. They'd watched last year's parade together in person from VIP viewing seats he'd secured, then strolled in the crisp fall air hand-in-hand along the twenty-five or so blocks back up Sixth Avenue to his building on Central Park West. But with those memories also came the gut-wrenching and still-fresh pain of her discovery a few weeks ago of his callous betrayal of their commitment. She'd made her decision that she couldn't stay with a man who would so quickly and casually betray her trust. The rightness of that decision was made clear to her in the maelstrom on the bridge, when another man had so willingly risked his own life to save hers. And Rose Ellen's and her father's. But it still hurt. She forced down the unhappy thoughts and focused on the delight of watching her young patient experience her first Macy's Thanksgiving Day celebration. Just as the parade drew to a close, and Santa finally made his way down the avenue on his sleigh, an aide brought in Rose Ellen's lunch, and it was time for Maggie to go.

"I'm going to head back to Caddo Bend now. Miz Hendri is expecting me back by two. You enjoy your turkey and dressing – and eat all your lunch, OK?"

"Do I have to eat this?" Rose Ellen pointed with a doleful stare at the jellied cranberry slice on her plate, then popped a neon orange cube of Jell-O into her mouth. The thought instantly entered Maggie's head: *if she can eat that wiggly, orange glop, she can eat anything.*

"You should try it," Maggie advised. "It's kind of sweet and tart all at once; you might like it. But if you don't, it's not a holiday requirement. Just be sure to eat all your turkey and drink your milk, OK? I'll be back soon."

"OK. Will you take this to my daddy," she asked, handing Maggie the drawing.

"I will, sweetie. I'll be sure he gets it."

Maggie took the drawing down the two flights and directly to the nurse's station where she explained what she needed to the charge nurse. Together, she and the nurse walked the artwork down to the officer at Waylon's door, let him examine it, and the two of them sweet talked him into allowing the nurse tape it to the wall beside Waylon's bed where he could see it. "There's nothing like the unconditional love of a child to help a wounded soul heal," she told the officer. And he had agreed.

Maggie pulled into the back lot of McSwain's Boarding House—or Miz Hendri's place as everybody in town called it—and came through the back door into the warm kitchen awash in a symphony of aromas of roasting poultry, sage, garlic, onion, brown butter, nutmeg, and cinnamon. And to Miz Hendri, herself, hoisting a golden-brown turkey out of the oven.

"Wow! He's beautiful!" Maggie exclaimed. "Can I help?"

"No, no," the robust old lady said, setting the heavy roaster on the stovetop grates and tenting foil over the bird, then continuing in her thickly German-accented English, "I think in here everything is just about ready. You could fill the water glasses and light the candles, if you would," she said, wiping her hands on the white apron she always wore in the kitchen. "And open the wine."

"Wine?" Maggie asked, incredulous. *Did I hear her right?* She'd never seen Miz Hendri take so much as a sip of liquor. There was a little sherry for the guests kept in a decanter on the sideboard in the front room, but that was all Maggie had ever seen in the way of alcoholic refreshment in the five months or so she'd lived there, apart from a bit she'd bought herself to keep in her room. Since Miz Hendri was a regular on Sunday at the non-denominational church in town, she'd assumed that maybe the woman opposed drinking on religious grounds.

"It's cooling. In the ice box," Miz Hendri said with a nod in the direction of the refrigerator.

Maggie looked inside with a little trepidation, fearing the worst about what sort of wine might be chilling within, and had to admit both her relief and delight to find a few bottles of a nice, dry rosé from the Rhone Valley. A lovely wine, she thought, perfectly suited for turkey and all the competing flavors in its variety of traditional trimmings. Maggie wasn't much of a cook herself, but she enjoyed a good meal – and good wine – whole heartedly. She grabbed the ice bucket from the counter, filled it from the big commercial ice maker on the back porch, and went to the formal dining room to fill the water glasses.

The table was set for six with a pale gold damask cloth, darker gold and sage green striped linen napkins, silver flatware, and sparkling crystal. The ivory china had a delicate gold-rim outside an ornate, vibrant band and a central cornucopia of fruits and flowers. Maggie picked up a plate and turned it over: Lenox Autumn it was stamped. *Simply beautiful.* And a lovely contrast sitting on heavily beaded forest green chargers. An impressive, low arrangement of autumn flowers, fruit, and greenery sat center table, flanked either side by groupings of pillar candles of differing heights.

"These flowers are incredible," Maggie said loudly enough for Miz Hendri to hear her as she came waddling in from the kitchen with trivets to protect the buffet from the hot dishes of food.

"Yes. They came this morning if you can imagine."

"I didn't know they delivered flowers on Thanksgiving," Maggie said, admiring the lush arrangement – clusters of orange and deep crimson roses, yellow button mums, pale green hydrangeas, deep purple anemones, shocks of wheat and silvery eucalyptus, broad shiny green magnolia leaves, brown lotus pods, and interspersed with apples and oranges. It was simply magnificent.

"*Ach*! I was very surprised, too. And so lovely and large; I didn't think you'd mind if I put them on the table."

"Why would I mind?" Maggie asked, puzzled.

"They are for you. From an admirer, maybe? There is a card," she said, indicating the envelope on the table beside the arrangement as she headed back to the kitchen.

Maggie picked up the envelope and opened it. The card inside read:

"Happy Thanksgiving. Wishing you were here with me and

praying you'll find a way to give me another chance. I love you~ J"

Maggie stuck the card back into the envelope. They were from Jeff, the man she'd been in a relationship with for the past three years. Uber-rich, fun-loving, drop-dead gorgeous, Manhattan-trauma-surgeon Jeff. The guy who'd recently shattered her heart. She hadn't divulged to Miz Hendri or anyone else much about Jeff. At least no one locally. Only her dearest friend, Charlotte, her college roomie, her 'sista from anotha motha' knew every detail. Her staff at the clinic and everyone at the boarding house knew that Maggie had a boyfriend – a beau as Miz Hendri charmingly called him – back in New York, and that she'd flown there a few weekends ago to surprise him with a visit. And she figured they'd probably surmised that the visit hadn't gone smoothly, as she'd come home somewhat less attached than when she left. But not the why of it.

What they didn't know was that when Maggie had tip-toed into his darkened bedroom early that Saturday morning and opened the draperies to enjoy the surprised look on his face, she'd been the one surprised. Shocked, more like, to find him in a tangle of sheets with his former girlfriend. She hadn't been gone from New York but a few months, and he was cheating on her with Judith Rawlins! Even now the remembered image nauseated her. She'd fled back to Arkansas. He'd followed, and she'd sent him away, telling her she would need lots of space to see if she could forgive it and trust him again. And she forewarned him she wasn't sure she could. She had too much loss and pain in her past to sign up for anyone she couldn't count on to be there for her one hundred percent, to have her back, to be true always.

And then JD had come into her life. Actually, he'd done more than just come in, he'd *saved* her life that terrifying night on the bridge. And she'd realized he'd always quietly been there since the moment they'd met on the road as she first drove into town—steady, solid, kind. He was charming, and they'd become easy friends from the jump. But a powerful bond had formed between them that night when they'd saved one another, like the instantaneous vitrification of sand struck by lightning, the substance itself forever changed in a blinding flash. And the relationship that formed had blossomed with each passing day. She took the card to the kitchen and dropped it into the trash can.

The doorbell chimed.

"I'll get it," Maggie said, heading for the front hall. She opened the door to find Velma Bradford, Miz Hendri's cousin by marriage and the local postmistress, smiling back at her, and behind Velma, her son Ben, holding a beautifully decorated pumpkin cheesecake. Maggie opened the screen for them and saw JD just pulling up out front and getting out of his truck.

"Sugar free, Doc" Velma pointed a thumb to the cheesecake, somehow knowing Maggie's thought before she could even voice it. She was a patient of Maggie's and a type 1 diabetic. And eerily prescient. "With a nut crust," she added with a lift of her brows and knowing nod.

"Sounds fabulous," Maggie replied. "I may have to join you in a slice of that! Come on in; dinner's almost ready."

Giving each of them a warm hug, she invited them to make themselves comfortable in the dining room. Then she waited on the porch as JD came up the walk carrying a bottle. He was dressed simply, as he usually was, in a pair of dark jeans, a sage green chambray shirt, and a buttery soft cognac leather bomber jacket. A broad smile lit up his tan, handsome face reaching all the way to the crinkled corners of his mesmerizing gray eyes. When he met her at the door, he tipped her chin up with his fingertips and bent to graze her lips with a light kiss.

"Happy Thanksgiving, gorgeous lady," he said.

"It is," Maggie agreed. "I honestly think I feel happier and more thankful today than at any Thanksgiving in memory," she added standing on tiptoe to kiss him again. Breathing in the scent of the cold air on his skin, the faint undercurrents of sandalwood soap and leather, she was truly grateful and felt blessed.

"That's just what I was hoping to hear," he said. He wrapped an arm around her, and they went inside.

Emmanuel Purifoy came into the dining room carrying a side dish to the buffet. White-haired, fit, and trim, the 70-something gentleman had been a dear friend of Miz Hendri and her late husband Robert's for over fifty years, and since Robert's passing had helped her take care of the property. When he saw Maggie, he beamed. "Happy Thanksgiving, Maggie!" He set down the casserole dish and oven mitts and came to give her a warm hug, then offered his hand and greeted JD.

"Same to you, Papa," Maggie said, using the familiar honorific they had agreed to on her arrival, when she'd asked him to call her Maggie instead of Doc or ma'am, and in return he'd asked her to call him Manny instead of Mr. Purifoy, which as someone young enough to be his granddaughter she simply couldn't bring herself to do. So, Papa had been their compromise, and she freely admitted, as a woman without parents or grandparents or for that matter any living family at all, that simple gesture made her happier than something so seemingly small had a right to do.

Miz Hendri came in from the kitchen bearing the golden-brown turkey perched regally on an ornate serving platter. She set it down with a flourish on the buffet to the oohs and aahs of everybody there.

"JD, would do us the service to carve?" Miz Hendri said, clasping her hands in front of her good 'Sunday' apron and backing away.

"Yes, ma'am. I'd be honored," he said with a slight, almost courtly, bow. "And this," he said with a wink as he handed her the bottle he carried, "is for after this beautiful meal."

"Calvados! My favorite, you know," she said.

"Yes, ma'am. I do. You and my mama."

JD picked up the antler-handled carving set beside the platter and went to work, quickly removing the leg quarters and slicing up dark meat, then removing the breast halves and slicing them so that each piece got some of the delicious crisp skin. Maggie was fascinated by his hands and loved watching them work. Their shape was strong and yet refined, their movements graceful like those of an artist, efficient and effortless. As she watched him carving, Maggie found her thoughts drifting back to the memory of those hands and the delights they'd brought to her body not so very many nights ago, and she was only able to pull herself forcibly back to the present when she heard Miz Hendri's voice.

"Please, please," Miz Hendri said, "everyone, bring your plate; eat while it is hot." And to a person everyone was happy to comply.

The food was delicious, and Maggie had just sat back down with a most uncharacteristic small second helping of almost everything – turkey, cornbread stuffing, roasted Brussels' sprouts, candied yams, whipped potatoes and gravy, homemade whole cranberry sauce. She had some of everything except the yeast rolls and butter, but she made up for that with a double second helping of a green pea and asparagus casserole in a cheesy cream sauce. It was a once or twice a year dietary splurge, so she refused to feel any guilt. Everything was delicious, including, she felt sure, Velma's pumpkin cheesecake, which she needed to leave at least a smidgen of room for.

"Hendri," Mr. Purifoy said, "you have outdone yourself this year."

"*Ach*! Thank you, Manny," she said, patting his hand. "It is nice to have appreciative people to cook for. And besides, Thanksgiving has been my favorite holiday since Robert brought me to America. 1962 it was. We had just been married in my hometown in Germany. Munich." She gave his hand a squeeze and another pat. "Manny remembers; he was Robert's best man."

"That I was. That I was," he looked at her with a bit of mischief in his eyes. "I remember how nervous he was and how pretty you were. I was a little jealous; I can tell you that now. Fifty-year rule," he chuckled. She smiled warmly and went on.

"Robert and I came across on a ship," she said, shaking her head at the memory. "High winds and rough seas tossing us for days," she said with some exasperation. "Never have I been so sick! Then we arrived at last in New York, and it was like I was dreaming when we sailed by the Statue of Liberty. My heart nearly burst with joy to see it. Then we took a train half the way across the country. So vast! I couldn't comprehend it. Finally, after more than two days," she said, raising her brows and two fingers for emphasis, "we arrived at the depot in Hot Springs. Robert's father met us at the station and drove us here. I was very nervous to meet his parents; I was young—just 19—and my English wasn't so good as it is now, but they welcomed me right away." She dabbed the corners of her mouth with her napkin, then smiled, eyes unfocused in a misty way at the memory. "It was just a few days after we arrived that we enjoyed our first Thanksgiving together right here at this table," she said, patting and smoothing the cloth on either side of her plate. "After all my family had been through in the years of the war and after the war—the turmoil, the scarcity, the devastation I grew up in—to come here, a young bride of a handsome American soldier, to come to all this beauty and bounty, it was unbelievable. In all my life I think I have never been more thankful than I was that day, and I try to remember that feeling every year."

Everyone was quiet for a moment when Ben broke the silence. "I'd really like to see New York," he said. "Go see Miss Liberty and the 9/11 memorial and all. Pay my respects."

"It's amazing," Maggie said quietly. "I've seen it several times. My..." she stopped short then continued, "my friend and I got to go there on September 11th a year ago when it opened. It's very moving, and the museum is completely awe inspiring. And heartbreaking. You'd really," she stopped again then continued, "no... I almost said you'd enjoy it, but you won't enjoy it, because of what it is; it's not enjoyable. But it's important, and you'll definitely be deeply moved by it."

"I sure would like to go," Ben said, and then after a pause he grinned like a kid rather than the deputy sheriff he was and added, "and I'd like to see that big lit-up Christmas tree." Two things as different as night is from day, but that was quintessential New York City— something for everybody.

"Well, Benji, you better put that on your Christmas wish list then," Velma said. "How's Santa supposed to know you want something if it ain't on your list?"

"Mama," he laughed, "I'm 23 years old. That's a little big to sit on Santa's lap."

"Don't be too sure. Santa's got a big lap," JD added with a softly exhaled *hmph*. He reached across the table and squeezed Maggie's hand. "How was Rosie this morning?"

"Good," she nodded. "She's good. Drew a picture for her dad, which by some miracle the charge nurse and I persuaded the duty officer to let her tape up in his room. We watched the Macy's parade, which I couldn't believe she had never seen, and she enjoyed that. Physically she's doing great; she'll probably be released in a day or two. And emotionally I think she's starting to heal finally," Maggie said.

"That poor child," Miz Hendri said. "What will happen when she is released? There is nobody for her."

"Yeah," Maggie said, "that's the major issue. Child Protective Services has spoken to a couple here in town – you all know Tom and Becky Davis – and barring any complication, they're willing to foster her until things are sorted out with Waylon's case, and we see what happens there.

"They've got a baby girl coming before too long, don't they?" Velma said.

"They do in about 4 months, but even I don't know the gender."

"Well, I do. It's going to be a girl," Velma said with a nod of complete confidence.

"We don't know for sure yet, but far be it for me to go against your intuition, Miss Velma." Maggie raised her brows and pursed her lips, "Either way, boy or girl, they've still got plenty of room, and it's a loving family atmosphere. And she'd have Charlie—who's only a couple of years younger and a little ball of fire—for company. If it works out, I think that would be a wonderful placement for her, until whatever's going to happen with Waylon happens."

"And what will that be?" Miz Hendri asked, looking to Ben.

"Well, ma'am, I reckon it depends on how much he cooperates with the case against Freeman," Ben said, reaching for the plate of crudité. "They say he admits he was there when it happened, so they could go for a felony murder charge. I figure they might offer him some leniency, though, for helpin' the prosecution." He took a green onion and several carrots and pieces of celery from the tray and deposited them onto his plate. "Then he did cover up the killing, too. Maybe his lawyers can make the case he was under duress." He crunched a bite from a piece of celery.

"And Nicholas? What will happen to him?" Miz Hendri asked, her eyes sad.

"I reckon he's going away for a long spell, but innocent until proven, you know," Ben said. "Even if his story holds up—he claims he didn't mean to kill Ruth—it's involuntary manslaughter at least. Probably with enhancements, being he did it while committing a felony and then covered up the crime, so that right there's probably enough for a felony murder charge. Then there's charges for the GBH and assault with a deadly weapon and attempted murder of three additional individuals on top of that. I don't see him getting out for a good long while, if ever. They could go for the death penalty on it."

Miz Hendri closed her eyes and put a shocked hand over her mouth. "*Ach*! He always seemed like such a nice young man." She shook her head in disbelief. "Polite and funny. Helpful. How does somebody like that do such things?"

"He's a classic sociopath," Maggie said. "Charming, engaging, persuasive. They make great con men; they fool people all the time. And sometimes do terrible things that nobody saw coming. I'm a doctor, and I didn't see it."

Maggie stood and began to clear the table. Miz Hendri protested that she'd do it, but Maggie insisted. "You cooked. Now you relax. JD and I will get the dishes into the kitchen. Velma, would you slice the cheesecake? And we'll sit together and enjoy our dessert and coffee."

"And Calvados," Miz Hendri added with a sly smile at JD.

JD and Maggie brought the stacks of dirty dishes to the kitchen and sat them beside the big farmhouse sink. JD scraped the bits of food into the trash; Maggie rinsed and stacked the china and loaded up what could go into the dishwasher. When they'd finished, he handed her a dry towel and then put his arms around her and drew her into a long embrace. She wrapped her arms around his waist and nestled her head against his chest, feeling utter contentment.

"Did anybody ever tell you what a beautiful person you are, inside and out?" JD murmured against her hair. "I feel like I'd been waiting my whole life for the woman of my dreams, and then one day there she was, stranded on the side of the road outside my hometown, trying to change a flat tire."

Maggie pulled away a bit, looked into his eyes, and smiled. "I could have done it, you know."

"Oh, yes, ma'am, I do. But then if I'd let you, you might have gotten away, and from the instant I saw you, I knew couldn't risk that." He cupped her face in his hands and kissed her so deeply and tenderly it made her knees go weak. She'd heard people say that, but until now she hadn't truly ever experienced it.

"Well," she whispered, "I've got no desire to get away, except maybe together out to your place after dessert, so you can show me all night long how special you think I am."

"Eat fast," he said.

CHAPTER 2
A Place Called Home

Maggie sat, staring into the fire, on the sofa in JD's comfortable living space, wearing his sage green chambray shirt from yesterday and not a lot else. She pulled the collar of his shirt up over her nose and breathed in the intoxicating combination of his scent mingled with her own. And with it came a warm, tingling rush of memories of last night. Admittedly, they hadn't gotten a lot of sleep, and the thoughts of what they'd done instead made her smile. She'd awakened early in the circle of his arms with her mind a-whir, and when she couldn't calm it, she'd kissed his shoulder softly, eliciting from him no than the merest twitch of one corner of a lip. So, she'd eased out of bed.

It was early still, but she'd already made herself a cup of press-pot coffee and managed to get the fire going in the grate of the big river rock fireplace that dominated one wall of the living room. Coffee in hand, she perused the eclectic selection of books in the floor-to-ceiling shelves that bracketed it, spotting one she'd read before, a novel by Patrick Suskind called *Perfume* and pulling it down. *That one ought to distract the monkey mind.* She wrapped herself in a soft handmade quilt she'd found folded neatly on the arm of the sofa pulled up before the fire and settled in with the book. But after re-reading the first two paragraphs over twice, she still couldn't corral her brain. So much had changed in her life in such a short time that it made her dizzy to think about it. She'd finished a residency, moved across the country to take over a rural medical practice in a place she'd seen only in pictures, and learned that a serious relationship she'd believed was solid and would remain solid at a distance wasn't so solid. And to top it off, she'd nearly been killed. *But at the end of it*, she thought, *there was JD.* He was now still peacefully asleep beneath a cozy down duvet in his bedroom down the hall.

Her head was spinning with it all. And when she felt like this, confused or unsettled, her go-to confidant was her best friend, Charlotte. Or *Charlotte from Charlotte* as she called her, because that's how she'd introduced herself in her sweet Southern drawl their first day of college over ten years ago, *"Hi, I'm Charlotte Ainsley. From Charlotte, North Carolina."* She and her young family still lived there. Eastern time, an hour ahead of Maggie. *Is 7 am too early to call?* She texted her instead.

CFC - RU up? Call when u can.

Maggie's phone rang almost immediately. She thumbed the screen to accept the call on the first ring, hoping it hadn't awakened JD.

"Maggie May, what's up, girl? It's early where you are."

"Pretty early where you are, too."

"Not in Mommyland, honey. Gotta get the heathens up, fed, and spit shined. We're going over to get pictures with Santa at the mall. Counting the days 'til Christmas vacation."

"I'm sure they are," Maggie said.

"No, not them. Me!" Charlotte laughed. "Maggie, hang on a sec; Ford's headed to the airport for a golf tournament in Dubai. Let me see him off."

Maggie heard Ford's voice, distant, "Mornin', Maggie May. Wish us luck!"

"Tell him I hope he tears the course up," Maggie said to Charlotte. "And you can call me back later."

"Maggie says to give 'em hell, Ford. No, just hang on, Maggie." Then she turned her full attention to her husband, and Maggie was left to eavesdrop on Charlotte's end of the conversation. "Give me a kiss, sweetie. Have you got everything?"

For all her seeming fun-loving flightiness, of which there was plenty, Charlotte was one of the most organized people Maggie had ever met. The whole Schaflien clan – the twins and Ford, for that matter – were a well-drilled ensemble under Charlotte's baton. Maggie unwrapped herself from the quilt and padded barefoot over to the kitchen island to make another press pot of coffee half-listening in as Charlotte went through a full run down. Maggie could envision her standing in her pretty kitchen, black hair coiffed, make up perfect, already dressed to the nines at 7 am, probably in heels, ticking each item off on her fingers.

"OK, pay attention, Ford. Got your suitcase? Carry on? Phone, chargers, tickets? Wallet? Passport? Visa? OK." Maggie could hear his soft 'uh-huhs' as she ran down the list. "Those new clubs should be at the course when you get there. The rep promised me. Now *you* promise me you'll be careful, and you'll miss me and the twins every second you're not on the course. On the course you think only about the next shot," she admonished him sternly. Spoken like the top-notch golfer she was herself. "Text me when you're on the plane and when you land. And when you get to the hotel call, whatever time it is. I will not sleep until you do. I love you."

Maggie could hear the twins' raucous 5-year-old good-byes to their dad, the pleas to bring them something cool from the trip. They were used to his traveling, Maggie knew. It's the norm in the life of a professional golfer not the exception with nearly every week during the season spent on the road, and that provided many opportunities for trip gifts for the kids. But Dubai was a new and exotic exception to the usual US and European repertoire. Maggie found herself feeling a little guilty, like she her quiet presence was somehow intruding on them, and it made her unexpectedly wistful to listen to them. The love that was so evident in their marriage, really within the whole family, was just beautiful to watch or in this case hear.

Then a door closed, and she heard Charlotte say, "Ainsley, Caroline, finish your breakfast. I need to talk to Auntie Maggie for a minute." And then she was back. "So where are you, and why are you up and texting me at 6 am?"

"I'm at JD's. I spent the night last night." The water in the electric pot boiled, and Maggie poured it over the grounds and stirred.

"Uh huh. And?" Charlotte asked, drawing the single syllable of *and* out to three as only a Southern girl can do.

"And, once again, it was pure magic. Honestly. And it's not just that he's beyond fabulous in bed; it's that for sure, but" she heard Charlotte's low snicker and paused for a moment, pondering, then continued, "it's just that I've never felt so completely loved and protected since my parents died. Not even with Jeff. And for the first time since I lost them, a place feels like home. But..." her voice trailed off.

"But what?"

"But do you think I'm rushing into this? Am I just on a rebound from Jeff?"

"Honey, nobody can answer that but your heart. What I can say is that I've known you for more than ten years, and in all that time I've never seen you make a rash or foolish decision. If anything, you think a thing to death. You told me yourself when we were at The Greenbrier last summer that you had some doubts about whether Jeff was your forever guy, which at the time I thought you were crazy and told you so. Anybody looking in from the outside would say he ticked every box: successful doctor, handsome, charming, fun, rich as Croesus, great chemistry, said he loved you. But with all that you were still unsure."

"Yeah. And then he hopped into bed with Judith before my side of it was cold." She pressed the plunger on the coffee pot with a touch more vigor than was completely needed.

"He did, the rat, but men do sometimes think with their wrong head – not that I'm condoning it. I'm not! But you know what I mean. And you know what else? What I've never heard you say before? That a place feels like home. So, ask yourself this: is it Caddo Bend that feels like home, or is it JD that makes wherever you are feel like home?"

"Hmm." Maggie didn't answer for a moment, considering that possibility. "Too soon to say for sure, but maybe." *Yes, maybe he is*, she thought with a smile.

"Oh, my sista, hearing you say even a maybe makes my heart happy," Charlotte said.

"Speaking of," Maggie looked up at the sound of the door opening in the back hall, "I think he's up."

"OK, I need to wipe the grape jelly off a couple of little faces and get over to the mall before the line extends all the way to the North Pole. Speak later?"

"Yes, later. And thanks."

"Anytime, my sista. Love ya'."

Maggie turned to see JD, dark hair still ruffled from sleep, walking into the sunny kitchen in a pair of soft flannel pajama bottoms that rode low on his slender hips, leaving his smooth, muscular torso and belly invitingly bare.

"Now *that* is a vision I could get used to seeing every morning," he said, walking up behind Maggie at the counter clad only his far-too-big chambray shirt. He wrapped his arms around her and nuzzled her ponytail aside to kiss her lightly on the back of her neck. "Aren't your bare legs cold, darlin'?"

"They are a little," she said, snuggling back against his warm body. "I got the fire going, for which I need some major kudos, by the way. That's a first."

"*Bravissima* on the fire," he kissed the other side of her neck, "darlin'," he added with another nibbling kiss.

"And, I've just made a fresh pot of coffee, which about hits the limit of my culinary skills. Want a cup?"

"I do. And then there's something else I want, and I'll just bet you know what it is," he said, turning her in his arms and pressing her tightly to him, where she could feel for herself quite plainly what that something else might be. "Come sit with me by the fire, and let's have our coffee."

They sat together on the sofa, and he wrapped the warm quilt around them both. Maggie snuggled into the circle of his arm and watched the flames dance in the grate as they sipped their coffee, content in the comfortable silence. After a bit, JD sat his cup on the table and took hers from her hand, setting it aside as well. Then he tipped her chin up so that he looked into her eyes, his gaze so deep and penetrating that she couldn't look away. He bent his head to let his lips hover over hers, almost touching and yet not, and she could feel the warmth of his breath against her skin, and the warmth of his hands as they roved down to caress her bare thigh. Her own pulse quickened, fluttering like a tiny bird in the hollow of her throat, and she flushed all over with a suddenness that left her skin feeling hotter than the fire blazing in the grate beside them. Her breath came faster and when she couldn't wait any longer for him to kiss her, she leaned up to kiss him, fully, and with a passion that she could feel coursing throughout her limbs. She threaded her arms around his neck, fingers wound in his dark hair, and pulled him to her. He groaned softly and wrapped her in his arms, tipping her back onto the softly-yielding down cushions. She gave a sharp intake of breath when he came to her, welcoming his body hungrily into her own, wanting nothing more than to be here, wrapped in his arms, joined with him, oblivious to the world outside themselves.

Afterward as they lay entwined under the quilt, he spoke softly, "There's something I need to tell you, so I'm just gonna say it." Maggie started to speak, but he put a finger to her lips, and she let him go on, "I think you know... hell, it's pretty obvious," he shrugged, then Maggie's cellphone rang, interrupting him, its harsh sound jangling in the intimate stillness of the room. JD gave a sigh and closed his eyes, lightly resting his forehead against hers.

They both ignored the intrusion for several rings, hoping it was a wrong number or spam call, but it persisted until Maggie finally said, "I'd better answer. It may be medical." She threw off the quilt and reached for her phone. "This is Dr. McKinley," she said.

"Doc," Donna Farmer, her clinic receptionist, said in a shaky voice. "We need some help."

"What's wrong?"

"It's Noah, my brother." Maggie could hear the panic in her voice. "We can't wake him up."

"Where are you?"

"At home. He's in his room. We couldn't wake him up this morning."

"Is he a diabetic?" Maggie asked, a crease of worry appearing between her dark brows.

"No, ma'am."

"Has he taken any medications?"

"I don't know," Donna replied.

"OK. I will be right there. Give me the address."

JD touched her arm and mouthed, "*Who is it?*" Maggie mouthed back "*Donna. From the clinic.*" He nodded.

"It's 148 D Street. Doc, please hurry."

Maggie grabbed a pen from her purse and wrote the address down, showing it to JD.

"I know where it is," he said. "I'll take you."

"Donna, are you with him now? Is he breathing?" Maggie was up and walking to JD's bedroom. JD right behind her.

"Yes'm, I'm in his room. And, uh, is he breathing? I don't know. I think so." Then after a beat, "Yeah. Yeah, he is. A little." She sounded to Maggie like she was perilously close to losing it completely.

"I will be right there. Donna. Stay calm. Turn him onto his left side if you can and keep trying to rouse him."

"How?" Donna asked frantically.

"Pinch him, slap the back of his hands, shake his shoulder. Just keep trying and hang on."

Maggie threw her jeans on under JD's shirt and stepped into her trainers. JD grabbed a hoodie and slipped on his boots, and they were out the door in under a minute, heading for the Farmer home.

"JD is the clinic on the way?" Maggie said.

"Yeah," he said. "Right on the way."

"Stop there. I need the crash suitcase. It won't take a minute to grab."

The Farmer's house was a neat two-story clapboard house with a wide front porch, just three blocks off the square. Every light in the house was on when they arrived. Donna opened the front door before they could knock.

"Doc, he's messed up. Totally. Mama's with him, but we can't get him to snap out of it," Donna said, leading Maggie to a ground-floor bedroom in the back.

"Have you called 9-1-1?"

"Yes, ma'am, we called them first thing, but they're on a call nearly all the way over to Mt. Ida. It'll be a bit."

Maggie and JD entered the small bedroom to find Noah's mother, Barbara Farmer, in tears on the edge of the bed, wringing her hands in the lap of her flowered shift. Beside her a thin young man—20-something he looked to be with longish hair and a scruffy light beard—lay clad in ragged, mud-caked jeans and a hoodie on his side passed out on the bed. JD helped the woman up and took her out to stand with her daughter in the hall.

"Let the doc do her work," he said gently. "Donna, y'all stay here. Look after your mama." Then he returned to the room to help as he could.

Maggie knelt beside the young man, loudly calling his name, and digging the knuckles of her right hand into his breastbone. "Noah? Noah, can you hear me?" Getting no response, she felt at his throat for a carotid pulse and was relieved to find a weak one but more than a little concerned to notice the blue tinge of his lips and nails. She clipped a pulse oximeter to his finger and put her stethoscope to his chest to listen. *Breath sounds slow and shallow but present, thank God.* The pulse ox beeped, and the display showed 72. *Low oxygen level.* Maggie held the lid of first one eye and then the other open and shined a penlight into each of them. His pupils were tiny pinpoints. *Opioid OD?*

"JD," she said, pointing to the crash kit, "hand me that vial on the far left." He pointed at one, and Maggie nodded. "Yeah, that amber one." She took the naloxone from him, popped the glass ampule, and drew the solution into a syringe, then diluted it with saline. Wrapping a latex tourniquet around Noah's bicep, she was gratified to see a useable vein showing itself in his forearm. *Thank God!* Intravenously the drug would work much faster, so Maggie popped a butterfly IV line into the vein, giving her a safer route to push in the narcotic antagonist a bit at a time. She immediately pushed the first dose, then she waited. Too fast or too much of the antagonist and he could become agitated, even seize, or vomit, and she wanted to avoid any of those possibilities.

"Now hand me that oxygen cylinder," she said pointing to the canister. He did, and she connected a mask and tubing to it, positioned it over his nose and mouth, and opened the valve. Finally, she wrapped the blood pressure cuff around his other arm and took his pressure. *Low but adequate for now.*

She continued to monitor him and call his name for the next few minutes, until finally Noah began to respond to the narcotic-reversing effect of the naloxone. His breathing strengthened, becoming a bit deeper and fuller, and with it, his blood pressure and oxygen saturation began to improve.

From outside the room, Maggie heard her nurse Therma Faye's voice in the hall, "Donna, what the hell happened?" Then heard Donna reply to her.

"Tee, I don't know for sure. Noah went out last night with some friends, just drinkin' he said, and he came in real late. Or I guess you'd say early. I didn't hear him, but I didn't get to bed 'til after midnight myself. Ben and I went over to Mt. Ida to the late show to see that new 007 movie. Then this morning, Daddy hollered at Noah to get up and run over to Medlock's to get today's *Gazette* out of the box there, and when he didn't answer Daddy told me to go in to get him up. And he was stone out. When he wouldn't wake up, I called 9-1-1, then I called Doc, and then you. She's in with him now."

Therma Faye entered the room in rumpled sweats, hair a frizzy, crumpled mess contained somewhat by a stretchy headband, looking like she'd just fallen out of bed herself, which Maggie suspected was exactly the case. "Doc? Is he gonna be OK?" Maggie looked up to see the worry on her nurse's face. Noah and Donna were her husband Jimmy's younger cousins; she'd known them both since they were kids.

"He's alive; I think we got to him in time, but it looks like he overdosed on some kind of narcotic. Is he a known user?"

"No, ma'am. Not as I know of. Smokes a little weed, I imagine, like they all do, but he's not a hard drug user." She turned a sharp questioning look back at Donna. "Is he?"

"No," Donna said quickly at first. Then whimpering, she added, "I don't know." She shook her head and looked down, not meeting her aunt's gaze.

"Donna?" Therma Faye said more forcefully.

"Tee," she said, her voice breaking, "I really don't know what he's into. Lately he's been hanging with some guys he used to work with before he hurt his back and got laid off. They're not from here. I don't know 'em." She snuffled and blew her nose. Her mother, beside her, sobbed loudly. Donna put her arms around her mother, and the two seemed to be holding each other up.

JD went to the hallway and took Donna and her mother by the arm. "Where's Bill, Barbara?"

"He's in the kitchen," she said in a weak, shaky voice.

"Come on," he said, turning them away from the door, "let's go find Bill and make everybody some coffee. I know I could use a cup." Maggie looked up at him and gave a small nod and an appreciative smile.

Then she checked Noah's vitals again. *BP 110/78, O2 saturation 88%, breath sounds clear, pulse stronger.* "He seems to be holding steady," she said to Therma Faye.

"Thank Heaven for small favors," Therma Faye said. "He's really a good boy, Dr. Mac. I don't know where he got this crap."

"Plenty of it out there, but there'll be time to sort that out later. For now, he'll need to be watched for several more hours, preferably at the hospital, since we don't have a clue about exactly what he took or how much or what his level of narcotic tolerance is." *Where is that ambulance?*

She breathed a sigh of relief when she heard a distant siren, and soon after the EMTs arrived to transport Noah to the hospital. Maggie gave them a quick, full account of what she knew and what she'd done, and they loaded him up in the wagon. Maggie, JD, Therma Faye and the Farmers stood together on the porch, watching the ambulance pull away.

"Bill, I can drive y'all over to Mercy," Therma Faye said.

"Thanks, Tee. Appreciate it. And thank you, Doctor," Bill Farmer said hoarsely, his arm around his wife's small shoulder and hers around Donna's, the three of them huddled, shell-shocked, together.

"Thank the Lord you're here," Therma Faye said, looking at Maggie.

JD quietly reached down and took Maggie's hand, threading his fingers through hers, then leaned close to her ear. "Couldn't agree with her more." Maggie looked up into his soft gray eyes and squeezed his hand in return.

CHAPTER 3
Happy Returns

On Monday morning, Maggie awoke early, and sadly alone in her room at Miz Hendri's. She'd spent the remainder of the long Thanksgiving weekend at JD's house, much of it wrapped in his arms, feeling very lucky that no other medical emergencies had interrupted what had proven to be a glorious couple of lazy days together. She basked in the warm afterglow. They'd been so preoccupied, in fact, that she only now realized he'd never gotten back to whatever it was that he'd so needed to tell her when Donna's call had come in. She'd have to remember to ask.

She climbed out of bed and spent a few peaceful minutes doing her morning yoga routine—just a single sun salutation—then she bundled up and went down to the garage to do this morning's WOD. Today was lifting, heavies of squat, press, and deadlift. She worked her way up in steady increments, then maxed out each lift for a single rep. In a bit over an hour, she'd finished the set, gotten showered, dressed in a comfortable pair of black wool slacks and a soft sweater, twisted her long blonde hair up in a claw clip, and headed out.

She'd come home late last night knowing she needed to get going early this morning to make a nine o'clock appointment in Hot Springs to pick up her new car at the dealership. She was surprised and pleased it was ready, and thankful all over again that she had listened to Jeff's advice to not skimp on a good policy from a cooperative insurance company. In just a week—and a holiday week at that—they'd come through not only with a loaner the next day, but now with the full new car replacement. The guy at the rental car company, where she returned the loaner, even agreed to give her a ride to the dealership when she dropped it off.

Her new car was pretty much a carbon copy of her recently destroyed one, a silver sport utility vehicle just one model year newer. For that matter, the other one had been nearly new; she'd had it a mere five months when it had been swept down the raging Caddo River. And she'd liked it a lot, so no need to change horses if you had one that rode just fine. The dealership even handled the licensing paperwork for her, saving her that brain damage. *On a lucky roll like this, I should probably buy a lottery ticket,* she thought.

Her next stop was at Mercy General Hospital to follow up on Noah with the team who had cared for him and to check on Rose Ellen and Waylon. The girl was due to be released later today, and Child Protective Services would be transporting her back to Caddo Bend and putting her officially into the hands of the Davises for a while. Maggie wanted to be there to smooth the transition. She headed straight for the pediatric floor and Rose Ellen's room, tapping lightly then pushing open the door. The bed was empty. She went to the nurse's station and found the charge nurse.

"Hi, again," Maggie said. "I came by to check on Rose Ellen Prescott, but she's not in her room."

The nurse looked up blankly for a moment then recognized her. "Dr. McKinley, right?"

"Yes," Maggie answered.

"She's down in her father's room on 4. Plan is to discharge her today, but her care team felt it would be good for her to visit with him for a little while before she goes. Fortunately, law enforcement cleared it, so long as an officer remains in the room and CPS is also present."

Maggie nodded. "Oh, good. I completely concur," she said. "It's going to be a difficult enough transition for her as it is. That's sort of why I came today. Thought a trusted face might make her feel more secure."

"I know it will, doctor," the nurse said. "Anything else I can do for you?"

"Actually, yes. I'd like to follow up on another patient of mine from Caddo Bend. Noah Farmer. OD, brought in a few days ago."

The nurse typed in a query and in short order pulled up his digital chart. "Yes. Looks like he was released yesterday afternoon; as referring physician, they should have notified you about it."

"They may have done. I haven't been into the clinic to check messages yet today. Any of the toxicology back on him yet?" Maggie asked.

The nurse scrolled through several screens of information, finally locating his laboratory results. "Some reports are still pending. There was a positive on THC and opioids. Confirmatory showed oxycontin," she said, turning the computer screen toward Maggie and pointing to the result. "Opioids aren't really surprising," she continued, tapping the screen showing his birthdate on the report. "Lotta guys his age in the same boat nowadays: get laid off or hurt on the job; benefits run out before the pain does. Crap ton of stuff out there to dull the hurt if you know where to look. Oxy, heroin, even fentanyl's showing up now. That's something new."

"Yeah, I saw plenty of opiate use and abuse in the ERs in New York, but I guess I just didn't expect it in a pretty little town like Caddo Bend," Maggie said.

"Welcome to small town middle America, Doc" the nurse said with a shrug and a sad smile. "That I-40 drug-distribution corridor runs from coast to coast."

The elevator doors opened, and the CPS case worker pushed Rose Ellen in a wheelchair out into the hallway. The child's tear-stained cheeks told the story better than words could have. Maggie approached her and, with a nod to the case worker, squatted down in front of the wheelchair.

"Hey, sweetie," Maggie said, putting a comforting hand on the girl's knee. "Are you all packed up and ready to get out of here?"

Rose Ellen nodded and stared silently at the tissue in her lap that she'd worried into a pile of white crumbs. For a moment Maggie feared that she'd again lost her speech, but after a moment she heard the child's soft voice. "Yes, ma'am."

"OK then," Maggie said with a glance at the caseworker's ID badge, "if Ms. Saunders approves, I'd like to tag along."

"If Rose Ellen agrees, I'd be happy to have you join us," Ms. Saunders said.

A sad hint of a smile touched Rose Ellen's lips. "Yes, please. Come." She looked up earnestly and wrapped her small hand around Maggie's. The three of them headed down the hall to gather her things.

Back in Caddo Bend, Maggie pulled into the Davis's driveway behind Ms. Saunders' sedan and climbed out. Tom and Becky Davis were standing, smiling, at the door with 5-year-old Charlie between them holding a colorful, hand-lettered sign proclaiming: WELKUM ROWSE! She couldn't suppress a smile. *Such a sweet little boy; such a sweet family*, Maggie thought. And such a perfect placement for Rose Ellen right now. Charlie would be just the stimulus she'd need to be drawn back into normal, happy, carefree child's life. Or as close to that as was possible in her current circumstances.

"Hi, Dr. Mac!" Charlie squealed, waving vigorously.

"Hey, Charlie. I love your sign."

"It's for Rosie," he said, grinning ear-to-ear as he proudly handed his artwork to the girl, who accepted it almost shyly.

"Good to see you, Doc," Tom said, opening the door and stepping aside to invite them in. "Ms. Saunders, Rose Ellen, y'all come on in. It's cold out this morning, and we've got a nice fire going inside. Becky made an apple spice cake."

The house was indeed cozy and warm, and filled with good vibes and delicious aromas. Becky Davis gave them a quick tour of the downstairs living areas: a front room, a comfortable family room and big open kitchen, dining room, playroom, and laundry/sewing room. Then up the central stairs to see the small bedroom that had been furnished for Rose Ellen in shades of pink, lavender, and cream. On the foot of the twin bed was a neatly folded quilt that the girl spotted straightaway.

"My quilt!" She ran to the bed and gathered the coverlet to her chest, burying her face in the soft, faded fabric.

"We asked Ms. Saunders to get something of yours to help this room feel more like home. I think this was a good choice," Becky said, kneeling down beside her.

Rose Ellen looked up, her eyes shining, "Yes, ma'am. My mama made it."

Maggie felt the sting of her own tears now and blinked them back, but with them came the certainty that this would indeed be a good place to let Rose Ellen heal.

"Rosie," Charlie said from the doorway, "come see my room now! I got a Furby," he giggled, "It's so funny. Come see what it does," he added, and the two children scampered off down the hallway to put the toy through its paces.

The adults took their conversation to the living room to enjoy a little coffee and cake. Once Ms. Saunders was satisfied that Rose Ellen was well settled for the near term, she took her leave, and Maggie did as well, heading to the clinic for a later than usual start to the day.

Coming in the back door of the clinic, Maggie ran immediately into Therma Faye in the back hallway.

"Hey, doc," she said walking with Maggie to her office. "We got all three rooms loaded up for ya' and a couple of walk-ins still waiting to come back. Nothing urgent there."

"OK," Maggie said hanging her coat and bag on the rack and slipping into her labcoat. She lifted the Scarlet Maple bonsai JD had given her from its current perch atop her filing cabinet and moved it to the sunny windowsill, cracking the window just a bit to let in some cool air. She noticed a sprinkling of fallen leaves, but JD had told her that was normal. It was a deciduous tree, and it would lose leaves in the fall and winter just like its larger kin. She stuck her index finger down into the soil and decided watering should wait until tomorrow. "What's first?"

"Lyla Green and her sweet little one; they're in Room 1 for a well check. Then you got a DOT physical in 2, and Noah's in 3 for a follow up visit."

"That was quick. How's he doing?"

"Noah? He seems to be doing OK. I think what happened scared the livin' crap out of him. I hope it did anyway. His daddy wanted him to come in first thing, let you talk to him, look him over."

Maggie started with Lyla and her chubby-cheeked new baby girl they'd named Isabella after Lyla's grandmother. Mother and baby were fine. Bella's height and weight were each a little under 50th percentile, which was amazing considering Lyla's pre-eclampsia. Lungs clear. Heart sounds normal. Fontanelle soft. Reflexes normal. She was eating well, gaining weight, and bright-eyed, with a head of soft wispy dark brown curls she'd probably lose most of. And Lyla was doing well, too. Weight appropriate. Blood pressure normal. Blood sugar normal. Eyes and vision back to normal again. No more headaches.

"How are things going at home? Everything OK?" Maggie said.

"Yes'm. I'm tired, but that's normal I guess with a new baby," Lyla answered.

"It is. Her weight's increasing as it should, so I'm guessing no trouble getting her to take the breast."

"No, ma'am. She latches right on; she's a good eater. I'm a little worried about Kenny, though. He thinks he needs to wake up whenever I feed her. He just stands there beside the rocker while I nurse her, asleep on his feet. Then he has to go to work all day. At least I can nap a little when she naps."

"Well, I applaud his impulse. Good for him. He's a good man; he's going to be a good father. But you guys need to spell one another. So, work out a schedule. Pump when you can and bank some breast milk in your freezer or even use one of the acceptable formulas, so Kenny can actually feed Bella and let you sleep through a feeding. Then he'll feel more like he can sleep guilt-free when you get up. Just getting those four connected hours of sleep is a real benefit to you both right now. Do you want me to talk to him?"

"No. We'll work out a plan."

"OK. I'm holding you to it," Maggie smiled and pointed a teasing finger at her. "And I will want to see this little one back at 2 months for her well check and shots."

"Thank you, Dr. Mac," Lyla reached out to take Maggie's hand and gave it a squeeze. "Thank you for everything you did for us."

"I'm glad it all turned out well," Maggie said, squeezing her hand in return then cupping the baby's head gently. "She's just precious. See you in six weeks."

Maggie entered the next exam room to find a very anxious, slightly overweight man, fidgeting on the end of the table. She glanced at the chart: *Boyce Dugan, 34 y/o.* Here for a Department of Transportation physical. She recognized him as one of the regulars who hung out on the bench at Eddie Ray's Service Station waiting to pick up odd job construction work in the mornings and jawing and blowing off steam together in the afternoons.

"Mr. Dugan," she said, extending her hand to him. "What can we do for you today?"

He took her hand and gave it a limp shake, casting his eyes down as he said, "I gotta get a physical to drive a truck."

Maggie took a seat on the rolling stool and looked over the DOT history and physical form. *Height 5'10", weight 195 lbs.* No significant history of any medical issues, non-smoker, occasional drinker, dipstick urine was normal, urine drug screen collected, blood drawn for their required lab analyses, pulse rate was a little elevated at 94 and his blood pressure was borderline high at 150/94. Therma Faye had put those pulse and BP numbers on a sticky note rather than recording them. Anything over 140/90 would likely fail him on the physical.

"I notice your blood pressure's a little high, Mr. Dugan," she said. "Is that unusual?"

"It's, uh, Boyce…ma'am," he said, licking his lips. "Yeah, it's usually OK, I think. I'm just kinda nervous."

"Why are you nervous, Boyce?"

"Well, uh, I finished the diesel driving academy program and got my commercial license last summer, but I hadn't been able to find anything permanent. Then a couple of months ago I applied for a job at JC Hurst, and last week they called me in for an interview and sent me to get the physical. I really want to get this job. It's more money than I've ever made in my life. By a lot. And benefits, too. But I have to pass the physical and all the screens."

Maggie could see from the thin film of sweat collecting on his upper lip how anxious he was. And how important this job was to him. "OK. Let me step out so you can get undressed. Put this gown on," she stood, handing him a folded gown, "and here's a paper sheet to cover up with. Crack the door when you're ready, and I'll be back to do your exam." Boyce's eyes grew large as saucers. "We're going to get all this out of the way," she continued, "because I think some of your blood pressure elevation is about the exam."

Boyce looked away, embarrassed, his ears suddenly gone scarlet.

Maggie went on, "And then we're going to let you get dressed, and we'll turn the lights off, put a little soft, peaceful music on in the room, have you lie down quietly for a few minutes, and Therma Faye's going to sneak back in to take that pressure again when you're relaxed. It's going to be OK."

And it was. After the exam and 20 minutes of quiet relaxation, Boyce's pressure had dropped to 138/88, which Maggie duly recorded on the form. He was good to go.

"Boyce, your pressure's down to below the cut off, but I want you to take how high it was before as a wake-up call to change some habits." He looked a bit confused, so she added, "Long haul trucking isn't an ideal occupation to keep weight and blood pressure under control. It's the exact opposite, in fact. Or can be. Endless hours of sitting and driving, the stress of the road, trying to meet deadlines, late nights, no end of unhealthy food choices available at every pit stop. You'll have to really work to combat those tendencies. But if this job is as important to you as you say it is, I'd recommend you commit to a common-sense program of getting off some weight, getting leaner and healthier and stronger, so you can keep doing it for a long time."

"What all do I need to do?" he said, looking up and holding her gaze for the first time.

"Well, for starters, eat mostly whole foods, not junk. Food that doesn't come in a plastic wrapper with a label. Get regular exercise, especially out on the road since that's where you'll be most of the time. Cut back on those sugary soft drinks I've seen you drinking up at Eddie Ray's." She handed him a sheaf of papers. "Here are some materials I'd like you to read, and then we can talk about it again if you have questions."

"Thank you, Doc," he said with a bob of his head and a grin that split his face from ear to ear. "I promise I'll read it."

"If you want to start working out, I'm thinking of starting up a group to work out together a few times a week. You'd be welcome to come if you're interested."

"Really?" he said.

"Yes, really," she said. "I'll let you know when we get it going."

Maggie took the next chart from the holder on the door of Room 3: Noah Farmer. She was looking it over and about to go into the room when Donna stuck her head out of the office doorway and said, "Dr. Mac, there's a phone call for you. It's Dr. Jeff. From New York."

"If it isn't an emergency, please tell him I'm in with a patient." She doubted it was an emergency and had no desire to speak to Jeff. She opened the door and walked in to find a thin young man, spit-shined clean, neatly dressed, his light-brown hair newly cut high and tight, face freshly shaved, and not at all looking like the bedraggled person she'd rescued from an opiate overdose only a few days ago.

"Hi, Noah," she said. "I'm Dr. McKinley. It's good to see you."

Noah looked down at his hands held tightly clasped together in his lap. "Thank you, ma'am," he said quietly. He cleared his throat and went on, "First off, I know I owe you big. Otherwise, I might not be here at all."

Maggie gave his shoulder a gentle pat. "I'm glad I was nearby. Are you ready to talk about what happened?"

Noah looked at her for an instant, then at the ceiling. "Yes, ma'am, I reckon I better."

Maggie sat on the stool and crossed her legs, waiting quietly for him to begin.

He took a deep breath and let it out in a long sigh. "I'm not sure what happened. Me and a couple of friends went over to Buck's for some beers, just hanging out."

"Who's Buck?"

"Buck's Bar. Beer joint out 27 toward Mt. Ida. One of the guys, I can't remember who, said we could get some weed that was 'killer special' from this waitress there. So, we all put in some cash, and I think it was Gil who went over to talk to her- "

"What was her name?" Maggie interrupted. "This waitress."

"I don't know. I've seen her at Buck's before, though."

Did you give all this information to the sheriff's office?"

"Yes'm, I told em at the hospital all I could remember then. I'm supposed to go talk to them again."

"Good. Then what?"

"Then we went down by the river and smoked a few joints. And I started feeling really weird. Couldn't talk straight, real dizzy, couldn't walk."

"Did you take anything else? Any pills, for instance?"

"No, ma'am. Just the beers, probably a few more than I shoulda had." He looked down at his hands again. "And smoked a couple."

"Do you take any prescription medications normally? For anything at all?"

"Not anymore. I hurt my back at work maybe four, five months ago and took some prescription pain pills for a couple weeks. Then when they ran out just some ibuprofen. My back feels fine now, but I got laid off a couple of months ago, so I've been kind of at loose ends lately." Maggie thought his story had the ring of truth to it.

"Let's take a look." She said as she stood and put her stethoscope to his chest, listening to his heart and lungs. *Normal.* She checked his eyes and reflexes. *Normal.* "Can you lie down, Noah?" Maggie pulled the foot extension out as he lay back for her to examine his belly. *Liver, normal, no tenderness anywhere, spleen not enlarged, bowel sounds normal.* She took a seemingly casual look at both his forearms for any scarring that might be evidence of chronic drug use. *None.* Then she gave him a hand to sit up and remained standing beside him.

"Did you know the drug screen they did on you turned up a narcotic—oxycontin—as well as THC? Marijuana," she clarified.

Noah's eye widened, and Maggie thought he looked genuinely surprised by the news.

"Where do you think that came from?" she asked, never taking her eyes from his face.

He drew his brows together and seemed puzzled, not answering for a moment. "Honest, ma'am," he shook his head slowly, "I don't even know what that is." He looked up at her with earnest blue eyes.

"Did you take any pills? Shoot up? Snort anything?"

He looked stunned. "No! It was just beers and weed. None of that other stuff." Her gut again told her he was telling her the truth. At least as he knew it. But somehow, he'd ingested oxy.

"Everything looks normal now, Noah. But it might be time for a new group of friends," she said as she opened the door.

Therma Faye was standing just outside the door when it opened. She pinned Noah with a stern look, "Doc's right about that, bud." Then to Maggie, "You got a call on line 2. Dr. Jeff... again. He says he wants to hold."

"What do we have left?"

"Nothing else scheduled. The two walk-ins is all. Looks like might be a UTI in Room 1 and, yes'm before you ask, I already got the urine spinning. And a twisted ankle in the trauma room."

Maggie didn't hesitate a minute. "He'll have to call back. Or just let him hold while I finish up with those two. Nothing more uncomfortable than a urinary tract infection; I've been there a time or two myself. If he hangs up, he hangs up."

"I'll put the urine under the scope for you," Therma Faye said as Maggie opened the exam room door. "Do you want a culture and sensitivity?"

Maggie glanced at the history: young woman without a chronic urinary tract infection history. "No, I don't think we'll need it. Not yet." She went into the exam room and shut the door.

CHAPTER 4
Cues and Miscues

About a half hour later Maggie had dealt with the walk-ins, one leaving with prescriptions for an antibiotic and a bladder antispasmodic medication and the other with his ankle expertly taped and wrapped and a prescription for physical therapy in his hand. As she headed back to her office, Maggie smiled to overhear Therma Faye instructing him to go by and grab the set of crutches that Eldon kept in the corner of Medlock's for lending out should someone in town need a pair. The custom had apparently been started decades ago, when Eldon's grandfather had run the General Store and was just one more charming thing in a long list of charming things Maggie had learned to love about this tiny, tight-knit town. She sat down at her desk and stared at the lone flashing 'on hold' light on the desk phone. After a moment, she picked it up. "Hi, Jeff. Sorry it took me so long; I was with a patient."

There was silence on the other end of the line for an instant, and she thought he must have finally hung up, then she heard, "Uh… Maggie, it's JD. Sorry to disappoint. I'll catch you later."

Before she could respond, the line was dead. *Damn it!* She dialed JD's number; it rang repeatedly then, "Hey, you've reached JD. Can't take the call, so leave me a message." *Double damn it!*

After the beep, she spoke to the machine. "JD, it's Maggie. Please call me back so I can explain."

The phone rang almost immediately, and Maggie snatched up the handset. "JD?"

"Mags? Is that finally you?" Jeff's voice was most certainly not the one she expected and definitely not the one she wanted to hear. "I waited on

51

hold forever, but I had an urgent page from the recovery nurse, so I had to hang up a few minutes ago."

"Hi. Yeah." She tried to keep the disappointment out of her voice. "Sorry to have kept you waiting so long. I had an urgent patient on this end, too."

"I would have waited all night, if that's how long it took to get through," he said.

"Jeff, I ..." her voice trailed off.

"Did you like the flowers?"

"Yes, they were beautiful. And big. Miz Hendri liked them very much."

"Good. I wasn't sure how capable a local florist might be, so I had them flown in from New York and delivered by courier."

Ah, that explains the unusual Thanksgiving delivery. She didn't say anything for a bit then asked, "What is it that you want?"

"I want you. Isn't that pretty obvious?"

Just not enough to keep your pants zipped were the words that leapt to her mind and almost out her mouth. Instead, she took a big inhale and exhaled before she spoke. "We've been through this Jeff. I told you when you showed up here, after my...uh...shall we call it my surprise visit to see you? Because I know I was surprised."

"Maggie, I told you it was nothing."

"It was whatever the polar opposite of *nothing* is to me. And I think I was pretty clear with you that night that I might not be able to get past this. And that if I ever could – a big if, mind you – I would need time. What's it been? A few weeks?"

"We just need some face-to-face time together to work through this. We can go anywhere you like for as long as you like. Together. I'm going to send the jet for you, OK?"

"No. Not OK. I have a practice. I have responsibilities to my patients. I can't just drop everything because you want to jaunt off."

"All covered. I've already got a *locum tenens* scheduled for you. Tentatively, of course."

Oh, you do, do you? Maggie said nothing aloud but felt her blood pressure rise and a flush climbing her cheeks; she struggled to keep her temper in check. This was their long-standing issue: money. Well, her issue, at any rate, and his money. His bred-in-the-bone belief that money and connections were always the answer to everything. Whatever it was, you could buy or schmooze your way out of it. Her voice was glacial when she finally spoke, "Cancel the doc. Do not send the plane. I'm not going anywhere with you."

"Mags, you're being unreasonable. Give me a chance. Please. Give *us* a chance."

My God, she realized, *you clearly have no idea what I've been through recently! None.* And then it dawned on her; he really didn't know. He'd have to be a mind reader to know. She'd cut off contact with him after the Judith debacle and had told him not to contact her. She hadn't told him about any of what had happened, which she now realized was because she hadn't felt the need to. And that she still didn't. Someone else had been there that night; someone else had her back.

"If you want to force the issue at this moment, then I can tell you this: I'm moving on. You should, too."

"Maggie, you don't mean that. We…"

"Jeff, there isn't a 'we' anymore. There just isn't. You saw to that."

There was only silence on the other end of the call.

"I honestly wish you nothing but the best," she said. "I wish you happiness and joy and love with someone you can really commit to. And I fully intend to have the same thing for myself. But I really need to go now. Goodbye, Jeff." She hung up the phone without waiting for a response, and with some measure of sadness for their past that was over and done, but with complete confidence that it was the right thing to do.

She dialed JD's number again. "Hey, you've reached JD. Can't take your call, so leave me a message."

With no more patients on the schedule and her phone calls to JD going to voice mail, Maggie decided to drive out to his place to see if he was there. When she pulled up in front of the house, neither of his vehicles was visible but maybe they were in the garage in the back. She walked up onto the wide, shady front porch of the house, a pleasing, woodsy mix of native river rock, planed cypress, and lots of mullioned glass under a verdigris copper roof. Clean, modern lines with a cabin-in-the-woods soul. She hesitated a moment, then rapped the bronze knocker. No answer. She rapped again. Nothing. *Maybe he's with his trees.*

She stepped off the porch and walked around to the back of the house, to where his bonsai greenhouse stood. Through the glass panels between the interlacing beams of the architecturally-jaw-dropping structure, she could see his dozens of tiny trees, rowed neatly on shelves. Not long ago, he'd introduced her to few of them, and that memory brought a smile to her lips. She recognized Benjamin, his *Ficus benjamina*, and Cio-Cio-san, his amazing Autumn Cherry, still fully blossomed out in pink-crowned glory.

But no JD.

She walked across to the detached garage at the back of the drive and peeked into the glass of the carriage doors. His vintage Jeepster ragtop was there, but not his truck.

"Can I help you, ma'am," the man's voice made her jump away from the door.

She turned to find a slightly built man in blue jean coveralls and Wellingtons eyeing her quizzically. She felt like a peeping Tom. "Uh, yes, sorry. I was looking for Mr. Langston. Is he home?"

"No, ma'am, he's not here," the man said.

"Oh. Well, when he comes back will you tell him Maggie McKinley stopped by?"

"McKinley. Sure will. But he said he might not be back for a couple of weeks. He asked me to watch over the trees."

A couple of weeks? WTF? He didn't say anything about being away! Her mind was reeling. None of this made any sense. She tried to gather some semblance of poise.

"Was he called away suddenly? I only ask because we were supposed to, uh, supposed to meet today," she added, as if that would justify her being there snooping around.

"I don't rightly know," he said. "He called me a few of hours ago about the trees. Asked if I would watch them for him 'til he got back."

"Well, if you'll tell him I was by, Mr...?"

"Furr, ma'am. Darrell Furr."

"Mr. Furr. Thank you."

"Darrell, ma'am."

"Darrell," she repeated. "I'll let you get to your work then. Thank you."

Maggie climbed into her car and immediately texted Charlotte: **Can u talk?**

For answer, her phone buzzed before she could get the car turned around to leave.

"Sista," Charlotte said when Maggie answered. "Whatcha need?"

"My head examined? An exorcist? A shot of Jameson?" Maggie said. "All three?"

"Oh, mylanta. What's happened?"

"Can you talk for a minute?"

"Sure, Dinner's in the oven, Ford's still in Dubai, and the kids are watching *Frosty the Snowman* for the umpteenth time."

Maggie filled her in on the conversation with Jeff, how she'd ended things with him, and about JD's abrupt ring-off in the confusion of who was holding on the line. And that he now wasn't answering her calls, so she'd gone to his house to apologize for the mix up and explain what was going on only to find he had left. For a couple of weeks.

"And he never mentioned a word about going on a trip?" Charlotte asked.

"No, nothing. We were together non-stop over Thanksgiving weekend, as you know. And he didn't say anything about it."

"Well, you don't really know what might have prompted it. Some family emergency, maybe?"

"Doubt it. He's like me; both his parents are gone. And as far as I know, he doesn't have any siblings. At least he's never mentioned a brother or sister."

"Yeah, but when you think about it, you guys have been friends for a few months, but you haven't been a *bona fide* thing all that long. What's it? Few weeks, really. Smokin' hot weeks, I'll grant you, but still. You're just getting to know one another, right? Maybe there's family you don't know about yet. A favorite uncle or aunt or a sweet, old white-haired granny gumming her food and rocking away in a home somewhere."

"Even so, that doesn't explain why he won't return my calls. I've left multiple messages."

"You want my advice?"

"You know I do," Maggie said with a deep sigh, as she pulled onto the main road into town.

"Let it be for a little bit. If he had an emergency, he'll call. If he was upset about the confusion with Jeff he'll think about it and come around, I'm sure. Just give him a little space."

"I know you're right." Maggie said, then heard Caroline crying in the background.

"Hang on a sec," Charlotte said to Maggie, then spoke to her daughter. "What's wrong, sweetie?" Maggie couldn't quite make out the child's response, drowned as it was in sobs. "Oh, no!" Charlotte said. "Well, he'll be back again next year, just like always. Right?" Then she came back to Maggie, "Sista, I need to run and deal with this. Frosty has melted, and Caroline is broken hearted about it. Again. Happens every time they watch it. Ainsley thinks it's hilarious, which doesn't help. She just needs a snuggle and a little maternal reassurance."

"You run. Give them both my love and a big hug. And thanks."

Maggie drove down Main Street, heading for Miz Hendri's. The streetlamps had come on, and she noticed that the workmen had been busy today decorating the tiny downtown for Christmas, each lamppost around the square was now bedecked with a tinsel angel, bell, or star aglow with lights. Some garlands of lighted tinsel and greenery had been stretched across the street between Molly's Café and the central green, and by the look of things, more garlands were on the way. And the huge, shaped cedar that grew opposite the gazebo on the green was surrounded by ladders and huge plastic tubs of what she assumed were lights and decorations, poised for the workmen to get busy again tomorrow. She could see the unlit shape of a large star already affixed forty-odd feet up at its top.

All the tinsel and lights made her a bit nostalgic for Manhattan at the holidays: buildings wrapped like gigantic presents, the beautifully decorated storefront windows at Bergdorf's and Tiffany's and other landmark establishments, the lit-up angels trumpeting in the alleyway that led from Fifth Avenue to Rockefeller Center, and the world's most famous Christmas tree. New York City was a magical place at Christmas, and she couldn't deny she would miss it. But this would be a new and different kind of magical, she was sure. Shaking off the melancholy vibe she headed home, where by now Miz Hendri would be putting dinner on the table.

And, indeed, when Maggie walked into the kitchen, the smell of roasted pork filled the room. She hung her coat on the rack by the door and went into the dining room to find Miz Hendri and Papa P in conversation at the table. Since Nick's departure, there wasn't yet another full-time lodger, and Papa had taken to joining them for dinner when there were no transient guests to keep Miz Hendri company. Tonight, there was just the three of them together for dinner.

"There she is," Papa said. "We were about to start without you."

Maggie sat down, and Miz Hendri immediately began passing her food, putting a thick slice of mushroom-stuffed pork tenderloin onto her plate, and settling a large mound of mashed potatoes and a pile of roasted green beans beside it before she could protest.

"Gravy?" Miz Hendri said, lifting the gravy boat.

"No, thank you," Maggie said.

"Would you like a biscuit?" Miz Hendri asked.

"No. I think this is plenty. It looks delicious," she said, eagerly taking a bite of the potatoes to please the cook, but relishing the pork and green beans, which truly were delicious. Miz Hendri filled her empty glass with tea, and Maggie took a sip to be sure it wasn't sweetened. *Unsweet.* What she felt she really needed was a glass of wine or maybe a good stiff drink, but that would have to wait until she was in her room.

"Did you get little Rosie settled in?" Miz Hendri asked, buttering a biscuit for herself.

"Yes. She's at the Davis's, and I think it's going to be a very good place for her.

"And Waylon?" Miz Hendri asked. "Did you see him?"

"Not today, but they allowed Rose Ellen to visit with him before she left, and though she was sad, I think that helped her. Not so sure about him, though. When I saw him on Thanksgiving, he looked good physically, but he's struggling, I think, to come to terms with everything that's happened: Ruth's death and his role in covering it up, almost losing Rose Ellen, the risk she may grow up without either parent. And doing it all without the liquid crutch he's relied on for years to calm the demons inside. He's got a rough road ahead."

"I pray for him every Sunday," Miz Hendri said. "And for little Rosie. And for you, too, after everything you've been through."

Back in her room after dinner, Maggie dialed JD's number again, getting the same recorded request to leave a message. This time, she did not. *Where is he? What's going on?*

She slipped out of her work clothes and carefully hung them to air, grabbing a warm pair of cashmere lounging PJs off the closet hook and pulling them on. She poured herself a shot of Jameson, thumbed up a favorite album from her iTunes library, and settled into the rocker in the semi-darkness of her room. From her desktop speaker, Bob Dylan's distinctive, whiny voice first remind her she *should not feel so all alone* and that *everybody must get stoned.* And then a few songs and another shot of Jameson later he offered up a lyric that went straight to her aching, confused heart: *You say you're lookin' for someone who's never weak but always strong, to protect you and defend you whether you are right or wrong, someone to open each and every door, but it ain't me babe. No, no, no, it ain't me, babe; it ain't me you're lookin for, babe.*

"Oh JD," she murmured, "where are you?"

***

JD settled into the wide leather seat of the 747 and nursed a neat double shot of Blanton's that the perky brunette flight attendant had brought him once they'd gotten aloft out of Dallas. The captain had just announced that they'd reached cruising altitude, and the dinner service would begin shortly. The business-class cabin was only about half full, and as fortune would have it, he'd drawn no one in the seat next to him. So, he'd plugged in his dead iPhone to charge and laid it on the empty seat beside his book and the plastic-wrapped pillow and blanket provided by the airline. He knew he'd need both the sleep and a fully charged phone when he landed.

The flight attendant came down the aisle and stopped beside his seat. "Have you made your choice for dinner this evening, Mr.," she glanced down at her list for his name, "Mr. Langston?" He noticed she had a light sprinkling of freckles across her nose and cheeks. Pretty.

"Yes, ma'am," JD said giving her a trace of a polite smile. "I'll have the beef, please."

"Good choice," she said, returning his half smile with a much fuller, brighter one of her own. "And with that would you care for another Blanton's, or would you prefer wine?"

"I think I'll stick with the bourbon. And some ice water, please."

"Are you going to Tokyo for business or pleasure?" she lingered, continuing to chat.

"Neither one really," he said, looking away, reaching for his book, and opening it. "My wife's ill."

"Oh, I'm so sorry," she said. He noticed her quick glance at his unadorned left ring finger. "Well, I hope she recovers soon," she said in a more subdued tone and moved on down the way to get the dinner requests from the next passengers.

Thirteen and a half hours later, the plane landed, and after clearing customs and passport control JD stood alone in the taxi line in a light drizzle. He was directed to the next taxi by the line attendant, who opened the cab's door for him; JD climbed into the car while the driver stowed his bag in the trunk.

"*Tōkyōdaigaku iryō sentā onegaishimasu,*" JD said to the driver when he returned, directing him in Japanese to take him to University of Tokyo Medical Center.

"*Hai, wakarimashita,*" the driver responded – yes, I understand – and pulled away from the curb. JD booted up his phone and checked his messages. A wistful sadness clouded his features as he listened; he closed his eyes and rubbed a hand across his face as the taxi sped on its way through the rainy streets into Tokyo.

CHAPTER 5
A Bruised and Broken Heart

Maggie woke feeling a bit thick-headed and cotton-mouthed, courtesy of a little too much Dylan and Jameson last night. She immediately reached for her phone but found no notification of messages or missed calls. Her heart sank. *Why doesn't he call? Where is he?* She wished she could just see his face, lose herself in those gorgeous gray eyes, talk to him. She looked instead at the photographs of her and her parents on the chest beside her bed—the three of them one Christmas morning and the three of them one summer in Paris—kept there as a constant reminder that she hadn't always been alone. Some days she needed that more than others, and today was one of those.

She climbed out of bed, made it up neatly as was her habit, then began her morning yoga on her knees, settling her butt onto her heels and folding her body forward to assume Child's Pose. Focusing on the movement of her breath, riding the wave of each inhale and exhale, she worked to blot out the anxiety and worry swirling within her and make her mind a blank. It took her a full five minutes of breathing into the pose before she felt calm enough to begin her flow, rising to her hands and knees for Tabletop, alternately arching her back into Cat and letting it sink into Cow, then pushing her hips up to hold Downward-facing Dog. Finally, she walked her hands back to her feet to assume a Forward Fold and then rose to Mountain. From there she flowed from pose to pose for another ten minutes, until she was satisfied that she'd loosened the kinks and grounded her emotions enough to begin the day.

She dressed in workout clothes and braved the chilliness of the unheated garage where her weight rig was set up. She'd stretched and warmed up with yoga already, so she was able to get right into this morning's WOD, which was a 10-minute AMRAP – cross-training lingo for as many repetitions as possible in ten minutes. In this case, it was a ladder of increasing numbers of burpee push-ups and ring dips, each round followed by 50 double-unders with the jump rope. Like her morning yoga, the workout let her blank her mind, at least for the duration of it.

After completing the WOD and taking a soothing hot shower, she dressed in a soft mauve turtleneck sweater over a black wool midi-skirt and boots. Slipping her mother's quartz and silver pendant around her neck, she headed to work.

Today, she decided to stop by Molly's Café for her favorite take-out breakfast carb splurge—scrambled eggs and diced bacon on an everything bagel. She didn't eat bread often, but her belly felt completely hollowed out and just coffee and a cup of protein-spiked yogurt wasn't going to cut it this morning. She parked on the street in front of the café and went inside to find Velma sitting at the counter eating an omelet and some fresh fruit.

"Mornin', Doc," Velma said. "Buy you a cup?"

"I'm just picking up a bagel sandwich to go, but I'd join you in one while I'm waiting."

"Bagel, huh?" Velma's brows shot up with skepticism. She was an insulin-dependent diabetic, and she and Maggie had had many discussions about the deleterious effects of refined carbs on blood sugar and their mutual avoidance of them as a general rule. "Pour Doc a cup on my tab, hon," Velma said to Molly, who promptly filled a crockery mug with steaming hot coffee and sat it on the counter in front of Maggie. "Guess with JD in Japan, we'll see a little more of you over here." She cut off another bite of the omelet and a long string of gooey cheese followed her fork on the way to her mouth. She took her fingers and tugged to break it, then wrapped the strand around the tines.

Japan? Maggie's heart lurched, and she struggled not to betray her surprise. Stirring cream into her cup she nodded and said to Velma, as casually as she could manage it, "Uh huh, you probably will. He left in such a rush that we hardly had a chance to discuss it." *Zero chance, actually. No hardly about it.* Her mind was a whirl of confusion.

"Yeah, when he called and asked me to hold his mail and packages, it seemed like he was flying low. I asked him how long he'd be gone, and he said he didn't know for sure. Really didn't say much more, just that it was something to do with his daughter."

Daughter? The word hit Maggie like a blow to the chest. *Daughter? WTF?* She took a sip of her coffee and scraped together as much poise as she could manage before speaking. "Well, nothing's more urgent than that," she said with a tight smile.

Molly brought her order, and Maggie took the sack, handing over her credit card, grateful for the interruption. She quickly downed about half her coffee and signed the chit. "Well, off to the salt mines," she said with what she hoped didn't sound like forced cheerfulness.

"Have a good one, Doc," Velma said, "and when you talk to JD, give him our best."

"Will do," Maggie said, her mind now more unsettled than when she'd waked up. *I will if he ever calls me back.*

Maggie's first stop at the clinic was the breakroom to make herself a double Americano to go with her bagel sandwich. She could hear Therma Faye and Donna arguing in hushed tones in the front office but couldn't make out what they were saying. And to be honest, her mind was elsewhere; she didn't much care what they were on about today. While she waited for the water to boil in the electric kettle, all she could think of was that word Velma had so casually dropped: *daughter. JD has a daughter. A daughter who presumably has a mother. Would she be meeting him in Japan? Had they been married?* She felt a jealous twinge tweak her heart and immediately tried to brush it aside. *Obviously in this day and age having a child with someone doesn't demand being married*, she reminded herself. But the JD she'd come to know wasn't the kind of man who would love 'em and leave 'em to put it bluntly and somewhat crassly. *Divorced, maybe?* He'd told her long ago that he was single. No qualifiers. Just single. He'd never mentioned being divorced or having a child. *Charlotte's right; we really are just getting to know each other.* There was probably a lot she didn't know about him and his past, just as there was still much he didn't know about her and hers.

Coffee and bagel sandwich in hand, she headed back to her office, so she could eat in peace before the morning appointments began. The office door was closed, which she found odd since it was rarely shut when she wasn't in it. Just as she was about to open it, Donna popped her head out from the front office, looking flustered.

"Dr. Mac," Donna said, "uh, you have a visitor waiting."

"Give me a minute to eat," Maggie said. "Then send them back. Who is it?"

"He's, uh, already in your office." Donna winced and shrugged. "Sorry."

Maggie pushed the door open. Even from the back, his tousled, sun-streaked head of hair was unmistakable. "Jeff!" she said. "What are you doing here?"

Jeff stood and turned around, casually buttoning his jacket as he did. As per usual, he looked like he'd stepped directly off the pages of GQ in perfectly tailored clothing, grey wool slacks and a black mock turtle under a muted charcoal plaid cashmere blazer. It was a sight that not so long ago would have set her heart doing somersaults, now it just made her stomach churn.

"I think we need to talk, face to face," he said and started to approach her.

Maggie sidestepped and went around to her chair, pointedly putting the desk between them. "You've wasted the trip," she said, setting the coffee down and opening the sack.

"I hope not," he said, unbuttoning his blazer and settling again in the chair he'd just vacated.

Ignoring him, she unwrapped the bagel sandwich and took a bite. And a sip of coffee. A hint of Paco Rabanne cologne drifted across the desk, evoking a rush of memories of their time together; she tried to force them away and casually took another bite.

After a long silent moment, he said, "Come with me so we can talk. Away from here."

"I already said no to that offer. I have responsibilities. I have patients scheduled, starting in," she looked at her watch, "fifteen minutes."

"OK," he said, "I'll wait until you've seen them, and then we can go."

"Go where?"

"Anywhere; name the place. The jet's on standby at the FBO in Hot Springs." Maggie started to protest, but he went on. "Your sub is on stand-by, too."

Maggie closed her eyes, counted to ten, and sighed heavily. "I'm not flying off somewhere with you. I told you that on the phone."

"Just give me the afternoon, then. We'll grab a late lunch around here somewhere." He leaned forward and extended his hand across the desk, flashing that boyish smile she'd first seen across a surgical scrub sink at the hospital more than three years ago. The one that had instantly attracted her to him. The one that had always made her heart dance. "And maybe dinner," he added lifting his brows in invitation.

She looked up and met his gaze but didn't take his hand. *Do the three years of my life I invested in our relationship demand at least hearing you out?* After a long moment's consideration she said, "I warn you there isn't much in the way of fine dining in Caddo Bend."

"We could drive to Hot Springs, then, or even Little Rock. That's the capitol, right?"

"It is. Let me see how the day goes," she said, "I'll call you when I finish here."

"Fair enough," he said with a shrug. "I'll go somewhere and amuse myself until I hear from you." He stood and buttoned his jacket. "Is there some place around here to get breakfast?" he said, eyeing her bagel.

"Molly's Café," she said. "On the downtown square, out the front door and down the street. It's not far."

"Thanks. I'll give it a try." He turned and left, pulling the door closed behind him. Maggie dropped her head into her hands and wondered what the hell she was doing, and why the hell he had to be so gorgeous and charming and smell like heaven itself? They were done. She'd decided that. She was with JD now; they were starting to build something good together. Then the thought of him so far away and out of touch, maybe even now somewhere with the mother of his child instantly made her heart ache. She willed herself not to think of it.

She was just finishing her last bite of bagel when Therma Faye rapped on the door and stuck her head in. "Sorry about springing the visitor on you," she said. "I told Donna he should wait out front. But golly Bob is he a looker! Donna's still fanning herself with a file folder."

Maggie gave her an eye roll but didn't engage in the commentary. "It's OK," she said finally.

"Anyway," Therma Faye continued, "the rooms are loaded up. Go to the treatment room first. Eldon Medlock's boy Scooter's in there. He's complaining that he's having some trouble breathing."

Maggie donned her labcoat and got to work, always a good remedy for forgetting your own fears and worries. She took the tablet reader from the door and gave silent thanks again to whatever State agency's grant money it was that had finally enabled them to bring their facility's charting into the 21st Century. She quickly scanned what Therma Faye had noted: *19 y/o WM c/o chest pain & difficulty breathing. BP 120/68; P 90; R 22; T 98.4. Normal BP, both pulse and breathing a little too fast. No fever.* She opened the door to find Scooter Medlock, tall and rangy like his dad, sitting on the exam table scanning the screen of his phone, not looking particularly distressed. When Maggie walked in, he put the phone back into his jeans pocket.

"Hi, Scooter," she said. "What's going on?"

"Mornin, Dr. McKinley," he said. "I'm not sure, but I think maybe I pulled something in my chest. It kinda hurts to breathe."

"OK, tell me what happened."

"Well, nothin' I can remember. I was unloading a delivery of 50-pound bags of pea gravel last night, hoisting em up onto my shoulder to carry. Stuff I do every day at the store, and I really didn't think nothin' about it. Then I woke up this morning a little sore and kinda having a hard time getting a deep breath. My dad made me come over. I think it's overkill; just probably pulled something on this right side here."

"Does it hurt when you take in a breath, or does it feel like you can't get a good breath in?" Maggie asked.

"Both, really," he said.

"Have you had a cough?"

"No ma'am," he replied. "Not really."

"OK. Let's take a look at it. Can you take off your shirt for me?" As he unbuttoned and shrugged out of his shirt, Maggie pulled her stethoscope from the pocket of her labcoat and rubbed the chest piece between her palms to warm it, taking note as she did that there were no visible bruises or scrapes on his skin. When she put the stethoscope to his chest to listen to his heart he immediately sucked in a big breath and winced. "Just breathe normally. I'm going to listen to your heart first," she said, patting his shoulder and continuing to listen. *Regular heart rhythm, a bit fast. No murmur or rub.* She moved the stethoscope to his back. "Now give me some slow, deep breaths, in and out through your open mouth." She listened first on the left side of his chest, then moving to his back, she listened from the top to the middle and down to the base of his lung at the bottom of his ribcage. *Breath sounds clear on the left.* Then she shifted to the right side and listened. A puzzled look crossed her face, and she lifted the head of the stethoscope and twisted it on its stem back and forth several times, then tapped the diaphragm of it a couple of times with her nail; she heard those taps loud and clear in her earpieces. She repositioned the instrument on his back and listened again, more intently, then moved to the side and the front. *Nothing. Not a sound on the right. Collapsed lung?*

Maggie pulled the earpieces from her ears and dropped them around her neck, then reached across to calmly open the top drawer of the crash cart and remove a pulse oximeter.

"What's that?" he asked.

"It measures the oxygen in your blood. Here, give me your index finger, I'll show you." He gave her a curious look. "It won't hurt," she said as she clipped the pulse ox onto his finger and activated it. "It'll give us a read out in just a few seconds."

In a moment the device beeped, and the display read 84. *Lower than it should be.* She found herself wishing, and not for the first time, that she had x-ray capability on site. She felt hamstrung without it. And the closest machine was in Mt. Ida, about 25 minutes away.

"Dang, how does it do that?" Scooter marveled. "It's like on Star Trek or something."

"Uh huh," she agreed. "And what it tells me is your oxygen is a little low," she said, reaching for the oxygen cylinder beside the table and pulling it closer. She removed a fresh mask and tubing from the crash cart and connected it. "I'd like for you to breathe a little oxygen for me, OK?" She positioned the mask over his nose and mouth and slipped the elastic strap over his head.

"What's wrong, Doc?" his voice sounded muffled behind the mask, like he was in a barrel.

"Well, I don't think you pulled a muscle," she said, putting a reassuring hand on his shoulder. She paused and let that fact sink in before she went on. "Don't be alarmed, but I think that your lung may have collapse."

Scooter's eyes widened. "What? How?"

"I suspect the repeated blows to your chest from hefting those bags of gravel may have caused it. Sometimes there's what's called a *pleural bleb*, which is just a fancy medical name for a blister or bubble of air on the filmy covering of your lung. Occasionally those blisters can rupture following a blow to the chest or back, and when they do it allows air to leak into the chest cavity – what's called a *pneumothorax* – and sometimes the lung collapses."

"Holy shit," he whispered, then winced. "I'm sorry, ma'am."

"My ears have heard worse, trust me," she smiled at him. "Just know that you're going to be OK. We need a chest x-ray to be sure of what's going on and the extent and nature of the collapse if that's what it is. I could send you over to Mt. Ida to get the x-ray, but if I'm correct that the lung is down – and I'm pretty sure I am – we'll need to send you over to Mercy General in Hot Springs, so you might as well get the x-ray there. If your lung is down, they'll want to admit you and monitor you for a day or so, keep you on oxygen, and see how things go. Sometimes these things will heal on their own. Sometimes it requires a surgeon to put a chest tube in place to restore the proper pressure in the chest and let the lung return to normal."

"Dang," he said, shaking his head. "Can you call my dad?"

"Sure," she reassured him. "Meantime, let me help you over to this chair to wait; you'll be a lot more comfortable there than on this table." She got him settled in the infusion chair in the corner, reclined it a bit, and covered him with a blanket. "I'm going to call your father and make arrangements to get you over to Mercy General. Then I'll be back to check on you. Everything's going to be fine."

Maggie left the treatment door cracked and went to her office. She buzzed Donna on the intercom line.

"Yes'm?" Donna answered.

"Donna, can you call EMS and tell them we have a patient with a pneumothorax we need to transport over to Mercy General? I don't feel comfortable just sending him in a car without an x-ray to be sure it's not a tension pneumo."

"A what?"

"Pneumothorax. Collapsed lung."

"Oh my gosh! Scooter?" Donna said.

"Yes. Tell them he's stable. And get Mr. Medlock on the phone for me, please. Is Therma Faye up there?"

"Yes'm, she's right here," Donna said.

"Tell her I need her to keep a close watch on Scooter in the treatment room until EMS gets here."

"Will do."

After Maggie had spoken to Eldon Medlock and called the ER at Mercy to alert them what was coming and what she'd done thus far, she checked in on Scooter, who was resting comfortably in the chair, scrolling through social media. His oxygen saturation was up to 90%, and Therma Faye was with him.

"Let me know if his ox sat falls," Maggie said quietly to Therma Faye. "Or if anything changes. And come get me when EMS arrives."

By half past one, when Scooter had been safely transported to Hot Springs and Maggie had worked her way through the remaining patients on her schedule, there was nothing standing in the way of her calling Jeff except her own reluctance. She spent another twenty minutes or so stalling, finishing up some charting, and intermittently checking her phone for messages and missed calls. *Still nothing from JD.* It was now almost two in the afternoon in Caddo Bend, so five in the morning in Tokyo. Doubtful she'd hear anything from him in the next few hours. *For heaven's sake, quit stalling,* she chided herself.

She texted Jeff that she was finished at the clinic and to meet her at the boarding house, so she could drop her car and let Miz Hendri know not to plan on her for dinner tonight. She was glad of the chance to have a moment alone with her to explain a little of what was going on. Miz Hendri had known JD all his life and was more than a little fond of him. Maggie didn't want her to get the wrong idea about this late lunch with Jeff. For his part, Jeff must not have been amusing himself too far away, because she'd only been home a few minutes and was still in the dining room talking with Miz Hendri when they heard him pull up in front. His knock soon followed.

"Will you let him in, please? I want to take this upstairs," she said, putting a hand on her laptop, "and run a comb through my hair."

"Of course," Miz Hendri said, "but *leibchen,* are you sure this is what you want to do?"

"Not in the least sure," she admitted. "But he's here, and he's asked to talk. After three years, I think maybe I owe him at least that."

When Maggie came back downstairs, she found Jeff sitting alone by the fire in the front room. He stood when she walked in and gave her an openly appreciative stare. She'd slipped into a pair of black skinny jeans, boots, and an ivory cashmere V-neck tunic that clung in all the right spots. Her long hair fell in silken, ash blonde curls onto her shoulders and caught and reflected the fire light.

"Damn," he breathed out the word in a whisper.

"Where's Miz Hendri?" she asked, ignoring his comment.

"In the kitchen, I think," he replied. "She deposited me in this cozy spot and offered me a glass of sherry. Which I declined." There was that smile again. "Ready to go?"

"We could just stay here and talk," she suggested.

"I'd like something a little more private, and something to eat. My breakfast at Molly's was surprisingly good, but it's long gone, and I'm starving."

"OK, where do you want to go?" she asked.

"Wherever you usually go is fine with me."

"I eat dinner here at Miz Hendri's most nights," she said, unable to suppress the image of JD, shirtless, whipping up something delicious at the stone counter of his kitchen. "As I mentioned before, there's not much in the way of fine dining around here."

"I did a little research on my phone while I waited for you. There's a place in Hot Springs called Bistro TinTin that gets good reviews online. Do you know of it?"

"No," she replied. "But I really haven't spent much time there, except to go to the hospital and the airport. I'm sure it's fine."

"Shall we then?" He inclined his head toward the door and flashed that disarming smile.

On the drive over, he chatted as if nothing had gone amiss between them. Nothing was said about their split, and Maggie wondered when he was going to get to the point. Or maybe that was his point, just reminding her how easily they got on, which had always been the case. When they arrived at the restaurant it was late afternoon, and the place was nearly deserted with just a couple of other tables occupied. The space had the look and feel of a classic French bistro, reminding her a little of a restaurant on 57th St. that had been one of their regular late night dinner haunts in Manhattan; she wondered if online photos of this place were what had drawn him to it. Though it wasn't as large or nearly as raucous as Rue 57, it was eerily similar, just a bit brighter and airier and easier for conversation, at least at this hour.

The waitress, a pretty, buxom, twenty-something woman with thick dark hair woven into a heavy braid, came over to offer menus and drinks almost as soon as they were seated.

Maggie asked for mineral water and lime.

"We have a local water. Mt. Valley. And it's delicious," the waitress said.

"Sure you don't want a glass of wine or prosecco?" Jeff asked.

"No, thanks. A little early for me," she said. *And I need to keep my wits about me.*

"OK. A large bottle of the water."

"Still or sparkling?"

"Still, please, and two glasses," Jeff smiled charmingly at the waitress. Maggie noticed his smile seemed to have the same effect on this woman as she'd experienced herself the first time she'd seen it. The poor thing just stood there staring at him, blushing pink under the sprinkling of freckles across her cheeks.

"Do uh, do you," the waitress stammered then found her voice again and continued, "Do you want ice?"

"Sure," he said, then added as she turned to go, "Thanks." The smile she gave him as she turned back his way was priceless. She knew the feeling.

Maggie scanned the menu for a moment in silence. "What looks good?" she said.

"You," he responded. "Always."

"I meant the food," she said, giving him a look.

"Can't go wrong with steak frites in a bistro," he shrugged.

"I was thinking about the fresh oysters and clams, maybe," she said.

Jeff grimaced. "Not sure I'd trust the raw bar this far inland. I had a near-death experience with bad oysters at a conference in Scottsdale once when I was a resident, and I made a vow that if I didn't die—which from my perspective for about 24 hours seemed by far the likeliest outcome—I'd never to eat them again unless I could see the ocean."

"And never in a month without an 'r'," Maggie added.

"Yeah, that too. But even though it's November," he said, looking around him, "I see no ocean, so I'll pass."

When the waitress returned with their water, Maggie could swear she'd glossed her lips in the interim and spritzed on some cologne, maybe a little too much of it. Jeff had that effect on women, and she knew he wasn't entirely unaware of it. He ordered the steak frites, medium rare, and a glass of a Rhone red. Maggie eschewed the raw bar, opting instead for bowl of steamed Little Neck clams in white wine broth and a salad. And stuck with the water.

Once Jeff's new admirer left them alone, he spoke, softly and earnestly. "Mags, I know I've hurt you. My lapse was stupid and meaningless, but I've told you that already."

"And I've told you it wasn't meaningless to me."

"I know. I know. Just hear me out. Please?"

Maggie looked at him and acquiesced with a single nod.

"Judith knows there's nothing serious between us—between her and me, I mean. What you saw meant nothing to either of us beyond two old friends who found themselves at loose ends on the wrong side of too much liquor."

"We've been over this ground," she said looking away from him and taking a calming breath in. Finally returning his gaze with a steely one of her own, she continued, "But you're wrong about it meaning nothing, and I don't just mean to me. I've seen the looks Judith gives you. I'm not blind and never have been. You may consider her a casual hook up with an old friend from boarding school, but it's painfully obvious that's not how she sees it. She wants more. She wants a serious relationship with you. Now."

"It may be what she wants, but I made it quite clear to her the morning you, uh," he hesitated a moment, and Maggie could almost see the gears turning as he searched for a less damning way to describe her finding him naked in bed with Judith, "...saw us together. I told her then all I want is you. I love you, Maggie. I. Love. You. And I want us to be together." He reached across the table and laid his hand over hers; she couldn't deny the warm, familiar sensation was inviting, and his touch, even such a casual one, could still send a jolt of sexual energy through her. She looked away and tried to shake off the feeling.

"Look at me," he said softly, and she lifted her eyes again to meet his. "If I need to take a vow of celibacy for the next year and a half, show me where to sign the papers. I promise you I will abide by it." He paused again and raised a brow suggestively. "Other than when we're together, of course."

Her phone buzzed on the table beside her, and when she glanced down at the display her heart leaped. JD's name and cell number appeared on the screen. *Really! Now?* After several more buzzes, she pulled her hand from under Jeff's and picked up the phone. "Excuse me a minute. I need to take this call," she said. "It could be the clinic," she added and immediately felt guilty for the impulse to shade the truth. She answered as she pushed through the side door to the privacy of the outdoor patio.

"Hello? JD? Hello?" But she'd missed the call; it had already gone to voice mail. *Damn it!* In a moment, the alert sounded to tell her that a voice mail had been left, and she clicked over to listen.

"Hey. It's JD." He paused a moment then went on, *"I got your messages, and I'm not ignoring you; I'm in Tokyo. That's what I called to tell you the other day, when,"* he didn't finish the sentence. Then he sighed audibly and continued in another direction, resignation evident in his voice. *"I've got some business that's going to keep me here for a week or more. I'm not exactly sure when I'll be back, but I'll let you know when I figure it out. There's some*

stuff I need to talk to you about but not on..." The recording ended abruptly, and she was unsure whether the call had dropped, the message had been clipped, or he'd been interrupted by something. Or someone. Maggie shoved that thought away and kept the phone to her ear long after the message ended, not wanting to break even this tenuous connection with him. Then she replayed the message and listened again. And then a third time. She thought for an instant about calling him back but didn't want to have Jeff walk in on the conversation and be put in the position of having to explain his presence to JD or send the wrong message. Or worse, reach JD in the middle of a situation with someone there. If that was a real thing, she'd rather not know about it just yet. Finally, she put the phone into her pocket and headed back to the table and a conversation that was surely going to be like walking across an emotional mine field.

"Everything OK?" he asked, sipping the glass of Rhone that the waitress had delivered.

"Yeah, all good" she said, nodding, but not offering more and lapsing into silence. *What is it that JD needs to talk to me about? His child? Her mother? Us? Is there still an us?* And even the possibility there might not be made her feel hollowed out and sad.

"This is surprisingly good wine. You sure you don't want a glass?"

"Actually, I could use one," she said, "but I think I'd prefer white with the clams."

He signaled for the waitress, who materialized at his side almost instantly.

"The lady would like a glass of white wine with her meal. Maggie, what sounds good?"

The waitress seemed loathe to tear her eyes away from Jeff but grudgingly turned them Maggie's way and said, "By the glass I can recommend a lovely white Côtes du Rhone, the Saint-Esprit 2009. And we offer a Pouilly Fume and a Sancerre by the glass as well, both also 2009. Any of those would pair nicely with the clams."

"May I have the Sancerre?" Maggie said.

The waitress brought her a glass of the white, and Maggie took a few sips in silence. Her thoughts had wandered back to JD's message when Jeff's voice jolted her back to the present; she realized he had been talking and that she had no clue what he'd said.

"...and obviously I understand it's going to take time and that I'm going to have to earn back your trust, but I swear to you I'm willing to do whatever it takes," he finished.

"Jeff, it's more than just trust. You should know there's some- " she began, but the waitress arrived with their food, giving Jeff a beaming smile and Maggie a temporary reprieve.

Once they were alone again it appeared that Jeff wasn't keen to resume the previous conversation; perhaps on some level he'd picked up on its direction and didn't want to go there. Instead, they chatted easily through-out dinner and on the ride back to Miz Hendri's about everything but the future of their relationship. She felt quite certain that it wasn't because he'd accepted the end of things as they had been between them—he wasn't one to give up so easily on something he'd set his mind to—but rather that he felt he'd said his piece, apologized, promised to do better, and from his perspective that was that. Case closed.

Jeff parked the rental car in front of Miz Hendri's and killed the en-gine. "Well," he said, "here we are." He turned to look at her, not saying anything more for a moment, then he reached out and stroked her hair with his hand, twisting a tendril around his finger, and smoothing it down over her shoulder. "You know your hair looks like spun gold in the moon-light." He leaned closer to her.

"Jeff," Maggie began, "there's something I need to tell you before you go."

"Shhhh," he said softly. "I'm not going anywhere yet. Just let me look at you."

But she was not to be put off this time. "You should know, there's some-," she began again but he pulled her close and interrupted what she had been about to say with a sudden kiss, tender and filled with longing. His nearness and the familiar, masculine scent of him in the warm car made her head swim, and she felt her resolve start to crack. *Don't do this*, she thought. *You can't do this.* Her gut had told her things had ended with Jeff the morning she found Judith in his bed. She'd been sure she couldn't build a life with someone she couldn't trust. Surer still after spending time with JD almost non-stop since that awful night at the river. But now JD was halfway around the globe; gone without warning. And there is a child. And a mother of that child. *Where does that leave me? Where does it leave us?* But with Jeff's lips soft on hers she couldn't think rationally, and it occurred to her that it would be oh, so easy to give in to this moment, to slip back into a relationship with him. "Oh, JD," she whispered.

Jeff instantly pulled away from her. "Who's JD?" The look on his face was a mix of disbelief and pain. "Did you just …?"

Maggie pulled further back from him and looked down. "Jeff, I'm sorry. I can't do this," she said softly. "I tried to tell you earlier." Tears glistened in her long lashes. "There's someone else in my life now."

"What do you mean someone else?"

"Just what I said," she met his eyes again. "I've been seeing someone. Here in Caddo Bend."

"Since when?" he asked, incredulous, angry.

"Since after I found you naked in your bed with your ex-girlfriend," she hurled the anger back at him.

He winced at that then after a beat narrowed his eyes in question. "Is it that post doc? The one that lives here?"

"No!" The thought of Nick revolted her, and she almost said so, then reminded herself once more that Jeff didn't know the whole story; they'd split up before all the drama with Nick had happened, and they hadn't spoken about any of it. He knew nothing of her abduction at gun point or her near death in the raging river. "It doesn't matter who," she said. "It's just not as straightforward anymore as my getting over your cheating and taking you back."

He just sat there, stunned, and said nothing, disbelief etched on his features.

"I was totally up front with you from the jump that I wasn't sure I could ever get over what you did," she continued. "I'm still not."

"And in the meantime, you've been hooking up with some local yokel you've known, what, ten minutes?"

"It's not like that. He's local, yes, but he's not a yokel. And he's most definitely not just a hook up." She felt her anger rise at his cavalier, hypocritical assumptions far more than she let on. "I think you'd better go," she said with quiet resolve, then opened the door and climbed out into the chilly evening air. Jeff opened his door to follow her, but she held up a hand. "Don't. I need you to not be here right now. I need to think all this through alone. Go back to New York."

"Maggie, please," he began.

"I'd advise against pressing me on this, Jeff," she said, fixing him with her stare. "If you do, you'll be disappointed because the answer I'd give you right now would be to reiterate what I have told you before, that we're done."

She turned and walked up the stairs and into the boarding house, immediately enveloped in the warmth of the space. In the front hall she stopped and listened until she heard the crunch of the gravel outside as Jeff's car pulled away. The night lighting was on in the front room and hall, which meant Miz Hendri had retired, for which she was grateful. She really didn't want to field any questions about tonight.

CHAPTER 6
Autumn Child

As Maggie climbed the stairs to her room, she checked her phone and found only one bar. *Damn it!* She wanted to return JD's call. *What time is it in Japan? Eight thirty pm here, fifteen hours difference, so add three and flip: 11:30 am.* But she still had only a single bar of service and didn't want to risk dropping the call at a critical moment if it went through. She could Skype, if the internet at Miz Hendri's wasn't utterly unpredictable, but unpredictability was its default state.

Thumbing up the *Essential Roy Orbison* on her iTunes playlist, she selected one of her mother's favorites, music she'd grown up listening to and singing along to with her. In moments Roy's amazing voice filled the semi-darkened space. *I love you even more than I did before but darling what can I do-oo-oo-oo? Cause you don't love me, and I'll always be crying over you.*

She took off her clothes and shoes and slipped into her favorite pair of lounging sweats. Then, she poured herself a healthy shot of Jameson and settled into the rocker in her room to think it all through, slipping her feet up under her for warmth.

After a few quiet moments, she unfolded herself from the rocker and padded over to open the drawer of the desk beside her bed. From it she removed the framed photo of Jeff she'd tucked out of sight the night she'd come back from that painful surprise visit to NY. Settling again in the rocker she took another sip of the Jameson and looked at the photo of him: shirtless, leaning against the deck rail of a racing yacht; his sun-streaked hair ruffled by the breeze; his tan flat belly; his disarming smile, caught in mid laugh. *Three happy, near-perfect, fun-filled, years together. Just not perfect enough to keep him from falling into bed with Judith when I was barely out of sight.* How could she believe him now? How could she ever trust that he would put her and their relationship first? She realized there were women for whom fidelity wasn't the *sine qua non*, but she simply wasn't one of them. Even if she could forgive, and she intended to work on that for the benefit of her own psyche—or rather as the nuns at boarding school would have admonished her, her immortal soul—she knew she couldn't forget. Couldn't unsee that image of them in the tangle of his sheets. Sheets she'd slept on with him not so very long before.

She looked up at the double oval frame on the dresser beside her, at the photos of her parents. "What do I do?" She asked aloud, searching their faces, wishing for the millionth time that they could answer. Wishing she could just pick up the phone and call them, tearfully pour out her hurt to them, and receive their wise counsel and the assurance that everything would be OK.

The ringing of her phone startled her and interrupted Roy in the middle of begging a pretty woman to look his way. She reached for her phone on the table beside her, and her heart nearly stopped when she saw the display.

"JD?" she answered eagerly. "JD? Is that you?" *Oh, God, please don't let the call drop.*

"Hey, sugar," he said softly. "Yeah, it's me."

She could hear the fatigue and strain in his voice. And something else she couldn't quite lay her finger on. "Oh, thank God," she said. "It is so good to hear your voice. Where are you? Are you OK?"

"I'm fine," he said and went silent for long enough that she feared the call had dropped before he continued. "Well, not fine, really. I'm in Tokyo."

Then she recognized the something else in his voice: sadness. Profound sadness. She heard him deeply inhale and blow out that breath in a long release.

"Yes," she said. "I got your voice mail. Why are you there? Why didn't you tell me you were going? I've been so worried."

"I called to tell you I had to go, but-" he paused and blew out another audible sigh. "This isn't a conversation I wanted to have over the phone."

"What's going on?" When he didn't continue, she broached the subject she most feared, "Are you having second thoughts about us?"

"God no!" he interjected. "No! It's not that."

In the background Maggie could hear what sounded like the rhythmic bleep of medical equipment and the drone of overhead paging, a soundtrack she was intimately familiar with. "Where are you, exactly?"

"I'm at the hospital at the University of Tokyo," he said and took a long pause before he added, "with my daughter."

There it was. That word Velma had uttered in the café. "Your daughter," Maggie repeated softly, more statement than question.

"Yeah," he blew out another breath. "I have a daughter. Here in Japan." He went quiet for a bit. Maggie took a swallow of the whisky and waited. "Her name is Akiko."

"That's a beautiful name," she said gently, not knowing exactly what to say next. "What does it mean?"

"Autumn child," he said softly, then after a long pause added, "She was born in October."

"And she's ill? In the hospital?" Maggie could imagine a beautiful Japanese woman with silken raven hair and worried almond eyes standing beside him.

"No, but her mother is very ill. That's why Namiko-san asked me to come right away."

"Is that her mother?" Maggie asked as casually as she could manage with her heart thudding from apprehension in her chest.

"No. Grandmother. Namiko is Akiko's grandmother—Katsumi's mother."

"And she's there now?" Maggie asked. "Katsumi, I mean."

"Yes," he said, pausing. Maggie could almost feel his anguished hesitance from 6,000 miles away and waited until he finally went on. "Sort of." He hesitated again, and she heard him take another deep inhale and exhale. "Not really. Katsumi was injured…severely…in an accident, a train derailment, just eight days before Akiko was due to be born. They airlifted them to the hospital, but Katsumi never regained consciousness. The doctors delivered Akiko by emergency C-section; it was a miracle she survived."

"Oh, JD," Maggie said sadly, "I'm so, so sorry." Her medical training allowed her to fill in the details about what that would mean. "That must have been so…horrible to… When did this happen?"

"Five years ago, this past October."

That surprised her; it was nothing new then. She couldn't process for a moment what it meant. "Where is your daughter now?"

"Outside. Her grandmother, Namiko-san, took her outside for a walk on the grounds."

JD went on to explain that after Akiko's emergency delivery, Katsumi remained unresponsive. Her brain scans showed massive damage, and EEG traces continued to show severely depressed electrical activity. That's how she'd been for the last five years.

The doctors told them her brain would never recover; she'd been too long without oxygen following the accident and during the traumatic birthing process. She would require total respiratory support and care for life, however long that might be. And worse and more painful yet, she would remain completely unaware of her surroundings or those around. And she had.

Since her birth Akiko and Katsumi had been cared for by Namiko in her home in Atami, a small coastal city near Tokyo. Because JD's work kept him away so much of the time it seemed like the best option for the girl, really for them both. So, he arranged and provided for around-the-clock skilled nursing care for his wife at home with her mother and daughter. He visited them often when he still lived in Japan to hold his daughter, read to her, sing to her. And he'd kept in regular phone and video contact with Namiko and Akiko in the two years since his mother's illness had first brought him back to Caddo Bend, but he'd traveled back to Tokyo only a few times in that interval. His business commitments there had ended for the most part, and he no longer wanted to be in Japan full time, but he felt he couldn't take Akiko from Namiko-san. The child was her living connection to Katsumi, her precious only child.

About a week ago, JD told her, Katsumi had spiked a high fever. The doctors diagnosed influenza but felt comfortable allowing her to remain at home in the full-time care of her nurses. Then her symptoms worsened, and they admitted her to the hospital in Tokyo a few of days ago, where her condition deteriorated further. Already on mechanical ventilation and not responding to antivirals, her doctors predicted an increasing struggle for her with no further course of action open to them. They were advising removal of life support to shorten the struggle. Her mother was fiercely resisting that option.

"So," he said, "that's why Namiko-san called urgently and asked me to come. Although the divorce had been legally and completely finalized years ago, when it was glaringly apparent Katsumi would never recover, by some odd twist of a Japanese legal technicality I'm apparently still the medical decision maker for her."

"JD, I'm so sorry. It's a nightmare position for anyone to be put in." Her heart ached for him. "How can I help?" She wanted desperately to reach out and touch him. To hold him. To comfort him.

She heard him take a deep, shuddering breath and let it go forcefully before he went on. "That's why I'm calling you. Well one reason, anyway. I need somebody with some perspective to walk me through this decision. I can't even discuss it with Namiko-san. Katsumi is her only child. For all intents and purposes, she's been gone for five years, but I don't think she can bear to contemplate losing her completely. But losing her is what she's up against."

"What do her doctors say?"

"Exactly that. She isn't responding to the medications they've given her; she's struggling more; her oxygen numbers are falling despite mechanical ventilation."

"Is she suffering?"

"How can we know? And if I give them the OK to...well..."

"Yeah. What does her brain activity show?" Maggie asked gently.

"Nothing," he said after a pause.

"And they don't think she'll ever recover any brain function?" she asked.

"No," he said simply.

"And without hope of even limited recovery, without hope of improvement, what purpose do heroic measures serve?"

"None," he said after a long pause. "None that I can see. Just prolong the inevitable and the suffering."

Maggie didn't respond but let him sit with his thoughts a moment.

"Thank you," he finally said, so quietly she almost didn't hear it. "I need to go now to talk with Namiko-san and my daughter and speak to the doctors."

"Go," she said, her heart breaking for him in what she knew were the coming gut-wrenching conversations. "Go be with them for as long as you can. I'll be here if you need me."

"Thank you," he said again. "I'll," his voice broke, and she could hear the strain in it when he cleared his throat and continued, "I'll call you in a day or two."

"I'm here," she said. "Any hour of the day or night. Just call."

From across an ocean and half a continent, Maggie became aware of the changed situation before JD did, alerted by the sudden shift of the ambient background medical sounds and the new urgency in the overhead pages, even when uttered in a language she didn't understand. And closer and more clearly, the rhythmic bleep of a heart monitor that had been replaced by the monotone whine of a flatline.

"JD," she said with some urgency, but before she could continue the emergent sounds of the responding code team filled the background void.

"*Dō shita no?*" JD said, then in English as well for Maggie, "What's going on?"

"*Kokoro teishi!*" someone barked at him. "*Doite!*"

"JD," Maggie said, "what are they saying?"

"Her heart has stopped. They're ordering me out," JD said.

"Then you have to act quickly if you want to stop her being coded," Maggie said in a rush. "You're her medical advocate. Even if you haven't signed a DNR yet, you can tell them not to code her if that's what you want, if that's what you think is best for her. Or you can let them proceed. It's your call."

The urgent clamor of the code process continued, then JD's clear voice cut through it. "*Sosei shinaide kusasai!*" The background chaos abruptly stilled. "Please do not resuscitate her," he added softer in English. Then more quietly he said, "*Kanojo ni heiwa o ataete kudasai.* Please give her peace."

"*Yoroshīdesu ka?*" the physician asked.

"*Hai.* Yes. I'm sure," JD said quietly, but firmly.

"Oh, JD," Maggie whispered. "I'm so sorry."

"I need to go now. I need to find Namiko-san.

"Go. Do what you need to do. I'm here," Maggie said. The whine of the background flatline alarm stopped. She realized that meant the team had turned the monitor off. She could hear them speaking in hushed tones, almost inaudible and completely unintelligible, but she'd been there so many times. She knew what they were saying, what was happening; it was the same in any language. Removing tubes and disconnecting leads, rolling them up, gathering discarded paper trash.

"Maggie, I…" he began but stopped.

"Go now and find her mother and your daughter. Let the nursing team make things peaceful there for them to say goodbye."

"OK. Thank you," he said softly. "I'll call you soon."

"I know," she replied simply.

"Goodbye, love."

"Bye," she said, and the connection ended. *Love. Love, he said.* Maggie held the phone to her ear in the darkness of her room, loathe once more to let him go.

She sipped the Jameson in silence, then finally dropped the phone to her lap; the display glowed brightly in the dimly lit space. She imagined the pain in JD's soft gray eyes, imagined them bright with gathering tears as he explained to a 5-year-old child what was happening, maybe held her small hand, and she felt her own tears slip quietly down her cheeks.

CHAPTER 7
Full Moon

The following Friday afternoon Maggie sat at her desk with a cup of coffee, enjoying a short break after what had been a completely crazy morning at the clinic. The last several days had been remarkably slow, but today, on top of an already-full appointment book of check-ups for blood pressure, diabetes, heart disease and all the usual chronic ailments, the schedule was further clotted up by several oddball accidents that she could only attribute to the waxing moon – it would be full tomorrow. She was just thankful that there was no Saturday clinic scheduled this weekend and that she had no pregnant patients close to delivery at present. The full moon often filled labor and delivery suites everywhere, irrespective of specific due dates.

Her fervent hope was that she could rest up and maybe get a little Christmas shopping done. It wasn't like she had that many people to buy for. Outside Charlotte's family, which was as close to family as she'd had since she lost her parents, in the last few years there'd been only Jeff and the odd secret Santa colleague gifts to think about. She was pleased that this year there'd be a few more: Miz Hendri and Papa, Tee and Donna. Rose Ellen. And now JD. With a full moon in the mix, a weekend of peace and quiet wasn't likely, but a girl could dream…and shop some.

Whether you'd previously believed in cosmic hocus pocus or not, a few years in medical practice would make the most ardent non-believer swear by the power of a full moon to inspire lunacy, wreck schedules, and create upheaval. She'd been advised that this was most assuredly so by her chief resident early on in her training, and she'd been instructed to keep careful track of the phases of the moon and to alert him when their team's scheduled ER call would coincide with its full phase. And based on that to endeavor to trade days with another less moon savvy team in advance if possible. She'd thought it a joke. Experience proved otherwise.

So far this morning, she'd had to sew up a deep gash in a woman's big toe made by the blades of a food blender—long story that one—and splinted what she was sure was a forearm fracture in an elderly gentleman who decided it was a good idea to crawl out the dormer window onto his roof to retrieve his cat. He'd slipped on the steep slant and fallen into the bushes below. And the cat hopped down safely on its own. It's a wonder the man hadn't broken more than his arm. His injury had reminded her yet again of how badly the clinic needed an x-ray machine; she'd only been able to evaluate his motor/sensory/circulatory integrity, splint him, and send him over to Mt. Ida for x-ray and casting. She hoped to remedy that deficiency and thought she'd located a suitable used machine in Little Rock; next she'd need to locate the $24,975 to secure it. And get it installed. And update Therma Faye's lapsed x-ray tech credentials. *One step at a time.*

"Break time's up," Therma Faye said, poking her head around the door. It had been a hellish day already and thanks to that and the dampness in the air her unruly hair stood out in a disorganized bleached blonde frizzle. "Roy Owens is in Room 2 for follow up. And we're getting the last two scheduled patients in 1 and 3 now."

"OK. Be right there. Just want to finish the last of my coffee."

Maggie lifted the tablet from the chart box beside Room 2. It read: *Owens, Roy. 61 y/o WM, recent MI. BP 145/85. P 88. R 12. Wt 227. Here for follow up.* She walked into the room.

"Mr. Owens, it's so good to see you up and about," she said.

"Roy, please," he said. "And I believe I have you to thank for still being here." Maggie extended her hand, and he enfolded it in both his and shook it gently. "And I need to apologize to you. I can't tell you how sorry I am for putting you in harm's way with those bones. I still can't believe how that all turned out."

"It's OK. All's well as they say," Maggie said, gently extracting her hand from his grip. "I'm more interested right now in how you're feeling. I've got the discharge notes from your cardiologist in Hot Springs," she said scanning the digital records. "He seems to think your heart muscle damage wasn't too extensive, and that the stent he placed in your artery will do the trick. There was, apparently, one tight blockage in the left anterior descending artery but not much anywhere else. Which is unusual, but good news for you." She didn't add that a blockage of the particular artery in question was often referred to in medicine as the *widow maker*. If he hadn't already heard it, she'd let that sleeping info lie. "And I see he put you on a statin," she looked puzzled as she read the summary, "though your cholesterol values aren't really all that high." She sat on the rolling stool, pulled it up in front of him, and spoke to him directly. "Your age and a documented heart attack do put you in the one category that has been shown to get a very slight overall benefit from taking a statin: men under 65 who have had a documented heart attack. So, although I'm no fan of the knee-jerk use of statins, I won't argue, at least not too vigorously, against their use in your case, if you tolerate taking them. Any issues so far?"

"That's one thing I wanted to ask about." He rested his meaty hands on his knees and leaned forward. "My arms and legs feel sore and tired, like I did a long day of hard physical work, but I haven't. I've been just laying around most of the time since the heart attack, walking a little every day like they told me to's about all, but everything feels sore. And he told me that's something I ought to watch for and let you know if it happened."

"When did this start?"

"Really just a few days ago. But it got so bad yesterday that I couldn't hardly reach up over my head to get a glass out of the kitchen cabinet, without a lot of moaning and groaning anyway."

"Let me look you over, and then we need to get a urine specimen, if you can provide us with one. And I'd like to draw some blood to be sure everything's OK with your liver, muscles, and kidneys." She keyed in the requested labs on his digital chart.

"Already provided one on the way in, far as the specimen goes. Been out there waiting a spell and needed to go. Therma Faye put a plastic cup in my hand just in case."

"Sorry about the wait. It's been one of those days," Maggie said.

"I heard that," he said, nodding his head. "I'm barely back at work, and if you can believe it, we've had a pair of what look like overdose deaths just this past week in Montgomery County."

"Really?" Maggie's eyes went wide.

"Yes ma'am," he said. "I don't know when that's ever happened before."

"I had an opiate overdose here in Caddo Bend last week, too. Not a death, thank God. We got to him in time. Have you got the tox reports back on those two?"

"They both came in DOA, and we don't know the final tox on them yet."

"The one here was oxycontin." The shock on Roy's face underscored his honest surprise and told Maggie he understood the implications of a substance that was both highly addictive and potentially deadly suddenly turning up in the area.

"Hate to see oxy on the rise here." He whispered the words with a concerned shake of his head. "How'd he get it? Or she?"

"He. And not taken knowing what it was, I think," Maggie clarified. "Might have been smoked in oxy-laced marijuana or maybe the pot was accidentally contaminated with it." She let that sink in for a moment. "To borrow from the Wizard of Oz, I don't know if it's a good witch or a bad witch that the victim took it unawares."

"Bad witch, I fear. I don't like the sound of it," Roy said.

"No. Neither do I. The guy who made the buy called it 'killer weed,' and he wasn't far off the mark. But first things first. Let's get you thoroughly checked out."

She listened to his heart and lungs, looked into his eyes, and palpated his abdomen. "I want you to stop taking the statin until we get all the lab results back. Drink plenty of water over the next couple of days." She took her prescription pad from her pocket and scribbled on it. "I'd like you add these supplements. One is bicarbonate salts that I want you to mix with some of the water you drink; it'll help reduce the acidity of your urine. The other is coenzyme Q10, ubiquinol, which is important for your heart. The statin squelches your body's production of it, so you should replace it for a bit. You can get both these at the Natural Food store over in Hot Springs or online." She tore off the prescription sheet and handed it to him. "And let me know right away if your muscle soreness worsens or your urine gets dark. And lastly, we need to talk about your diet. There are some changes I'd like you to make if you're willing."

"Doc Grayson over at Hot Springs gave me a diet sheet. Or well, his nurse did."

"And?"

He made a grimacing scowl, like he'd tasted something foul, and shook his head. "I stay hungry all the time, and it all tastes like cardboard." He winced, then dropped his gaze to his lap. "I can't stand it, ma'am. I know I need to do it, but to be honest I swear I'd rather starve than live on steamed rice, kale, and low-fat dressing."

"Then you'll be glad to know that's not at all what I would recommend you eat. I'll have Therma Faye give you some information about the kinds of foods I'd like to see you eating, but in a nutshell, I'd like you to stick to meat, fish, and poultry grilled, broiled, or roasted, not breaded or deep fried. You can have eggs, green and colorful vegetables, and leafy greens – doesn't have to be kale if you don't like it—and some fresh fruit.

Avoid vegetable oils. Use olive oil or butter for cooking and eating. Or coconut oil.

"Butter?!"

"Butter," she nodded. "Stick to nuts and seeds and solid dark chocolate for occasional snacks. Stay away from bread and baked goods, starchy vegetables, and sugar as much as possible. Avoid anything boxed or wrapped in cellophane with a label. Eat real food, not packaged junk. And in a month, we'll recheck all your bloodwork and see how you're doing." She stuck out her hand. "Deal?"

"Deal," he said and for the first time seemed to smile with genuine pleasure. "Oh, and can my wife eat the same? She's been takin' a statin for a while now."

Maggie rolled her eyes again. "I probably need to take a look at her. Ought not to be making recommendations for patients I've never seen. But, in general, what I can tell you is that there has never been a single medical study that showed any all-cause mortality benefit of taking a statin for women of any age. But she needs to come in and talk to me about it."

Roy's specimen cup was sitting on the counter when Maggie walked into the lab. The urine in it was dark amber, but not deep red or brown, which was somewhat a relief to her. Statins were known to cause muscle damage in five to ten percent of people who took them, although Maggie honestly thought that might be an underestimation of the problem. The fragmented muscle proteins wound up in the urine and could seriously damage the kidneys, even cause kidney failure. She opened the bottle of urinalysis test strips and dunked one into the cup. *Not too bad. pH 6.5, no ketones, no glucose, no bilirubin, maybe a trace of blood.*

"Tee, would you draw a red top and a purple top on Roy, please, for SMAC 25 and CBC? I need to see his muscle CK levels and liver and kidney function tests. Is this Roy's urine under the microscope?"

"Yes'm."

Maggie focused the lens on the specimen slide under the scope and was relieved to see a few intact red blood cells and the occasional white blood cell in the field. *Probably just a little prostatitis.* Absent those, the trace of blood in the specimen could indicate muscle damage after all. "Send this urine to the lab for complete chemical and micro analysis. Just to be sure we aren't missing something."

"Will do, Doc." Therma Faye poured the urine into a lab specimen tube, capped it tightly, and labeled it. Then grabbed the phlebotomy tray to draw the blood.

"And, Tee, Roy told me there have been two possible overdose deaths in the county just this past week." Maggie's statement stopped Therma Faye at the doorway, and she turned and gave Maggie a concerned look. "Did Noah for sure talk with somebody at the Sheriff's office to tell them what he knows about what he smoked and where it came from?"

Therma Faye pursed her lips and arched her brows dramatically. "Oh. Yeah." She punctuated each word with a nod. "Barbara—you know, Donna and Noah's mama, Jimmy's sister?"

"Yes, of course I remember her."

"Well, she told me he went over and gave a statement this morning to Dub. His daddy took him over there himself and waited outside the office to be sure."

"Good. Two ODs in a week is a scary trend here. In Manhattan it would be a light week, heck, a light afternoon, but here, it's a big deal. They need to get on this before it gets completely out of hand," Maggie said. "Oh, I almost forgot. Give Roy a Diet and Nutrition packet. What's left to finish up?"

"Becky Davis is in Room 1 for a maternity visit. Vitals are all good and, yes, I got her urine already; no blood, no protein, no sugar on the stick," Therma Faye said. Maggie gave her an appreciative nod, and in return the nurse twitched her brows and playfully mimed a lick of her finger that she touched to her hip with a '*sssssss*'. "And then you have a blood pressure follow up in 3. And then—if the good Lord's willing, and nobody else shows up with some weird something or other—I think we can stick a fork in this crazy day."

"Your lips to God's ears, Tee."

By the time Maggie got back to Miz Hendri's, all she wanted was a quick, light dinner and a long, hot soak in the tub. She handled the first half of that equation with a serving of salad and a couple of juicy roasted chicken thighs from the full evening spread Miz Hendri had laid out, then slipped away upstairs as soon as she could manage it without being insulting. There was a retired couple staying at the house this week—crystal hunters—and she felt she ought to at least be passingly sociable, much as it pained her. Her feet hurt and her back ached, and she just wanted to be horizontal. But she'd asked the nice couple to be on the lookout at the crystal fields for a small quartz needle and let her know if they found one. She was thinking she would surprise Rose Ellen with her own crystal pendant for Christmas if she could find a suitable one to have mounted. So far, although they had found plenty of nice crystals, they had not seen what she was looking for but were headed back out there tomorrow to search again.

Once in the quiet of her room, she kicked off her shoes and began to fill the tub with steaming water, adding a healthy scoop of Epsom salts and lavender buds. From her playlist, she selected the soundtrack from the movie *Midnight in the Garden of Good and Evil,* and soon kd lang's easy rendition of *Skylark* colored the silence. Soothing, soft, mellow. Just what she needed physically and emotionally right now. Emotionally because she hadn't heard from JD in the three days since Katsumi had died. She reminded herself almost hourly that there must be a jillion-and-a-half details he had to deal with, and she trusted, implicitly, that he would call when he could. She just wished the opportunity would present itself sooner rather than later.

She undressed and hung her clothes to air, then slipped into the steaming, fragrant bath. *Aaaaaaah!* The track changed, and just as Rosemary Clooney's rich voice began to remind her that *fools rush in where angels fear to tread* her phone rang. She lifted the bath towel from the stool beside the tub and dried her hands then picked up the phone beneath it. *Charlotte.*

"Hey there," Maggie said, putting her on speaker and setting the phone safely aside on the stool again.

"Hey, my sista," Charlotte said in her sweet drawl. "Just wanted to check in and see how you're holding up. Have you heard from him?"

"No. Nothing since the other day, but I can only imagine what he's going through with this." She had filled Charlotte in on what she knew of where JD had gone and why. And what had transpired with Jeff.

"I hear ya, Sista. The pain of a mother losing a child and a child losing a mother. I can't even…" Charlotte's voice trailed to a whisper, and she went uncharacteristically quiet. After a bit she cleared her throat and continued. "Did he mention how long he'd be there?"

"No. Just that he'd be home soon, whatever soon means. And that he'd call."

"And what about Jeff? Have you heard from him again?"

"No. Not since the night he left here after I told him about JD. And to be honest, I hope I don't. At least not for a while. For him to have accused me of infidelity, of having a mindless hook up, after what he did with that…that…"

"Hussy?"

Well-timed humor had always been one of Charlotte's best weapons in diffusing any emotional situation, and Maggie couldn't suppress a laugh. "Yes," she agreed. "Couldn't have said it better myself. That hussy. It was all just so hypocritical. So out of character, or at least a side of his character I'd never seen."

"He revealed a lot with that, I'd have to agree. But it's all still hanging out there waiting to be dealt with, isn't it?"

"What?" Maggie asked.

"The whole issue of whether you're willing to take him back in spite of it. Whether you even want to consider it. That's what he showed back up on your doorstep asking for is it not? And you told him you'd give him a definitive answer." She paused, and when Maggie didn't respond she pressed her. "Right?"

"Yeah. And I will," Maggie said quietly. "I just want JD to get back and see if everything's OK first."

"Hedging your bets?"

Charlotte was one of the few people Maggie trusted enough to let tell her hard truths and from whom she could accept them in the spirit offered. In the last fifteen years, perhaps the only one.

"No!" Maggie protested. She could almost see Charlotte's perfectly plucked brow arch up as she heard her muffled *hmmph*. Char's palette of snorts could display a dizzying variety of meanings sculpted into a single sound that from their many years' friendship Maggie could read like a script. This one silently said '*Oh really? Honey, I didn't roll off the turnip truck last week!*'

"Sounds a little like it." Charlotte said at last.

"No. Really," Maggie explained. "My decision about Jeff has nothing to do with JD or my feelings for him. Or his for me. It's not that at all. It's just… Listen, I've thought about it 'til my brain hurts, and I'm very sure I can't take Jeff back after what he did with Judith. I know I simply wouldn't ever be able to trust that he would resist temptation if the occasion offered itself up again."

"I get it, Sista," Charlotte said. "But he needs to know that. Definitively."

"I thought I'd been definitive on the phone the night of the flood when I told him I wasn't coming back to the City." Her voice trailed off, and she blew out a long breath.

"No, you said you weren't coming for the holidays. That's not definitive."

"OK. But then again when he called and wanted to whisk me away to Shangri-La or wherever, I specifically told him not to come. I told him to go have a life! That was definitive."

"But apparently, he didn't think so, or he wouldn't have showed up there. From what I can see, he's not going to give up easily on something he's after," Charlotte said.

"No. He's not. I guess I shouldn't have been surprised he'd come. I all but told him it was over and done again that night; maybe I should have just said so flat out right then and there. But I was so shell-shocked by the new bits and pieces I'd learned about where JD was and why he was there, and so pissed at Jeff for his condescending 'hooking up with a yokel' dig, it didn't seem a good idea to blurt out something in the raw emotion of the moment."

"Well, you don't ever do anything half-cocked," Charlotte said with an amused snort. "That's for sure."

The bath was starting to cool, and Maggie turned the tap to add more hot water. "Even if once JD gets back home he decides to call it quits, whatever *it* is or turns out to be, I can't see myself going back to Jeff. Not now. Not after what he did. And I will tell him so. Again. Definitively," she said pointedly. "I just need to see JD first and get the whole story. See where we stand. Figure out if we're facing the future together or if I'm facing it alone."

"You know you're never alone in this world, my sista," Charlotte said gently. "Not ever."

"I know," Maggie said gently back. "What would I do without you?"

"Muddle through just fine, I'm sure. But I'm here anyway. Call me when you hear anything."

"I will. Night."

Maggie was just laying the phone back on the stool when the ding of a text alert sounded. She looked at the display: *JD*. Grabbing the phone back up quickly, she almost dropped it in the tub. She juggled it, narrowly preventing disaster, and opened the message.

Hey, sugar. Hope you're asleep now. Been hard few days here. Otsuya tonight, ososhiki tomorrow. Memorials daily for a week, then home, I hope. Will call when I can. Take care.

She texted back: See you in a week. Call if you need me.

Then she googled the Japanese words. *Otsuya*: a funeral wake. According to wiki an event not unlike the wakes of Western tradition where friends and family gathered in proximity to the deceased to reminisce, pay respects, and keep vigil. The *ososhiki*, she learned, was the funeral rite itself, which was followed ninety-plus percent of the time by cremation and then seven days of memorial prayer, incense burning, and chanting. Then finally interment of the funeral urn in the family grave with the ancestors. For the extremely devout, the memorials continued every seventh day thereafter until the forty-ninth day. Then again on the hundredth day. And then repeated once a year. All very well-prescribed by Buddhist tradition. Sounded like—and she selfishly hoped—his plans skewed to the less devout end. She couldn't bear him to be there for the next three months plus.

She lay the phone aside and climbed out of the now-cool tub, drying herself vigorously with a towel. She slipped into a light silk night shirt and brushed her long, blonde hair until it shone, before gathering it into a high ponytail. The bed was going to be more than welcome tonight.

CHAPTER 8
To Dust Return

After all the final arrangements had been made at the hospital, JD, Namiko-san, and Akiko had traveled the hour and a half from Tokyo to the coast by private car yesterday in almost complete silence, arriving at about half past six in the seaside town of Atami where Namiko-san lived. The afternoon had been sunny and unseasonably warm, the sea calm, and thankfully there'd been no rain, though it was common on the coast of the peninsula in the late autumn. Today had been cooler, and as evening fell the temperatures had dipped into the 30s. Despite the chill, the air inside the temple seemed close and sultry. And heavy with incense.

JD closed his eyes and took in a deep breath, trying to relax as he exhaled slowly. The priest's soft chanting of the *sutra* echoed from the stone walls and filled a space that was illuminated by dozens of candles, though their light failed to relieve the darkness much. His friend, the mother of his child was finally truly gone, and it filled him with an odd sense of regret for all Akiko had never known and would never know. Custom required him to stay nearby throughout the official period of mourning, and though he absolutely knew he needed to be there for his daughter, and intended to be, he wanted nothing more at this moment than to be with Maggie, to hear her voice, to hold her in his arms. And those thoughts filled him with a sense of guilt so dark for wishing to be elsewhere that a thousand candles couldn't dispel it.

He opened his eyes and stared ahead at the elaborately carved, wooden coffin sitting on a pedestal before an altar surrounded by flowers, candles, and sculpture. Beside it, as was traditional, an easel displayed an image of Katsumi, smiling and pretty, as she'd been before. The flickering candlelight reflecting off the dark, polished cherry wood of the coffin was almost hypnotic to him and offered a welcome distraction to his thoughts, letting him blank his mind.

Akiko stood very still beside her grandmother, both of them dressed soberly in unadorned black kimonos. Beside the coffin Namiko-san took up a third pinch of *makko*—powdered incense—touching it to her forehead, then sifting it through her fingers into the burner as she'd done with the two pinches that preceded it. Her weathered face bore witness to the weight of her grief in severing the last earthly connection to her beloved daughter, other than the small girl whose hand she gripped tightly in her own. For JD the connection to her had been severed long ago. When they returned to their seats, Namiko-san swayed and her steps faltered; JD immediately stood to take her elbow, guiding her gently onto the chair beside his daughter. It was his turn now to say his formal goodbyes.

He'd been raised in the Christian tradition, of course, and still considered himself to be one, but Namiko-san was devoutly Buddhist, as Katsumi had been. For their sakes he intended to honor their traditions as far as he was able. And, he admitted to himself, it was comforting to embrace their certain belief in her reincarnation, to imagine that his good friend, the mother of his child might return whole and strong to live a longer, easier life than the one she'd just departed.

He breathed in deeply, and the cloying scent of incense filled his lungs and made him dizzy. He shook his head to dispel the sensation, lest his own steps falter, and walked to the coffin. Through the glass pane in its lid, he gazed upon her serene face, softened now in the stillness of death, framed by wisps of silken black hair. No longer trapped in a body her damaged brain could not command, now at peace and free of worldly cares and pain. Three times he gathered the *makko* between his thumb and forefinger and brought it to his forehead, tapping lightly as he honored her memory,

wishing her divine energy a speedy journey closer to *nirvana*, then sifting
the grains of powder into the burner. With a last look at her face, he returned slowly to his place beside Namiko-san, who sat rigidly beside his
child in the front row of seats and constantly worried the strand of funeral
beads she held in her hand. Together they waited in silence as the other
mourners—cousins and other more distant family, loyal friends, even a few
of JD's closer former business associates—offered incense and prayers to
the departed soul and acknowledged the bereaved family trio, who accepted the condolences with silent head bows.

When the *sutra* chanting ended, the coffin lid was lifted, and one by
one those paying their respects approached it bearing blooms taken from
the surrounding floral displays to lay within it beside her body. Then each
mourner departed the temple in silence, the only sound the muted shuf-
fling of their feet on the stone floor. Once everyone but the three of them
had gone, a slight, older gentleman in a black funeral kimono lowered the
coffin lid and nailed it shut, each hammer blow that reverberated off the
ancient walls elicited a soft whimper from Namiko-san and struck JD to
his core with finality and sadness. Not sadness for himself, but rather sadness for his child, for all the things that would never be. But that die had
been cast five years before.

The attendant set the hammer aside and with the help of another
man transferred the coffin to a cremation tray and rolled it to the doors of
the crematorium. JD, Namiko-san, and Akiko rose and followed them,
stoic, black-clad figures walking stiffly together and watching as the box
disappeared behind the doors. JD laid a gentle hand on Akiko's shoulder,
then cupped her head and smoothed her raven hair pulling her closer
to his side. She glanced up at him with a curious wide-eyed stare. he
was sure she was confused; he knew she didn't completely understand
what was happening. She'd never known her mother as anything but a
non-responsive form that lay in a hospital bed attended by a succession of

nurses around the clock. She'd never felt her warm embrace, never heard her laugh, never seen her smile.

Namiko-san had declined to participate in the feast that would occur during this cremation interval, although it was traditional. JD would be expected to play the host, high on his list of things he didn't want to do, and he dreaded it mightily. They'd agreed to send the mourners on to an arranged meal catered in a pavilion nearby, choosing instead to wait outside the doors in silent vigil until the process began. Then they departed in silence; Akiko and Namiko-san to her home, and JD to join the guests at the funeral feast. It would be several days before the cremation process was complete, and there was nothing left of Katsumi but ashes and bones.

When that interval had passed, as custom demanded, JD and Namiko-san returned and used a pair of special chopsticks—one made of willow and one of bamboo to represent a bridging of the earthly and ethereal worlds—to pluck the pieces of white bone from the still-warm ashes and place them one by one into the funeral urn. Namiko handed her chopsticks to Akiko, as was also the custom, and helped guide her small hands as she too plucked a whitened bone from the powdery ashes and dropped it into the urn. When the ritual was finished, they would take the urn to Namiko's home, where it would sit in a place of honor beside their *butsudan*, the home shrine. In seven-days' time, after as many memorials, they would lay the urn with Katsumi's bones into the family grave alongside that of her father and those of the departed generations who came before them.

CHAPTER 9
Many Happy Returns

"No! Noooooo!" Maggie and Charlie cried in unison as the spinner landed on 4. They sat cross-legged on the floor and watched helplessly as Rose Ellen bounced her pawn four places on the board *bop bop bop bop* and slid it up the ladder to reach the number 100 space to win for the third time in a row.

"Ta da!" Rosie grinned from ear to ear and hopped up to take a bow. Maggie and Charlie could do little else but offer a sporting high-five to the victor.

"Congratulations." Maggie stood and smoothed the wrinkles from the lap of her slacks. "Again," she smiled and tousled the girl's honey-colored mop of hair.

Becky Davis came in from the kitchen, wiping her hands on a kitchen towel. "Lunch is ready, kids. Dr. Mac, won't you stay and join us?"

"Please, please, please, Dr. Mac," Charlie and Rosie squealed.

"Thanks, but I can't today. Much as I've enjoyed getting thoroughly trounced by you two at Chutes and Ladders, I've got to run. I have some work to get done, before I meet a friend later."

"Let me walk you out then," Becky said. "Kids, wash your hands and get to the table."

On the porch, Becky pulled the front door closed behind them and whispered, "OK, now tell me what it was you heard about Waylon Prescott."

Maggie gave a head wag toward her car, and they walked together to it down the neatly manicured gravel driveway in the late morning sun. "I got a call yesterday from his defense counsel, telling me that I wouldn't be needed for the video deposition they'd scheduled for next week. He said that because of Waylon's cooperation with the prosecution and his willingness to testify fully against Nick, the DA has offered a plea deal. They'll charge him only on aiding and abetting and accessory after the fact in exchange for his testimony and a guilty plea to those charges. Waylon's planning to take the deal to avoid a trial that Rose Ellen would likely get pulled into. Not to mention all the lurid publicity that would surely surround it. Can't say I disagree with his decision. The statute says 3-to-5 years; lawyers expect he'll get less."

"The last thing that sweet girl needs now is to suffer through a 3-ring circus of a trial; she's been through enough. Always such a little trooper and a joy to have around. Tom and I are more than happy to have her here for as long as she needs a home. She and Charlie have become best buds. To be honest, I think having her here's been good for the both of them."

"Yes, I believe it has. And she and Charlie are going to have another little buddy before we know it. How are you feeling?"

"Fine." She wrapped her hands across her round belly. "Getting to be big as a house," she laughed. "Carrying this one totally different from Charlie, though, for whatever that's worth."

"Well, if baby folklore and Velma's intuition are to be believed, you and Tom might need to be focusing on girl's names. I'll see you in the clinic next week."

In the car, Maggie immediately checked her phone for messages, finding nothing new. JD's text yesterday had said he was flying home today, but not exactly when. She'd texted him that she'd be happy to drive over to Little Rock to meet him, but he replied not to worry, that it was all arranged; he'd see her in Caddo Bend. There were only a few flights daily from Tokyo to Dallas, and she'd looked them all up online. The earliest one should have arrived hours ago, if it was on schedule, but she didn't know if he'd been on it. The next didn't arrive for a few hours yet. Then there was one more that would arrive later tonight. Once in Dallas, he'd then have a short hop to Little Rock on one of the many daily connecting flights; there were several possibilities there, too. Then the hour and half drive to Caddo Bend. She estimated the earliest he could be home was sometime between noon and one, and if he was on the next flight after that maybe seven or eight tonight. If he was on the latest flight, it could be midnight or after. It was just coming on noon now, and as she still hadn't heard from him her mind whirred with all the possible scenarios. *Just calm down*, she scolded herself. *If he was on the early flight he's landed in Dallas by now*, she thought, *unless under the moon's lingering influence the flight was delayed or cancelled. Surely, he'd text if so. Wouldn't he?*

As she turned onto Main Street, she couldn't suppress the bizarre feeling of having arrived at Santa's village. Tinsel fluttered in the light breeze on every garland-wrapped streetlamp pole on the square and the enormous cedar on the green as well. The sight lifted her spirits, and she decided to kill a little time and distract herself with a bit of Christmas shopping. So instead of going back to the boarding house, she headed for the Jewel Box, the tiny jeweler's shop on the square.

She entered the store, and the bell above the door tinkled merrily, right in keeping with the soft carols playing through the speakers. Max Rosenthal, the jeweler, greeted her from behind the counter where he'd been carefully arranging a display in the glass case.

"Dr. McKinley! What a pleasure to see you. How can I help you?"

"Hi, Mr. Rosenthal," she said, walking up to the counter. She took off her mother's crystal pendant and held it out to him. "I was wondering if you might have access to a quartz needle something like this one."

He took the pendant from her and inspected it, drawing his bushy grey eyebrows together as he did. "I don't usually deal in quartz, but I can likely find one. Arkansas's quartz country, you know. Where'd you come by this one?"

"My grandfather found it not far from here. He was a part of the original Caddo mound survey back in the 1940s and 50s. He had it made into this pendant for my grandmother."

He laid the pendant out on a suede pad on the counter. "OK if I take a photo of it?"

"Absolutely. Go right ahead."

He pulled his phone from the inside pocket of his suit coat and snapped shots from several angles, laying a small ruler beside the crystal to capture its size correctly. The high-tech smart phone looked incongruous in his spotty, old hands, but perhaps no more incongruous than his sharply pressed broadcloth shirt and 3-piece suit looked on the streets of rural Caddo Bend, where the typical mode of dress tended more toward dusty denim than pressed serge. She'd heard from Velma (who else?) that he and his family had moved to the Caddo River area from Chicago years ago, when Max was a teenager. Being Jewish, itself something of a curiosity in a small rural Arkansas town back then, as well as hailing from north of the Mason-Dixon line, he must have felt a bit of a fish-out-of-water transplant like herself though by now he'd been here 45 or 50 years. His father had started a little shop in Glenwood, not far from here, where he sold a bit of estate jewelry, precious metals, and coins and repaired watches and clocks. The last a highly marketable skill he'd taught his son. But Max had set his sights on bigger things; he'd gone to college at Vanderbilt, obtained a degree in business there, and stayed in Nashville, Tennessee to work in a big bank, where he had met and subsequently married a girl from Caddo Bend, and they come back together to open The Jewel Box and raise a family. Interesting how things work out sometimes. The road you take to get away leads you right back home.

"Doctor?" Maggie jumped when he touched her arm. Apparently, he'd been talking, and she'd missed most of it adrift in a brown study.

"I'm sorry," she said. "I got lost there for a minute. You were saying?"

He smiled and nodded. "I was saying that I believe I know where I can find a similar needle. Do you want it mounted, like this one?"

"I'd prefer a slightly smaller needle, if possible. It's for a young girl. But similar and mounted with silver like this or as close to this as you can manage." She picked up her own necklace and slipped it over her head.

"OK. Just give me a few days to locate one of the right size. I'll give you a call." As she headed for the door, he called after her, "Merry Christmas!"

She started to respond in kind then stopped herself, wondering if with his being Jewish she ought to wish him Happy Chanukah. She opted instead for "Thank you. And a happy holiday to you!"

From there, she headed to the clinic and the luxury of high-speed internet to do a bit of online shopping. With no patients scheduled today, there'd at least be peace and quiet. She walked through the silent back hallway and directly to the break room, where she made herself a double Americano and thumbed up her Christmas music play list to keep the holiday spirit flowing, then settled at her desk to shop...and wait.

Soon, she'd ticked Therma Faye and Donna off the list, getting each of them a cashmere wrap from *Maison 1367*, her favorite purveyor of fine cashmere. What she loved most about their products—besides that they were lusciously soft and warm—was their durability. As their tagline suggested, they feel like velvet and wear like iron. She'd dragged her *M. 1367* wraps all over the country; she'd slept snuggled in them on planes, trains, and call room cots, and they still looked good enough to wear to a black-tie affair. Unlike some cashmere, they never pilled or frayed. The ladies would love them.

She'd already gotten JD's gift, cashing in to grab it on a half-price discount over the Black Friday weekend sale. She'd seen it on social channels and ads and even featured in the *NY Times:* a sous vide water oven. It was pricey, but worth it, she decided. She'd done her research, and, although there were cheaper options, they looked like toys or DIY projects. He'd never want such a contraption on his elegant stone counter. Besides, JD was a serious cook; he needed a serious appliance. A sleek and sophisticated appliance. *Like this one*, she'd thought when she clicked the Buy Now button on the SousVide Supreme product page. She even knew where on his counter it would fit. And she was certain beyond a doubt that he would love it. Plus, she had other ideas about a few less-tangible gifts she hoped to give him that she was equally certain he would enjoy.

Next, she decided she'd go with something experiential for Miz Hendri — a weekend package to take the healing waters of Hot Springs. She'd just gotten onto the Arlington Hotel website to purchase a gift certificate when the text alert dinged on her phone interrupting Karen Carpenter's rich alto rendition of *Merry Christmas Darling*.

One glance rewarded her with the notification she'd been praying to see. Just two simple words: I'm home. Yet they made her heart sing.

She texted him back: Be there shortly! Welcome home! Then grabbed her purse and coat, not bothering to put it on in her hurry, even though the temperature outside had dropped sharply toward freezing as the dusky evening deepened to dark.

The drive to JD's was just 15 minutes when the low water bridge was passable, which it ought to be; there'd been no rain in the last week. The prospect of seeing him filled Maggie with both joy and more than a little apprehension. *After all that's happened will we be OK? Will 'we' even still 'be'?* She didn't want to think about it and pushed aside all thoughts that they might not be OK. All she knew was she needed to see him so they could talk. He'd explain; she'd know then.

When she arrived at his home, smoke was rising from the stone chimney and the windows were softly lit with what she judged to be firelight.

She hurried up to the front door and knocked. No response. She knocked again, louder. Still no response.

She walked around to the back of the house to where his bonsai greenhouse stood, and through the transparent panes she could see him lovingly tending one of his dozens of incredible tiny trees. She stood for a moment, just watching him snipping, watering, talking. *A bonsai whisperer*, she mused. It charmed her that he had given names to some of them. *Such a complex person*, she thought, *a real Renaissance man – soldier, scholar, singer, scientist, artist, adventurer, music lover, book collector, cook.* The list too long to recount. Seeing him standing in the greenhouse brought a vivid torrent of recent memories of the unanticipated passion that had first ignited between them in that stunning space. The images instantly filled her mind and made her go faint with desire. *OK, add fantastic lover to the list,* she thought. She tapped on the door.

JD turned, and when he saw her the merest hint of a smile tugged at the edges of his lips then it was gone. He laid his pruners down on the workbench and crossed to open the door. The earthy smell and warmth of the greenhouse poured out around him as he enveloped her in his strong, warm embrace. She reveled in the moment, but when she pulled away, she noted a hurt sadness in his gentle eyes that she hated to see.

"Hey," he said softly. "I wasn't sure I'd hear from you today."

"I left a text on your phone," she said.

"Hmm," he breathed the sound out and tipped his head toward the house. "It's inside. On the charger. I don't usually bring it out here when I'm working."

Is there a slight distance, a wariness to his demeanor that wasn't there before? Or am I imagining it? She decided to lighten the mood, keep it casual. "Then let's go inside, and I can pour you a glass of wine. Or make you a welcome home cup of coffee." She smiled at him and raised her brows in invitation, then extended her hand. "Or maybe tea? I think I can manage that, too."

His gaze held hers for a long moment. "Sure." The hint of a smile returned. "No wine, though. Too jet lagged for that." Reaching out to take her proffered hand he pulled her gently toward him again and scanned her face, now just inches from his own, as if he were trying to reacquaint himself with its every line and pore. And then he kissed her lips softly, slowly lingering, letting them both savor the moment of reconnection and dispelling the wary undercurrent she thought she'd glimpsed, driving any remaining doubts from her mind.

In his kitchen, she filled the electric kettle and set it to heating. "So will it be coffee or tea?"

"I think I'm in a tea mood. Will you join me in that? I brought back a new batch of gyokuro," he said.

"I will if you'll tell me where the tea is," then added with a shrug and a smile, "And the tea pot."

"Why don't we do this together," he said, the smile coloring his voice. "That'll speed things up." He came to stand closely behind her, leaning closer still to reach over her to open the cupboard and fetch down a graceful side-handled, hobnail tea pot. She could still smell the warm, loamy greenhouse on his shirt as she allowed herself to settle lightly back against his chest.

He placed a light, playful kiss on the top of her head then crossed to the farmhouse sink to fill the pot with hot water and set it on a trivet to warm. "The tea's in the cabinet to the right of the stove," he said.

She opened the cabinet to find neat rows of various types of tea and quickly skimmed the labels in search of the one he'd mentioned, gyo-something or other. "This one?" she said, picking up a cardboard tube and handing it to him.

"Yeah," he said. "It's my favorite green. Jade Dew, they call it. The growers protect it from sun for twenty days before harvesting, which gives the leaves their deep green color. And makes it less astringent, smoother than some other varieties. You'll like it." He emptied the warming water, spooned leaves into the pot, and filled it with fresh water taken just off the boil, then he set the pot and a pair of black raku tea bowls on a tray and took it to the sofa before the fire to wait for the tea to steep.

Maggie sank into the seat beside him and tucked her feet up under her, leaning comfortably against his side. He wrapped an arm around her shoulder and absently twirled an escaping tendril of her hair. Neither of them spoke for several minutes, seemingly content just to be close instead of half a continent and an ocean apart. There was much, she knew, that needed saying, some of it she may not want to hear, but the truth of it mattered to her. Still, this was JD's story, and she intended to let him tell it in his own time, in his own way.

Finally, he said, "I was never in love with Katsumi." He let the words hang there for a moment. "I cared deeply for her, but it wasn't love."

"But you married her," Maggie said softly. A log collapsed in the grate sending a shower of popping sparks as it did. She focused on the glowing embers and waited for him to go on.

JD drew in a deep breath and blew it out. "I did." He paused for a moment as though trying to sort out the best way to explain it all. "We'd known each other for almost a year—she worked in upper management at the company that had bought a couple of my patents. I was still going there regularly on a consulting basis. We had a few casual dates, then a few... uh...less casual ones." He sent her a meaningful glance; she nodded that she understood the drift. Then he sat forward and poured the tea into their cups, handing hers to her and settling back beside her. "We'd been dating, I guess you'd call it—although it was something less formal than that really—for maybe six or seven months when she told me she was pregnant.

I was stunned. Completely blindsided. I think she was, too. She'd assured me she was on the pill the first time we were together, and I believe she was, but nothing short of abstinence is foolproof."

"No. It's not." Maggie sipped her tea and stared into the flickering fire.

"She said she'd wrestled with the idea of terminating the pregnancy for a few weeks, but when she'd ultimately decided to keep the baby, she felt it would be wrong not to tell me. She made no demands on me, financial or otherwise; she just wanted me to know. We weren't in love and didn't pretend to be, but we were friends, and we got along well. And now we were going to be the parents of this child we'd conceived together, although that was something neither of us had ever even considered. So, we married in a quiet civil ceremony to make my paternity official, with the agreement between us of living separately and divorcing amicably once she was born, but with the intent to share in the raising our child and do it in a way that ensured she would know she had two parents who loved her."

"And then the accident," Maggie said, turning her head and glancing up to look at him, instantly saddened to see pain cloud his handsome features.

"Yes. And everything changed." He sat forward to pour them each more tea. "I became the single parent of an infant girl. And Katsumi… well, you know the end of that story."

But not the rest of it, she thought. "JD," she said, turning in his arm to face him fully and twining her fingers with those of the hand that draped over her shoulder, "I'm so sorry. For your loss, for your pain. I wish there was something I could do to take it all away."

He sat his cup on the table and took hers from her hand, then wrapped both his arms around her and pulled her closely to him. "Just holding you in my arms is all I need right now, Sugar," he murmured against her hair and placed a gentle kiss on the top of her head.

Maggie tipped her face to his, inviting his kiss, and he obliged. "Are you sure that's all?" she whispered against his lips, then kissed him again, more deeply.

"Well, maybe not all I need," he said with a soft chuckle.

A chilly morning breeze swept in from the bedroom window that JD kept slightly raised at night and sent Maggie burrowing more deeply under the down duvet. She'd slept in. An uncommon enough occurrence, but one she welcomed today. Stretching out her arm she found that JD was no longer beside her, and for a moment she experienced a frisson of anxiety that she might have only dreamed he'd come home. But no, she was indeed in his bed, wearing absolutely nothing but a smile that broadened as she recalled last night's passionate reunion. That memory, one that sent warm shivers shimmering again throughout her body, along with the muted sounds now emanating from the kitchen put her worries to rest that it was an illusion.

Maggie tossed back the duvet and climbed out into the chill; her bare skin instantly prickled with goosebumps. JD had warned her the first time she'd stayed over with him that he kept his bedroom cool year-round for sleeping, which she confessed she enjoyed, especially under a warm duvet and nestled in his arms. *But in December? Brrrr.* She wrapped her arms across her chest and rubbed them vigorously. She hadn't expected to stay the night and with nothing of a warm, lounging nature to put on, she stooped at the foot of the bed to grab his discarded shirt. She threw it around herself, closed a few buttons, and rolled the sleeves up to above her wrists. It smelled of him, and she inhaled deeply to enjoy the sheer intoxication of it. The shirt swallowed her, reaching nearly to her knees; it warmed her somewhat, though she wished she had some socks. As soon as she stepped onto the polished flagstones of the hallway, however, all was well, and she gave silent thanks for the radiant floor heat that gently warmed both the air and her bare feet.

The savory smell of bacon drew her to the kitchen, where she found JD standing at the stone counter. She padded in and stood quietly in the doorway for a moment, watching the muscles of his bare back tense and relax as he broke eggs one by one into a glass bowl. An ethereal soundtrack was playing, the soft music drifting from speakers, audible only in the kitchen; she'd heard nothing of it in the bedroom or even in the hallway. Though she wasn't familiar with this precise piece of music, having been raised and educated in a Catholic girls' boarding school, she immediately recognized the Latin words as well as the musical form. It was a requiem, a Catholic mass for the dead. She'd heard enough of them in the course of her years at St. Bonaventure's. But this one, far from being forbidding or angry in its mood as some were, was otherwordly. Harp and string arpeggios and a chorus of female voices singing the familiar Latin words in tight harmony: *Sanctus Domine Deus Sabbaoth. Hosana in excelsis. Benedictus qui venit in nomine Domini.* Holy Lord of Hosts. Hosana in the highest. Blessed is he who comes in the name of the Lord.

Their voices sounded like a distant chorus of angels, soft at first, then building to a glorious crescendo of joy as they drew nearer, then fading again as if the celestial visitors had appeared and rejoiced and now winged away again to Heaven. And then a single female voice took over, crystalline, pure, and rich, and filled with deep emotion and tender pleading. JD stopped what he was doing and stood quietly, enraptured, unmoving, the whisk in his hand poised motionless over the bowl of eggs. She listened to the words the woman sang: *Pie Jesu Domine dona eis requiem sempiternam.* A simple plea: Gentle Lord Jesus give them rest without end.

When the final, almost-inaudible note faded to nothingness, she saw his shoulders relax visibly as though the music had been supporting him or he'd been holding his breath and had finally released it. Maggie realized she'd been holding her own breath as well. She didn't want to disturb the moment, but when she softly exhaled he turned, and she could see tears glistening in his lashes. The corner of his lip twitched into the suggestion of a lopsided smile, and he reached out his arm to gather her to him.

"You OK?" she said quietly, laying her cheek and palm softly against his bare chest.

"Yeah," he said after a beat. "Yeah, I'm OK. Just needed to hear this." He pointed a small remote control in the direction of the stereo system in the adjoining living room and the music stopped.

"I didn't mean to interrupt; it's so beautiful. A requiem." A statement, not a question. "I recognize that much, but not one I'm familiar with. Whose?"

"Maurice Duruflé." He placed a soft, lingering kiss on the crown of her head.

"For Katsumi?"

"Yes. And for me," he added quietly. Then he drew in a deep breath and whooshed it out as if pushing the sadness away. "My favorite recording of it, mainly for that cut. Kiri Te Kanawa's *Pie Jesu*. It always does this to me. The most perfect rendition ever laid down in vinyl. In my humble opinion, at least." He smiled genuinely, finally, and casting off the somberness returned to his whisking. "I thought maybe we could use a little nourishment after last night," he laughed lightly and stretched over to plant another playful kiss on her forehead. "Truffled eggs sound good?"

"Mmm. Yes. And I believe I smell bacon."

"You do. And I'd lay odds you want some coffee." He tilted his head toward the electric kettle on the counter. "Heat the water. There's French Roast already ground and in the press."

"So, you're telling me you think I can at least boil water, then?"

"I am. Don't let me down." His low laugh was almost musical, and the slightly mischievous smirk that accompanied it warmed her heart and filled her with relief to see the cloud of sadness lift.

As they sat together on stools at the counter enjoying their breakfast Maggie marveled yet again at his culinary skill. A simple meal but stunning and accomplished without any seeming effort. He'd shaved paper-thin slices of black truffle over the creamiest scrambled eggs she'd ever tasted and added slices of crisp bacon and fresh berries brightened with a sprinkling of lime zest to round out the plate. She'd even indulged in half a slice of buttered sourdough toast with jam. Delicious beyond belief.

Afterward, they'd taken their coffees and moved to the comfort of the sofa and warmth of the crackling fire, where they sat side by side, talking easily about one thing and another. A bit less easily about the sad events of the last week or so: the death, the funeral, and the seemingly endless series of required memorials that followed it. After the first seven days of mourning, there would be a memorial to mark the 49th day since her death and another at the 100th day. Then annually for many years. That was the Buddhist custom, and he said he intended to honor the tradition to the best of his ability. Mostly for Akiko's sake. That meant he would need to go back to Japan in mid-January for the first of those memorials and then again in March.

He'd been staring into his coffee cup as he recounted the litany of funereal duties, then he looked up and met her eyes. What he said next took her by surprise.

"Come with me. To Japan." He laid his hand over hers.

The intensity of his gray eyes underscored the sincere intent of his words; the invitation, completely unexpected, stunned her, and for a moment she just stared blankly at him, finally finding her voice. "W-would that be appropriate? Would I be welcome? I mean by your, uh, your former mother-in-law?" When he didn't immediately respond, she continued, "And your daughter?"

"She already knows about you," he said without further elaboration. That news surprised Maggie even more, and she wasn't quite sure what to make of it. *Who is it who knows?* She waited a bit longer for him to say more, but he didn't. Her mind was drowning in questions. *Is his child is staying in Japan with her grandmother? Or is he going to retrieve her? Does he just want me to meet her? Or is she coming home with him? Is she who knows about me? Or who?*

"I've never been to Japan," she said finally, enjoying the warmth of his hand holding hers and the pleasant sensation of his thumb gently, rhythmically, almost absently rubbing the back of it. A gesture seemingly insignificant, yet so intimate. It made her realize that her physical attraction to him, strong in its own right, was perhaps but the prelude to something much more serious and lasting. Honestly, she wasn't yet completely sure how she felt herself, let alone whether he felt that same *something more*—he'd never said as much directly—but she admitted she'd begun to hope so. Were that to be the case, it would require being open and honest with each other about everything, including Jeff's recent visit. And she wasn't sure she was up to piling that emotional burden onto a psyche recently weighed down with so much sadness. *It can wait*, she thought. *I'll tell him everything, but not now.*

"I'd love to go with you," she said at last, surprising herself. She meant it, too. She wanted to go with him, be with him, help him through this.

"Good," he said.

"There's a lot to figure out. I mean, how long would I need to be gone? I'll have to get coverage at the clinic and…"

"See which date fits your schedule best, and we'll figure it out, whatever it is." He tipped her chin up and kissed her lips. "But right now, I was thinking we might see how some other things fit."

CHAPTER 10
A Heavy Lift

Monday had dawned cold and clear, and Maggie's breath came in visible rhythmic clouds in the chilly air as she powered through the last nine chest to bar pull ups and dropped, catlike, from the chin bar to immediately heft the barbell up to rest across her collarbones. Lowering herself into a deep squat, she pushed in one fluid motion to a stand as she thrust the bar overhead. Eight more like that and she completed her morning's workout. Breathing heavily, she glanced at the timer app on her phone: 6 minutes 8 seconds, a personal best time for Fran, the infamous WOD that, done at full prescriptive level, consisted of a series of twenty-one chest to bar pull ups, followed immediately by twenty-one thrusters with the 45-pound barbell and a pair of 25-pound weights—ninety-five pounds total—followed immediately by fifteen repetitions of each exercise, and capped off with a last set of nine of each of them. Performed for time with as little rest as possible between the sets. She took a long chug of water and sat on a box to recover, breathing in deeply through her nose and exhaling clouds of foggy breath.

To her surprise, she'd come outside this morning to find there'd been a dusting of snow last night, an occurrence Miz Hendri had informed her—while clucking about her not having on warm enough clothes for such a cold morning—was unusual but far from unheard of in December in Caddo Bend. She'd shivered in the brisk air on her way to the garage, even bundled up in an insulated jacket and headband. But she wasn't cold now. Quite the opposite. She positively radiated body heat after that workout, steaming like a draft horse pulling a heavy load uphill in a Maine winter. And she'd sorely needed a good hard workout, having missed last Saturday's scheduled one visiting with Rose Ellen and fretting over when JD would arrive and whether everything was okay between them. Of course, she'd spent the rest of the weekend in his arms answering the last question to her satisfaction and getting plenty of exercise of a different sort, for which she was equally grateful. And she was unable to suppress a smile at the memory.

At the crunching of footsteps, she stuck her head out the garage door. It was Boyce Dugan, one of her patients.

"Boyce?" She was starting to cool off now and shrugged into her jacket again. "What can I do for you."

"Mornin' ma'am," he said with a bob of his head and nervous shuffle of his feet. "I, um, got the job," he said, his voice filled with a measure of pride.

"Congratulations! That's wonderful!" Her enthusiasm was genuine. She'd seen how much landing the trucking job meant to him when he'd come in so stressed for his physical.

"You, uh…you said last week to come by today at seven if I wanted to learn how to work out." She noticed he was decked out in a thermal jacket and winter tights—camo of course—an outfit she suspected was usually used for sitting on a deer stand, not doing a WOD. His longish hair escaped from under the edges of a Day-Glo stocking cap. At least he had on athletic shoes and not hunting boots.

"Oh, of course. Absolutely." To be honest, the weekend with JD had pushed that invitation completely out of her head. But no problem. "Perfect timing," she said cheerfully. "I just finished my own set, so we can get you started."

She'd spent the next forty minutes or so guiding Boyce through a gentle warm up and stretching session and showing him proper form for sit ups, pushups, and planks, and when he'd struggled with them, scaling the techniques with less demanding options for his less-than-fit beginner level. She'd taught workouts at her box in Manhattan over the years and had a first level certification for coaching; and though it had lapsed, she knew what to do. She pulled a length of one-inch PVC pipe from a barrel beside Papa's workbench to use in lieu of a barbell to demonstrate proper lifting technique, coaching him through his own attempts at the deadlift, squat, and overhead press maneuvers. They'd done little, by her standard, but Boyce was red-faced and puffing like a steam engine by the end of it; his camo t-shirt showed sweat stains on the chest and back and in large dark crescents under each arm. But at least he was here, he was trying, and she had to applaud his willingness to give it a go.

"How's the diet going, by the way?" She tossed him a towel, and he wiped the sweat from his face and neck.

"Pretty good." He puffed a time or two before going on. "Lost about 5 pounds already, I think." He looked down, avoiding her eyes.

"That's not just pretty good. It's great. And when you combine that way of eating with this way of exercising, you'll even amplify the effect."

"Never thought I could do that." He puffed again. "Lose weight, I mean, eating meat. Figured I'd be munchin' rabbit food." He grinned up at her somewhat sheepishly.

Maggie smiled and nodded. She'd seen that dawning revelation in other minds before. "Just keep at it, and you'll see."

"But what about on the road…"

She waved off his concern. "Let's just get you going, and I'll show you a routine you can do with minimal or no equipment when you're on the road. Just remember that what you put into the tank—the food part of the equation—sets the stage for everything. It accounts for about 80% of the positive changes you'll experience, so focus on that. The resistance and cardio do the rest."

He looked up, finally meeting her eyes, and smiled. "Thank you, ma'am. I seriously mean it. And I mean to try." *What more could a doctor ask?*

After a quick, hot shower, she dressed, grabbed a protein shake—no time for more—and headed out the back door. If she hurried, she'd just make it in time for the first patient scheduled for 9 am. But what greeted her was a giant rental truck completely blocking the back drive of the boarding house and a swarm of men with dollies ferrying boxes from the shed in the back into the truck. The shed had been where Nick Freeman had kept the artifacts he'd extracted from the archeologic dig he'd supervised on a Native American mound nearby. As he was now cooling his heels in jail awaiting trial for murder and more, she supposed someone had come to take custody of the stuff.

She sidled up to Papa, who was standing to the side watching the men working, collar pulled up against the chill and hands stuffed deep into the pockets of his barn jacket.

"What's going on here?" she asked him.

"Moving crew sent by the University. Come to take all Nick's Caddo pots and such back over to Little Rock. They have a court order; Sheriff Perkins came with them, so I unlocked the shed."

"Great. And I'm late to get to the clinic. How long do you think they'll be?" She stamped her feet against the cold and blew onto her hands.

"Oh, a good while, I'd reckon. Still a lot in there," he said. "I'd run you over, but they've got me blocked in, too." He nodded at the garage housing his Jeep. "I was planning to go over to Waylon's myself this morning to gather the eggs and feed and water the hens, but it looks like that will have to wait a bit."

"Well, if it's going to be the rubber sole express," she said, "I'd better get moving. Think I'll grab a to-go cup for the walk. Want one?"

"That'd be nice. Chilly this morning," he said, following Maggie inside.

In the warm kitchen, Maggie pulled her insulated coffee tumbler down from the cabinet, along with a mug for Papa and turned to fill them from the pot Miz Hendri kept going every morning, finding it curiously almost empty. *Won't take long to make another pot,* she thought. She quickly filled the water reservoir and spooned grounds into a new filter, then pulled her phone from her purse and texted Tee at the clinic: **Car blocked. Walking. CU in a few.**

"You said that you were going out to deal with the hens at Waylon's?"

"I am," he nodded. "They need care; Hendri needs eggs; and little Rosie needs the money, or at least she will at some point, and it would be a shame to let what's there go completely to seed while Waylon's gone. I'm taking most of the eggs to Medlock's to sell and trying to be sure Waylon's few other customers' orders get filled. We opened a savings account for Rosie with the help of the folks at the Child Protective Service, and the money gets deposited there."

"That's really so kind of you."

He shrugged the compliment off. "Still trying to figure out the vegetable patch. Course it's dormant now in the winter, but come spring we'll want to do a bit. JD has something in mind, he said. Not sure what, exactly. I know he spoke to Darrell Furr about maybe taking it over for the near term, plant in the spring and harvest as needed to sell at the Farmer's Market, but I don't know that he will have time to do it ongoing, or if he even wants to."

When the coffee finished brewing, she poured them each a cup and peered out the window, confirming the large truck still blocked her in. "Well, I'm off on foot. See you tonight."

As soon as Maggie opened the back door of the clinic, a cacophony of unintelligible wails emanated from the treatment room down the hall, intermingled with Therma Faye's loud and repeated reassurances that everything would be all right. Okay anesthesia, they called it in medical school. Just utter OK confidently, rinse, and repeat: *It's OK. It's OK. It's OK.*

"Doc's on her way," Therma Faye said. "It's gonna be OK; just hang on."

Maggie bypassed her office and walked straight into the room. "I'm here, Tee. What's going on?"

"Says he can't close his mouth. Well didn't say it, wrote it."

The man sitting on the exam table bellowed something sounding like 'Ghahngh!' Even from the doorway Maggie could see that his lower jaw was stuck open.

"I'm Dr. McKinley. I need to examine your jaw to see what's going on; is that okay?" He nodded, and she dropped her purse and coffee in the chair by the door and moved to stand before him, placing her hands on either side of his jaw, just in front of each ear, feeling the landmarks, feeling for point tenderness. His lower jaw, the mandible, had slipped out of its joint socket in the skull. *Dislocation.* She'd have to reduce it.

"Tee, get me 20 milligrams of IV diazepam." Then to the most-un-comfortable patient she explained, "Your lower jaw has come out of its socket on this side. I'm going to need to put it back in place, but first I'm going to give you some medication in your vein to relax these very power-ful chewing muscles here." She touched the sides of his cheeks. "It won't take long to act, and it will be much easier for us both. Is that OK?"

He nodded his assent.

"Are you allergic to any medications?"

He shook his head no.

"Did this happen from some kind of trauma? Did you have an acci-dent? Get hit or fall?"

He shook his head back and forth several times and uttered another "Ghahngh".

"Here you go, Dr. Mac," Therma Faye said, laying the filled syringe, a latex tourniquet, butterfly IV catheter, and alcohol swab on the ring stand beside the table.

Maggie pushed the man's grubby hoodie sleeve up over his elbow and wrapped the tourniquet around his arm, noting as she did the intricate tattoo of a bald eagle on his forearm. Swabbing the area quickly with the alcohol pad, she slipped the butterfly needly into a vein near his wrist and secured it, then released the tourniquet and slowly pushed in about half the medication though the catheter. Depending on his tolerance to it, he could require more, might require it all. Within about two minutes, however, he began to relax and by three he was calmer and still.

"OK," Maggie said, "I'm going to ask my nurse to stand right behind you and brace your head securely. I want you to lean back against her and keep your head still. I'll have to pull down on your jaw quite firmly to free it up, possibly on both sides, in order to get it in the right position, then we'll let those strong muscles guide the jaw back into place. It's going to feel very odd, but the pain will stop soon. Ready?"

The man nodded his head again and closed his eyes.

Maggie put her thumbs into his mouth, careful to position them outside the molars; the last thing she needed was a crushed thumb. She then wrapped her fingers under the jawbone on either side, and exerting a strong steady downward pull, she was able to distract the jaw enough to dislocate the other side, and for just a moment the jawbone was floating free in her hands. Then she rocked the mandible down and toward the back of his head and suddenly both sides slipped into the notches in the skull where they belonged, and the jaws snapped forcefully shut. The pain relief was instant. Maggie removed her hands and stepped back, giving him some space.

"Ahhgh," the man said gingerly working his now-function jaw, opening and closing his mouth in tiny movements that made him look a bit like a fish. "That's better now." He cupped his cheeks in his hands and gently massaged the muscles. Maggie noticed his nails were as grubby as his hoodie, and both fingertips and nails were stained dark orange with nicotine. His lank brown ponytail looked like it hadn't had a wash in a while either. "Much obliged, ma'am."

"You're welcome. Let me take a look now." Maggie paused, then reached again to feel with her fingers below and in front of his ear, all along the joint line of the jaw. "Any pain here? Or here?" He shook his head. She pushed down the length of the jawbone. No point tenderness anywhere; nothing at all painful to pressure. Satisfied that there wasn't likely a fracture, she breathed a little sigh of relief and wished for the umpteenth time she had an x-ray, then removed the IV and put a band aid over the blood droplet that appeared. After a moment she asked, "What happened, Mr, uh…?"

"Yawned." He shrugged and looked up at her. "Not even out of bed yet. Hell of a way to wake up." He stuck out a grubby hand to her. "Marty Bledsoe."

"Maggie McKinley," she replied, taking the filthy hand. "Good to meet you Mr. Bledsoe. If under less than pleasant circumstances."

The man started to open his jaw wider, but Maggie stopped him.

"No. Don't do that yet. I want you to take some care in talking, laughing, and especially in yawning for the next few days. As a precaution, I'd like to send you over to Mt. Ida to get an x-ray of your jaw to be sure nothing is broken."

"Naw. I don't need that. I'll be fine."

"Your choice, but it's what I'd recommend you do," she said, pinning him with a firm and she hoped authoritative look. He stared back at her in silence. She shook her head and sighed, realizing he probably wouldn't keep the appointment even if she made the referral. *C'est la vie. You can only lead the horse to water.* "I'll have the receptionist give you an authorization for the x-ray in case you change your mind."

He gave a non-committal shrug, and Maggie sighed again. "You're probably going to be a little woozy for a while from the muscle relaxant. Do you have someone here with you who can drive?"

"Yeah," he said, continuing to massage his sore chewing muscles. "Couple of the boys brought me in. They'd be out there waiting, I reckon."

"OK. Tee can you go be sure he has someone to drive him?" Then back to her patient, she continued, "Mr. Bledsoe, let me run through your care instructions." His mouth curled into a smirk, and he folded his hands in his lap and sat up primly in a display of mock attentiveness. Maggie ignored his patronizing posture and pushed on. "For several days, as I said, try to avoid opening your jaw wide and eating any food that requires much forceful chewing – solid pieces of meat, jerky, nuts, hard vegetables like raw carrots. Just let things heal. Eat soft foods like soup or scrambled eggs, maybe canned chicken or tuna or grilled fish."

"Ice cream, OK? I love ice cream."

"Sure, that would qualify as a soft food. But don't eat just ice cream." He waved away the suggestion and puffed out a dismissive sigh. Maggie tried, apparently without much success, to suppress a buddy-you're-work-ing-my-last-nerve-here look, but he must have finally noticed because his posture relaxed, and the smirk vanished. *Good,* she thought. *Score one for the home team.*

She continued with her care litany and his more genuine attention. "Get some protein in from eggs or fish. Even a protein shake. You need it to heal those traumatized tissues. If you have a heating pad or hot water bottle and an ice pack, you can alternate the hot and the cold and that will help as well. And I'm going to give you a prescription for a few more of the diazepam to keep any spasm of the muscles at bay for a few days. I don't think you'll need anything for pain, now that it's reduced, beyond maybe some Tylenol or ibuprofen. If you do, I want to know about it." She jotted down the prescription on the pad and handed it to him.

"OK, doctor. Whatever you say," he shrugged and mumbled without much moving his mouth.

"And I'd like to see you back in a week to recheck it. Sooner if it gives you trouble in some way. Say unusual pain or maybe it acts like it wants to come out of joint again."

"Got it."

Maggie stepped into the hall just as Therma Faye was heading back to the room. Maggie pulled the exam room door closed behind her.

Therma Faye whispered, "Well, his 'boys' as he calls em are out there waiting, but they reek to high heaven of pot and it not even ten in the morning; we're gonna need to air out the waiting room once they're gone or all the patients'll be higher'n a kite. You ask me, those two might be less fit to drive than him even after that IV tranquilizer."

"Well, unless you really think that's the case, help them get him to the car or truck or whatever it was they brought him in. I need to scrub my hands, and then I'll get busy with the rest of what's scheduled. And on that score, who's first?"

"In room order. Sprained ankle recheck in one; annual pap smear and pelvic in two; and a toddler with a cold in three. And a couple left out front still to come back."

"Onward and upward, then." Maggie picked up the iPad from the chart box beside Room 1 and opened the door.

CHAPTER 11
Best Laid Plans

Papa pulled up into the dirt driveway of Waylon's empty farmhouse and parked. The yellow 'Crime Scene Do Not Cross' tape was still wrapped around the front and fluttered in the light breeze. It wasn't exactly a crime scene, but in the ongoing investigation of what had happened a few weeks ago and the discovery of Ruth's bones at the Caddo mound on his property, the police had cordoned their house off in the event it might yield evidence regarding her murder or the abduction and attempted murder of Maggie, Rose Ellen, and Waylon himself. No one was living there now, so no one had bothered to take it down.

Papa walked around to the back of the house to where the hen houses stood and was greeted by a flock of agitated birds, clucking and flapping, clearly unsettled by something. He opened the gate to enter their coop yard and stopped first and checked their water reservoir, then looked around curious as to what had them in such a state. Not seeing anything, he quietly walked up the ramp, and ducked through the doorway to enter the roost. Inside shafts of sunlight filtered through cracks between the boards of the house and illuminated the startled brown face of a man inside. A light-blue bandana tied around his thick black hair accentuated his heavy dark brows and mustache; he was dressed in a threadbare jacket and loose, worn jeans and held a basket filled with eggs.

"What are you doing here?" Papa made a move toward the man, who was about his own height but younger by half a century and stockier by forty or fifty pounds.

"*Joder*!" The man uttered the curse and lifted a stout, short section of tree limb he had tucked into his belt, clubbing Papa's head with a vicious side stroke before he could react.

As Papa crumpled to the floor of the hen house, the man fled, eggs and all.

***

By the time Maggie returned to Miz Hendri's at supper time, she was exhausted. What she craved most was not dinner but a nice, hot, relaxing bath and a generous pour of wine. She entered the kitchen to find Miz Hendri in a state. Pots bubbled vigorously on the stove behind her, threatening to boil over, but the normally efficient woman just stood in front of the oven twisting her white apron in her hands, oblivious to the incipient mess.

"What's wrong?" Maggie immediately crossed to her and put a hand on her arm, then reached around her to turn the burners down to simmer.

"Manny," she said, the worry evident in her bespectacled, hazel eyes. "He told me when he left earlier that he would help me with something this afternoon, but he has never come back. I tried to ring him, but he does not answer his phone."

"He mentioned this morning that he was going out to Waylon's place to see to the chickens," Maggie reassured her. "Maybe he got a late start or had another stop to make. I'm sure he'll be here shortly."

"No, no, no." Miz Hendri shook her head vigorously and redoubled her efforts to twist the apron into a Celtic knot. "He left here before noon. He should be back. *Ach*! Something is wrong; I feel it."

"It's going to be OK. I'm sure it is," Maggie said, now a little less confident. "Listen, I'll drive out to the Prescott farm. Maybe he's still there."

"No! You must not go alone, *leibchen*. It's almost dark."

She was right about that. Maggie had to admit her recent experience had left her with no desire to be alone in her car on a desolate country road in the dark. "Let me see if JD's around. Maybe he could go with me." Maggie slipped her phone from her pocket and dialed JD's number.

He answered on the first ring. "Hey, sugar." Just the sound of his calm, deep voice made her feel less anxious.

"JD, can you meet me at Waylon's farm in a few minutes. I'm leaving Miz Hendri's right now."

"Sure. But why? Is something wrong?"

"Papa went out there earlier today and said he'd be back by now, but he's not come in. Miz Hendri is worried something might have happened because he's not answering his phone."

"OK. But come to my place; we'll go together."

"On my way," Maggie said, heading out the door.

"You will call me just as soon as you know something?" Maggie heard the worry in Miz Hendri's voice as the old woman hobbled behind her to the back porch. "Please."

"I will. I promise."

On the drive to JD's house, Maggie turned over the possibilities of what could have happened. Papa was up in his seventies, an age when the list of things that can go wrong – heart attack, stroke, broken hip from a fall – gets longer, likelier, and more worrisome. But he was hale and hearty, mentally sharp, and very fit for his age. *Doesn't rule out a slip and fall,* her medical training reminded her. *Or some other accident.* And she was well aware that seemingly good general health didn't entirely rule out those other medical possibilities either. She crossed the low water bridge and gunned the motor to pull up the incline on the far side, glancing left, but scarcely stopping at the intersection with the highway as she made the turn that took her to the road to JD's property.

When she pulled up to JD's house, he was on the front porch waiting for her and hopped down to meet the car. He opened the passenger door and stuck his head in. "Want me to drive?"

"No, I'm fine. I know the way."

He raised a brow and gave a short nod. "OK, let's go."

The SUV bounced down the rutted country road that led to the Prescott farm, situated a couple of miles or so beyond the entrance to JD's property. The road was unlit, and since the moon had set early, the twin high beams illuminated only the immediate roadway ahead leaving the surrounding fields and woody parcels cloaked in gathering darkness.

"Whoa! There's the turn to the house," JD said abruptly, bracing himself on the dash.

Maggie stomped on the brakes, and the car skidded on the hard-packed dirt. "Sorry. It's getting so dark I didn't see the mailbox." She backed up, then edged forward across the stile and into the long, narrow dirt drive. The house was dark, but she could make out the tail of a flapping strand of yellow Crime Scene tape in the headlamps as they pulled up. And Papa's old burgundy Jeep Cherokee sitting in the scrubby brown clumps of dead grass beside the house. Cold dread gripped her heart.

"Stay here," JD said to her in a low voice. "Let me see what's going on. I'll call you if I find anything."

"No." Maggie grabbed his arm. "I'm going with you. If he's hurt or ill, I need to be there."

JD narrowed his eyes, as if weighing the option, then he gave a brief nod and opened the door. "Stay behind me."

Maggie tossed the strap of her medical bag over her shoulder and climbed out, falling in behind him as they made their way quietly around the side of the house. When her eyes became accustomed to the darkness, she noticed for the first time the pistol tucked into the back of his belt and shuddered. *A necessary precaution*, she reminded herself. *No former Ranger would ever go blind and unarmed into an unknown situation.* But somehow the knowledge didn't calm her racing heart.

They stopped at the back corner of the house and listened for a full minute. She could hear her pulse pounding in her ears, but no sound outside herself except the occasional call of a night bird. JD motioned for her to follow, and she stayed close behind him as they skirted the dormant garden behind the house and headed around to the chicken coops. The chicken-wire gate stood open slightly; JD eased it open wider, and they advanced step by silent step into the enclosed pen, until JD held up a hand, stopping to listen again. Then he slowly drew the gun from his waistband – *had he heard something?* Maggie strained her ears, and finally picked out a scrabbling sound from inside the hen house. JD tensed, dropped to a knee, and leveled the barrel of the pistol across his forearm toward the dark opening to the roost, poised and ready. Momentarily, the bobbing head of a rooster poked out from the door of the roost and looked around. With a flap of its wings, it strutted down the ramp. JD visibly relaxed and waited a few moments more, then motioned them forward, up the ramp, and into the hen house. It was silent and black as pitch inside, but as they entered, the hens roused in their nests and began to cluck and chatter softly among themselves. One carefully placed footstep after the next, they moved down the row of nest boxes until JD stopped abruptly and nearly toppled forward.

"There's something on the floor here." Squatting down and tucking the pistol back into his belt, he pulled out his phone and snapped on the flashlight. The bright glare shattered the dark stillness and illuminated the object in front of him.

"Papa!" Maggie gasped as she moved up beside JD.

He was lying face down on the floor of the coop; blood from a gash in his scalp had dried and matted his white hair and pooled on the floor beneath his head; the contents of a couple of broken hen's eggs merged into the viscous, dark puddle. And beside him lay a thick short length of a tree branch. Maggie knelt and felt immediately for a pulse at Papa's neck, breathing a sigh of relief when she felt it strong under her fingertips. She turned him face up. He was out cold and didn't respond when she called his name or lightly slapped his cheek. She pressed her thumbnail hard into the nail of his middle finger, and the painful stimulus elicited a soft groan.

"Give me the light," she said. JD handed her his phone, and she lifted each eyelid to shine the flashlight into Papa's pupils. She was rewarded with a sharp contraction on one side, but a sluggish response on the other.

"Oh, God, "she whispered and turned worried eyes to JD.

"What?"

"His left pupil's not reacting as it should. Could be a stroke but judging by the head wound and blood and this," she said pointing to the branch, "more likely an intracranial bleed – subdural or epidural hematoma." She breathed out the words, almost fearing to say them aloud. She looked at JD. "We've got to get him to a hospital right away. I don't think we can wait for the EMTs to make it out here and all the way back to Hot Springs. And if it's what I think it is, there isn't a lot they would do anyway that I can't do."

"OK. Help me get him onto my shoulder." In the close confines of the hen house, maneuvering was a challenge. Maggie stepped over Papa's still form to the back of the space and squatted to help JD raise the man's upper body. Then when JD squatted low Maggie looped Papa's arms over JD's broad shoulder and gave the assist needed to lift the man's dead weight as JD rose to a crouching stand. Maggie shone the flashlight toward the doorway as JD carried Papa out into the fresh night air. Once outside, when JD could stand again, he immediately took off at a trot, easily carrying the old man's slighter frame back around the house to the car. Maggie latched the gate and then ran ahead to open the hatch and drop the back seats so JD could lay him into the cargo space. She tossed in her medical bag and crawled into the back with him.

"How long will it take us to get to Hot Springs?"

"About 45 minutes from here, I expect," JD said as the engine rumbled to life. He backed around, spinning dirt and rocks as he did, and tore down the drive.

They arrived at Mercy General's Emergency entrance in just shy of 38 minutes, a testament to the fortunate absence of traffic and JD's willingness to push the speed limit.

JD unfolded his tall frame from the chair he'd been sitting in for hours and stretched, extending his arms toward the harsh fluorescent panels on the waiting room ceiling, then rolled his shoulders forward and back, working out the kinks. "Want something to drink? Some tea or coffee?" He turned back to Maggie, who sat leaning forward, elbows on her knees, staring at the floor. JD bent slightly down to her, lifted her hand, and gave her fingers a gentle squeeze. "There's a machine. Or I could go find the cafeteria."

"Coffee would be good," Maggie said returning the squeeze. Stiff herself after so long a time in the dubious comfort of a molded plastic chair what she really needed was a good long yoga stretch, but a waiting room full of the sick and injured wasn't exactly the place for it. "I'm going to ask to speak with the duty physician," she said, standing and shrugging away a few of her own kinks.

Behind the admission's desk a short, round woman sat filing a set of very long, very bright acrylic nails. She wasn't the same person who had been there when they'd come in earlier. The crew had changed at seven pm and it was now well past eight. Maggie shifted from one foot to the other, waiting none too patiently for said clerk to finish what she was doing and acknowledge her presence. Finally, the woman glanced up and arched her penciled brows in a *what-do-you-want?* expression but said nothing as she continued to work the file across her hot pink talons and smack the large wad of chewing gum in her cheek.

Maggie cleared her throat. "Has there been any word on the patient we brought in with the head injury. Emmanuel Purifoy?"

"Are you immediate family?" She wielded the file back and forth.

"No. I'm the referring physician. Dr. McKinley. I'd like an update from the duty physician or charge nurse."

"Dr. Simmons is on break," she chirped. "Nurses are all busy with patients. You'll have to wait."

"We've been waiting," Maggie countered firmly, "for about two and a half hours."

The woman sighed deeply and laid down her file, then scuttling sideways like a rotund crab, her chair creaking under her, rolled over to the computer screen and tapped a few keys with the talons. "He's still in surgery is the last update here. McKinley, you said?"

Maggie nodded. "Mmm hmm."

The woman ran a pink dagger down the screen, searching, then finally stopped and tapped the glass. "Yeah. You're on here. When Dr. Beasley's done, he'll come out to speak to you." She gave the gum a loud *pop* and shrugged her meaty shoulders in an unspoken *nothing more can I do* gesture. "Just have a seat." Clearly dismissed, Maggie bit back the retort that sprang to her lips and returned instead to her perch on the hard orange plastic.

JD handed her a vending machine coffee. The thin cardboard cup was almost too hot to hold; she cradled it gingerly with her fingertips and blew across the surface to cool it before taking a tentative sip. JD didn't seem affected and blithely sipped from his cup. She mused that perhaps the Army issued its Rangers heat-resistant, silicone-coated mouths and fingers, with a lifetime warranty.

"What'd they say?" he asked.

"Nothing helpful." She ticked the list off on her fingers. "He's still in surgery. The doctor will be out when it's over. And I should go cool my heels."

"Did you get ahold of Miz Hendri?"

"I did earlier. She's going to call Papa's daughters and let them know." She took another tentative sip. Still too hot. "I hate that she's there alone. She's worried sick."

"I spoke to Sheriff Perkins," JD said. "They're going to send a car out to Waylon's. See if they can piece anything together tonight about who did this. But I doubt they'll –"

The double doors to the back hallway swooshed open, and a distinguished-looking, scrub-clad surgeon with the erect bearing of someone who'd done a long stint in military service walked briskly through. He pinned JD with a questioning look and walked his way. "Are you Dr. McKinley?" he asked. JD pursed his lips and raised his brows as he gave his head a slow shake and tipped it with a glance in Maggie's direction.

"I'm Dr. McKinley," Maggie said, standing and joining JD and the surgeon. She held out her hand, and when the man shook it, she noted a flicker of confusion and something else in the eyes behind the round tortoise-shell glasses, but it quickly vanished. That other something was a thing she'd seen many times before, a sizing up of sorts, that momentary dilation of the pupils that betrayed subliminal, baser interests, though he was easily old enough to be her father. Men, she had long ago realized, couldn't suppress the tell-tale tweak of their sexual antennae when coming face to face with an attractive female. At least none she'd met so far.

"Apologies, ma'am. The note only said…uh…I assumed…" His voice trailed off, but he quickly recovered his poise and directed his further remarks to her. "Cameron Beasley," he introduced himself, releasing her hand. "You're Mr. Purifoy's physician, then?"

"Yes. Is he OK?" Her voice sounded professional and calm, but beneath the surface she was working mightily to keep out any trace of the anxiety she felt.

"He took quite a blow, as I'm sure you know, and it fractured his skull. X-rays show it wasn't depressed though." Dr. Beasley had fully regained his professional demeanor and was all business now. "Fortunately, you got him here in time."

"That's good." Maggie nodded and breathed an audible sigh of relief.

"We drained what turned out to be a very large epidural hematoma," he continued.

"Was there any deeper damage?" Her coffee had cooled enough to permit a generous swallow of it, and she drank, grateful for the warmth and the caffeine.

"The scans don't show anything subdural. At least so far. But as I'm sure you know, that doesn't always show up right away."

"Can we see him?"

"Not yet. He's still in recovery. Could be a while. I can put your cell number in the chart and have the ward clerk call you when he gets settled into a post-op bed. He'll be in the ICU tonight at least."

"ICU?" Maggie dug into her bag, coming out with a pen and scrap of paper on which she scribbled her cell number, handing it to the surgeon. She really needed to get some business cards. *Add that to the to-do list.*

"He was unconscious when you brought him in, as you're aware, and hasn't regained consciousness yet though he's responding normally to stimulation, and that's a good sign. Still, at his age, there's always the worry of a deeper tear, a slow leak accumulating over the next bit. Fragile older vessels and all. I'll want to watch him very closely tonight and scan again tomorrow." He put his hand somewhat paternalistically on her upper arm. "Why don't you go get some rest, maybe grab a bite to eat." She appreciated that he didn't call her *dear* or *honey,* but she heard the unspoken moniker in his voice nonetheless, and she stiffened slightly but said nothing. "We'll know more in a few hours."

JD took Maggie's other elbow and gave it a gentle admonishing squeeze. "Doctor's right, Maggie. Nothing more we can do right now."

Maggie looked up at JD, reading the *slow-your-roll* warning in his eyes, and after a momentary pause she gave a scarcely perceptible nod, then turned back to the surgeon, all business herself. "Thank you, Dr. Beasley." She extended her hand again. "We'll be nearby. Please ask them to call if there's any change."

JD kept her elbow firmly in his grasp guiding her through the chilly night air to her car. "You wanted to paste him," he said with a soft snort of a laugh. Maggie started to reply but had to admit it was true; he just smiled down at her, amused, and released her arm. "You were thinking it so loud I could hear you from where I was standing." He opened the door for her, and she climbed in. "Must be a pain in the ass."

Maggie nodded her head. "It is." She looked up and found his gentle eyes on her face, and her anger instantly faded. "You'd think you'd get used to the patronizing and condescension, and I guess you sort of do after a while, but it still rankles sometimes. It doesn't help that I'm hungry and tired."

JD climbed into the driver's seat. "That I can fix. I saw a 24-hour pancake shop around the corner on the way in. Not far. We could at least get an omelet or something."

"Yeah, that's fine. What I need is a stiff drink."

They were half-way through plates of steak and eggs when JD's phone rang. "It's Ben Bradford," he said, thumbing to answer.

"Hey, Ben," he said, "find anything?" JD listened for a minute and cocked his head in question. "That's good." Then after another few moments, "Hmmm, that's interesting. Is there a chance they can recover a print?" Then another pause. "No, he hasn't waked up yet, but the surgery went well according to the doctor. We're going to stay the night in Hot Springs," he looked over at Maggie for her approval of that notion. She nodded, and he went on. "We'll be back tomorrow sometime, if all goes well with Manny." He said goodbye and put down the phone.

"What did he say?"

"First off, Velma went over to stay with Miz Hendri tonight."

"That makes me feel better," Maggie said with a relieved sigh.

"Me, too. And the crime scene investigators are going back out to Waylon's first thing in the morning. Ben said they're hopeful they can maybe raise a print off the broken eggshells. Maybe DNA off that piece of branch. Maybe the perp held them. He's staying out there tonight himself to make sure the scene's secure." The waitress arrived with the bill, and JD handed it back to her with his credit card. "Thank you, ma'am." Once she departed, he reached across the table and took Maggie's hand. "And speaking of staying somewhere tonight," the wanting of her was evident in his eyes, readable from across the room, "let's find a place that's not too far away."

He brought her fingertips slowly to his lips, and that simple, sensual act set a quiver of desire pulsing in her belly. "Yes," she responded softly meeting his gaze. "Let's."

The hotel room was dark and smelled faintly of holiday spices. Maggie thought she detected evergreen, orange peel, cinnamon, clove, and maybe black currants. Must be a dish of potpourri somewhere. Not unexpected, as it was after all the height of the Christmas season; still she appreciated the nice touch. But the air in the room was close and too warm. JD helped her off with her coat and tossed it and his own leather jacket onto the chair. Then he turned down the heat, drew back the draperies, and threw the balcony doors wide open to let in the fresh, cold night air. The Christmas lights twinkled below, painting the dark room in muted flashes that danced on the walls like multi-colored fractals.

Maggie opened the mini-bar and squatted in front of it to examine the offerings. "What's your pleasure?" The cool white light of the refrigerator illuminated her face, making her flawless skin almost glow. "There's champagne and white wine, and beer if you want something cold. I see a red blend of some sort. And the usual whisky, vodka, gin." She riffled through the cabinet's contents. "And brandy."

She hadn't heard JD come up behind her and flinched slightly when he touched the back of her neck, just grazing her skin with his fingertips as he traced a line down to where her pulse was suddenly fluttering in the hollow of her throat. He bent down, his voice was deep and husky in her ear. "My pleasure, darlin'," he said, placing a gentle kiss at her temple, "won't be found in a bottle."

He took her hand and closed the mini-bar door returning the room to semi-darkness, lit only by the twinkling lights beyond the balcony. She rose and stood before him, looking up, meeting his gaze. His eyes never left hers as he loosened the top button of her silky blouse, then the next and the next in a slow progression that left her breathless. Then he slipped the garment off her shoulders and arms and let if flutter to the carpet behind her.

"Your turn," he said.

Her fingers trembled slightly as she worked open the buttons of his soft flannel shirt, exposing the smooth, warm expanse of his sculpted chest and releasing the intoxicating, masculine scent of him. He bent his head to kiss her, softly, lingering on her lips, then moving to plant a trail of slow kisses down her neck, his breath warm against her skin; kissing each shoulder he slipped the straps of her silky camisole over them and let it drop to her waist. Then with exquisite slowness he pressed kisses down her neck and chest, each one lower than the next.

She threaded her fingers into his thick hair to pull him closer to her as he made his way lower. Unbuttoning her slacks, he knelt to ease the zipper down, planting light, tickling kisses on her abdomen as he went. In one fluid motion she pushed her slacks over her slender hips and let them drop to the floor. JD stood and wrapped his arms around her waist, kissing her lips slowly, then picked her up to lay her gently across the bed.

Maggie awoke sometime later and found JD propped up on one elbow, watching her in the still dark room. He trailed a fingertip languidly from her shoulder, across her collarbone, and down the center of her chest and abdomen, then along the gentle curve of her waist, finally letting his hand come to rest at her hip. Then he leaned over and kissed her forehead tenderly. "Now that was the very definition of my pleasure," he grinned at her.

"Can't say I disagree," she smiled up at him and shivered slightly, snuggling closer to his warmth.

"Too cold?" JD got up to close the slider, leaving just a crack for fresh air. "Maybe we should actually get under the covers," he chuckled. "And grab a few more hours of sleep."

Maggie pulled back the fluffy duvet, slipped between the cool sheets, and held the covers open, her large dark eyes inviting him to join her. "What's your pleasure now?"

CHAPTER 12
The Life You Save

The next morning Dr. Beasley stood outside the ICU doors looking much less crisp than he had last night, like he hadn't slept much or maybe at all, Maggie thought.

"His vitals have been stable all night," he said to her, "and follow up scans this morning look good. He's talking, and his neuro exam is amazingly normal for the extent and type of injury at his age. We're transferring him now to the floor." He took a long drink of his coffee and ran a hand through his wavy, salt and pepper hair in an unsuccessful attempt to bring some order to it.

"Long night?" Maggie knew that up-all-night, hollow-eyed feeling all too well. She'd experienced it herself often enough and seen it in Jeff and many others. Awake and functional, but totally depleted.

"Mm," he nodded and took another swig from the cup. "MVA, multiple cars and a semi. In the OR most of the night."

"How'd it go?"

He cocked a brow and shrugged. "Win some, lose some," he said with a trace of sad resignation. She'd been there, too; it was tough to work hard to save a life and fail. Every loss hurt.

JD returned just then with a hot cup of coffee in each hand, handing Maggie hers and laying his now-liberated hand protectively—and perhaps a little possessively—on the small of her back.

"He's awake and alert," she said to him. "We should be able to see him shortly."

"Thank God." JD extended his hand to the surgeon then returned it immediately to Maggie's waist. "Thank you, sir. We appreciate all you did to bring him through."

"Well," Beasley said, "he's not fully out of the woods yet, but he's doing better than I would have expected. We'll keep him here a few more days and see how it goes. He's going up to 3, if you want to go to the waiting room up there, they'll let you know when you can see him. Shouldn't be long."

"Thank you, again," Maggie said.

The family waiting room was furnished in what she assumed was intended to be a calming color palette of creams and blues and greens that somehow came off looking a bit more seasick than seafoam. Small clusters of other patients' concerned families and friends were scattered about the room, conversing in hushed tones, or trying to sleep. Maggie and JD had just settled into chairs in a quiet corner away from the others when Deputy Ben Bradford's tall, slender frame filled the doorway.

"Ben!" Maggie said when she spotted him. His creased shirt and the hint of stubble on his normally smooth cheeks attested he'd had a sleepless night of his own.

"Mornin', Doc," he smiled and came toward them. "How's he doin'?"

"Haven't seen him yet today, but his surgeon thinks he's past the worst of it."

"That's sure good to hear." He took a seat. "Ma'am," he said to Maggie, "much as I don't want to bother him, we need to see if he can remember anything about what happened. Forensics said it's Mr. P's blood on the limb, and they lifted a thumb print from one of the eggshells this morning; they're putting it into AFIS. Maybe they'll get a hit."

"He may not be able to remember much," Maggie warned. "He was knocked unconscious, and there's often amnesia surrounding the traumatic event itself, sometimes even including a period of time leading up to it."

"Yes, ma'am. I understand, but I still gotta ask."

A nurse's aide appeared, scanned the waiting room, and called from the door, "Purifoy?"

Maggie and Ben both looked over at him and raised simultaneous hands. "Here," Maggie said. Ben dropped his hand, deferring to Maggie, who smiled her thanks and stood. She shot Ben a glance and nodded toward the door, inviting him to join them.

Maggie, JD, and Ben entered the room to find Papa with his head swathed in a gauze turban, tethered to a plethora of tubes and wires, lying flat on his back. His nurse was at his bedside, fussing with his pillows.

"I was just getting him settled," she said, "but if you'll keep it short." She raised the head of the bed, but only slightly.

Ben stepped up to the bedside. "Yes, ma'am. I just have a few questions." The nurse nodded and left them.

"We can come back later," JD said to Ben.

"No. I'd like y'all to stay. You two found him. I'm gonna need to ask you some questions, too."

Ben pulled a small notebook and pen from his shirt pocket and flipped it open. "Mr. Purifoy," he began, "first off, I'm real sorry about what happened to you. But I promise we're gonna do whatever it takes to find out who did it."

Papa looked tired and pale to Maggie, but that was expected. The deep purple bruising that had settled around and below his left eye didn't improve the look, but she was heartened when he smiled weakly at Ben to see both sides of his lips raise equally. *No facial paralysis. That's good.*

"Thank you, son." His voice was soft and rasping, but that wasn't uncommon either post op from the intubation and the drying effect of the anesthetic gasses and oxygen. "What is it you want to know?"

Maggie closed her eyes and offered up silent thanks for a second time in as many minutes. Papa's speech, though slow and deliberate, was clear.

That was also a very good sign, since blunt force trauma to the left side of the head can sometimes damage the left hemisphere of the brain housing the speech areas.

"Well, tell me anything you can recall about it." Ben stood, pen poised to paper, waiting.

After a long pause, Papa took a deep breath and blew it out through his nose. "Well, I remember driving out to Waylon's place. Remember that the hens were agitated by something, outside raising a ruckus when I got there." He paused a moment, closing his eyes, as if gathering his thoughts, straining to recall then looked again at Ben. "I checked the water reservoir outside before I went into the hen house to see what had them in such a state. Thought maybe a snake or something had gotten into the nests." He stopped and closed his eyes.

Maggie moved over to the other side of the bed and quickly scanned the monitor displays. *BP, heartrate, respirations all look good.*

"Do you remember seeing anything or anyone inside?" Ben continued to scribble on the pad.

"I couldn't see clearly. My eyes hadn't quite adjusted to the dark inside." He paused again, then finally continued, "When I first went in, I noticed a smell. I thought maybe a skunk had gotten in. They'll raid a chicken coop if they can get in the fence. But it wasn't a skunk. It was someone, a stocky shape. He had… I say 'he', it seemed like a man; voice sounded like a man, anyway."

"He spoke? What'd he say?" Ben prompted.

"Just one word."

"Did you understand it? The word, I mean?" Ben was all eagerness.

"Ho-dare is what it sounded like."

The look on JD's face was priceless, and he worked to suppress a laugh, but it snorted out anyway. Ben looked quizzically at him. "A little Spanish profanity, I think," JD said. "J-o-d-e-r, most likely. A curse word. Spanish F-bomb."

Ben nodded and wrote it all down dutifully. "Can you describe the person at all?"

"Nothing too specific. Stocky. About my height. Black hair I think and a mustache."

"Anything else?"

"Had a light blue or white cap or maybe a cloth or bandana of some sort on his head. I remember the color stood out against all the darkness. Then… nothing. Next thing I know after that, I woke up with a powerful headache and a pretty nurse standing over me, patting my shoulder, asking me if I knew where I was."

"OK, that's good." Ben flipped the notebook closed. "If you remember anything else, you just let us know."

"I will, Benji."

"We're following all the leads, Mr. Purifoy. I promise you we'll find who did this to you."

"Ben," JD said, "if it's OK with you, we'll stay and visit a few minutes more, and then we'll come give you a statement."

"That's fine, JD. How 'bout I just meet y'all in Caddo Bend later today? I need to head on back." He bobbed his head, turned, and left.

When Ben departed, JD took his place beside the bed. "We're not going to stay too long today, but I just wanted you to know that I've got everything worked out with Darrell to handle the chickens at Waylon's for the short term. And I've been working out a longer-term plan, too, but we can talk about that when you're rested and stronger."

Papa absently picked at a snagged loop of thread on the pale green coverlet. "I'm worried about Hendri. She'll need some help at the house."

"I know. I'll handle whatever she needs myself, Manny," JD patted his arm to reassure him. "Don't worry about that. We'll take care of things there."

"And I'll be there with her every night." Maggie said, glancing up at JD and suppressing a laugh at his startled expression at the prospect of an unspecified period of enforced celibacy. Papa nodded and smiled at her, but his eyes were heavy with fatigue and lingering traces of post-anesthesia lethargy. "We're going now so you can get some sleep. Don't worry about a thing. Just rest and recover. We'll see you in a day or two."

In the elevator, alone, JD drew Maggie to him in a strong embrace and kissed her ardently. Pulling away at last, he looked down at her and brushed a tendril of hair away from her cheek. "Every night? What were you thinking?"

"Well, I didn't say I'd be there alone every night, did I?"

He kissed the tip of her nose playfully. "No, ma'am. I guess you didn't."

The elevator doors opened on the Lobby, and he wrapped an arm around her shoulders as they squeezed around an aide and a patient in a wheelchair waiting to board.

At the main entrance, JD handed the parking stub to the pimply, bored teenaged attendant manning the booth, who did a comical double take at Maggie before he took off at a trot to retrieve the car. He returned with it in short order and wheeled up under the portico, hopping out and holding the door for JD, pocketing the bill he palmed to him, then hustling around to the passenger side to help Maggie in, staring at her like a moon-struck calf. She rewarded him with a smile and a soft 'Thank you' as she tried to pull her door closed.

"My pleasure, ma'am," he stammered, blushing to the tips of his ears, but not letting go of the door handle. "Y'all drive safe now and have a nice day."

"I think you have an admirer," JD said when the door finally slammed shut and they pulled out of the lot.

"What's your plan, by the way?" she asked once they were back on the road.

"Plan?" JD looked momentarily confused and didn't elaborate as he negotiated the traffic to merge onto the highway.

"You told Papa you had a plan for Waylon's property," Maggie said.

"Oh, that plan." He nodded toward her phone. "Put something good on for us, and I'll tell you what I've got in mind."

"What's your pleasure?" she asked, all wide-eyed innocence at the clear reference to last evening's most-pleasant interlude.

"You already know the answer to that," he said with a twitch of his brows. She rolled her eyes. "Oh, you meant musical pleasure," he said. "In that case, surprise me. Actually, darlin', in either case surprise me."

Maggie scrolled through her iTunes library and finally settled on a mellow playlist of classic rock. Good for background and conversation. She queued it up, hit play, and the tinkling harpsichord intro of Elton John's *I Need You To Turn To* filled the space.

"Mmm. Good choice. I love this song," he said. A half smile curved his lips "Always have. I remember the first time I heard it. Must have been ten years old, eleven maybe. My mother was listening to it on the cassette player in the car—that tells you how long ago it was! I looked over at her and saw tears in her eyes. I said, 'Mama what's wrong?' and she just smiled at me and said, 'Nothin' sweetie. Just a beautiful sentiment. Listen to it. That's how I feel about your daddy.' I didn't understand what she was even talking about. Then she said, 'Someday when you're all grown up, I want you to be able to feel that way about someone.' She played it non-stop. My mama was a big Elton fan."

"Mine, too," Maggie smiled, and he reached over to lay his hand on her thigh, comfortable in their shared moment of reminiscing.

"She about wore the tape out on *I Guess That's Why They Call It The Blues*," he said. They laughed together, then lapsed for a bit into easy silence. He signaled and accelerated to pass a slow-moving tractor trailer chugging along uphill ahead of them.

"I'm not sure why—maybe because of my own parents' leaving me so early—but I'm drawn to the music of their era. Much more so than my own. My dad loved vintage vocal jazz—I think I've told you that before—but my mom was more a creature of her time, musically speaking. Dylan and Elton. James Taylor. The Eagles. The Stones and the Beatles. Seals and Crofts. CSN. Queen. Even The Dead. Listening to the pop and rock classics keeps her closer to me, somehow. She loved this one, too."

"So different from anything else he did," JD paused for a moment, thinking. "Except maybe *Your Song*. The feel of *Turn To's* almost classical. Like Bach or Haydn, almost, in the keyboard and strings. And his voice on this one," JD just shook his head in admiration. "Such a perfect combination those two: Elton's musical genius and Bernie's poetry."

He listened for a moment then his rich baritone voice joined in, singing, "Did you paint your smile on when I said I knew that my reason for living was for loving you. We're related in feeling, but you're high above. You're pure and yet gentle with the grace of a dove." He reached over and took her hand, brought it to his lips and placed a soft kiss on the back of it.

Maggie found herself wondering if he knew all the lyrics to every song ever written. Sure seemed that way. She felt her throat tighten and swallowed hard, surprised by the sudden rush of a sense of belonging that his singing those lyrics inspired. Not trusting her voice, she just smiled at him, and they listened in companionable silence to the end of the song. Before the next cut began, she cleared her throat. "You were going to tell me about your plan."

"Oh, right. Have you ever heard of Joel Salatin?" Maggie shook her head. "Polyface Farm?" Again, the question drew nothing but a blank look and a negative shake of her head. "He's a journalist-turned-farmer who owns a 500 or so acre piece of land in Virginia that he's turned into a totally organic, totally integrated, working, profitable farm. His method hinges on growing good grass – he calls himself a grass farmer, but that's just the foundation of what he does. It's a beautifully integrated, sustainable, complete agri-ecosystem.

"I read about it a few years back in a book by Michael Pollan called *The Omnivore's Dilemma,* and I happened to notice that book on the shelf the other night, looking for something else. And that got me to thinking about Waylon's place; he's got a lot of fertile, rich pasture, oak woods, and plenty of room. He's already got the chickens and a stream-fed stock pond. And a good-sized vegetable garden. We could build on that. Renovate the farmhouse; build some out-buildings; fence the pastures; replicate the Polyface model.

"Salatin teaches courses on how to lay it all out and make it work. I was thinking maybe I could go to Virginia, learn about it, and while Waylon's gone, hire a crew and try to do something like that on his place on a slightly smaller scale. He's only got about 200 acres, maybe 250. But once he's out and back home, he and Rose Ellen are going to need something more than selling eggs and a few vegetables out of a truck patch. And he's going to need a purpose. A reason to stay sober and productive. A way forward."

Maggie was amazed yet again at his thoughtful, generous spirit. "I think it's a great idea. Will he go along with it?"

"Can't see why he wouldn't." He pulled into the passing lane to accelerate around a pickup full of hay bales. "But I'll go talk to him about it once he can have visitors. He'd never take it as charity I know that; but it wouldn't be. I'd put up the front money to get it set up and operating as an investment that he could pay off as the farm becomes profitable. And for me, it'd be a way to repay him for helping me find my compass after my dad died. Don't know where I'd have wound up without his guidance back then, but it probably wouldn't have been here, now… with you. And for that alone, I owe him."

They turned off the main highway onto the gently rolling two-lane road that wound through a landscape of winter pastures, pine forest, and bare stands of hardwood that would take them home. The skies had grown sullen in the last few miles and threatened rain.

"Want to grab a bite?" JD asked. "We're almost to Glenwood; we could get lunch at The Nest."

Maggie's stomach rumbled at the suggestion; they hadn't eaten since the eggs last night. The broiled catfish at The Fish Nest was indeed a draw, truly the most succulent and delicious catfish anywhere, but Maggie was no fan of driving in the rain and fervently hoped they could make it back home ahead of whatever storm seemed to be brewing ahead. She leaned forward and peered out the windshield again at the gathering dark in the sky and felt her heart rate quicken. "Tempted as I am, do you mind if we don't? It really looks like rain, and besides I want to check on Miz Hendri."

"No. That's fine. We can fix something there."

As if on cue, several fat raindrops splattered against the windshield and splotched the dry pavement ahead. In the space of a few minutes, those few were joined by an increasing torrent of drops interspersed with the *tick tick tick* of sleet pellets hitting the glass. Maggie clenched her fists in her lap and took a deep inhale, releasing the air through parted, trembling lips in a soft *whoosh*, trying to calm the panic that always simmered just under the surface anytime she traveled on a rain-slick road. Or at least had done so for the last fifteen years.

JD gave her a quick sideways glance. "You OK?"

"Yeah," she said, her voice a little shaky. She cleared her throat. "I'm fine."

"You don't look fine. You're pale as milk." He reached over and wrapped his large hand around her clenched fists, massaging the back of one hand gently with his thumb until it relaxed.

A loaded logging truck barreled past them in the other direction and threw a momentarily blinding spray of slushy water onto their windshield with a hard, loud *splat*. Maggie screamed and grabbed JD's hand with both hers.

He tapped the brakes and gradually slowed, steering the car into a widened turn out and stopping. He activated the emergency flashers and turned off the music, unbuckling his seat belt so he could turn in the seat to face her. He reached out to cup her cheek and smooth back the hair that hid her face, gently hooking it behind her ear. "What's going on, sugar? Tell me." She closed her eyes and shook her head. Her throat was so tight she couldn't speak. A solitary tear escaped and slid down her cheek, and he wiped it gently away. Then he reached across to take her in his arms, holding her, murmuring soothing words, and placing soft kisses into her silky hair as she trembled in his embrace.

Other than the drumming of the rain on windshield and roof, only the *tik-tok tik-tok* of the flashers broke the silence inside; the only other disturbance came when the occasional big truck jostled the car as it rushed past and plastered the side window with slushy spray. He rocked her gently in his arms and let her softly cry until the heavy downpour outside slackened, slowed to a *pitter patter*, then finally stopped.

He cupped her chin and tipped it up to look into her dark luminous eyes; tears still glistened in the thick black lashes. "Now can you tell me what all this is about?" His soft voice was as welcome and soothing as his caress, and Maggie felt the tension that had gripped her melt from her forearms, shoulders, and back. She reached into her bag and pulled out a tissue, daintily dabbed the corners of her eyes, and then blew her nose loudly.

"Sorry," she smiled weakly at him from behind the tissue and blew loudly again. Then she sniffed and relaxed once more into his arms and began to recount the story at the deep root of her panic, the full story she'd never told to anyone but Charlotte and under similar circumstances. The story of the night that had forever changed her life, the night in the cold rain when her parents' car had skidded off the road, flipped over the guardrail and into the river below, the night they'd been killed, and she had lived. The night that had left her alive but alone.

When she'd finished, still wrapped in his warm embrace with the steady thump of his heart comforting against her cheek, she looked up into his eyes. He scanned her face and murmured, "I'm so sorry," stroking her hair tenderly. "You're safe. And you're not alone anymore. I'm here."

CHAPTER 13
Pot of Gold and Sorrow

Yesenia flattened another ball of yellow corn masa dough between her hands and flopped the thin disc onto a piece of scrap aluminum heating over the coals. Her expanding belly made the reach over the hot brazier more difficult, but she managed, and when she'd settled the tortilla successfully on the smoking hot metal with the others, she rocked back on her heels and caressed her abdomen with both hands. When she and Domingo had migrated north, fleeing Matamoros and the dangers of the drug cartel there, she hadn't known she was expecting, but that fact had become abundantly clear a few months later. They'd believed they were coming to a better life, a safer place, but when no work had materialized and their food and money had run out, hope had run out as well. And a couple of months ago when she'd been physically unable to continue the arduous journey on foot, Domingo had told her there was no option but to take whatever work he could find here, distasteful as the work might be. They had to eat; they had to survive. If harvesting illegal hemp for these Americans was all he could do, he'd told her, he would do it. For her. For their unborn child. After the child came, he'd promised they would continue north to Colorado as planned, to his mother's cousin there, who'd offered to help them find better work.

They had pitched their small tent near a trickling stream that afforded them water for washing and cooking, in a spot well away from his dodgy employers' sometimes-raucous main camp in the clearing over the hill. There was privacy here, and it was quiet, but Domingo didn't like to leave her alone when he worked, especially at night when they had sometimes harvested until dawn. Now the process of trimming, curing, and drying had begun. Today he had been gone since early morning, and the stars were already peeping out in the dusky sky overhead.

At the sharp snap of brush behind her, Yesenia froze like a frightened squirrel.

"*Huevos, mi amor.*" It was Domingo's voice, and Yesenia's tight shoulders visibly relaxed.

"*¿Por qué llegas tarde?*" She turned a look at him, her pretty, dark eyes echoing the question she'd asked: why had he been gone so long?

He stepped out of the brush, his own dark eyes smiling, and laid a basketful of fresh eggs like a trophy beside her. "*Para ti y el bebé.*"

"*Gracias, mi corazón. Y para ti.*" He was her love, her heart, and he needed the nourishment as much as she and their child, but she knew that without her insistence he probably wouldn't eat the eggs himself.

She smeared a couple of the fresh tortillas with a generous spoonful of warm, refried beans, rolled them up, and handed them to her husband. Then rolled another for herself. They sat side by side on the ground, grateful for their meager supper, and he told her about running into the man at the chicken house and the circuitous route he'd taken on his return, the reason for his prolonged absence.

Then Domingo, exhausted from the long day, the unsettling incident with the man, and the many extra miles of walking, kissed her hand and turned in. Yesenia rolled the last of the freshly grilled tortillas in sheets of paper towel and smoothed out another lightly used piece of aluminum foil to wrap them securely, laying them along with the eggs into the beat-up plastic cooler they used to keep what little food they had away from scavenging animals. She banked the fire and joined him in their flimsy tent, closing the zippered opening securely. She stripped off her shift, laid it carefully beside his clothing to air through the night, and burrowed down beside his warm body under their blanket.

The next morning, Domingo emerged from the tent to find her already up, warming tortillas and frying two of the eggs on the makeshift griddle laid over the fire. She looked up and smiled when she saw him, put an egg and some cooked parsnips onto a warm tortilla and folded it over, holding it out for him.

"*Come. Come, mi amor.*" He took it from her, shrugging in reluctant acquiescence, his eyes shining with love for her, and ate it as she'd asked. She folded the remaining egg into another with a smile and joined him.

She had put on her sweater and thin cotton jacket, the only outer garments she owned, over her cotton shift, but all together they offered little warmth. He stepped into the tent and brought out the thin woolen blanket from their pallet and wrapped it around her against the December chill, letting his hand pause to caress her belly. The baby gave a strong kick, and Domingo jerked his hand away and let out a joyous whoop!

"*Fuerte. Muy fuerte!*" So strong. He placed his hand again on her round abdomen, feeling another strong kick, then rubbed her belly with gentle circles, cooing softly to the baby within. "*Mi hijo!*"

"*O tu hija*," she gently reminded him. It could be a girl.

"Sanchez," a voice barked from the trees on the crest of the hill above their camp. "Marty wants to see you."

Domingo bent to whisper in her ear, "*Volveré pronto.*" He would return soon. With a gentle squeeze of her shoulders and a soft kiss to her cheek he was gone, swallowed by the cold gray mist of the morning, and she was alone again by the fire.

***

Domingo and the tall, lanky man who'd come to get him, a man called Gil, stood at the door of Marty Bledsoe's fifth-wheel trailer in the main camp. Gil knocked loudly and waited. His long blonde hair was loose, and he raked his hands through it and pulled it back into a stringy ponytail he secured with an elastic band.

"Yeah, what is it?" The voice from inside had an angry, impatient edge to it.

"Got Sanchez here," Gil responded.

"Bring him in, Gilly."

The door opened from within, and Gil shoved Domingo, somewhat roughly, ahead of him up the steps and into the trailer, ducking in behind him. It was warm inside, almost too warm Domingo thought after the long walk up the hill in the frigid morning air.

Marty Bledsoe reclined in a high-backed captain's chair, his feet propped up, smoking a fat joint that permeated the space with its sweet aroma. A skinny young woman with blue streaked hair sat on the edge of the desk beside his feet. He gave a jerk of his head toward the door and said, "Tiff, take a powder, honey. We got business to talk about." She gave him a smirk but bit back whatever she may have been about to say and hopped off the desk, brushing past Domingo on her way out the door. Once she was gone, Marty swiveled around and rocked the chair forward to face them, his feet landing with a solid *plunk*. Domingo gave a startled jerk and sharp intake of breath, and the man smiled at him, but not in a friendly way. He didn't speak for a long moment, just continued to stare at Domingo.

"You been across the wood stealin' eggs again?"

Domingo stared wide-eyed, not responding at first. He spoke a little English, enough anyway to understand the gist of the question.

"Answer him, dickhead," Gil said, shoving him in the back.

Domingo swallowed and gave a single quick acknowledging nod.

"I thought I told you not to go back over there." Marty's eyes were cold and hard above the thin line of his mouth.

"*Mi esposa-*" he began, but Marty cut him off.

"Don't give me any more crap about your wife and what she needs. The whole woods between here and there is suddenly crawling with Mounties and dogs. What'd you do? Can't just be a wetback stealin' eggs."

Domingo felt his cheeks flame with anger, but when he spoke his voice was soft and controlled. "There was a man," Domingo said in halting English. "He saw me. I hit him."

"You hit him," Marty cocked his head to one side, his voice very matter of fact. Then he slowly leaned forward and propped an elbow on each knee, the doobie smoldering in his stained fingers between them. "Did you kill him?"

"I dunno. I run."

"Straight back here, no doubt."

Domingo held his boss's gaze but shifted his weight from one foot to the other and back. "I walk long time."

"But you came back here." Marty pointed to the floor. "Here."

"*Sì*," he answered quietly.

"You disobeyed my direct order. And your boneheaded carelessness has endangered our business." Marty stared at him and let the tense silence hang in the room, heavy as the cloying smoke, until Domingo finally dropped his gaze to the floor. Then Marty went on, "Gilly, round up Dak and the rest of the crew and have 'em bust camp. Load up everything that's already cut and baled and dried and get it the hell out of Montgomery County tonight. I don't want to lose any of this harvest. Stuff's got a kick like nothin' I've ever seen. Even before we lace it. Don't leave anything behind, not even trash, nothing. Take it all over to the barn in Mena for now." He took a long drag on the joint, its tip glowing bright red orange. He held it in, then waved the hand holding it dismissively at Domingo. "And get him out of my sight."

"OK, boss," Gil said and coughed into his hand. "What you want me to do with him?"

Marty narrowed his eyes and kept his voice similarly low. "Whatever you need to do, bud. Just clean this up."

***

On Friday afternoon, Maggie stood in the clinic breakroom waiting none too patiently as the espresso machine slowly chugged out her double shot. *A watched Nespresso never shoots.* That was the nonsensical first thought that flitted through her mind. *Probably ought to clean this thing* was the second, not nonsensical and clearly necessary one. She made a mental note to order some of the cleaner solution packs online.

It had been a ponderously slow afternoon owing to several cancellations that had left a large open block on the schedule after lunch. She'd occupied it catching up on her medical reading and earning a few credit hours of CME by completing the quizzes at the end of the journal articles. And solving the *NY Times* crossword. When she'd finished the puzzle, it was mercifully almost time for the last scheduled patient of the day, and she'd come in here to make herself a quick coffee. Or that was the plan, but it was taking its sweet time. The machine finally spewed out the stream of coffee, and double Americano in hand, she headed back to her office.

"Doc," Therma Faye's voice called from the front office where she was filling her downtime knitting. Donna was filling hers absorbed in scrolling through the social media feed on her phone, as usual, and the two of them jointly by catching each other up on all the latest in celebrity news and town gossip. "Any update on Mr. P?"

Everybody was naturally upset about what had happened to Papa; he was a beloved fixture in the town, but the gossip mainly centered on who could have done it and the fact that whoever it was that had cracked his head open was still out there loose. She backtracked with her coffee to join them.

"Well," Maggie said, drawing up a chair, "he's doing OK. Recovering anyway."

"Thank the good Lord for that." Therma Faye kissed the knuckle of her index finger and pointed it to the sky then looked in horror at her handiwork. "Aw shoot! I dropped a stitch back here." She peered at the rows, unraveled some stitches, and shook her head, muttering in disgust.

"They transferred him this morning to a rehab setting for about a week or so," Maggie continued. "He's got a little weakness in his right leg and hand, so they want to keep him there for physical and occupational therapy."

"See, Tee," Donna gave her aunt a smug smile, "that's what I mean about you can't believe half of what you hear. I heard down at Molly's it was his left side of his head that got whacked. And it's his right!"

"No, it wasn't. It was the left," Therma Faye assured her. "The left controls the right and right controls left. Isn't that right, Doc?" Her needles were *click clacking* rhythmically again.

"It is for the body. The left hemisphere of the brain controls the left side of the face, but the right side of the body. And *vice versa*." She took a long sip of her coffee and enjoyed both the rich aroma and the pleasant warming sensation it left all the way down. "His injury was to the left side of his head, but thankfully his speech center, which is on that side, wasn't damaged. He's doing very well considering, and I suspect he'll be back to his old self before we know it."

"Ben told me they had a lead," Donna said, looking up briefly from her focus on the screen of her phone. "He couldn't say what, though."

"Well, I hope it turns up something solid," Therma Faye added. "Folks are jittery. I mean first there's Ruth's murder—now granted that happened a couple of years ago, but still we only just found it out. And you and Rosie and Waylon almost getting killed by that... that," she shook her head, apparently unable to come up with a fittingly damning pejorative. "And now folks are getting clonked on the head doin' nothing more than gathering in the eggs! Criminently! What next?"

"Don't ask," Donna interjected, looking up from her phone and pinning Therma Faye with a wide-eyed stare. "Mama says that just brings more bad luck."

"Unwilling to argue with that logic," Maggie said, getting up to head back to her office. But just then the front door burst open, ushering in a blast of cold air and the imposing silhouette of the town's mayor, Coot Raines, who sneezed loudly into a white handkerchief and then blew his nose with an impressive honk. His diminutive wife, Billie, completely obscured at first behind his bulk, stepped around him and closed the door, then gently took his elbow, and guided him into the waiting room. He shuffled into the room in slippers, the loose legs of his flannel pajamas incongruous below his tailored navy dress coat and scarf. A shock of his unnaturally dark brown hair hung in damp, limp strands over his clammy forehead instead of being swept back in its characteristic highly-styled coif, and his rosy nose stood out in vibrant contrast to the sweaty pallor of his face.

"Mr. Mayor," Therma Faye exclaimed laying aside her knitting and getting up from her chair. She opened the waiting room door, "You don't look so good. Donna, pull up the mayor's chart. C'mon Billie, bring him this way."

Maggie took the iPad from Therma Faye as she came out of the exam room. "His temp's 103, Doc. Pulse and respirations fast. Pressure's OK. Says his throat's sore, and he aches all over like he's been beat."

Maggie entered the room to find Billie Raines hovering nervously beside her clearly miserable husband, rubbing his broad back, a worried look on her face. She nodded to Maggie and moved to sit in the side chair out of the way as Maggie approached him. "Mr. Mayor, what's going on? Tell me when it first started? And how?"

"Yesterday evenin'," he answered hoarsely. "I was drivin' back from a meetin' over at Mt. Ida, just sittin' in my car at a red light." He covered his face again with the kerchief, sneezed, and was immediately seized by a fit of coughing. "Sorry 'bout that," he said when he was finally able to continue. "I was just sittin' there, and out of the blue my back started to ache. All across it. Like I'd been used as a tackling dummy at a Hog's practice." She'd been an Arkansas resident for less than half a year, but that was plenty long enough to know he was referring to the beloved college football team in Fayetteville, where he'd been a legendary offensive lineman. And at his size, likely never a tackling dummy. *At least his sense of humor is still intact,* she thought. He sneezed again into the handkerchief and blew his red nose. "By the time I got home I couldn't hardly get out of the car and into the house. Billie put me straight to bed. Felt my head and said I had a fever. I coulda told her that," he chuckled weakly. "Gave me a dose of something for it, Tylenol I guess, wasn't it hon?"

"It was," Billie nodded. "Two extra-strength."

"And made me a hot toddy."

"OK," Maggie said, pulling her stethoscope from her pocket and settling it into her ears. "Let's see what's going on."

Maggie listened to his lungs and was mildly concerned, but only that, to hear a few scattered wheezes and rales, the whistling and crackling sounds that suggested constricted airways and fluid in the air sacs, though nothing localized into one spot. Her face betrayed nothing of even the mild concern she felt. Heartrate was fast but sounded normal otherwise. The mayor's throat, she noted, was red and inflamed. Ears clear. The lymph nodes in his neck were a bit swollen and tender. Nothing remarkable on her exam of his abdomen. Her mind sifted through the likely diagnoses: *Flu? Strep? Pneumonia?*

She opened the exam room door and walked into the hall, pulling it closed behind her. "Tee?"

"Yes'm?" Therma Faye called out from the lab.

"Can you please get rapid strep and flu tests on Mr. Raines? And a white count."

Maggie's first impression, now her worry, was borne out when the rapid test came back positive for Type A influenza. She hoped a case this early in the flu season didn't presage a bad year in the making—like the one four years ago. She'd been a senior med student then at Columbia in Manhattan and on the front line dealing with the non-stop stream of flu patients that filled the clinics and the wards and the morgue that year.

The mayor's white blood cell count was low, common in viral illnesses like the flu, but at least his strep test was negative. There was still the possibility of pneumonia, which wasn't uncommon in patients with the flu when their immune system was already struggling to fight off the virus and failed to mount an effective assault against some bacterial opportunist. And no easy quick test to determine it.

She'd written him a prescription for an antiviral for the flu and weighed the need to cover him with a 5-day pack of antibiotic to give him protection against the most common bacterial culprits causing secondary pneumonias. She decided to wait and see a few days on that. And last she'd recommended something over the counter to help thin the mucus in his airways and quiet his cough, though she suspected he'd default to the hot toddy remedy, and she couldn't really argue with that. Lemon juice provided some vitamin C and was not a bad mucus thinner itself. The honey and hot water soothed the raw throat, and the honey itself was a pretty good antibacterial agent. And alcohol, whisky in this case, is an excellent cough suppressant that for her money made a toddy much more pleasant to take than standard cough medicine.

Then she'd sent him home in Billie's care with instructions to give him plenty of fluids and rest, and if the fever got too high and he was uncomfortable, some more Tylenol or ibuprofen. Because flu is spread mainly by droplet transmission, she reinforced the importance of frequent handwashing, told her to make liberal use of disinfectant spray in the air and on surfaces, and to isolate the mayor as much as possible from others in the household. One of them should sleep in a guest room, if possible, or on a couch. And she asked her to chart his temperature every few hours – with a thermometer, please, not a hand—and let her know if it spiked higher than it had been or persisted longer than 48 hours or if he got worse. She added an electronic reminder to the chart for Therma Faye to call and check on them on Monday. Although Billie had told her she'd taken the annual flu shot, it didn't offer one-hundred-percent protection, and Maggie still worried she might come down with it, too. And a lot of others, unless they were lucky.

By the time she'd finished with the mayor, her last scheduled patient was ready for her. It was just an insurance physical, and she thanked the powers that be that it wasn't anything complicated. She was beat. Sitting bored, she'd learned long ago, is almost more exhausting than being busy. She was ready to put paid to today.

Maggie had just slipped off her labcoat and was debating whether it ought to go into the laundry, deciding in light of the mayor's flu that it did, when the intercom buzzed and Donna's voice said, "Dr. Mac, JD's holding on line one."

She tossed the labcoat into the hamper in the corner, flopped down in her chair, and grabbed up the receiver. "Hey, there! I was just thinking about you."

"Oh, I like hearing that," he said, and she could almost hear the smile in his voice. "Are you finished there?"

"I am, thanks be to all that's holy."

"Mmm. Bad day then?"

"No, not really. Just a lot of unremitting boredom." Her stomach growled loudly. "And I'm starving."

"So I hear," his soft, sexy chuckle was like a refreshing balm to her spirit. "I happen to have a cure for both your boredom and your hunger, I think."

"I'm in. Whatcha got in mind?"

"We-e-ll," he stretched the word out and launched into his pitch, "tonight's the peak of the Geminids meteor shower, and miracle of miracles, the skies are going to be perfect. So, I thought we might take a picnic supper and a bottle of wine out to a good vantage point and watch the show."

"That sounds lovely. Let me call Miz Hendri and beg off dinner."

"I'm standing in the kitchen with her right now, so you're set on that end." Miz Hendri loved JD, and Maggie knew she'd agree to any plan that paired the two of them up. "Come on home, put on something comfortable and warm, and we'll go."

"But I promised Papa I'd be there with her every night," Maggie teased.

"Yeah, I recall. Got that covered, too. Velma and Benji are coming over to have dinner with her, and Velma's going to stay the night."

JD had taken down the ragtop of his old Jeepster for optimal viewing, but without either roof or actual windows to protect them, the sharp crosswind made Maggie's eyes water and burned her cheeks and nose as they drove through the empty darkness of the countryside. He seemed impervious to the elements, but Maggie felt the cold even bundled in multiple layers, woolen socks, fleece-lined boots, her puffy jacket, and warm gloves. And a stocking cap pulled low to cover her ears. Despite all that, she was still grateful for the heat of the dash and floor vents that she trapped under an old Hudson Bay Point blanket he'd thrown over her legs. She'd secured it behind her shoulders and draped it across to the dashboard pinning that end with her feet. It made a pretty cozy cocoon. They bounced along, ultimately going off road, through a shallow stream, and across a wide expanse of rolling pasture toward the top of a hill on the far back corner of JD's property, a point where, he'd told her on the way, his land met Waylon's.

The moon had set early, and away from the lights of town the inky skies were awash in a nebula of blue-white stars, like brilliant gems strewn thickly across the impenetrable darkness by the hands of the gods. They chugged at last up the steep slope to the dome of a high hill and came into a broad clearing protected on all sides by woods, where they stopped. It was silent here but for the whistling of the wind, and the clearing offered an unobstructed view of the vast universe that spread above them like a gigantic IMAX screen. JD pressed himself up by his hands, hopped both feet onto his seat and, in one fluid motion, levered himself between the seatbacks and into the rear of the Jeepster. He'd already removed the back seats to make a roomy platform behind them and in a trice had unrolled and spread out a pair of self-inflating camping pads onto it. Then he unzipped two thick, down sleeping bags and zipped them to each other again to make a cozy double-wide sack that he laid out on the pads.

"Join me?" He kneeled and held out his hand to help her climb from the front seat to the Jeep bed.

"You look like you've done this before," she smiled taking his hand and stepping over the console, dragging her warmed blanket along with her.

"I have." He smiled and placed a courtly kiss on her knuckles. "But usually alone. On a river somewhere. Gotta admit, tonight I prefer having company to being on my own. Your company anyway." He glanced up, scanning her face.

His eyes mesmerized her, as they'd done the first day she'd met him on the road into Caddo Bend. Their soft gray seemed more luminous in the starlight, as always full of intelligence and laughter and, right now, more than a little desire. The look was so penetrating, in fact, that she felt her knees wobble a little as she sat down cross-legged beside him on the pallet.

From a large backpack he first produced the infrastructure of their feast: bamboo plates and cutlery, thick ceramic mugs, wine glasses, napkins. Then a large thermos that he set aside. And a bottle of wine, a white burgundy; he opened it and held up the cork, rolling it between thumb and fingers, then gave it a sniff, smiled, and nodded. Taking that gesture as his approval of the evening's wine selection, she held out their two glasses for him to pour.

He replaced the cork in the wine bottle and tucked it into a safe corner of the Jeep's bed, where it would stay nicely cool in the chilly air, then took his glass and raised it to her. "I will love the light for it shows me the way; yet I will love the darkness for it shows me the stars." They touched glasses, and each took a deep sip.

"Mmm," Maggie nodded appreciatively and took a second sip.

"That's not me, by the way, that quote; it's Og Mandino."

"Well, whoever said it, it's beautiful." She lifted her glass and gave the wine a swirl. "And this is remarkable."

They sipped their wine in silence, staring at the starry night, JD pointing out the winter constellations to her: Orion the Hunter, Canis Major, Taurus, and of course Gemini, the namesake origin of the December meteor shower they'd come to witness.

"There!" Maggie cried out in delight, pointing to the heavens as the flash streaked in a fiery arc across the sky. "Do you suppose there's a pot of gold at the end of that arc? Like a rainbow?"

JD shrugged and raised his brows. "Who knows? Nice to think so."

"It's incredible!" Her eyes shone with childlike joy.

"Wait until it peaks later tonight. There will be a hundred or more an hour. Better than fireworks on the Fourth of July." Her stomach rumbled loudly. "But I hear you're starving," he said with an amused soft snort and set his wineglass into a cup holder.

From an insulated hamper he lifted out and unwrapped a stunning charcuterie board of Parma ham, several types of salami and various cheeses, olives, pickled vegetables, dried cherries, and nuts and laid it between them on the pallet along with a foil-wrapped and still-warm half-baguette. He spooned out a big dollop of grainy mustard and another of quince paste onto the board, capped the jars, and put them back into the hamper. Then he poured steaming chowder from the Thermos into their mugs.

Maggie took her mug, grateful for the warmth of it on her hands, and brought it to her nose. It smelled of black pepper and the sea. And its rich and savory creaminess warmed her from the first mouthful. Which was followed in short order by more mouthfuls until the mug was empty. She sat the mug aside and rolled a thin slice of salami, dipped it into the mustard, and held it out for JD. He leaned over and teased it with his lips, straight from her hand into his mouth. *How does he make something so simple and ordinary seem so sexy*, she wondered? Then, he reciprocated, feeding her a paper-thin slice of Parma ham rolled around a small Cornichon. The contrast of the salty ham and the piquant dill of the pickle was heavenly. And so it went, the two of them chatting, laughing, eating, drinking, and marveling at the occasional spectacle of a shooting star.

When they'd finished and gathered up the remains of their feast and stowed it and the now-empty wine bottle in the hamper, JD produced two more mugs and another Thermos from the backpack and poured.

"Kahlua and hot cocoa," he said. "Dessert and after-dinner drink rolled into one."

It was late, and the night had grown quite cold, but the thick, liqueur-laced cocoa warmed her to her marrow. Mugs in hand, they pulled back the top layer of the double sleeping bag and settled themselves side-by-side against the backs of the front seats, stretching their legs out beneath the thick down of the top bag and the heavy woolen blanket and sipping their dessert.

"You have a cocoa mustache," he said, slowly leaning in close to examine it and letting his lips hover just over hers. Then he kissed her, sucking lightly at her upper lip and letting his tongue tease the opening of her mouth. "Mmm. Delicious. And I don't mean the cocoa." He took her mug and set it and his own aside, then took her in his arms and kissed her fully and deeply.

"The Geminids?" she murmured against his lips.

"Won't peak for another couple of hours," he said kissing her again. "In the meantime, I was thinking we might set off some fireworks of our own."

They awoke some few hours later, naked under the down, Maggie wrapped in the curve of JD's muscular body in a cozy cocoon of warmth that contrasted sharply with the frigid night air. Their discarded clothing lay crumpled at the foot of the sleeping bag. JD kissed first her bare shoulder, then her temple, then her cheek. "Look up," he whispered, his breath tickling her ear.

Maggie turned her head to gaze skyward. Almost every minute a meteor or two streaked overhead, some just quick flashes, others burning long, brilliant arcs across the heavens before disappearing. She turned to lay on her back, and JD followed suit, burrowing his arm beneath her shoulders to draw her close to him, snuggling together under the warm down, as they watched the celestial light show unfold.

"I've never seen anything so glorious," she said softly.

He turned toward her and propped himself on one elbow half-covering her lithe body with the solidness of his own and looked tenderly into her eyes. Then, tracing the line of her cheek and jaw with his fingertip, he whispered, "I have."

Her breath caught in her throat, and she felt almost dizzy. He gently parted her legs with his knee, never taking his eyes from hers. They came together slowly, sensually, taking their time, their breaths and their bodies moving in unison, savoring each second of pleasure, riding the building wave to its shuddering completion as the stars streaked overhead.

JD rolled away, and they lay together, spent and sated, their slowing deep breaths the only sound. "As I said," JD whispered when he could finally speak, "glorious."

The quiet intimacy was shattered by a piercing scream from below them. "That's human," Maggie bolted upright. "A woman."

"Yeah," JD was already kicking out of the sleeping bag and pulling on his chilly jeans.

CHAPTER 14
Circle of Life

JD and Maggie hurriedly dressed and were soon bouncing down the hillside in the Jeepster in the direction of the screams, which intermittently continued to pierce the night air. They saw a light down below them beside the meandering stream, and when they got closer, they could see it was a campfire, and beside it a tent. Another agonized scream rent the air.

They pulled up beside the campsite, and Maggie was out before the Jeep stopped moving. She had forgotten to bring her medical bag with her tonight and cursed herself for it now. The tent flap was zipped shut, and she fumbled in the dark to raise the zipper, calling out a loud 'hello' as she did.

Inside, on a crude pallet, lay a young, pregnant woman, her dark hair plastered in long, sweaty strands to a pretty, brown face. Bloody fluid soaked the blanket beneath her. She was alone and clearly in labor. And something bad was going on.

"It's OK. I'm a doctor," Maggie reassured the woman. The uncomprehending expression in the frightened dark eyes told Maggie English wasn't going to cut it. She'd spent her residency handling emergencies in a multi-cultural neighborhood in uptown Manhattan and knew enough basic medical words in Spanish and a few other languages to at least get an idea of what was going on. She started with Spanish. "*Habla Español?*'

The woman grimaced and another guttural scream filled the tent. "*Sí,*" she hissed out, nodding. She drew her knees up toward her belly and groaned in pain, bunching up the blanket in her fists.

"*Yo soy…*" Maggie went blank for a moment on the Spanish word for doctor. All that would come to mind were the words from the familiar song, "*Yo no soy marinaro. Soy capitán.*" She shook her head to clear the earworm and finally dredged up the word: *médica*. "*Yo soy la médica.*" She knelt beside the woman to feel her round abdomen, assessing the baby's position, then positioned herself at the woman's feet. "*¿Su nombre?*" Maggie asked her name.

"Yesenia," the woman hissed between clenched teeth.

"*¿El dolor cuanto tiempo?*" Hoping she'd said something that approximated how long has the pain been going on?

The woman answered, "*Una hora,*" then grimaced and panted. "*Muy... mal dolor...diez minutos.*"

"*El...* Oh hell's bells, what's the word for bleeding?" she muttered aloud in English. Then it came to her. "*Sangrado. ¿Cuanto tiempo el sangrado?*" The bleeding, Maggie hoped she'd asked, how long on that?

"*El mismo,*" Yesenia replied between short pants, then her face contorted again in agony and another scream tore from her lips.

"El mismo?" Maggie asked aloud. *How long is that?* She didn't understand. Her Spanish didn't extend far past common medical terms.

JD, outside the tent, heard her and responded, "The same. *El mismo.* Bleeding's been going on ten minutes I guess is what she means. Or maybe she means an hour." He'd stuck his head in earlier, but Maggie had waved him away. She didn't think the poor woman would much like having two strangers in this confined space considering what was going on. *Thank God he's here now,* she thought.

Bright red blood continued to seep from between Yesenia's legs, and Maggie raised the shift over her knees to get a better look, but the woman clamped her knees together.

"JD," she called over her shoulder, "can you tell her I need to examine her?"

"*Yesenia, la médica necesita examinarte,*" came his soft, deep voice from outside the tent. Some of the woman's tension seemed to dissipate.

"Tell her I need to look and to feel her baby's position."

JD translated quickly from the opening of the tent, and the woman let her knees fall apart again and relaxed some. They continued this way with JD translating Maggie's instructions or questions and Yesenia's responses.

Maggie took her cell phone from her pocket, shined the flashlight between the woman's thighs, and bent to gently spread the lips of her vulva apart. At least the baby wasn't crowning. Her mind raced. *Likeliest cause of the bleeding's a placental abnormality at this stage. Placental abruption? Placenta previa?* The distinction was vital, because in previa, even inserting fingers to examine her could cause fatal hemorrhage.

"What's it look like?" JD spoke in a low voice.

"Can't be sure," Maggie said calmly in a light, even voice, keeping every scintilla of concern out of it so as not to alarm the woman. "Could be one of two problems with the placenta. And neither of them good. In one, the placenta is separating early from the wall of the womb. In the other, the placenta has implanted over the outlet of the womb blocking or partially blocking it. If the baby tries to come through, or my hands probe the opening, major hemorrhage could occur. Either one is potentially fatal even if we were in the hospital when it happened. Out here, with nothing to work with and labor beginning … JD, she could easily bleed to death. And the baby could die. We've got to try to get her to the hospital."

"As we recently found out, that's a good 40 minutes away. More if we wait for an ambulance to get here. Do you have that much time?"

Maggie shook her head. "No. I don't think so. The clinic then."

"Yeah. OK. I'll get her into the back of the Jeep."

Maggie backed out of the tent and let JD inside. He spoke rapidly to the woman in Spanish, telling her who he was, what they were going to do, asking was she alone, was there anyone they could contact? As he gathered her up and carried her out, she told him in rushed, anxious bursts of speech that her husband had left with his co-worker two days before and not come back. His name was Domingo Sanchez. They were from Mexico. They had no family here, but there was a cousin in Colorado, Guadalupe Morales. They'd been planning to go there.

JD gently laid Yesenia onto the soft down pallet in the bed of the Jeep and covered her with the Hudson Bay blanket. Maggie crawled in beside her and held onto the roll bar with one hand and Yesenia with the other as JD backed out, spun around, and barreled across the stream and pastures headed for the main road. The contractions seemed to have slowed, at least temporarily, and for that Maggie gave silent thanks for one small mercy.

In fifteen minutes the Jeepster skidded into the back lot of the clinic. On the way, Maggie had called 9-1-1 for an ambulance to meet them at the clinic and had waked Therma Faye and asked her to come in *stat* to help. Tee stood now at the open back door waiting for them, hair still in curlers, ample body wrapped in a pink terry cloth robe, the legs of her flowered flannel pajamas stuffed into a pair of Wellies. Maggie had said 'come now' and she had.

"I got the IV set up with Ringer's in the treatment room, Doc," Therma Faye said. Maggie nodded as they rushed past her. Yesenia in JD's arms was moaning and muttering unintelligible words, but there was no need to speak the language to understand the anguish and fear in them.

"Tee get her pressure. JD, tell her we need to start an IV," Maggie said, wrapping a latex tourniquet around the woman's arm and swabbing the skin quickly with an alcohol wipe. She slipped a 14-guage IV catheter into a vein, hooked up the tubing from the bag of fluid, and opened the line. "And get her on the cardiac monitor and some O2 going."

"Pressure's 100/75. Heartrate 100," Therma Faye said, applying sticky cardiac lead pads to the woman's chest. The trace soon appeared, sharp green spikes moving quickly across the display. Tee hooked tubing to the oxygen cylinder beside the cart and placed the mask over Yesenia's face, but she wrenched her head away, eyes wild, mumbling anxiously until JD spoke to her.

Maggie listened to Yesenia's abdomen with her stethoscope, relieved beyond measure to still hear a fetal heartbeat.

"JD, tell her the baby is OK. Tell her that we're going to examine her now, and we'll need to move her down to the end of the table." JD, standing at Yesenia's head, leaned close to her and translated the message in a calm, low voice. Maggie pulled the litho stirrups out from the end of the exam table and then pulled Yesenia into position at the foot of it, bending her knees and putting her feet into the stirrups. Seated now on an exam stool, Maggie could see they were in deep trouble. The bleeding was getting worse.

Yesenia grabbed the sides of the table and let out a low groan that crescendoed into a howl of piercing volume even muffled by the oxygen mask. JD leaned close again and whispered comforting Spanish words in her ear. A strong contraction gripped her again, and along with it came another scream and another torrent of bright red blood.

"Pressure's falling. Now 90/70." Therma Faye's worried expression matched Maggie's. "What the hell's goin' on?" she said, and her eyes sought Maggie's.

"Not sure if it's placenta previa or an abruption. Or possibly something else," Maggie said rapidly and quietly. "Can't tell without an ultrasound. Too dangerous to do a digital exam. Not good either way. Where is that damned ambulance?" Maggie grabbed a handful of towels and stuffed a few under Yesenia's hips, dropping the remainder to the floor to absorb the bloody fluid that had already accumulated there. "Give her 6 milligrams dexamethasone IV push and make sure that line is fully open. Do we have any terbutaline in the crash cart?"

Therma Faye drew up the steroid dose and pushed it into the IV port, then flushed the line with saline. She peered into the top drawer of the crash cart, found the vial of terbutaline, and held it up. "Yep. How much?"

"Give her 0.25 milligrams. We've got to stop these contractions if we can. At least give them a chance to make it to the hospital." *And maybe at least one of them a chance to survive.* She immediately pushed that thought away.

The distant wail of the siren was so faint at first Maggie thought she was imagining it, drowned as it was by Yesenia's throaty groans and pitiful wails. But it grew insistently louder.

"Shhhh," JD gently stroked Yesenia's hair. "*Necessita respirar, pequeña. Respire.*" She settled down, breathing as he'd asked, and, as the contraction abated, she loosened her white-knuckled grip on the table long enough to reach up and grab hold of JD's hand instead, gripping it as if it were a floatation device and she in danger of going down for the third time.

The loud wailing of the siren and throaty rumble of the ambulance's engine accompanied flashes of red light now visible outside the windows, and Maggie felt the first hint of relief and hope.

"JD, would you go out to meet the ambulance?" She glanced up at him, and though her voice was calm, the worry was obvious in her eyes.

JD nodded and grabbed Therma Faye's hand, gently transferring Yesenia's grip to it, murmuring reassurances in Spanish that he would be right back, that he wasn't going far away.

Momentarily he and the paramedics—a tall, wiry young man and a spiky-haired, 30-something woman with sleeve tattoos on both forearms—hustled through the back hallway and into the room. Maggie briefed them on the situation and what she'd done, the medications she'd given, her suspected diagnoses, and the need for getting her to Mercy General with all speed.

"She speaks little to no English," Maggie told the emergency team. "She's about 35 weeks pregnant, the best we can calculate, first child, and I suspect she's had no prenatal care."

"Family?" Spiky Hair asked as she and her partner lifted Yesenia onto their stretcher and transferred her oxygen, IV fluids, and cardiac leads to their equipment.

"A husband. And apparently he's missing."

Yesenia was rhythmically mumbling something in Spanish that Maggie couldn't at first identify, muffled as it was behind the mask. Then she recognized the words *Santa María, Madre de Dios* and knew she must be somewhere into the ten Hail Marys of the rosary. Raised Catholic, Maggie knew well what came next: pray for us sinners, now and at the hour of our death. She sent up her own prayer to the Virgin that this would not be that hour.

The paramedics covered the woman with a thermal blanket and strapped her securely onto the stretcher. JD laid his hand on her shoulder and spoke softly again to her in Spanish. She nodded and grasped his hand, bringing it to her damp cheek and muttering her thanks; her eyes above the oxygen mask were filled with fear and glistened with tears. He walked beside the stretcher, letting Yesenia cling to his hand until they loaded her into the back of the wagon. Maggie came to stand beside him as the team closed the doors and wheeled away. They watched in silence until the flashing red lights disappeared down the road, then he pulled her to him, wrapping both his arms around her slim torso; she relaxed into their strong circle, cheek against his chest, listening to the steady, reassuring thumping of his heart. He rested his own cheek on the crown of her head.

"Thank you," she said softly.

"For what?"

"For being there. For seeming to always know what to do. And doing it."

He gave a soft snort. "Does it seem like that?"

"It does," she said, tipping her head up to look into his eyes.

He placed a gentle, lingering kiss on her forehead, closed his eyes and inhaled deeply, then looked down again and held her gaze for a long moment. "Not always, but I'm glad you feel that way."

After another long moment she asked him, softly, "So how is it you're so utterly fluent in Spanish?"

He didn't answer immediately. Finally, he said, rather matter-of-factly, "Deployed to South America a few times when I was a Ranger. Columbia and Venezuela mostly. Special ops."

"And that was enough to become so fluent?"

"Mmm," he gave a dismissive laugh. "Languages have always come easy to me, I guess. Everywhere we deployed, seemed like I was the one tasked with learning the language and interacting with the locals."

"So, any others besides Japanese and Spanish?"

"A few." He kissed her forehead again, more playfully this time, and adroitly changed the subject. "Let's go finish up inside."

Therma Faye had already gathered the sharps and bundled the soiled disposables—towels, table paper, and assorted other bloody trash—and stuffed them into the bio-waste containers. Now she was moping the tile floor with disinfectant.

"Tee, that can wait 'til later," Maggie said. "Go on home and get some sleep."

"Aw hell no," Therma Faye continued to swab with the mop in vigorous strokes. "Jimmy and I have plans to go this afternoon to get our tree; promised the kids we could decorate it tomorrow after church. And remember J&J's not coming to clean 'til Monday night; Joy sprained her ankle, and Jolene's gone over to Mena; their mama's sick or something." A reference to the Culligan twins whose local cleaning business kept the clinic ship shape. Tee jostled the mop head up and down in the bucket of disinfectant and passed it through the roller wringer. "And I, for one, don't have any intention of leavin' this mess 'til Monday morning. Or comin' in early either. Y'all go on; I'm almost done."

"I'd just as soon not leave you here alone in the middle of the night," JD said. "We'll just hang if that's all right. Anybody want a tea? I could use something."

"Sure," Maggie said and headed down the hall toward the break room, but instead went to the supply closet and pulled two heavy duty trash bags and a couple of biohazard bags from a box and then went out the back door. She was still vibrating with the undissipated energy of the recent emergency and wasn't sure sitting down for a cup of tea was in the cards for her just yet. Outside, the eastern sky had gone from inky black to dark pewter, and the silhouettes of bare trees were becoming visible, though the sun still hadn't shown its face.

"Where're you going?" JD asked.

"To get the sleeping bags and that blanket from the back of the Jeep; they're soaked with blood. We can take them over to the Wash-O-Mat in Glenwood and use their big commercial machine."

"Like you told Tee," JD said taking the bags from her hand and surprising her by scooping her into his arms, "that can wait 'til later. And I'll deal with it then." She started to protest, and as his hands were full, he used a long kiss to silence her in mid-word as he carried her down the hall. In the breakroom he set her down gently in front of him. "And as soon as we're finished here," he went on rubbing her back gently with both his hands, "I'm taking you to Miz Hendri's and putting you to bed."

Maggie stood on tiptoe and weaved her arms around his neck, kissing him teasingly. "And joining me there?"

"Mmm. We'll see." He unwound her arms, kissed the back of first one hand and then the other, and went to fill the kettle.

Therma Faye appeared shortly in the breakroom door, purse over her arm. "OK, y'all, I'm done. And outta here unless there's anything else you need."

"Not a thing I can think of," Maggie replied. "Get some rest and have fun picking out your tree. I'll see you Monday."

The bright mid-morning sun streamed in through the mullioned windows of Maggie's bedroom; she opened her eyes a crack and promptly

closed them again. It had been nearly dawn, when she and JD had finally crawled under the duvet and gone to bed, which is to say to sleep as
they were exhausted as much from the late night's enjoyable activities as its
traumatic ending. *Thank God it's a Saturday with no scheduled patients*, she
thought. She could just lie here a while longer next to him, their bodies
nested together like spoons in a drawer, his muscular arm heavy in sleep
on her waist, his warm breath ruffling the fine hairs at her hairline, tickling
her neck.

A part of her wanted to call to check on Yesenia, and another part
feared making the call. She reassured herself she'd done what she could
to save mother and child, to forestall labor, and to help mature the baby's
lungs for what was sure to be an early delivery. At 35 weeks, he—or she—
was still more than a month from full term. She prayed that they'd made it
to Mercy in time. If not, she knew there was little hope for either of them.

She eased out of the warm circle of JD's arms, trying not to disturb
him, and took her phone into the bathroom to make the call to Mercy.

"This is Dr. McKinley." She spoke in hushed tones. "And I'm calling
to check on my patient, a young woman brought in last night by ambulance. In labor." She listened then added, "Yesenia Sanchez." And after a
pause, "Her birthdate? No, I don't have that." Then another pause. "Yes,
thank you. I'll wait." After an interminable interval of awful elevator music
on hold, a nurse on Labor and Delivery finally picked up.

Maggie identified herself and asked again about Yesenia, then listened for a moment. The tears welled in her eyes, and she put a hand over
her mouth to stifle the whimper that tried to escape, finally able to pull
her emotions together only enough to mutter, "Thank you. I understand.
Goodbye." Then she slumped to the floor against the clawfoot tub and
quietly wept.

There was a soft tap on the door, and when it eased open JD stood in
the doorway, looking down. He knelt beside her and took her into his arms.

"Shhhh," he murmured, gently stroking her hair. "Shhhh. It's OK."

She buried her face in his chest and, without further need to be quiet, let go a torrent of tears and gasping sobs. She was usually pretty stoic, not generally a weepy person, but twice in the same week she'd found herself sobbing in his arms. He held her close, rubbing her back, murmuring comforts, rocking her gently until she was calm again.

"What is it?" he said at last. She felt the rumble of his voice in his chest against her ear.

Maggie's throat was so tight she could barely make the words croak out. More difficult because she didn't want to say them out loud and make them real. She swallowed hard and whispered them. "She died on the table." And began to weep anew.

"And the baby?"

"A boy," she said, her voice tight. "He survived. By some miracle he survived." She reached for a tissue and blew her nose. "He's in the NICU."

"We need to try to find his father. It's hard for a child to never know its mother and grow up without a father as well."

Maggie glanced up at JD and saw the shadow of pain cloud his handsome features for a moment and knew his thoughts had turned to his own child, who'd lost her mother and whose father was thousands of miles away. She reached up and put her hand tenderly to his cheek. He put his hand over hers, pulling it away to place a kiss in her palm. Then held her hand to his chest.

"How's Akiko?" she asked softly.

"Reading my mind now, are you?" He gave her a sad half-smile and a bit of a shrug. "She's doing all right. I talked to her on FaceTime yesterday morning. Her bedtime in Japan. That's when we usually talk. She wanted me to read her the story of Momotora, the Peach Boy. So, I did. Again."

"Have you ever thought about bringing her here to be with you?"

"Sure," he kissed her palm again. "But for now, anyway, it would be too disruptive."

"For you or Akiko?" She asked quietly and almost instantly regretted her words.

He didn't answer her right away and seemed to be weighing the two somehow. "For her," he said finally, "but mainly for Namiko-san."

"Don't you miss her?"

"Of course. But she's better off there for the time being. With what's familiar."

They sat there on the bathroom floor for a long stretch, saying nothing, and not needing to say anything, Maggie's occasional sniff the only sound. She stirred finally within the comfortable circle of his arms.

"I could really use a coffee." She murmured the words without even looking up. "You?"

He stood and pulled her up beside him. She saw herself in the mirror, tear-stained cheeks, red-rimmed eyes. "Oh Lord, what a sight." She took another tissue and blew her nose again.

"Yeah, might want to splash a little cold water on your face and dry those pretty brown eyes. And maybe get dressed first, or Miz Hendri may kick you out for engaging in disreputable behavior above stairs."

CHAPTER 15
A Bittersweet Season

JD and Maggie walked into the big country kitchen to find Miz Hendri, Velma, and Ben already around the table drinking coffee. Maggie knew JD had arranged for Velma to stay over last night with Miz Hendri after their supper, and she supposed Ben had come back this morning to pick her up.

"Dub said they pulled him out just downstream of the high-water bridge," Ben was telling the women. He turned his head as they entered. "Hey, JD. Where'd you come from? I didn't see your car out front."

"No," JD said giving Maggie a conspiratorial glance. "I parked in back."

But for some odd reason didn't walk through the back door into the kitchen, Maggie thought and suppressed a smile when she saw Ben's expression that suggested he could add two and two.

"Some coffee?" Miz Hendri said, starting to get up.

Maggie put a staying hand on her shoulder. "Sit. I'll get it." She crossed to the cabinet, grabbed a couple of mugs, filled them, and handed one to JD.

"Somebody drown then?" JD asked and took a deep, long sip of his hot coffee.

"Yeah, maybe," Ben said. "Couple of kids canoein' upriver yesterday afternoon late found the body tangled in some brush in the shallows and called it in."

"Anybody local?"

"No. And no ID on him either. Don't know cause of death or much else yet."

"Will somebody tell me what the heck is going on around here?" Velma shot an accusing look at her son as if his position in local law enforcement somehow made him culpable for the recent spate of crime. "This used to be a quiet little corner of the world, and that suited me just fine. Then, in just this last two months we've had Ruth's body pulled out of the riverbank—God rest her soul—our town doctor and two other people almost killed by that murdering crazy person, Manny clubbed in a chicken house, and now a floater in the Caddo!"

"I know, Mama. And we're on it, I promise you. And speaking of..." He stood up and settled his uniform hat on his head, straightening it carefully. "I need to get over to Mt. Ida by ten a.m. for the post on that guy. Come on, Mama. Let's get you back to the house, so you can dress for the social."

Miz Hendri saw Velma and Ben out and returned to the kitchen. "JD," she said, "could I ask your help please with something?"

"Yes, ma'am. What can I do?"

"The men delivered our Christmas tree yesterday, and they set it up in the front parlor for me, which was very nice of them, but they put it the wrong side." JD appeared confused as to exactly what she meant. "With the *dürftig* ...uh, *ach!*" She searched for the English word, finally remembering, "the sparse side showing. Manny would always..." her voice drifted off, leaving the thought unfinished in a distracted way that was most unlike her, and Maggie hated to see it. Papa's injury had affected Miz Hendri deeply, that much was clear.

"You want me to turn it around for you?" he said, rising from the table.

"Exactly." They walked into the front parlor where the tall Fraser fir filled a corner between the fireplace and the front window. It nearly scraped the ceiling, with just enough space left for a topper. And a full, fluffy specimen it was, except for a scraggly gap created by a couple of misshapen branches on the side the deliverymen had bizarrely left facing out.

The air in the room was heavy with fir scent, and Maggie breathed in deeply and smiled. "Ahhh, Christmas by the lungful," she said. "Is there a better smell? But I gotta wonder, unless there's a worse bare spot on the back side, what were they thinking?"

"Ya," Miz Hendri gestured at the gap and nodded in agreement. "You see?"

JD reached in between branches to grab the trunk and eased the tree around on its axis until the bare area disappeared.

"Little bit more," Miz Hendri said. JD complied, and she eyed the result. "There. That is perfect. *Danke schöen.*"

Maggie eyed the stack of plastic storage containers that she assumed were filled with decorations. "Do you want some help decorating the tree?"

"That would be lovely," Miz Hendri clapped her hands together, clearly pleased with the notion, then glanced at her watch. "We have a little time yet before I must leave for the Christmas brunch at the church."

"We can get started, if you'd like," Maggie offered.

"Something to drink, then? We cannot decorate properly *die Tanne* without something festive to drink. I have not made eggnog yet, and there is not time for it, but I can make some cocoa. Or would you like wassail?" She was already headed for the kitchen.

"Cocoa for me," Maggie said. The idea of hot mulled wine this early in the day made her stomach heave. "I'll queue up my Christmas playlist to get us in the holiday spirit."

JD spread the boxes out in a single layer on the floor to better assess what was there, finding them separated sensibly into neatly packed tranches of the decorations that needed to go on first, such as toppers, garlands, and strands of lights, and the individual ornaments that would follow, with the fragile glass ones carefully wrapped in tissue and stowed in divided layers. The remaining boxes contained décor of other types—faux greenery, stockings, candles, figurines, ribbons, and bows—and in its own box, a carved wooden crèche.

"Want me to start with the star and the lights, Miz Hendri?" JD called out, unfolding the ladder that leaned against the fireplace and positioning it beside the tree. Receiving a go ahead shout from the kitchen, he climbed up and affixed a lighted Christmas Star to the tree's top, then began to unwind a strand of antique bubble lights.

"Ever seen these before? The real thing I mean," JD said, leaning over to show the strand to Maggie, who shook her head 'no'. "I remember Mama had a few of these old strands when I was little; they're so cool when they warm up. OK that's an oxymoron," he said with a chuckle. "The liquid inside the base bubbles up through this tube part when they heat up. I could watch 'em for hours when I was a kid."

"Do you still have them?" Maggie asked, propping her phone up on the mantle where they could better hear the music.

"Huh unh. They're long gone. Probably be a fire hazard anyway. Looks like Miz Hendri's had these re-wired."

"I'm not hearing the music very well," Maggie said. "I'll go get my speaker from upstairs."

She sprinted up the stairs, taking them two at a time, returning after a few minutes, speaker in hand, along with a tissue-wrapped parcel and a framed photo. She laid the parcel and photo down on the sofa and busied herself finding a suitable place to plug in the speaker. Soon she had Nat himself crooning about roasting chestnuts and tiny sleepless tots.

"Love the King Cole version of this," JD said looping the last of the strands of lights around the bottom and connecting the plugs. "What a voice."

"Yeah. My dad's favorite song of the season," she said, "but he was partial to Mel Torme; the Velvet Fog he said they called him." Suddenly, her eyes misted, and she turned away, hoping JD hadn't seen. Picking up the fire tool ostensibly to poke up the fire, she gave the logs a half-hearted push and sent a shower of sparks into the air. The last thing she wanted was to cast a pall on such a happy, festive moment; there'd been enough sadness already this morning, and she'd be damned if she'd succumb. But he must have seen because he came up behind her and gently put his arms around her waist.

"What's wrong?" His voice, a murmur beside her ear, was followed by a soft kiss to her temple.

She shook her head gently and stared into the fire. "It's nothing," she said. "Just always a bittersweet time of year for me." She reached over to pick up the photo from the couch and held it out to him.

JD took the frame from her and stared intently at the image of a family—mother, father, daughter—at Christmas, as evidenced by the tree, the stockings, and the detritus of present opening.

"You?" he said, tapping the child perched on her father's shoulders with his finger.

Maggie closed her eyes and nodded. "Mmm-hmm. I was three."

"And beautiful already. These are your folks then." A statement, not a question. He scanned the image a long time as if he were trying to memorize it. "Apple didn't far from that tree," he said, indicating her mother. She had the same coloring as Maggie, the flawless olive skin, the same dramatic dark brows and almost black eyes, the same slender, athletic body. The same smile that lit up her face and the room around her. "What was her name?"

"Liza," she said softly. "Well, Elizabeth, but Daddy called her Liza."

"And your father?" His eyes rested softly on her face, patient, waiting.

"Lach. Dr. Evan Lachlan McKinley. I always thought his full name sounded so distinguished." She smiled up at him, grateful again for his uncanny ability to soothe and calm her, to ground her emotions and, whatever the situation, to make her feel safe and loved.

"So, you're the second Dr. McKinley in the family?"

"Third. My parents were both PhDs. So was my mom's dad, but he wasn't a McKinley."

He stood the frame on the fireplace mantle and held out his hand to her.

"Well then, third Dr. McKinley. Let's get with it; this tree's not gonna decorate itself."

Maggie helped JD unfurl the multi-colored glass bead garlands next, and they wound them around the tree, then began to unwrap the delicate glass ornaments, hanging each one with care. There were many of them – old world Santas, sleighs, bells, balls and stars, gingerbread men, snowmen, rocking horses and wreaths. Each unique and all lovely.

Maggie opened a flat box filled with dozens of hand-crocheted lace snowflakes; their once-white cotton yarn gone ivory with age. Beautiful and homespun, they made a perfect counterpoint to the brightly colored blown-glass artistry. They'd almost placed them all when Miz Hendri returned.

"Here is the cocoa," Miz Hendri called out as she waddled in from the kitchen with a large tray. "*Ach*! So quick! And already so pretty!" She poured them each a cup, inserting a peppermint stick to stir and to flavor, and then disappeared down the hall.

Maggie took a sip of the cocoa, which was thick and rich with cream, the depth of bittersweet chocolate, and vanilla top notes. And it instantly transported her to Angelina's of Paris and the idyllic summer she'd spent in France eighteen or so years ago with her parents. The memories that surfaced were bittersweet, like the beverage, but this morning was about being with family of a new sort, and she found herself wanting to revel in the now, not the past.

Miz Hendri reappeared shortly with her handbag over her arm, hat on her head, a wrapped present in one hand, and a pair of white gloves in the other.

"This is sublime," Maggie said raising the mug of cocoa appreciatively. "Thank you. Are you not having some?"

"No, no. I'm off to the church. The Ladies' Auxilliary gathers every year for a Christmas brunch. We enjoy some food and caroling, and we each bring a small gift for one of the children on the Angel Tree. Miz Hendri's eyes fell on the tissue-wrapped parcel Maggie had left on the sofa, and she bent to look at it. "What is this? I don't recognize." She began to unwrap the tissue.

Maggie made a move to take it, but it was too late. The packet was opened. Inside was a needlepoint Christmas stocking. Actually, three of them stacked one atop the other. Emblazoned across the top one was the name MAGGIE in large block letters; under it there was another one for LIZA, and one for LACH.

Maggie reached over to collect them. "Christmas stockings. From my childhood. Mine and my mother's and father's as well. My mother made them for each of us for my first Christmas. Mama joked they decided to call me Maggie because she couldn't fit Mary Margaret on the stocking." She smiled sadly and clutched them to her chest. "I don't have much left of them." Then, as if she felt the need to explain, she added. "I just brought them down to show to JD; I'll take them back to my room."

"No. You will hang yours here on the fireplace," Miz Hendri said, pinning Maggie's tentative eyes with a brook-no-argument stare of her own. "All three, if you would like." She rose and went to one of the boxes, searching through its orderly contents. "Here." She handed Maggie three plain stocking hangers. "This evening I will set up the crèche on the mantle and arrange the garlands and candles. And then I will hang mine and Manny's stockings here beside your family's stockings. I have my Robert's stocking still. And Manny must have June's somewhere; I will ask him. We have not hung those since… well…not in a very long time. JD, do you have a stocking for Christmas?"

"I do, Miz Hendri, if I can find it in the things I have stored from Mama's house."

"Bring it over for Christmas Eve. And Kathleen's too, if you wish. We will put them all up together and remember the ones we love who are gone. They will all be with us again this year."

CHAPTER 16
Friends in Low Places

Ben Bradford winced at the shriek of the cranial saw as the patholo-gist, Dr. Bruce Glickman, bore down hard to open the dead man's skull. The sound made his teeth hurt. Ben closed his eyes and swayed slightly, then took in a deep inhale through his mouth and exhaled in an audible *whoosh*. He'd made it through the Y-incision and the removal and weighing of all the man's internal organs by counting the acoustic ceiling tiles back and forth and back again. There were 54 of them, if anyone cared to know. The tooth-shattering sound of the saw and the smell of saw-burned bone he couldn't escape.

The doctor glanced up. "You okay there, partner?"

"Yeah," Ben said, clearing his throat and straightening his shoulders. "I'm good. Just tired."

"I'm almost finished here, if you want to take a load off in the hall."

"OK. Maybe I'll do that."

Ben went into the hall, grabbed a drink from the vending machine, and found a seat on one of the metal folding chairs lined up against one wall, laying his uniform hat on the chair beside him and breathing deeply in and out a few times. He popped the tab on the can and took a swig. The whine of the saw from the autopsy suite floated into the hallway, but in a muffled version and was mercifully diluted somewhat further by the buzz of the fluorescent lights overhead. He pulled his phone from his pocket and texted Donna.

Hey, babe. Still in Mt. Ida. We on for tonight? He clicked SEND. The ding of her reply was almost immediate, and he smiled and took another big drink from his coke.

ya! where?

Buck's? He took another sip from the can and then another as he awaited the reply ding. Buck's was a seedy dive bar over on Highway 27, a little rough, OK maybe a lot rough, but served decent burgers and cold beers and occasionally had good music on a Saturday night. Finally, the alert ding came.

idk mama h8s

no worries ur w/me

After another long pause without a response, he added, Junkyard Funk's covering Garth.

Luv Garth she replied quickly, followed by three emoji hearts.

CU 7?

K

"Deputy," Dr. Glickman came out from the autopsy suite and pulled the mask off his face. Ben stood, slipped his phone into his back pocket, and took out his notebook and pen.

"Looks like your boy probably drowned. I say probably at this stage. Maybe aspiration contributed, too. There was some vomit in both lungs, along with water and river silt, so he was at least alive when he went into the river. Can't say yet if he had help getting there. Could have been drunk or stoned and just fallen in. Might have the preliminary basic tox screen in a couple of days, but the final confirmatory results will be at least a month or more. No overt signs of foul play, no bullet wounds or stab wounds, no head trauma or fractures, neck wasn't broken. Did have recent abrasions on the back of his head and his elbows, looks like he'd bit his tongue maybe, a little blood in his mouth, but that's about it. No pills in the stomach contents, but still had what looked like fried eggs, potatoes, and tortillas, typical beaner breakfast. Hadn't eaten it long before he bought it. They'll do chemical analysis on all that to confirm. No ID on him?

"No, Dub said not." Ben continued to scribble notes in his little book.

"Could be an illegal. There's a couple of tats that might prove helpful for ID. And you could get lucky if he has prints in the system.

"You got photos coming my way?"

"Indeed. Digitals should be up in an hour or two. Roy's away this week, you know, so we'll get everything in and bring him up to speed on Monday; he can send over the prelim on cause then."

Ben flipped the notebook closed and put it into his shirt pocket, then settled his hat on his head and adjusted it carefully. "OK. We'll continue to treat it as suspicious until y'all clear it. Thank you, sir."

***

Just after 7:30 that evening Ben pulled open the weathered wooden door of Buck's Bar and a dense cloud of smoky air billowed out. Donna grimaced and fanned it away then walked in ahead of him, showing her ID to the burly guy in the wife beater and hoodie seated just inside and getting from him the required BB stamped on the back of her hand. Ben handed him the cover charge and scanned the room by force of habit, getting the lay of the land. The interior was dark, lit mainly by a mishmash of neon beer signs that peppered the walls and the pendant lights that hung over each of the three pool tables in the back. And it smelled of stale beer and cigarettes, tinged with a cloying undercurrent of marijuana smoke. He made a mental note of that last bit, though it wasn't exactly unusual in a place like Buck's. The background soundtrack of the jukebox was punctuated occasionally by the sharp *clack* of billiard balls breaking and lusty shouts pro and con from the players as the balls found pockets or didn't. In a game of pool, every shot pleases somebody.

He made note of the three scruffy guys who were playing at one table. A young couple played at another, and Ben couldn't help noticing the way the young woman's ample cleavage spilled out of her low cut, clingy knit top when she leaned across to make a shot. Not really his type, but a guy couldn't help noticing a display like that. It wasn't lost on her partner either, who, judging by her response, must have made some comment that Ben couldn't hear before slapping her playfully on the rump. She swatted at his hand and laughed. The third table was free.

The room was already filling up with not a single stool available along the bar itself and only a couple of tables still empty on the floor. Ben put a hand on Donna's back and steered her through the crowd toward the open table for two that offered the better view of the stage area. He pulled out the chair for her, settled her in, and sat himself with his back to a half-wall, where he could see the door, the lion's share of the room, and the stage.

"I could use a beer," he said signaling a passing server, who came over. Ben pointed at Donna. "What you want, babe?"

"Beer's good," Donna said, then with a glance at the waitress added, "I'll have an Ultra."

"An Ultra for the lady and a Heinie for me," Ben said. They had a couple of beers on tap, but he preferred the taste of a Heineken, even from a bottle.

"Anything to eat?" The waitress snapped her gum impatiently. She was wiry and lean, with cobalt blue streaks in her dark hair and a hard look about her features, an effect enhanced by the strand of barbed wire tattooed on her left arm. It wrapped in a spiral from her wrist, across her forearm, circled her elbow, and ran up her bicep to disappear into the cut-off sleeve of her t-shirt near the shoulder. Ben wondered how much farther it went. Maybe it took a dive over her shoulder and went down her back and across her butt and down her legs as well. Interesting to speculate, but also not his type.

"Sure," Ben said looking over the waitress's head at the big blackboard menu above the bar. "I'll have the double Bacon-a-tor burger with pepper jack and fries."

"Can I have a single veggie burger? No mayo or onions," Donna cocked her head and looked up at the woman. "Or pickles," The waitress rolled her eyes and scribbled the omissions on her pad. "And sweet potato fries."

"How can you eat that crap?" Ben asked her once the waitress had left them. It actually surprised him that Buck's even had a veggie burger on the menu. *Sign of the times.*

"Sweet potatoes?" She gave him a look of wide-eyed innocence. He gave her an eye-roll to rival the waitress's.

"No, you know what I mean. That fake meat crap."

"It's not bad," she said, putting both palms on the table and leaning forward. "How can you eat a cow?"

"Because it's delicious?" He gave her a palms up shrug that all but screamed 'Duh!'

"But they got such pretty eyes and sweet faces."

"For a girl that grew up in the country, you don't know much about livestock. Cows aren't all that sweet if you want to know the truth. And not very smart either."

The waitress returned with their beers on a tray.

"Y'all want glasses or not?" she said to Ben.

"Yeah," Ben said. The waitress flopped a pair of cardboard coasters emblazoned with the Buck's Bar logo—double Bs joined by a strand of twisted barbed wire—onto the table, and Ben wondered if maybe her barbed-wire tat was just a required part of the uniform. She set down the chilled glasses and deftly poured a beer into each, then blew a large bubble with her gum, popped it loudly, and was gone.

"Humans are meat eaters, Donna," Ben said, taking a swallow of beer. *Aaaaah!* It was icy cold, another of the things he liked about Buck's, its overall seediness notwithstanding.

"But it's mean to kill 'em," Donna countered.

"C'mon, babe, think about it. Humans hunted all these giant, scary animals, like cave bears and mammoths and other shit that doesn't even exist anymore, with nothing but their bare hands and pointed sticks."

"So?" She took a swig of her beer and licked off the foam mustache it left.

"So, cows are still around."

"And your point is?" She folded her arms across her chest and sat back.

"Look, cows and pigs and sheep and whatnot all made a deal with humans a long time ago. You take care of us, and we'll take care of you. Domestication, they call it. That's why they're even still here. They're slow and stupid and don't have sharp teeth or claws to fend off predators. Humans protected the animals, and in return when their time came, they wound up as food."

"But why couldn't they just graze happily in a pasture until they died of old age?"

"Not how nature works, babe. Predators are gonna eat prey. And in the wild they're not too nice about it."

The *thwang* of an electric guitar chord and squeal of an overloaded amp interrupted her protest and drowned out the jukebox for a moment.

Donna clamped her hands over her ears. "What a gosh-awful noise!"

Musicians had begun to filter up onto the low stage, tuning guitars, adjusting mics. Soon, the not-so-friendly Ms. Barbed Wire returned with their burgers and sat the plates down with a thump.

"Ketchup, Tabasco, and mustard's there," she said pointing to the obvious rack of condiments on the table. "Couple more beers?"

Eyeing his full glass of beer, he gave her a quizzical look. "Maybe in a bit." Ben said. "But could we have some mayo?"

She pulled a squeeze bottle of mayonnaise from the pocket of her short apron and plunked it down on the table. "Anything else? Show's about to start."

"Naw. I think we're good." She turned on her heel, and he called after her, "And uh, thank you, ma'am."

"I wouldn't thank-you-ma'am her," Donna gave the departing Ms. Wire a scowl. "Who put a bee up her butt?"

"Don't fuck with me about that, bro! You know that ain't how it was!" The angry shout came from the pool table in the corner, where two guys were currently up in each other's faces, brandishing their cues like martial arts staves. The taller of the two ducked just in time to keep his head from being split open by the wide swinging arc of the shorter man's stick, which having missed its intended mark crashed into the overhead pendant light, smashing it to smithereens and sending a cascade of colorful glass shards raining down onto the green felt tabletop. The guy at the adjacent table grabbed his buxom date and shoved her behind him and into the corner out of harm's way.

"Stay right here," Ben whispered to Donna. "Get under the table if you need to." He was up and beside the pool table in two steps. "Hey! Y'all need to simmer down."

The shorter man was red-faced, chest heaving, his expression wild and angry, but he backed away as Ben and the night manager converged on them. A sweet miasma of pot scent hovered around the table like a fog. Ben had only taken one sip of his beer but feared he might get a contact high just standing by them.

"Do I need to call the law here?" the manager barked at them.

"I am the law," Ben said calmly. The manager squinted at him and cocked his head. "Ben Bradford," Ben said, pulling out his badge case and flipping it open to show it to the man.

"Aw hell, Deputy, I didn't recognize you in your civvies," the manager said.

The taller one laid his cue down on the table, put his palms up, and spoke. "We don't want no trouble."

"We all don't want trouble," Ben said. "What's your name, bud?"

"Gil Stevens," the tall man said, brushing back a greasy strand of blonde hair that had come loose from his ponytail during the altercation.

"And your friend?" Ben pinned the shorter one with an authoritative stare.

"Brandon," the shorter one said, looking away. "Ferrell. Brandon Ferrell."

"Is there some kind of problem y'all need to settle outside maybe?"

The taller one shot his short friend a look, Ben couldn't help noticing, filled with wordless communication.

"Naw," the short one said finally breaking the eye contact. "We're good. Our buddy's not feelin' too good, though. He's in the head."

"Y'all got some ID?" The two men nodded, removed their driver's licenses from their wallets, and handed them over to Ben, who examined them closely, then handed them back.

"Who's paying for this?" The manager gestured at the shattered fixture.

Over the shoulder of the one called Gil, Ben noticed the third man he'd seen in their party emerge from the men's room; he started toward them, pale and wobbly on his feet, then made a U-turn and slumped against the door jamb, as if trying to hold himself upright. Ms. Barbed Wire also spotted him, Ben saw, and he watched her hurry around the perimeter of the pool tables to where the guy lolled against the men's room door. She slipped her head under his arm and her arm around his waist and shouldered his weight, moving him in slow steps closer to the trashcan beside the door. *Probably cleaned up more than her share of puke and not looking to do it tonight*, Ben thought.

Brandon glanced toward the men's room and tapped Gil with the tip of his cue, giving a head nod toward their ailing pal. Gil turned to look behind him and returned the nod, then peeled several bills from a thick fold of money he took from his wallet, handing them to the manager. "That cover it?"

The manager counted the cash. "Yeah, ought to." He folded the bills and stuck them into his shirt pocket. "Why don't y'all call it a night. I gotta deal with this mess." He looked around and motioned to a gangly male server who had just pushed through the swinging doors from the kitchen. "Hey, Rusty! Go back and get the broom and clean all this glass up. Dust vac the felt, too. Damn glass slivers are everywhere. We'll have to close this table for tonight."

"We done here?" Gil asked Ben.

"Yeah, y'all go on," Ben replied. "Your friend gonna be OK?"

"Yeah. Just had a little too much fun tonight. He'll be fine."

Gil walked over and relieved Barbed Wire as the sole support of his unwell buddy and motioned with his head toward the door, "C'mon Dak; let's get you home." On the way by the pool table, he gave the third Musketeer a head bob in that same direction. "Let's go Brandon. I think maybe we've worn out our welcome. Gimme a hand here." Brandon joined him on Dak's other side.

Ben let the lopsided trio wobble out the door then followed them to the parking lot. They struggled to lever their friend into the back of a big, blue Dodge Ram extended cab pickup and climbed in front. Ben took his phone from his pocket and snapped a photo of the license as they pulled out, watching until the taillights disappeared down the road before going back inside.

"What was that all about?" Donna asked Ben. She was still wide-eyed and flushed from the excitement.

"Dunno. Just a couple of boys blowin' off steam, I reckon." Ben turned his attention back to his burger and beer.

"I recognize them," Donna said, taking swig. "Those two that were fightin'."

"Where from? They're not from around here, I don't think." Montgomery County didn't have a huge population, fewer than ten thousand people, and Ben had lived here his whole life. The guys were about his age, but he didn't remember any of them from school or sports.

"They brought a man into the clinic the other day with his jaw out of joint, and Dr. Mac had to put it back in place. They were both just reeking of pot at ten in the morning. Stunk up the whole waiting room."

"Reeked of it pretty good tonight, too."

She took a bite of her ersatz burger. "Mmm. Delicious. Want some?" She smiled flirtatiously at him around the bite.

"Lord, save me. No," he grimaced at the suggestion. "But you have ketchup on your cheek," he said, smiling back. He pulled a paper napkin from the dispenser and reached across to wipe the glob away.

They'd hardly finished their burgers when the stage lights snapped on, and the set began with the lead singer belting out—*Blame it all on my roots, I showed up in boots and ruined your black-tie affair*—in a passable rendition of *Low Places* that soon had the whole bar swaying and singing along to the chorus, Donna and Ben included.

CHAPTER 17
Which Witch?

Maggie's first patient of the day hadn't been on the schedule. Just before 8 am, a gangly boy of about ten arrived urgently, limp in his father's arms. Therma Faye had hustled them straight back to the treatment room, shouting for Maggie on her way. She dashed into the room to find the child unconscious, moaning, trembling, drooling, and sweating on the exam table. His father hovered anxiously beside him.

"I'm Dr. McKinley," she said to the father. "What's going on?"

"Ryan O'Connor, ma'am," the big man spoke with some urgency. "This is my boy, Tommy." His breath was ragged, as if he'd been running.

"Doc," Therma Faye stepped close to Maggie and said in a low voice, "just so you'll know, this is Molly's son and grandson. Molly at the café."

She nodded in understanding, but it really didn't matter to Maggie whose grandson he was. The bottom line was he was someone's precious child, and they treasured him. She'd pull out all the stops, regardless. But knowing the relationship gave an added layer of dread if something should go wrong. "What happened?" she asked again with more urgency.

"I can't rightly say," Ryan answered her question, anxiety and worry plain on his face. "He and a buddy apparently played hooky and took their poles down to the river this morning, and he came staggering back home just now. He puked right on the front porch and then just collapsed; I grabbed him up and carried him straight here." The eyes under his bushy auburn brows were distressed, frightened.

"It's going be OK, Mr. O'Connor. We're going to take care of him." Maggie put her stethoscope into her ears and listened. *Heart rate very rapid. Breathing shallow.* He was salivating copiously, the drool flowing in a steady stream down his chin, already soaking the collar and front of his shirt. She lifted each lid and shined her penlight into his eyes, finding both pupils dilated. *Head injury? Rabies? Poison of some sort? But what?* She felt his scalp carefully all over in search of any suggestion of head trauma and found none.

"Tee, help me get his shirt and pants off. See if he has any bites or a rash."

They struggled a bit, but soon had the boy stripped to his Pokémon underpants; examination found nothing unusual on his skin anywhere.

"Has he been well, prior to this?" Maggie asked.

"Yes'm. Seemed fine this morning before he went out. Oh, God," his voice broke, and he stifled a sob. "Please help him."

"Mr. O'Connor, did he say anything at all before he collapsed?"

"No. No." He shook his head pitifully. "But Billy, that's his friend, told me out by the river Tommy said his mouth burned and his stomach was cramping, and he said he got real shaky and weak, couldn't hardly walk. And he was drooling and slobbering something fierce, like a … Oh, God, do you think it could be rabies, Doc? He's out in the woods all the time, and there's skunks and 'coons and…"

"I certainly considered it, but I don't see any evidence of a healing bite of any kind. Some kind of poison's more likely. Tee, tell Donna to call 9-1-1." Maggie pulled a set of cardiac leads from the crash cart and ripped the package open, then attached the leads. "And you call poison control, STAT!" Next, she started an IV.

"Got Poison Control on the line," Therma Faye said when she came back in with the phone handset held to her chest. "Told them the symptoms. They want to know do we know if he ingested anything?" She looked to Ryan O'Connor for an answer.

He scraped his hand across his thick beard and shook his head back and forth. He looked like he was going to cry. "I don't know. He had cereal for breakfast, I think. Billy's out in the waiting room. He was with him."

"Tee go ask. Quickly!"

She returned to the room momentarily and motioned Maggie over to speak quietly to her. "The boy said Tommy licked or sucked on some kind of root on a dare, thought it was potato or something, but he says he doesn't know if he ate any of it but doesn't think so. Poison Control says administer charcoal anyway."

"He's unconscious. I can only administer it via gastric tube, and I'll need to intubate him to protect his airway if I do that in case he vomits. Go make the charcoal slurry. And warm a liter of irrigation fluid in case we need it."

"Mr. O'Connor, I'm going to need to intubate your son." He looked confused. "Put a breathing tube into his windpipe," she clarified, "and give him some medicine, some charcoal, through a stomach tube. Is that OK?" Ryan nodded, numbly. "Do you want to go sit out in the waiting room?" Maggie thought he looked like he was going to faint; he was quite a large man, and she didn't relish the idea of either having to pick him off the floor or stitching him up if he cracked his head open on the tiles. "Tee, take Mr. O'Connor out and ask Donna to get him some water. Then I'll need you back in here."

Once Therma Faye returned, Maggie inserted the breathing tube into Tommy's airway and slipped a gastric tube through his mouth and into his stomach, then pushed the charcoal slurry down the tube with a large syringe. She'd scarcely finished when she heard the whine of the ambulance's siren growing louder. *Thank God they were close by today.*

In a few minutes, once she had handed Tommy's care off to the EMTs, she breathed a sigh of relief and whispered a prayer after him that he'd be OK. His dad had insisted on driving behind the ambulance to Hot Springs, though she was less than sure it was a good idea in his distraught state. But his wife was home with their toddler, who had a cold; he'd assured her he'd be fine. She hoped so.

"I need a coffee," she said to Therma Faye as they cleaned up the detritus left scattered in the treatment room.

"Wonder what he got hold of?" Therma Faye said, stuffing the crumpled-up table paper into the trash.

"I don't know, but we need to find out."

After the excitement of the morning, the clinic had settled back into a more normal pace of scheduled appointments and a few work-ins. In the late afternoon, Maggie stepped out of exam room 2 and called down the hall. "Tee?"

"Yes'm? Back here," Therma Faye's voice drifted out from the lab, and Maggie followed it back there.

"If you'll get Becky Davis ready for her pelvic exam, I'll get started in 3."

"OK. Three's a woman with the fever, cough, sore throat, body aches, you know the whole package. That makes four so far today."

Maggie blew out a long sigh. It did make four, and that made her nervous that flu season was upon them in earnest and early. "OK. I'll go see her, but it sounds like I'm going to need another white count and a nose and throat swab. And, though it pains me to say it, I fear we're also going to need to order a bunch more rapid flu test kits."

"Already done it," Therma Faye assured her. "Be here tomorrow."

Donna popped her head out of the office doorway. "Dr. Mac, Roy Owens is on the line for you."

"OK. Tell him I'm just going into a patient's room and unless it's urgent, ask if I can call him back."

About an hour, one pelvic exam, one chest cold, and one more case of documented flu later, Maggie sat with a coffee at her desk to return Roy's call. She dialed his number, put the phone on speaker, and rocked back in her chair with her aching feet up on her desk. Today's challenging early morning WOD along with the unexpected emergency of Tommy

O'Connor's poisoning plus four unscheduled patients this afternoon had exhausted her, and she just needed to close her eyes and get off her feet for a few minutes.

"This is Roy Owens," the voice answered from the speaker.

"Hi, Roy. It's Maggie McKinley returning your call."

"Yes ma'am, thank you," Roy said. "I just wanted to give you a little follow up on those suspected opiate ODs we spoke about the other day. Turns out it wasn't opiates at all. Tox showed THC, but no opiates."

"Hmm. Maybe the good witch, then, not the bad one. I sure didn't like the prospect of three opiate ODs in the space of a week."

"Me neither, I promise you," Roy agreed. "Interesting thing, though. Something unusual's turned up in those two cases here that I'm not sure what means. Some kind of a plant toxin they called it, high levels in both of them. And here's the weird part: same combo turned up in that guy they fished out of the Caddo last week. THC and this plant toxin."

"Plant toxin?" She immediately thought of Tommy. *Could it be the same thing?* If so, the other three had all died, and she prayed again the same fate wouldn't befall Tommy. "I had a boy in this morning with what I think was poisoning, and we don't know exactly what yet, but might have been from a plant. Not sure I like the sound of this witch any better," Maggie said.

"No. Not at all better."

"Any idea when they might know what the plant is or the toxin?" She jotted a note to call the hospital and at least alert them to the possibility of a connection. Her mind was whirling; she needed to try to identify this root Tommy had licked. Maybe his friend Billy could take someone out to where they'd been fishing.

"Likely to be a while," he said. "I'll let you know when I hear a result. And there's one other thing that I guess I can tell you since you're still technically my deputized assistant until the end of the year."

The unwanted role of interim coroner he'd foisted off on Maggie in the immediate moments after he'd collapsed with a heart attack while pulling bones from the riverbank by Frenchman's Mound a few months ago had almost gotten her killed, and she wasn't sure she wanted to know whatever it was he was about to tell her now. Before she could object, he went on.

"Fingerprints on this fella they pulled from the river popped on AFIS. He's a Mexican national. Tried to cross the Southern border illegally in California two years ago and got apprehended by CBP/ICE. They printed and ID'd him and shipped him back to Mexico, but I guess he made his way back over. Name's Domingo Sanchez."

Maggie lurched forward in her chair, nearly spilling her coffee as she dropped her feet to the floor and landed with a loud *thump*. "Domingo Sanchez?"

"That's right. Why? Does that name mean something to you?"

"Maybe," she said quietly. "I'm not sure, but I may have taken care of his wife. She was named Sanchez, and I'm pretty sure she said her husband's name was Domingo."

"Wife? Huh. We'll need her to make an ID and claim the body then. Can you give me her contact info?"

"No," Maggie replied softly. "I can't. She died Saturday night over at Mercy. I can give you the name of the doctor who operated on her. You can get the full story from him."

"OK. Text me his name, and I'll follow up with him, but here's the other shoe. This Sanchez's prints match the ones the crime scene techs lifted from the broken eggshells in Waylon's hen house. Looks like this is the guy who attacked Manny Purifoy. Description matches what Manny remembers, too."

"Are you absolutely sure?" she finally said quietly.

"No doubt about it," Roy confirmed.

Maggie was too stunned to respond for a moment, staggered by the realization that this news made clear: that a tiny baby boy fighting for his life in the NICU in Hot Springs was officially an orphan. She felt the hot sting of tears behind her eyes.

"Thanks for letting me know." She cleared her throat and said, "Let me know about the toxicology when you hear. Bye, Roy."

The next call she made was to JD to fill him in. He'd been with her during her fight to save Yesenia and her child; she felt he deserved to know what she'd learned.

"Damn," he said. "So, Yesenia and her husband are both gone. And their baby son is in the hospital fighting to live, with no parents to come home to."

"That's about the size of it," Maggie said. "And it just breaks my heart."

"I know, Sugar. I know," he said softly. "It sucks. But at least we know the name of the cousin. The one in Colorado."

"Right. Guadalupe Morales. I've given her name to the CPS caseworker, Mrs. Saunders. They're trying to locate her now, but who knows if they'll find her. If she's illegal, she may not be on anyone's radar. And then there's the issue of what to do with their bodies. Right now, Domingo's is in the county morgue here. And Yesenia is lying in the morgue in Hot Springs. But at some point, they'll both be released. And then what? I don't want them dumped in some pauper's grave somewhere. Or worse given over to science." She shuddered at the thought.

"Let me work on that. We'll figure something out," JD said quietly.

"But what —" she began, but he cut her off.

"I'll take care of it. I promise you. First let's just hope they can find the cousin."

Maggie's low back and neck were in an aching knot, and she reached around to massage an especially tight spot with one hand. *That's not going to cut it.* She put the phone on speaker so she could continue the conversation, then stood up beside her desk and bent backward to stretch out the kinks in her spine, then dropped forward and put her palms on the floor. "Mmm. That feels so good," she said, her voice muffled behind the veil of long blonde hair.

"Well, whatever's bringing you such pleasure, I wish I was there to be the proximate cause of it," he said. "Are you about finished for today?"

"Yeah, actually, I am as far as scheduled patients go. Why?" she said, standing again and rolling her neck and shoulders, enjoying the *pop pop crunch* as things loosened up. She raised her arms high over her head to stretch in that direction as well, then sat, feeling more relaxed.

"I was thinking," he said, "that we should maybe go back out to where Yesenia was camped and collect all their things. Not sure there's much there, but whatever it is, it belongs to their son now."

Maggie hadn't thought along those lines yet. Hadn't allowed herself to think beyond trying to save Yesenia and her baby. And it pained her that she'd failed in at least half of that goal. She didn't want to think about what the future might hold for that innocent, tiny survivor. Living a life without your parents was something she well understood, but this child wouldn't even have the joy of memories of them or photographs or Christmas stockings with their names. Maybe there is something in that ragged tent that would someday bring him comfort. Offer a small connection to the parents he would never know.

"Yes, we should do that," Maggie agreed.

"I'll loop Ben Bradford in first, let him know it's there. Now that they've identified the body from the river as Domingo's the police might want to take a look at the area where they were camped. Tell you what, why don't you come over to my place for dinner tonight, and we can work out a plan. And maybe after that maybe I can encourage you to make a few more of those delightful little moans I just heard."

"I was not moaning," she protested, laughing.

"Oh, you were," he chuckled softly. "And I'd like to hear it again."

She could find no argument with that stellar idea, except her promise to Papa that she would be at the boarding house for the evening meal and at night until he was able to come home. It was clear to Maggie that Miz Hendri was not nearly as anxious now that she knew Papa was on the mend and would soon be discharged from rehab. *She's tougher than anyone gives her credit for,* Maggie thought.

"Let me touch base with Miz Hendri," she said. "I think there's a guest couple due to check in this afternoon, and if so, she wouldn't be alone for dinner... or after."

"Mmm. I like the sound of that, too. Let me go figure out what I can throw together for us then, and I'll see you in a little while."

"Looking forward to it," Maggie couldn't suppress a smile as she disconnected the call, her earlier fatigue having vanished at the dreamy prospect of an evening of good food and wine and whatever might follow.

When Maggie got to JD's house it was half past five and already dark, but dark came early in late December. She gave the knocker a couple of quick raps then let herself in. JD was standing at the stone counter talking on the phone. CSN's *Southern Cross* played softly from the speakers. *Have I ever mentioned to him that's one of my favorites?* The lyrics of that song always made her dream of sailing the coast of South America under a boundless night sky lit by a blanket of stars. Bucket list trip, that one. Someday she'd do it. But in the here and now, the intoxicating aromas of cooked bacon, roasting poultry skin, butter, and garlic made her mouth begin to water. She deposited her purse on the sofa, quietly, so as not to disturb his call.

When JD saw her, he motioned her over, gave her a quick peck on the lips, and mouthed that it was Ben on the other end. She nodded and pointed to the open bottle of white in a chill sleeve on the counter, raising her brows in question. He held up two fingers, which she took to mean he'd like a glass as well, so she poured one for each of them and sat his on the counter beside him. Then took a long and welcome sip from her glass. She recognized the label; it was a New Zealand sauvignon blanc, not a particularly expensive one, but one he liked and kept around in volume for everyday drinking. She took another sip and swirled it in her mouth, inhaling the perfume of it up the back of her throat and out her nose. Hints of tropical fruit on the front and a crisp, refined finish.

"Mmmmm," she purred softly, giving him a teasing, smoky stare.

JD smirked and bit his lip to keep from laughing, then mouthed 'Was that a moan?'

She shook her head and gave a non-committal shrug.

"OK, thanks Ben," he said. "I understand. We won't touch it until y'all say otherwise. Just make a note that when you're finished with it to let me know; I'll be sure whatever is claimable goes to their baby boy."

JD ended the call and laid down the phone and his wine glass; he took Maggie's from her hand and set it beside his on the counter, then cupped her face in his hands and kissed her tenderly. She smiled up at him, and he fully wrapped her in his arms and kissed her properly.

"Mmmmm," she purred again, pulling away to find his eyes. "Now that *was* a moan."

"Happy to be of service, ma'am," he said. "And I hope to be of even greater service to you shortly, but dinner first. It's just roasted chicken and a wilted spinach salad, I'm afraid. Nothin' fancy, but we won't starve."

He quickly reheated the drippings that remained in the skillet from frying the bacon, and when they were warm, he drizzled them into the mustard, herbs, honey, and vinegar in a bowl, whisking vigorously. He poured the warm dressing over the fresh spinach, sliced eggs, mushrooms, crumbled bacon, and red onions and tossed gently. The pungent smell of the vinegar permeated the air, cutting through the savory scents of bacon and chicken.

"What did Ben say?" Maggie asked when they were seated and had enjoyed a few bites.

"That we should hold off until he gives us the go ahead. He confirmed that the body they pulled out of the Caddo was Domingo's, which I knew already, and that autopsy showed cause of death was probably drowning, which I also knew, but he said there's something unusual that turned up—didn't say what—and he said they'd like to go over the campsite and take a look. I told him I'd take him out to it tomorrow morning."

"I'd like to come with you," she said.

"OK, but why?"

"I don't know. I just feel Yesenia needs an advocate, somebody that's on her side if they're going to rifle through her personal belongings. It's crazy, I know. But as Roy reminded me, for better or worse, I'm still a deputized member of his staff for a few more weeks, so it's kosher."

She cut off a piece of her chicken and popped it into her mouth with her fork. JD picked up a thigh in his hands and took a big juicy bite.

"Finger food," he said, wiping the greasy, buttery residue from his lips and fingers with his napkin. "Chicken, I mean. In the South you don't want to be caught cutting chicken off the bone or eating a drumstick with a knife and fork." He raised one brow. "Marks you as a Yankee."

She ignored him and cut off another bite, daintily plucking it off the fork with her fingers and putting it into her mouth, then sucking the tips of her fingers suggestively.

His eyes narrowed slightly. "I'm gonna need you not to do that, or I may need to put the rest of this in a to-go box and move straight on to dessert."

She smiled at him. "OK. But about tomorrow, I'm pretty sure we don't have any appointments before 10. Could we go early?"

"First light's what Ben had in mind." He refilled her wine glass and topped off his own. "You good to go about 7?"

"Depends on how late I'm up tonight," she said with a grin and a wink.

CHAPTER 18
Evidence of Harm

Gil pulled the big truck up behind a large, prefab metal warehouse, parked it in the scrubby, brown grass, and climbed out. A night-watcher lamp shown a cone of yellowish light that illuminated most of the dirt and gravel parking lot. *Power company's already repaired it.* He gave his head a disgusted shake. They'd shot the light out just the other day to cover their clandestine night-time delivery of the product and supplies after they'd cleared the camp. *Hell, if you wanted the bastards to come fix it, you'd wait a damn month,* he mused. He took a last drag on his cigarette and flipped the butt down in the dirt beside the building, stomping it well out. The last thing he needed was to start a grass fire here. The thought amused him – *a grass fire that could start a 'grass' fire.* He knocked three short raps on the roll-up loading bay door and then after a 3-count pause rapped once again, and immediately the door creaked up about three or four feet so he could duck under it, then it rolled back down. The air inside the warehouse was heavy with the skunky funk of green marijuana; it hit him square in the face, strong and musky, and made it hard to breathe.

"The hell took you so long?" Marty Bledsoe sat in the back of the space, feet up as usual on his desk. Smoke curled upward from the cigarette in his hand, visible in the light thrown by a gooseneck desk lamp, which was about the only light in the dark interior.

"Checking on Dak," Gil said. "He's better and all, but he still ain't quite right. I went to the store and got him some more Gatorade and pop-sicles. Brandon's staying with him tonight."

"Dak makes three who've got sick just in the last few weeks. You seen those other two?"

Gil shook his head. "Naw, not in a week or so."

"What the hell's goin' on? Where'd they go?" Marty took another long drag and blew out a stream of smoke. "Didn't even come to pick up their pay yesterday."

"They hadn't been back to the motel either; I know that. Not sure where they went. Maybe back to Tennessee. I think they were from somewhere up by Memphis," Gil said.

"Well, we're gonna need more hands to load this shit up when the trailer comes in. What about that kid you used to work with?"

"Naw. I don't think so. Hadn't seen him around in a while either."

"You handle that other matter I needed done?" He took a last long drag from his cigarette and stubbed it out in the overflowing ashtray beside him, then dropped his feet from the desk and swung around to face Gil. "Well?"

"Yessir, it's handled. But-" he looked away from his boss's cold stare.

"But what?"

"Dude's dead," he said and then quickly explained further. "We didn't kill him. He just died."

"Whatta you mean, *he just died*?"

"Well," Gil cleared his throat, "what I said. He died. Me and Brandon had him in the truck takin' him over here to Mena; figured we'd put him on the plane heading back across the border after it made the oxy drop. Send him back to Mexico, to his roots, back to his people."

"And?" There was impatience in Marty's tone.

"And we hadn't hardly got to the high-water bridge when he started moanin' and shakin' like a leaf. We thought he was just scared, ya know? We gave him a doobie to calm him down when he first got in the truck— he'd been ravin' about *mi esposa mi esposa* and jabbering all that shit like he does, and it did seem to shut him up. He got quiet anyway, but after a while we saw he was slobberin' like a mad dog. And then he puked. Right in the cab of my truck! I won't get that smell out for a month. I was so damn pissed; I stopped the truck right on the bridge and dragged his ass out. I threw him a rag, told him clean it up right there. But his legs were like jelly, and he couldn't hardly stand. And then he fell over and started jerkin'— his arms, legs, everything floppin' around on the bridge. And then he started gurglin', chokin' on the puke I guess, and gaspin' for air. We didn't know what the hell to do. And then in a few minutes he quit movin'. His eyes were still open, but it didn't look like he was breathin' anymore."

"So, you didn't kill him, Gilly, you just didn't help him. Have I got that right?"

"Pretty much," Gil said looking down at his feet. He wanted very much to light up a smoke but fought down the urge. Marty didn't like people smoking near the drying product, other than himself, of course.

"And where is he now?"

"We were gonna bring him back here, keep him on that flight back to Mexico. But we could see a car coming down the way toward the bridge, and we didn't have time to heave him back up into the cab, so we just rolled him off the edge of the bridge into the river and took off."

"Dumb fucks." Marty closed his eyes and shook his head. "And what about when he turns up?"

"Figure it'll just look like he drowned," Gil offered with a shrug.

Marty took a deep breath in and glanced around at the stacked bales of pot that filled the warehouse. "What about his *esposa*, hmm? Dom harvested, baled, and dried plants; he crushed the oxy to lace the product." He walked over and stood close enough that Gil could feel Marty's breath on his face. "The wife knows what's going on here. Don't think she doesn't.

She might only be able to tell it in Spanish, but plenty enough people can understand it if she does. Go over to where they camped first thing tomorrow and tie up that loose end."

***

Tendrils of early morning fog swirled over the dead tops of bitterweed and leafless clumps of sumac bushes that dotted the ground as Maggie and JD bumped their way in his truck across the pasture to the campsite. Ben and a crime scene tech followed behind them in the patrol wagon. She'd gotten home quite late from JD's place, had dragged up at 5:30 to work out and shower, and was still nursing her first cup of coffee when he'd pulled into the back lot of Miz Hendri's just before 7 am. She'd poured most of the rest of the pot of coffee into a Thermos and brought it with them and was just unscrewing the vacuum stopper to pour herself a second cup when JD stomped on the brakes and came to an abrupt stop. The coffee sloshed in the bottle, but mercifully not out onto her slacks.

The dome of the blue nylon tent, though right in front of them, was almost invisible in the gray early morning light, obscured further by the patches of fog that still hung in the low spots along the stream; she hadn't even seen the campsite until they practically ran over it. Ben pulled to a stop beside them, and he and the tech climbed out. JD opened his door, but Ben put up a hand.

"Let me and Steve go in first," Ben said, referring to Steve Vlasavic, the tech. "see if there's anything we need to preserve. I mean, I realize both y'all have been in here already, but still… protocol and all."

JD climbed out and stood beside the truck. Maggie scooted across the seat to the driver's side and rolled down the window so she could hear what was going on. It was cold enough out that his breath came in visible puffs, yet he was dressed only in jeans and a light pullover sweater. In a minor bow to the elements, he'd added an oiled canvas Barbour jacket, unzipped, but apart from having turned its collar up and putting his bare hands in the pockets, he appeared impervious to the damp chill. She on the other hand wished she'd worn electric ski socks. She'd never dreamed it would get so cold in Arkansas.

"Do you think they'll find anything that explains what happened to Domingo?" she said, rubbing her gloved hands together for warmth.

He shrugged and shook his head. "Who knows? Guess we'll find out soon enough." His phone chimed, and he took it from his pocket and looked at the display. "I gotta take this." He walked some bit away from the truck and spoke quietly.

Maggie could make out enough of the conversation to recognize he was speaking in Japanese. Then she heard the sing-song patter of a higher pitched young voice as well and realized it must be a FaceTime call from Akiko. It was just after seven in the morning in Caddo Bend, which meant after ten pm in Japan. *A late bedtime for a five-year-old.* She could hear his gentle, soothing voice, and though she couldn't understand the words, the sentiment was clear: a parent comforting a child. Then she heard him singing, soft and low. And after a few minutes, he ended the call and came back to the truck window.

"My, uh," he paused, looking almost apologetic as he held up the phone, then slipped it into his pocket "my daughter. She had a nightmare. Been quite a few of those lately."

"Oh, I'm sorry she's having a hard time," Maggie said.

"No, I'm sorry."

"For what?" she asked.

"Well, for that, of course, that she's having a hard time; it hurts when she hurts. But for… a lot of things." She noted a far off look in his eyes, a sadness.

"There's nothing more important than for a dad to make his daughter feel safe and loved." Maggie rubbed her hands together again and blew on them to warm them.

JD opened the driver's door and motioned her to scoot over as he climbed back inside and rolled up the window. "Here," he cranked the motor and turned the heater to high, "let's warm you up." He opened his Barbour and wrapped it around her, pulling her in closely to him, then kissed her lightly on her forehead. She buried her nose against the warmth of his chest, breathing in the scent of winter air and the heady combination of oiled canvas and the sandalwood and cedar that clung to it. "Better now?" he said, resting his cheek on the crown of her head.

"Mmm hmm. I think I could stay like this all morning." She looked out the windshield to see Ben emerge from the tent and come toward them. "But it looks like Ben has other ideas."

Maggie moved back to her own cold seat, and, as Ben approached, JD rolled the window down admitting a new blast of chilly air. "Find anything yet?"

"Nothing much important; you can come take a look if you want, Doc. Steve's still at it though. He's photographing outside right now, then he'll head inside. Sheriff just called. Death's been ruled as drowning, so this isn't a crime scene. Says he wants us to photograph and take a few samples. Just in case."

Maggie climbed out from the cab of the truck, reluctant to leave JD's warmth, but she braved the cold, zipped her jacket all the way to her chin, and resolutely walked over to the tent. Ben held the flap aside as she ducked under it. The low morning angle of the strengthening sun streamed through the opening, lighting the interior sufficiently to see the blood-stained pallet that still lay in a crumpled pile on the floor and the meager stack of neatly folded clothing resting against the opposite wall of the cramped space. Beside the clothing lay a small bound book. She bent to pick it up—*Santa Biblia* was stamped in fading gold letters on its black leather binding—the Holy Bible. A wooden bead rosary lay beneath it. These items she mentally marked should be saved for the baby. At least once the county gave the OK. There wasn't much else but a near-empty plastic water jug, a lantern with a half-burned candle in its socket, and a battered plastic cooler tucked in the corner. She carefully opened the lid of the cooler and saw eight or nine eggs, something rolled in foil, a can of evaporated milk, a gnarly light brown vegetable of some sort, an opened bag of corn masa, and a box of safety matches. All that remained of two young people in search of a better life. From outside she could hear the *click whir* of the camera shutter as Steve documented the campsite itself. She pushed back out of the tent flap and saw Ben standing a little way away talking to JD. She walked over to them.

"You can smell the weed inside. But the green, skunky odor, not sweet like what floats in the air at a concert or bar or whatever," she heard Ben saying as she joined them. "Seen what you need, Doc?"

"Yeah," Maggie nodded, saddened once again that there was so little to see.

"All pretty much like it was, then?" he asked her.

"Best I can remember. We were so focused on Yesenia and getting her out of there, I can't say I really took much of a look around that night."

"Alright, thanks. Why don't y'all head on back, then? Steve and I'll finish things up here and call when we're done, and y'all can come get it later. No sense all of us freezing."

"OK," JD said. "I promised the good doctor I'd have her back at the clinic by…" he looked the question to Maggie.

"Ten," she answered, then said to JD, "We could go by Molly's and grab some breakfast on the way, if you're up for it."

"Always," he gave her a half smile. "Just give us a call, Ben."

After a quick bite at Molly's JD had dropped Maggie at the clinic. The mood at the café had been subdued without Molly's jovial face and easy Irish banter, and her absence had reminded Maggie that she needed to call to check on Tommy this morning before she got wrapped up in the flow of patients. She flipped on the lights in her office, closing her eyes to shield their sudden, cold, fluorescent glare and making a mental note to find some full spectrum light tubes for the fixture. She hung her puffy coat on the rack and donned her labcoat, then sat down at her desk and picked up the phone. She dialed the hospital and put it on speaker, leaving her hands free to transport her maple bonsai to its happy place on the sunny windowsill, cracking the glass an inch or two to give the tree some air.

"Mercy General, how may I direct your call?"

"Hi," Maggie began, "Dr. McKinley calling regarding a patient of mine from Caddo Bend. Tommy O'Connor. He was brought in with suspected poisoning yesterday." Maggie could hear the *click clack* of keystrokes.

"Transferring you to Pediatric ICU, doctor." And with another *click*, she was gone.

The music on hold was all instrumental renditions of Beatles' tunes, which at least made the interval passably bearable, but, as the minutes dragged on, she found herself wishing she'd grabbed an Americano on the way in. Her mind automatically filled in the absent lyrics of the song currently playing – *Here comes the sun, and I say, it's all right.*

"Four-A, PICU," the voice finally answered. "Mullins."

"Yes, Ms. Mullins. I'm Dr. McKinley. My patient Tommy O'Connor was brought in with suspected poisoning yesterday. I'm just calling to see if I can get an update on him"

"Sure, doctor. McKinley you said?" *Click click click.*

"That's right."

"Yes, I see you listed here as referring physician. Let's see… right now, he's been medically sedated, still on the ventilator. He had a major tonic-clonic seizure after they brought him in. EEG and brain scan this morning were within normal limits, though. They're keeping him sedated, at least for now."

Maggie breathed out a relieved sigh. *At least he's still alive.* "Any determination yet on what might have been the cause? The only thing we know on this end is he may have licked or sucked some kind of root and quickly got sick. And we've had a couple of other possible plant poisonings in the county recently, so there's some urgency in figuring this out."

There was a long pause punctuated by a few more keyboard clicks before Ms. Mullins spoke. "Nothing back on the toxicology yet. Would you like me to make a note in the chart to forward any results to your office?"

"Yes, please. That would be helpful. Thank you." Maggie supplied her email and the clinic fax number and ended the call.

The balance of the morning had been uneventful, but there'd been a steady stream of walk-in patients with flu-like symptoms throughout the afternoon, some positive for the virus, others not. Based on today, it was shaping up to be a doozy of a flu season and likely to derail holiday plans for some families as the virus made its rounds between now and Christmas, which was only a week away.

Therma Faye stood at the sink, scrubbing her hands for the umpteenth time today after the last flu-positive patient departed and complaining, "Dang, my hands feel like I've scraped all the skin off of 'em. I gotta remember to order some more of that pink soap; this iodine stuff just eats me up!" She dried her hands on a paper towel and tossed it in the trash, then pumped a puddle of lotion into her palm and rubbed it over her hands and forearms. "I think there's just Mr. and Mrs. Benson left on the schedule. They're in Room 1. And before you ask, it's not her foot this time, thank goodness. It's him; his ears are stopped up. Mrs. B says he can't hear her." She dropped her voice to a low whisper. "Between you and me, I think it's selective deafness, if you get my meanin'. That woman could talk the horns off a brass Billy goat. I didn't look in his ear, but I got my fingers crossed it's a middle ear effusion, not a wax plug. If there's a worse way to end a busy day than irrigating the wax out of an ear, I don't believe I've made its acquaintance."

By 3:30, everything had been cleared out, including Mr. Benson's ear to Therma Faye's dismay. Maggie made herself a coffee and took it back to her office to finish up crossing all the t's and dotting all the i's of the day. Donna had put a sticky note on her desktop screen, and she pulled it off to read:

JD called. Ben finished w/ camp. Pick u up 4-ish.

She smiled at the youthful penmanship—printing, of course—with circles for dots over the i's. Like most millennials and Gen Zs Donna didn't do cursive. Maggie had been stunned to learn this when she'd left hand-written notes for the young ward clerks at Columbia—and more recently for Donna. Most of them could hardly write cursive after third grade, and worse, they could barely even read it. And to Maggie that was a sad state of affairs; she was firm in the belief that there was no more artful form of written human expression than graceful cursive script. She herself wrote a beautiful hand, so striking, in fact, that one of her staff mentors at Columbia had even teased that she couldn't possibly expect be a doctor with such legible penmanship. Maggie was officially a millennial herself, having been born in 1984, making her only 7 or 8 years older than Donna. But unlike her, Maggie had benefited from a classic Catholic boarding school education in which precise calligraphy was enforced through grade 12 with the sharp rap of a ruler on tender knuckles. She'd hated it at the time, but in the rearview mirror, she was more than a little grateful for the skill it had ingrained.

She looked at the time. JD would be here in about half an hour, early enough for them to get out to the campsite and collect everything before it got too dark, if they hurried. But before they went, she wanted to check on the status of the Sanchez baby and speak to Papa, who was supposed to be released day after tomorrow. It would be very nice to have him home for the holidays rather than stuck at the hospital.

She made the first call to the rehab unit to let Papa know that JD would be there to pick him up on Friday when he was discharged and bring him back to Caddo Bend. Miz Hendri had insisted on his coming to the boarding house, instead of going to his own house alone, and though he'd protested it wasn't necessary, she would not be dissuaded, so that was the plan. Maggie had to admit she felt a little better herself having him in Miz Hendri's ground floor guest room, at least until she was fully satisfied herself of his complete recovery. Plus, she knew Miz Hendri would insist he get his daily rounds of home PT done.

Next, she dialed the main number for Mercy General and asked for the NICU, got put on hold, transferred twice, then finally connected to someone at the neonatal intensive care desk.

"Dr. McKinley?" The voice was young and pitched high in the male register with, Maggie noticed, the merest hint of rhotacism—difficulty with the 'r' sound. "Sorry to keep you on hold, but it's been crazy here to-day; the moon must be full." She heard him blow his nose then sniff loudly. "What can I do for you?"

"Hi, Mr…"

"Pearcy. Michael, please," he responded. Her short time in the South had already taught her that this was his invitation, more than that really, his formal request to call him by his first name. So, she made a mental note.

"I am the physician who first attended one of your patients… pre-de-livery that is. Baby Sanchez?"

"Oh, yes," he said, "the clerk told me you were inquiring about him. Such a sad story. Bless his heart. Give me a second to pull up his chart." He gave another rattling snort, and it made Maggie want to hand him a tissue through the phone. She heard his congested breathing and the quick clacks of his keystrokes over the line and entertained herself silently contemplating what might be giving him the stopped-up nose. *Seasonal allergies? Nasal polyps? A cold? No, surely not that, not if he's at work in the NICU.* Before she could settle on a presumptive diagnosis, he was back to her. "Yes, I see your name here as referring. As to how he's doing, he was several weeks early, as you know already, and had a rough start. But Milagro's a little fighter, and he's -"

"Milagro?" she interrupted him.

"Well, that's just so we have something to call him besides Baby Sanchez; since they've said he'll probably be here a while, so we sorta wanted to make him feel more welcome. And he is a little miracle, right?"

Maggie had to agree that he was indeed.

"He's doin' real well," Michael went on. "Weight's back up to almost 5 pounds now. Numbers look good this morning, blood gasses all OK, his bili's still up a smidge too high, so they've got him under the bili light. Breastfeeding would bring it down, but..." his voice drifted off, leaving the saddest part unspoken; he had no one to breast feed him.

"Right," she murmured. "Well, that all sounds hopeful. Thank you, Michael. I'll check back in tomorrow." She disconnected the call. *Well, he's alive,* she consoled herself. *But now what? Only one way to find out.* Maggie dialed the number for Ms. Saunders at CPS but got her voice mail, so she left a message inquiring about whether they'd located Guadalupe Morales and asked her to return the call. She was just hanging up when her cell buzzed with an incoming call from Melody Saunders.

"Ms. Saunders," Maggie answered. "I was just leaving you a message."

"Yes, I couldn't get my phone out of my pocket," she laughed. "Sorry about that!"

Maggie glanced again at the clock. *Ten 'til four.* She put the phone on speaker so she could finish tidying up before JD arrived.

"No problem. I was just checking in to see if you'd had any luck on the Guadalupe Morales front." Maggie walked to the window where the bonsai maple was perched and closed it, then picked the tree up to move it to its usual nightly spot on the bookshelf, sticking a quick finger under the moss to check the moisture. *Needs a drink.*

"We've had a little break there, I hope. We think we may have located the woman in the Greeley area. Right name anyway, but we're not a hundred percent sure it's the right person; Morales is a pretty common surname. They're sending someone from Colorado CPS out to check. But if so—and fingers crossed—that will be a stroke of good luck in a long string of misfortunes for that family."

"I know. My heart just aches for that sweet little boy." Maggie picked up her phone and cradled it on her shoulder and continued the conversation as she carried the bonsai down the hall to the break room and sat it into the sink, turning the sprayer on it for a good soak, then leaving it to drain she headed back to her office. "He seems to be doing well enough physically, and that's a positive. I just pray you find her. For his sake." She tossed the few file folders and papers scattered across her desk into an 'IN/OUT' box and put her desktop computer to sleep, then shrugged into her puffy coat and threw her purse and medical bag over her shoulder. She didn't intend to be caught unprepared again without it.

"I'll let you know the minute we have news," Ms. Saunders said. "Bye now."

Maggie ended the call and dropped her phone into her purse as she walked down the hall. She stopped by the storeroom closet and grabbed a handful of heavy-duty trash bags and a couple of bio-waste bags, just in case. She didn't know what the crime scene tech had bagged and taken, but better safe than sorry if he'd left the blood-soaked pallet.

As it turned out she and JD arrived to find the tent and all its contents had been removed. Nothing remained but the disturbed ground where it had been pitched, the cold campfire inside a circle of river rocks, and across the rocks, a blackened piece of aluminum sheeting that from the look of it perhaps had served as a makeshift stove top and griddle. There was a large tin can—the big fat kind like whole tomatoes come in—sitting on the metal sheet. The place had an eerie just-abandoned feel to it, as if the energy were still there, lingering in patches like this morning's fog, but the physical stuff was gone.

Maggie jerked her head up the hill at the noise of an engine gunning and tires spinning on rocky soil of the rise above them. "What was that?" she said to JD, peering toward the hilltop to see who or what it was. She saw nothing at first, apart from a hawk that made a visible dark blot on the dusky pale gray of the sky as it drifted in circles on an updraft above them, then her eye caught a flash of blue moving behind the scrubby undergrowth that rimmed the crest of the hill.

"Somebody hunting, probably," JD said, glancing up the hill. "Deer season's over now, but folks can hunt squirrel, 'coon, and 'possum year-round."

"People actually eat opossums and racoons?"

"They do. And squirrels, too. They taste pretty good, if you know how to cook them." He nodded toward the campfire. "Looks like Yesenia did a little cooking right there."

Maggie walked over to the campfire to peer into the can balanced on its edge, wrinkling her nose in apprehension of what sort of rural delicacy she might encounter there. It was about half-filled with a clearish liquid and slices of what looked like some kind of a pale root vegetable. "What's this?" she said to JD.

He joined her and squatted down beside the can, peering in. "Don't know. Remains of their dinner, looks like. Maybe sliced parsnips? Or could be fingerling potatoes, I guess. They're coin slices of whatever it is, too skinny to be a turnip. One way to find out." Curious and adventurous cook that he was, he reached in to grab several of slices from the liquid and took a bite of one, chewing thoughtfully. "Mmm. Pleasant tasting. Kind of sweet. Maybe a wild carrot?"

Maggie put her hand to her lips and gasped aloud when he thew the pieces into his mouth, then relaxed somewhat remembering their walk in the woods a few months ago when he'd plucked wild blackberries from a bush and eaten them. And offered them to her. She'd been reluctant at first, but they'd proven to be delicious. And it made her mindful again of this curiously different world she now inhabited where edibles grew wild all around.

"Will you just eat anything?" She shook her head in disbelief.

"Well, maybe not anything. But a part of Ranger training is a survival week. They drop you out of a plane into some remote woods somewhere with an empty canteen and a knife and your bare hands and come back to get you in a week. In the meantime, you've got to survive on whatever Mother Nature provides to you. You get over being squeamish pretty fast." He popped the rest of the coins in his hand into his mouth. "Want some?"

"Hard pass on that. I'm not much for eating things I don't know the name of, let alone ones that have sat outside in a tin can for God knows how long," she snorted out a laugh. "I'm going to call Ben and be sure they're hanging on to that Bible and the rosary for the baby. That's about all I saw in there that would be worth keeping." Maggie dialed Ben's number on her cell and put it on speaker so JD could hear as well.

"Ben Bradford," the voice answered, "I can't take your call now. Leave me a message."

"Hi, Ben. It's Maggie McKinley. We're out at the Sanchez campsite, and it looks like you guys got pretty much everything. There were two things I meant to mention – a Bible and a wooden rosary – that I think for sure ought to be preserved for the baby. So, when you're finished with the stuff, let me know, and we'll get those to the right place for him." She dropped the phone back into her purse and turned to JD. "Looks like there isn't much else for us to do here, shall we head back and get some real dinner?"

"Sure," he said, draping an arm loosely across her shoulder and giving her a quick peck on the lips as they walked back to the truck. "Your place or mine?"

"Miz Hendri would probably enjoy having us." She entwined her fingers in his. "You, especially; you know how fond she is of you. Besides, there's always more than enough."

CHAPTER 19
Med Flight

Ben sat alone on a barstool at Buck's, methodically peeling the label off the bottle of beer he'd been nursing for almost an hour. He was listening with half an ear to a very drunk man farther down the bar whine to the bartender – and there really was no other way to characterize it than whining – that his cheating wife had taken his two kids and worst of all his new F-150 and left. Ben shook his head. *Man up, bro!* With the other ear, Ben was keeping track of the two guys playing pool at a table in the back. One was the taller of the two yahoos who'd gotten into the scuffle the night he and Donna had come to hear the music; the other guy he didn't recognize.

He'd been driving back from Glenwood when he'd gotten Maggie's voice mail, which confused him, because he and Steve had taken nothing at all from the Sanchez camp in the end but photos and some samples and swabs. It should all have still been there. He'd called Maggie right back to ask if she'd seen anything unusual or anybody else around the campsite. She'd not seen anyone, she said, but had heard a truck up on the hill above them; it might have been blue, she said, but all she'd really seen was a flash of color.

As he was driving back toward town, he'd just happened to spot a blue truck in the parking lot at Buck's—the big blue Dodge Ram extended cab those two rowdy boys had gotten into with their sick friend the other night. He was officially off duty, but he decided to stop anyway. He'd picked up a weird vibe from them, one of those prickle the hairs on your neck kind of things, and he'd followed them out that night and snapped a photo of their plates and run them just to see what came up. Figured it would probably wind up to be nothing, but you never knew.

The truck, it turned out, was registered to a company called MB Storage and Transfer with an address in Mena. That was Polk County, not Montgomery, so he'd put out a feeler to his friend, Junior Davis, in the sheriff's department over there.

The address of MB Storage, he'd said, was a warehouse on an isolated stretch of farm road on the far west outskirts of the town. Junior told him there had been a few complaints in the last year or so from farmers in the surrounding area about planes circling and taking off at night disturbing the livestock, but as yet they hadn't been able to verify anything that seemed much out of the ordinary. Still, Ben had a hunch they were up to no good. Donna had said they were stoned at ten in the morning the day they'd come into the clinic. So, when he'd seen the truck, he'd come into Buck's to have another look.

"Can I get you a refill on that?" The bartender indicated Ben's empty beer. "Or a burger or something?"

Ben gave a casual glance at the pool tables. Didn't seem like those two were headed out soon; lotta balls on the table still. "I'll take an order of chili fries," Ben said, "and just a glass of soda water with ice and a lime. Don't open a can or nothing. Outta the gun's fine."

"You got it. Be right up."

Ben stood and walked over to the jukebox, which took him over by the table where the men were engrossed in their game, close enough to hear their conversation without seeming to. The jukebox was an old school model, a half-dome of backlit, molded plastic, chrome, and glass, probably been at Buck's since his grandaddy started the place back in the 50s, but the current owner—Cletus Buck III—had refitted it inside, and it now played from a digital playlist still accessed via push buttons with numbers and letters. He pushed C and 26 and queued up Darius Rucker's *True Believers* and hung there perusing the playlist as if looking for another selection, but with an ear trained on the table.

The tall one that he recognized was lining up a shot; looked like he was trying to hit the 6-ball into the 12 and bank it off the rail and into the side pocket. And it looked to Ben like it didn't have a prayer. *What the hell's his name? Bill something? No, that's not right. Gil. Yeah, it was Gil.* In his side vision, Ben watched as Gil drew back the cue and tapped the 6 which hit the 12 but sent it woefully off the mark. His somewhat shorter companion cackled around the cigarette that drooped from his lip, scattering ashes onto the felt. He drew on it deeply and laid the smoldering stub into an ashtray sitting on the rail, took a swig from his mug, then twirled his cue in his hand.

"I'm gonna run it now, bro!" the shorter one said, his broad grin revealing a missing first molar on the left. "Then we can get that greaser's shit back on over to Mena."

At the mention of the word *greaser* Ben's ears pricked. He took another moment to stand at the jukebox and select another song to follow Darius, settling on *Callin' Baton Rouge.* A little Garth in homage to Donna. Then he saw that the bartender had put his fries on the bar, and as there was nothing less appetizing in his book than cold fries, he returned to his seat still trying to catch the gist of their conversation. All he picked up was something about a camp stove, which made no sense to him. He popped a fry into his mouth and smiled. The fries were hot, and the chili was hotter. Just like he liked it.

The guy wielding the cue was as good as his word, and it was *click roll clunk* with ball after ball until he'd cleared the table of solids and had only the 8-ball left for a win. Calling the pocket, he sank it. "You owe me a twenty, bro!" He rolled his cue across the green felt and drained the rest of his beer.

"Shit," Gil muttered, jerking his wallet from his pocket, and peeling off the bill. "Let's get outta here."

Gil drained the remains of his own beer and lit a cigarette off the butt smoldering in the ashtray.

Ben signaled the bartender and laid a twenty and a five on the bar. "Keep the change," he said, rising to leave ahead of them. In the parking lot he got into his truck, and when he saw the men come out, he watched in his rearview as they walked to the blue truck and climbed in. He let them get a little way down the road before pulling out onto the highway to follow them. There was hardly any other traffic until they got close to Mena, so he had to hang back far enough not to be conspicuous. Once through town, the blue truck turned off onto Hwy 8 toward Rocky, a road Ben knew cut through mostly open pastureland. Not many businesses or houses that he could remember, so he didn't turn and follow but went on through the intersection, doubled back in the parking lot of an auto parts shop, and turned back onto Hwy 8 coming from the other direction. In a couple of minutes, he caught sight of the blue truck's taillights a good way ahead of him and saw it turn into a dirt entrance road that led to a metal building a couple of hundred yards off the highway. There was an unlighted sign affixed to the side of the building, but Ben couldn't make out what it said in the dark from this distance. He drove past the entrance and on down the desolate highway. When he felt he'd gone far enough to be well out of sight, he pulled into a gravel turn out and whipped around to head back in their direction.

A good distance away from the building, while he was still shielded from its view by a thick copse of hardwoods, he pulled the truck far off onto the shoulder, killed the lights and motor, and sat a minute thinking about what he should do. And shouldn't. He was off duty. He had no jurisdiction here. But he needed to know what was going on and what they'd meant about a greaser's stuff. *Did they take the tent from the Sanchez campsite?* Well, here they were. And here he was. So, he climbed out of his truck, quietly shut the door, and set off on foot across the dark open field toward the building. He could see the blue truck parked beside it, illuminated somewhat by a night-watcher high on a power pole behind it. He'd need to skirt that lighted area to keep from being spotted, so he veered back closer to the road, crouching low as he made his way through the tall stalks of dead grass and scrub in a drainage ditch that ran alongside the highway. He thanked the Lord they hadn't had rain in the last few days, otherwise he'd be knee deep in water. As it was, the ground at the bottom of the ditch just squished a little under his boots.

Then he heard the tinny, distant whine of an airplane engine and looked up to see a small prop plane making a wide, steep bank over the field on the opposite side of the building; it disappeared from his view for a moment and then reappeared, lined up for a landing, descending toward the field. He pulled his phone from his pocket and snapped a few photos, then texted them to his deputy friend at Polk County with a quick message: **Am at warehouse. Plane landing.**

He pocketed the phone and crept close to the building through the weeds. One dry stalk snapped sharp as a gunshot when he stepped on it, and Ben froze in a hunkered squat until he was satisfied the sound hadn't betrayed his position. With the plane coming in, he figured the attention of anyone inside would be focused that direction, so he inched his way around to the opposite side of the building where the truck was parked. Staying low, hugging its corrugated metal wall, he scanned the area and, seeing no one anywhere, dashed to the side of the truck and looked in the bed.

The blue tent and a jumble of its contents lay scattered across the floor. The gold lettering on the spine of the Bible glinted in the moonlight; he could see the edge of the cover just peeping out from the tumbled blankets and clothing, and he put a foot on the bumper to lever himself over the tailgate and into the bed. He grabbed the Bible and looked around quickly for the rosary Maggie had mentioned, flipping over and shaking out the blankets and clothing but didn't see it. He was about to give up when his eye caught a glimpse of a shape out of place, a disruption in the regular wales in the corner of the floorboard liner. Just as he reached down and his hand closed on the string of smooth round beads, the screech of the bay door as it rolled up stopped him cold. He hopped down and scrabbled away from the truck, flattening himself in the dirt and tall, scraggly weeds on its far side, well away from the cone of light thrown by the night-watcher.

He heard two voices—one he recognized as Gil's and another, much deeper one—and the crunch of their footsteps on the gravel as they drew nearer the truck. He breathed quietly through his open mouth, praying one of them wasn't heading for the passenger's side. He chanced a glance up and was relieved to see both sets of boots visible under the truck on the driver's side.

"Tiff's going to finish up lacing the high-end inventory tonight," the one with the deeper voice said. "Take all Dom's crap and bury it or better yet burn it. Get rid of it. Permanently. And find his woman before she finds someone to spill her guts to. I want her out of here."

"I got no idea where she is, Marty. She was gone when we went over there to get his stuff." There was a long pause before he continued. "She's knocked up, you know. About to pop, it looked like last time I saw her. I doubt she could go far."

"Then you oughta be able to find her. When the plane goes back South tomorrow night, I'll be on it. Be sure her ass is on it, too. Get rid of her and her anchor baby. A two-fer." The man—Marty, Gil had called him—chortled at the comment. "But first go round up the crew at the motel. Tell 'em the truck's coming tomorrow late, and I want this product moved out of here before Thursday night, and if it is, they'll get a bonus."

The truck's engine rumbled to life, and the Gil slammed his door. Ben laid in the weeds, still as a stone and watched the truck pull away. The other man ducked under the roll-up bay door and disappeared into the building, and the door rolled back down. Alone again in the darkness, Ben let out a relieved sigh and stuck the small Bible into the waist of his jeans and the rosary into his front pocket.

His cell phone buzzed with a text alert, and he pulled it from his pocket, shielding the light with his hands. *Probably Junior.* He checked the display; it was his mother, texting.

Benji, where are you? You oughta been home an hour ago. I need to eat soon.

Got held up with something. Don't wait dinner on me.

OK. Are you sure you're alright? You sound funny.

He couldn't help smiling. *How the hell does she know what I sound like? It's a text!*

Fine, Mama. Gotta go now.

He stuck the phone back into his shirt pocket and crept closer to the corner of the building, staying in the deep shadows, as far from the light thrown by the night-watcher as possible. When he peeked around the edge of the warehouse, he could see that the plane had landed on a dirt strip in the middle of the pasture and was rolling quickly toward him, the buzzing of its props getting increasingly louder. Ben pressed himself tightly against the cold corrugated metal, staying out of sight. The plane came to a stop beside the building, and the pilot emerged. Two others came out of the warehouse and met him—one he recognized as Gil; the other, a woman, he also recognized by the barbed wire tattoo on her left arm. The pilot swung open the back hatch, climbed in, and handed out six parcels, each about the size of a shoe box, but heavy from the way they hefted them. And the three of them took the stuff inside. Ben recorded all of it on video with his cell phone and texted it to Junior.

They were up to something; that was pretty clear. And he was more convinced than ever it was something no-good. He really wished he could get close enough to hear their conversations to confirm it, but there didn't look to be any substantial cover or shadow between where he crouched and the door they'd gone into. *Too risky.* And besides, he reminded himself, it was out of his jurisdiction; he needed to leave it to Polk County to handle. Once out of earshot, he decided, he'd call Junior and fill him in. Ben backpedaled quietly to the opposite corner of the building then skirted the dark edge of the field back to his truck.

Once safely inside the cab, he dialed Junior's number and put the phone on speaker so he could drive.

"Brother," he said when Junior answered, "where you at?"

"Work. Sprained my ankle, been sittin' the night desk all week."

"You get my texts?"

"Yeah. What the hell is it and where?"

"Out at that warehouse I had you run the address on. MB something or other. I followed a couple of guys I was curious about out here from Buck's. You said there'd been planes buzzing the livestock, and that's one of them landin' there in the pasture in the picture I sent you. I saw them unloading some boxes of something and was close enough to hear a little of what they were saying. Something's going down tomorrow night. A truck's coming to take away whatever's in there, and even from outside it smelled like a whole lotta pot. And one of them mentioned something about lacing high-end inventory. Sounds like it's not just pot. And there's more. I think these guys may be involved in the death of a guy we pulled out of the Caddo the other day. Coroner ruled it accidental drowning. Now I'm not so sure."

"Damn."

"Yeah. A guy called Marty seems to be in charge. I overheard him talking to the guy I followed – that one's name's Stevens, Gil Stevens, with a 'v'. I broke up a fight between him and a buddy a few nights ago at Buck's."

"Damn," Junior said again. "Tomorrow night, you say? How many are there?"

Ben took a quick glance as he drove past the warehouse without slowing; he didn't want to call any attention to himself. Everything seemed buttoned up and quiet. The plane was still parked beside the building, but all the doors were now closed, everything was dark.

"Don't know. I saw four for sure: three men and a woman. I recognized her; she waits tables over at Buck's. Then there was the pilot that landed the plane. But I heard the one in charge, Marty, tell Gil to round up the crew. I don't know how many that is."

"They armed?"

"I didn't see anything, but I would assume if it's illegal pot or drugs, they are."

"I'll get with the sheriff and see if he'll authorize somebody out there to watch tonight. Sounds like we may need more manpower if we're going to bust this thing up tomorrow. If it's like you say, this one probably goes over to the state boys or the feds."

"Maybe. Either way, it's not Montgomery County's. I'm headed home now. Let me know what goes down."

"I'm on it, bro. Thanks for the follow up. We'll get these dirtbags."

CHAPTER 20
Love and Loss

The colorful lights of the Christmas tree shone from the front parlor window of the boarding house, welcoming JD and Maggie in with a touch of holiday cheer. They'd stopped at JD's house on the way to grab a bottle of wine for dinner.

"You don't think Miz Hendri will object, do you?" Maggie asked as they climbed the stairs to the porch. "She usually doesn't serve anything but tea with dinner, except on special occasions." The soft light from the flickering gas lanterns on either side of the front door bounced off the silver and gold ornaments in the evergreen wreath hanging there, making them glow as if they were lit from within and, she couldn't help noticing, casting dancing shadows across JD's high cheekbones, bringing out the strong lines of his face and, if it was possible, making it appear even more handsome.

"No," he said. "And besides, even a random Tuesday night's a special occasion when I'm with you, Sugar." He winked at her, kissed her playfully, and opened the door. "She won't mind."

As usual, the delicious aromas of a homecooked meal permeated the whole downstairs. Tonight's fare was simple: a fresh green salad and a rich, savory stew with big chunks of fork-tender beef and a half dozen different colorful vegetables in a flavorful, thick broth. And cornbread, of course, with butter. And jam. The Santa Ynez Valley pinot noir JD had brought was the perfect compliment. It was just the three of them tonight, with Papa still not back, no transient guests, and as yet no new long-term lodgers, though Miz Hendri mentioned that one was expected just after the new year. A writer who was seeking five or six months of solitude and few distractions to finish a book. She'd laughed that Caddo Bend should do nicely on both of those fronts. Maggie and Miz Hendri had speculated back and forth about what kind of book it was, what it might be about, and the fun of having a writer in residence, both curious if it might be someone famous. The name didn't ring a bell, but maybe, they speculated, it was an alias. JD for his part seemed to be ignoring them.

The stew was delicious, and Maggie had just gotten up to ladle herself another small serving from the tureen on the sideboard, working diligently to scoop up just the meat, celery, carrots, eggplant, and squash and avoid the many chunks of white potato without seeming to. She glanced over her shoulder to ask JD if he'd like more and noticed his bowl was still nearly full. She tried to recall if he'd taken a second serving but couldn't remember his doing so. *That's odd,* she thought, *he said he was starving earlier.* And he'd hardly touched his wine, which was especially unusual.

"JD?" She laid a hand on his shoulder and was alarmed to find the muscles lightly quivering beneath her touch. "Are you OK?"

For answer he gave a tight shake of his head and swallowed visibly. And then swallowed again. Then with a low groan, clutched his lower abdomen. Maggie immediately sat her bowl down on the table and dropped to her knees beside him. "What's wrong? Do you have belly cramps?" The pained expression contorting his face gave her the answer before he could even nod yes. She'd dropped her medical bag in the front hall and leapt up to retrieve it, coming back with the stethoscope already in her ears. She knelt again and listened. *Slight wheezing in his chest. Heart rate slow but regular. Bowel sounds hyperactive.* She felt his forehead. *Not feverish.* She pressed her fingers into the four quadrants of his abdomen, searching for any specific points of tenderness, but nothing seemed especially so. His lips were pinched into a tight line, and his eyes were closed. "JD, look at me. Open your eyes." When he finally opened them, they seemed unfocused, and the pupils were so large that their normally soft grey color appeared black. She grabbed a penlight from her bag and snapped it on.

The response of his pupils was sluggish. *Oh, my God, no! Just like Tommy.*
"JD, can you move? Can you stand and walk?" His lips moved, but she
couldn't understand his response if that's what it was. "Miz Hendri, can
you help me get him to his truck? I've got to get him to the clinic now!"

Henrietta McSwain was at least seventy years old and heavy, but despite some arthritis in her hip, she was robust and strong. With more alac-
rity than was her habit, she was at Maggie's side. "Tell me what it is you
need me to do."

"He's too heavy for me to fireman's carry by myself, but I think if I get
under his chest and drape his arms over my shoulders, I can lift with my
back and legs enough to move him if you can support some of the weight
of his lower body from behind." Maggie ran to the front door and opened
it, then grabbed her purse and dashed down the walk to open the door to
the truck and toss her purse inside. When she returned, she shoved JD and
his chair back to make room and squatted low in front of him, her back
to him, so she could take on his weight across her shoulders and back. She
pulled his arms one over each of her shoulders. "OK. I need you to grab
onto his belt, and when I stand pull up hard."

Miz Hendri's wrapped her knobby fingers around JD's belt at a loop
on either side of his jeans. "Ready," she said.

"On three. One, two, three!" Maggie held tightly to JD's wrists and
drove through her heels until her hips and legs were extended, and at the
same time Miz Hendri pulled upward on the jeans from behind. Together they were able to bring JD's semi-conscious form to its feet, his body
resting across and supported by Maggie's back. Then step by laborious
step they walked him to the front hall, down the two steps of the porch,
down the walk, and to the open door of the truck. Getting him inside
the cab took a bit of maneuvering, but they managed to turn him to the
side and let him fall laterally onto the seat. Maggie was able to shove him
forward and fold him at hips and knees enough to wedge his legs into

the floorboard space. "Now, call 9-1-1 and get an ambulance to the clinic ASAP. Tell them it is a poisoning, and it's urgent."

Maggie climbed into the driver's seat and sent up a prayer of thanks for keyless ignition; she'd not thought to get the keys from his jeans pocket. She pulled her phone from her purse and speed dialed Therma Faye, putting it on speaker to keep both hands free should she need them.

"What's up, Doc?" Tee answered, chuckling cheerfully at her lame, long-running joke.

"Tee," Maggie interrupted her. "Meet me at the clinic immediately. It's JD. He's in a bad way, like Tommy O'Connor. Bring Jimmy if he's there. And hurry!"

Maggie gunned the engine, speeding down Main Street toward the clinic, and in a few minutes careened into the back parking lot of the clinic, almost skidding into Therma Faye's car coming into the lot from the opposite direction. Jimmy was with her, thank God, and the three of them were able to carry JD's trembling body into the clinic. Maggie's heart was hammering so hard she thought it might break through her ribcage, not from the exertion but from fear and dread. She willed herself not to think about what could happen, not to think about who this was lying unconscious and quivering in her hands. She simply had to divorce herself from the emotion of it, put her medical mind in gear, and act.

"Take him to the treatment room," she said, nodding in that direction as they made their way down the hall. "Tee, it's just like Tommy, same kind of poisoning symptoms. I'll need to lavage his stomach, and we'll need to intubate him to do it safely." As they lay JD on the exam table his back arched suddenly, and he began to convulse violently. "Get an IV going, biggest bore we have. Use Ringer's. Quick! And when it's in, get him on the cardiac monitor."

"Jimmy," Therma Faye said, pressing her thunderstruck husband into service, "hold his arm still for me." She grabbed a padded arm board from the crash cart and placed it under JD's flailing elbow. "Now hold his arm tight against this board while I tape it." She struggled to wrap the self-adhering bandage around the board and arm. "Now hold it flat on the table; keep it still as you can." He blinked, wide-eyed, but did as instructed.

While Tee went to work getting the line in, Maggie opened the crash cart and made a quick scan looking for a vial of sux—succinyl choline—a powerful skeletal muscle relaxant. She couldn't intubate him while his jaws were clenched with seizing; she'd have to essentially paralyze him with the sux. It was a dangerous but necessary step that could prove fatal if she couldn't get the breathing tube in place quickly, because once she gave the drug he couldn't breathe on his own. She quickly assembled the necessary equipment—laryngoscope and endotracheal tube—and had them beside her, then snapped the tip off the glass vial of sux, drew up the dose, and injected it into the port of the IV line that Therma Faye had managed to secure. As the sux took effect, the spasmodic lurching diminished and ceased. Maggie moved quickly to the end of the table by JD's head, tipped his chin up, crouched down, and went to work. She opened his now-slack jaw to insert the blade of the scope only find his mouth filled with saliva that immediately ran out the sides.

"I need suction," she said. Therma Faye flipped on the suction motor, uncoiled the loops of tubing, and handed Maggie the tip. She suctioned the saliva away, then sighting down the scope before it could reaccumulate, she hooked the tip of the laryngoscope blade under his epiglottis lifting it forward to expose the vocal cords. When the endotracheal tube slipped uneventfully between the cords and into place, she let out a deep sigh of relief. Inflating the cuff on the tube to keep it in place, she quickly attached the Ambu bag, and gave it a strong, steady squeeze. "Jimmy, can you bag him?" His brows shot up and his eyes went wide again. Maggie fixed him with a stare that repeated the question wordlessly: *can you?*

He swallowed and gave her a tentative nod. "Yes'm, Doc, I think so. If you show me." He stepped beside her at JD's head.

"Do it like this." She demonstrated the squeeze again. "One steady full squeeze about every 6 or 7 seconds. Count it in your head in Mississippis." He smiled at her then and looked a little more confident. Maggie put her stethoscope in her ears and listened, again relieved to hear good breath sounds on both sides. "That's good, Jimmy, keep it up. Tee, mix the charcoal slurry and get the bucket set-up."

Therma Faye crossed to the cabinet and took down the container of activated charcoal. They always kept a liter of sterile irrigation water at the ready beside the charcoal in the cabinet. She opened the bottle, poured some of it into a plastic kidney basin, added 100 grams of the charcoal, and mixed it together with a tongue depressor. She sat the remainder of the liter in the sink in a basin she filled with hot tap water to warm the fluid to closer to body temperature before using it for the lavage.

Maggie snapped on a pair of latex gloves and retrieved the lavage tube from the drawer of the crash cart, tearing open its sterile packaging. Then she stretched it across from JD's head to his belly, estimating the length needed to reach his stomach. She lubricated the tube and inserted it into his mouth, feeding it carefully down into his stomach, then attached a large syringe and pulled back the plunger to suck the stomach contents up into it. The appearance of yellow-green stomach fluid in the tubing verified she'd hit the correct spot. Without x-ray, it was the only means she had to know if she'd placed it properly.

Before they began the lavage, she reached into the crash cart again and withdrew a vial of diazepam—Valium—a longer-acting muscle relaxant and anxiety reliever. She unwrapped a new syringe and needle, drew up 10 milligrams of the medication, and injected it into the port of the IV line. The paralytic effect of the sux would last only a few minutes, and she didn't want him to begin seizing again.

Satisfied it was safe to begin the process of washing out his stomach, Maggie removed the large syringe from the lavage tube and attached a small funnel, so she could pour the warmed irrigation fluid directly down the tube. Therma Faye handed her the liter bottle, and once she'd instilled about a quarter of it, she lowered the funnel and tubing below the level of the table and let it siphon into a gallon zip bag in a bucket that Tee had placed on the floor beside the table. The fluid back-flowed readily into the bag, bringing stomach contents with it. They repeated the procedure several times more until the fluid coming out of the tube ran clear, then they poured in the charcoal slurry and removed the tube.

"They're here, Doc," Therma Faye said with a look toward the back hall, as she took the tubing from Maggie's hands and deposited it into the sink. "I'll go let 'em in."

Maggie had been so absorbed in her work that she hadn't even registered the wail of the approaching siren or the sharp knocking on the back door. She bent to the bucket and zipped the seal on the bag of stomach contents that she labeled quickly with all the pertinent identifying information: what it contained, JD's name, birthdate, today's date, and her own initials. The hospital would need it to identify the poison, though Maggie had a gnawing worry that the root coins he'd so cavalierly eaten at the campsite were at fault. *Damn fool!* She should have slapped them out of his hand. *What was he thinking?*

The sounds of Therma Faye and the emergency team banging down the hallway pulled her back from contemplating what she was going to do to him when this was all over, and he was well. She recognized one of the EMTs as the spiky-haired woman who had transported Yesenia to Mercy only a few days ago, although she'd tinted her short platinum spikes a striking red in the interim. She'd been oddly grateful, then, that at least one member of the team would be a female, nonsensical as the thought perhaps was. Maggie quickly briefed the pair on everything she'd done thus far and what she knew of JD's history, including what he'd eaten today both the legit, which hadn't been much, and the suspect.

"Take good care of him," Maggie said to Spiky Hair as she and her partner transferred JD over to their stretcher and started to wheel him away.

"Goes without askin', Doctor," the woman replied, taking the bag of stomach contents Maggie handed her and laying it on JD's legs, continuing to talk as they rolled the stretcher quickly toward the door. "Not that it would matter, but JD and I went to high school together."

Maggie was struck once again how much more intwined the lives of people were in small town America compared to an urban setting, how many fewer degrees of separation. "Small world," she said.

"Yeah, but I'd hate to have to paint it," Spiky's partner joked without breaking stride.

"Wait!" Maggie ran after them. "I need his keys."

"Might wanta get his phone, too, Doc," he said.

She slipped the phone from the right back pocket of JD's jeans and the key to his truck from the front, then, reluctant to let him go, grabbed onto his hand, and walked beside the stretcher the remainder of the distance to the ambulance, finding at least a little solace in the steady, light pulse at his wrist. Therma Faye and Jimmy followed in their wake to the back parking lot. In the light of the moon, low and still nearly full, JD's normally sun-bronzed face looked ashy gray, like carved marble, the effect made more pronounced by the sharp contrast of his dark hair and the long fringe of black lashes that rested against the clammy pallor of his face. It made her heart ache with worry. She backed away reluctantly as the EMTs hoisted the stretcher into the back of the wagon.

"Dr. Mac," Therma Faye said, coming up beside her and putting an arm around her shoulder to hug her close in a much more familiar and motherly way than was her usual custom, "he's gonna be OK. He's tougher than a boot. You know that. He'll pull through whatever this is."

He was tough. A survivor. Maggie knew that in the depth of her soul, but she couldn't dispel the image of JD's handsome, smiling face as he casually popped the coins of the cooked root into his mouth and chewed. It dissolved like a swirling fog into the ghostly white face she'd just seen, and then into the specter of little Tommy O'Connor still comatose on a ventilator in Hot Springs, the whole pitiful tableau narrated like an episode of CSI with a voice over of Roy Owens detailing the high levels of some unknown plant toxin in Domingo Sanchez's dead body and the other two unidentified corpses now lying in the county morgue, and it chilled her to the marrow. She felt herself trembling. Therma Faye must have felt it as well because she began to vigorously rub Maggie's arm.

"You're freezin', honey," Therma Faye said. "Do you want us to drive you back to Miz Hendri's? Jimmy, go start the car and get it warmed up."

"Thanks, Tee, but no. I'm fine. I'll drive JD's truck back over to there and take my own car to Hot Springs." Maggie could see the worry on her nurse's face as she pulled away from her arm to go back inside. "I'm fine," she repeated. "Or I will be when I know he's stable. Thanks for coming in and for…everything." She squeezed Tee's hand and turned away, blinking back the tears that threatened to well in her eyes.

"OK, but you call me the minute you know anything. And if you need anything, anything at all."

"I will. I promise. Right now, I just want to get to Mercy." Maggie hurried back inside with Therma Faye following in her wake. *She looks about as frazzled as I feel,* Maggie thought. In her office she threw her purse over her shoulder and then stopped at the treatment room on her way out.

"I'll get everything cleaned up here. You go on," Therma Faye said, picking up the detritus of their recent activities from the floor around the table and stuffing it into the trash and bio-waste cans. "What do you want me to do about the appointments for tomorrow?"

"Tell Donna to reschedule everybody for later in the week. I'm not sure when I'll be back, but I'll let you know what I figure out. I may need to get a *locum tenens* to fill in for a few days."

"You stayin' the night there, then?" Therma Faye stoppered the sink and poured disinfectant solution into it, then filled the sink with hot water to soak the tubing, bucket, and funnel.

"I'm staying however long it takes to be sure he's OK."

CHAPTER 21
Divine Intervention

In the dark hours since they'd moved JD from the ER to a bed in the ICU, Maggie had sat near his bedside, perched in a vinyl-cushioned side chair, nursing a wretched cup of tepid hospital coffee, and listening to the rhythmic *click whoosh sigh* of the ventilator. The ICU doc had elected to keep him sedated with phenobarbital to keep his seizures at bay, a medically induced coma is what it was called, while they awaited the final toxicological results on his stomach contents and blood samples to determine what if anything else they might be able to do.

As she wasn't a spouse or immediate family and not on staff at Mercy, she'd had to fenagle her way in by asserting she was his primary care physician, which was in most respects true, and by some miracle the night charge nurse in the unit had let strict protocol slide. A small mercy, to be sure, but one she was grateful for.

She'd spent some of the time on her phone, searching online for information about plant toxins, finding and taking screen shots of several reasonable possibilities to show to JD when he woke up, which he would do she reassured herself. *He must!* Based on what she'd seen floating in the tin can at the Sanchez campsite, she'd decided the most probable suspect was a plant called *water hemlock*, a close relative, she couldn't help remembering, of the poison the philosopher Socrates had drunk in 399 BC in fulfilment of his death sentence. She shook the thought away. *Sometimes ignorance is bliss, and a steel trap memory is a curse instead of a blessing.* She read on.

In summer, the wiki entry said, water hemlock bore clusters of delicate small white flowers on slender stalks with foliage that looked enough like wild carrot, parsnip, or parsley that it often fooled amateur edibles foragers, who mistook it for one of those with sometimes tragic results. In December the stalks would be dry and bare, of course, but apparently the plant was stoutly poisonous in all four seasons and in all its parts from blossom to leaf to root whether fresh or dry. It could cause skin rashes if merely handled but was markedly toxic if ingested and could even poison a person who inhaled its airborne essence during mowing or clearing brush or in the smoke if the dead stalks were burned. *Wicked bad stuff.*

She googled up a PubMed article that informed her that the plant owed its toxicity to a group of piperidine alkaloids, most abundantly a chemical called *coniine*, that at first stimulates the nervous system causing—among other things—trembling, excessive salivation, difficulty walking or moving, and in some cases convulsions. A look of deep concern clouded Maggie's features as she read. *All Tommy's symptoms. And JD's.* Then it depressed the nervous system and could lead to respiratory failure, kidney failure, amnesia, coma, and sometimes death. The last word gripped her heart like an icy hand and froze the blood in her veins. *Death.* She simply refused to entertain the notion. It wouldn't happen. It couldn't. She wouldn't let it.

Further reading, however, did nothing to allay her fears. If it was water hemlock, there was no known antidote, nothing to counteract the toxin, nothing to be done beyond supportive care: the ventilator that breathed for him, the drugs that kept seizures at bay, the fluids that kept his blood pressure up and his kidneys functioning, and time to let his system clear the poison if it could. *Or if not,* her mind whispered, *coma and death.* She pushed those frightening specters from her consciousness again and scooted her chair close enough to the edge of the bed to hold his hand. His strong, artistic hand, so graceful in movement, stilled now by the slow, steady drip of sedative-laced fluid through the subclavian line into his vein. She brought his hand to her lips and kissed the back of it tenderly, rubbing her thumb over the prominent veins on it, willing the toxin coursing in the blood within them to be gone.

A chiming melody came from her purse: JD's phone. She reached in and pulled it out. It was a FaceTime call. *Oh my God! Akiko!* She stared at the display, frozen, unsure what to do. Obviously, his daughter and her grandmother in Japan had no idea what had happened to him. If she didn't answer they would be worried because they couldn't reach him. And they'd be even more worried if she did answer. How could she tell them this news? Could they even understand her if she tried? JD had told her Akiko spoke some English, but even so, Maggie could not be the person to tell her this. And she had no clue if the grandmother spoke English. *Calm down! Think! What can you do?* Surely, a five-year-old didn't have her own phone; the phone must belong to the grandmother. Maybe she could send a text message to the grandmother explaining things. She could write it out in English and put it through Google translate and paste that into a text. Wouldn't be perfect by a stretch, but maybe at least the basic facts would get through.

She took a long, calming breath and exhaled, then put her thumbs to work.

She copied the incoming number showing on the screen into her phone and began the text, **Dear...** and then realized she didn't know the woman's last name. She'd only ever heard JD speak of her as Namiko-san, and she feared it might be too forward or maybe even rude by cultural standards to address her by her first name. She deleted what she'd started and began again.

IMPORTANT MESSAGE regarding JD Langston from Dr. Maggie McKinley. I am contacting you with important information about your grandchild's father, JD Langston. He has been taken ill and is in Mercy General Hospital in Hot Springs, Arkansas, USA.

What more should she tell them? How much should she reveal about his condition? Probably best to go gently, let them absorb the information and wrap their heads around it in small bites. She continued,

He is improving and expected to recover in coming days.

She prayed that was all true; she was counting on it herself.

I will update you with any news. Please feel free to contact me if you have questions.

She added her cell number and email then re-read the message. Satisfied, she highlighted and copied it, and scrolled over to the browser to paste it into the translation window. She clicked TRANSLATE and the resultant Japanese appeared in two forms, as picture characters and words with letters. It was unfortunately all gibberish to her, but she hoped it wouldn't be so to the recipient. Unsure which version to use, she highlighted them both, copied, and pasted the translations into the text window of her phone above the English she'd written. Would Namiko even receive it? Or open it if she did? Surely a woman who used FaceTime used text. If not, she'd done about all she could do for now. She clicked SEND.

Outside the room there was a sudden commotion and a calm, monotone voice from the overhead pager, "Doctor Quickstep. Doctor Quickstep to the ICU." Maggie understood what that meant. There was likely not a doctor named Quickstep; it was a pseudonym, a ruse used to disguise calling the on-call cardiac arrest or 'code' team to a specific location within the hospital—in this case the ICU—without alarming the patients or visitors. In some hospitals it was Code Blue. In her residency it had been Dr. Heart, which caused occasional confusion because there really was a Dr. William Hart on staff. The students and residents always had to wait a beat before tearing off in response to the page to be sure whether it was Dr. Heart... Dr. Heart and they needed to run ASAP or Dr. Hart...Dr. William Hart, and they could finish their lunch.

She rose and walked to the door of JD's cubicle and could see that the commotion had localized across the ICU on the opposite side of the central nurses' station. A team of scrub-clad nurses, physicians, and respiratory techs crowded around the bed of the patient who was coding, a woman it appeared from the pronouns the team used. She could hear them working and picked up the muffled urgency in their voices as they called for the sequence of drugs that might save her.

"Clear!" She heard the physician's directive quite plainly, followed by the thumping discharge of the defibrillator and the suspended silence that followed as every eye in the room turned to the heart monitor to assess her response. "Clear!" again and with more urgency. Another discharge, but this time followed by the return of the rhythmic chirp of cardiac activity. Immediately the tenor of the room changed, urgency replaced by relief and calm. Crisis averted.

Maggie turned to go back into the room but stopped when she heard her name.

"Dr. McKinley, isn't it?"

She turned to see a familiar face under a tousled head of wavy salt and pepper hair. "Dr. Beasley," she said, recognizing the neurosurgeon who had recently operated on Papa walking toward her down the hall.

"I was going to call you tomorrow about Mr. Purifoy being discharged on Friday. Funny to run into you here. What brings you to the ICU so late, ma'am?" Maggie noticed again the quick, unconscious widening of his pupils as he approached her, though his manner remained the essence of courteous professionalism.

"My, uh," she glanced over her shoulder to the bed where JD's still form lay. "My boyfriend was taken ill this evening." She'd never actually spoken aloud of JD as her boyfriend, and it registered at once as an odd and oddly comforting feeling.

"Oh, I'm sorry to hear that. This would be the tall gentleman I initially mistook for you in the ER the other night?" His tight-lipped grin sheepish and slightly embarrassed as he recalled his earlier gaff. An expression so genuine that Maggie could almost forgive him the *faux pas*.

"Yes, JD Langston. In bed seven." She inclined her head toward the opened slider of JD's room. "We think he accidentally ingested a neurotoxic plant. He became violently ill quite suddenly."

"Did he? What plant? I only ask because I have a bit of knowledge in that field—toxicology, I mean."

"The tox results aren't back yet on his stomach contents, but I think it could have been water hemlock he misidentified as an edible root." She could see his pupils dilate again and wondered if it was concern and apprehension they mirrored or simply avid interest in a medical curiosity.

"Could I buy you a cup of coffee? We can discuss it further if you like. I was just in to check on a post-op, and I'm waiting on a stat lab."

Maggie looked again into JD's room. "I don't really want to get too far afield just yet."

"No problem. We can just grab a cup from the machine and sit next door in the family waiting area. I'd really like to help if I can." His smile seemed kind and genuine.

And so, she'd agreed but just for a few minutes. They'd sat with their coffees and spoken briefly about Papa and his remarkable progress. Beasley admitted he was impressed at his recuperative powers but voiced relief that he wouldn't be going home by himself; he thought it best to have someone with him for a week or two as he got his feet back under him. And then Maggie had filled him in on how JD came to have eaten the toxic plant. He'd asked what it looked like, how long the delay had been before the onset of symptoms, and what they'd been. She told him about what she'd witnessed, how quickly he'd gone from joking and laughing to almost unconscious and the actions she'd taken after the symptoms had appeared. He reiterated what she already had read about hemlock: no antidote, no specific medicine or remedy available. Getting it out fast was the most important, then supportive care.

"He's very lucky you were who was with him. Very," Beasley reiterated. "Had you not been medically trained and right at hand, he would likely have-"

Maggie interrupted quietly, "Died. Yes, I know. And he's a long way from out of the woods even now, isn't he?"

Beasley shifted uneasily in his chair. "Yes," he said with some reluctance. "If it was hemlock, and from your description I'd lay odds on it, he's not out of the woods yet."

Maggie could feel a stinging begin behind her eyes that she knew wasn't just fatigue, but she refused to go weak and weepy in front of this man. She rose from her chair and extended her hand. "I'd better get back. Thank you for the information and the coffee, Dr. Beasley."

"Cam, please," he said, taking her proffered hand loosely in his.

"Cam," she repeated with an incline of her head. She gave his hand a firm shake and extracted her own. "If you'll excuse me, I need to check on JD."

She entered JD's dim room and out of habit scanned the screens on all the medical equipment arrayed around him, noting his heart rate, blood pressure, oxygen saturation, urine output. Forcing herself to think medically, analytically, and clinically helped keep her fear at bay. She touched his cheek and stared with an intensity that she prayed penetrated the fog of the meds and the poison with her message: *I'm here. I'm with you.* She sat in the chair and picked up his hand again. It was warm, but appropriately so, and that was good.

She must have drifted off, because she was jarred awake by the buzz of a text alert. She pulled her phone from her pocket. *Charlotte?* It was very late in North Carolina. The letters of the text swam in her sleepy vision, and she blinked several times to clear it up.

MM - RU OK?

She'd called Charlotte from the ER waiting room hours ago and filled her in on what had happened and promised to call again when she knew something. Technically, she had no new information, but really the time had just gotten away from her, and she felt a pang of guilt for leaving her dangling. There'd been no one in her life for the last decade who'd been more a rock to cling to in any storm than Charlotte, except perhaps recently the man who lay sedated in the bed beside her chair. She texted back

Yeah. Mostly.

How's our boy?

It made Maggie smile that she referred to JD as 'our' boy.

Still out and on ventilator.

Sista. So sorry. Can u talk?

Maggie kissed JD's hand and whispered to him, "I'll be right back." She walked next door to the family waiting room, mercifully empty now, and called Charlotte, who answered on the first ring.

"Char, it's the middle of the night. Why are you still up?"

"Couldn't sleep." She paused, and Maggie could hear her concern even in the silence. "Worried about you is all. Look, I just needed to hear from the horse's mouth that the horse is OK."

"The horse is fine. It's the rider I'm worried about. But thank you for caring, my sista."

"And as for the rider? Any news?"

"His vitals are good. They've got him intubated and deeply sedated for the time being. They're doing all they can."

"Any idea what it was?"

"Nothing more than I knew earlier. A toxin of some kind. I've been scouring the internet for possibilities and most of them are pretty scary."

"Do you need me to come? Ford's home and can handle the heathens. I can be on a plane out of Charlotte first thing in the morning."

"It's too close to Christmas. You need to be home with the angels. And I'm fine. Really. I'm just going to stay right here 'til he wakes up."

"What about the clinic?"

"I spoke with Dan Milsap, the doc who covered for me back in October when I went to New York, and he's booked up through the holidays, but he recommended somebody who can give me a few days of emergency coverage between now and Christmas at least. So, I'm set there."

"Do you have a hotel room? You can't just stay at the hospital around the clock."

"Well, I'm staying here tonight at least, and we'll see what tomorrow brings. JD was planning to pick up Papa when he's released from rehab Friday morning, so I'll need to do that. I'll probably just stay here until then. Once I get him situated at Miz Hendri's, I can shower and change and grab a few things. And I'd like to check in on Rose Ellen, then come back here."

"I'm praying he'll have turned the corner by then."

"Your lips to God's ear. But he looks so…" Maggie paused; her throat suddenly tightened, and for a moment she couldn't speak. She swallowed and tried clearing it a few times, but the strain was still evident in her voice when she finally continued. "He looks so pale… and fragile. And…" she felt the welling tears slide down her cheeks.

"And he's not fragile. He's strong." Charlotte's words were firm, but her sweet Southern drawl, as always, was a balm to Maggie's bruised psyche. "And you are strong. Remember that."

"Thank you," her words scarcely more than whispered.

"Get some sleep now, Sista."

"You do the same. Love you."

Maggie slipped quietly back into JD's room and took up her post in the chair. She laid her head on her folded arms, one hand resting on his, and tried to sleep, lulled by the steady chirp of the heart monitor and the *click whoosh sigh* of the ventilator that punctuated the silence.

***

On Thursday evening Ben Bradford was just getting out of the shower when his cell buzzed. Twice in rapid succession. He dried his hands and picked it up. A text from Junior Davis, his buddy at Polk County.

Got 'em!

That could only mean one thing: the MB Warehouse operation. Ben was running a bit late to pick Donna up, but he couldn't resist hearing how it all went down, a thrill even if a vicarious one. He called him back.

"Junior! What all happened?"

"All great, bro! I just came in tonight, and nobody can talk about anything else. It was mag-ni-freakin-fique! You knew the DEA boys took it. Vernon was pissed."

"Yeah, I bet he was." Ben knew well how galling it was for a small county department to do all the legwork and have the State or the Feds swoop in and scoop up all the glory. He put the phone on speaker, so he could shave and talk. "So, tell me everything." Ben wiped a port hole in the fogged-up mirror with a hand towel and smeared his face with foam. He didn't have much of a beard and could easily have managed with the slap-dash of an electric razor, but he liked the feel of hot water and foam.

"Team went out covert and early. In the wee hours. We—I say we, but it was half us and half Feds—scattered in the woods out south and east of the warehouse and had eyes on all day. Buncha guys in pick-ups showed up throughout the morning and then late afternoon a big black tractor trailer pulled in. Big. Like a fifty-footer."

Ben let the razor glide through the foam, rinsing it off in hot water in the sink after each stroke. "Big warehouse. Must be tons of weed in there." He tipped his chin up to shave the underside.

"I heard that. Anyway, once they'd got a good start on loading the shit up, we brought the big patrol wagon in and blocked the drive entrance. Ain't no other way out but over the pasture and through the woods. So, then we charged in on the warehouse from both directions and hoovered up the entire illegal contents of the warehouse – bales and bales of marijuana and multiple boxes of illegal oxycontin tablets. And the whole stinkin' bunch of em. All except the boss man himself. He lit out soon as the wagon showed up."

"How? If the only way out was blocked, I mean?"

"Plane. He and I guess the guy flying it took off—literally—apparently with whatever records and cash there was, since none was found on the premises."

Ben rinsed his face in the hot water and patted it dry with the towel. "Well, that sucks."

"Yeah, tail number on the plane was covered, too. FAA's alerted but who knows if they can track it? But, all in all, it was good. Lotta shit off the street. Lotta dirtbags, too. And all thanks to you, bro. Not that you'll get the credit you deserve for it."

Ben slipped on his jeans and shrugged into a t-shirt and thick wool sweater. "Thanks for the update, Junior, but I gotta run. I'm late to pick up my lady."

"Give her my condolences." Ben could hear the smirk in his voice.

"Later."

The other alert was a voice mail from Maggie. He listened on his way out the door and the news it contained of what had happened with JD made him heart sick. She'd also asked him to look in on Papa and Miz Hendri, which he would do and was glad to do. He closed his eyes and said a little prayer for JD's recovery.

CHAPTER 22
Homecoming

On Friday morning, Maggie pulled her car into the patient loading spot at the curb in front of the rehabilitation wing at Mercy and climbed out. Papa sat, bundled in a parka, waiting in a wheelchair under the entrance canopy. He sported a bandage still on the left side of his head, where a portion of his thick, white hair had been shaved away, giving him a bit of an asymmetric punk rocker look that she found amusing. She hopped out and came around to greet him. The patient transportation associate, aka the hospital aide pushing his chair, bent down and said something Maggie couldn't hear, but whatever it was left Papa smiling and chuckling.

Maggie helped the aide load Papa into the car, stowed his bags and a half dozen arrangements of get-well flowers in the back, and climbed into the driver's seat. He didn't yet know what had happened to JD, and it was going to be up to her to fill him in. Knowing how easily medical information became medical misinformation when related third hand by a layman, she didn't want to leave it to Miz Hendri, who herself didn't know the whole of it yet, to explain it to him. She decided to wait until they got back to Caddo Bend, and she could bring them both up to speed at once.

"So, what was so funny?" she asked as they headed down the hospital drive toward the intersection with the main road.

"Oh, back there you mean?" He chuckled again. "He wanted to know if you were my girlfriend or my daughter. Gave me a laugh. I told him you were my granddaughter. That's not technically true, of course, but true enough." That he would consider her so brought a joy to her heart and made her quite happy.

"I'm sorry the girls couldn't stay longer, but it's great you got to see both of them." The light turned, and she pulled out into traffic. "I'm glad I got to meet Julia, at least."

"Me, too. I knew you two would get on. She was here for three days which was nice. Eliza couldn't stay but just over night. She and Brooks are in the middle the wine production cycle at the vineyard, and what with the kids getting out for the holidays, she couldn't be away longer." He gazed softly into the mid-distance, and Maggie wondered if something was troubling him; he wasn't one to complain.

"Are you feeling OK, Papa?" she asked. He turned to look at her and nodded, then reached over to pat her arm affectionately.

"I'm fine. Just thinking about the girls. Warms an old man's heart to see them, but the visits always go by too fast. Julia wants me to fly to Atlanta for the holidays; I told her I'd like to, but I'm not sure I'll be quite up to the trip just yet. Maybe later in the new year."

"Well, I hope you're up for a big holiday celebration here. I know Miz Hendri plans to pull out all the stops food-wise in honor of your return. You know food equals love in her world."

"Indeed, I do. Her cooking can put about twenty pounds of love on you before you can turn around."

Getting out of town was a bit more of a hassle than usual and took substantially longer than Maggie had expected. They inched their way down Central Avenue, the city's main thoroughfare, with cars already bumper to bumper at half past nine. Most unusual in her—admittedly—limited experience with Hot Springs streets.

"What's the deal with all the traffic?" she drummed her fingers impatiently on the steering wheel. She was eager to get Papa home, gather her things, and get back to JD.

"Oaklawn. Racetrack folks coming in, I expect," Papa said. Maggie had no clue what he was talking about, and her expression must have betrayed her confusion. "Oaklawn Park," Papa explained. "Race meet starts in a couple of weeks, so all the track workers are starting to come in. It's one of the major old-line thoroughbred tracks in the country. Built just after the turn of the century. The previous one, I mean. Nineteen hundred and something."

"I had no idea," she said, tapping the brakes to arrest her glacial forward motion after gaining another few feet on their journey. "I went to Saratoga once to see the Travers Stakes with my, uh, my former boyfriend and his parents. Some close friend of theirs had a horse entered, I think."

"Another beautiful old track. Older than Oaklawn, but just by a nose, to put it in racing terms." He grinned at his joke. "June and I used to enjoy coming over for a day at the races years ago, but anymore I tend to avoid the crowds. Depending on your perspective they're both a blessing and a curse, the crowds I mean. The town's population nearly doubles in size during the season, and that brings big revenues to hotels, motels, restaurants, and bars, and other retail establishments. They welcome it; their success depends on those months. But the traffic it also brings is horrendous in a town built for half as many cars and people."

"Well, I can attest to the truth of that part," she said, eyeing the solid string of cars ahead. They were at a dead standstill now and a few frustrated drivers had begun to honk. She closed her eyes and took a calming breath. Despite having spent most of her adult life in Manhattan, where traffic jams and honking in protest were something of an official pastime, she'd never gotten used to the noise pollution of it. Honking ought to be reserved for when there was something important to honk about, like to warn of imminent danger. And she didn't view being frustrated as a just cause.

"The locals hate the traffic," Papa went on, "but what they hate worse is you can't get a table at a restaurant from January through April. It's no time to be in Hot Springs unless you're there to go to the racetrack. Much as Hendri loves to soak in the hot mineral waters for her rheumatism, we never even try to come over to take the baths during the race meet. Can't get a room. Or if you can, the price is sky high."

The day had started out with pale blue skies and even some weak sunshine, but a storm was in the forecast for this afternoon, and already the skies in the west had taken on that leaden look that usually meant rain. Maggie had found to her delight that late autumn in Arkansas could be glorious, crisply cool and colorful. It could also sometimes be gray, overcast, sullen, and rainy and that looked to be the order of the day today. She scanned the low clouds massing overhead and prayed the rain would hold off until she could get Papa settled at Miz Hendri's and make a quick turn-around. She wanted to be back at Mercy well ahead of the storm.

They escaped the snarl of city traffic at last and before long settled into a peaceful, companionable silence as they rolled through a bucolic tableau of pine stands, bare hardwoods, and golden-brown pastures on the two-lane highway toward Caddo Bend. Maggie was relieved, and a bit surprised, that so far Papa had not questioned why she'd come to retrieve him and not JD. She must have been thinking a bit too loudly about it, because like a gypsy mind reader he picked up on it.

"I assume, at some point, you'll tell me what's caused those dark smudges under your pretty eyes." The look in his own warm brown ones was kind and concerned but left little doubt that he expected an answer.

After a quick glance at him, she gave a nervous half smile and directed her attention back at the road. She'd sent a message to Papa yesterday that something had come up, and JD wasn't going to be able to drive him, assuring him that she would be there as scheduled. She hadn't wanted to speak to him directly for just this reason, afraid that he'd hear the worry in her voice. Apparently, he could hear the worry in her mind.

"Nothing. Just didn't get much sleep the last couple of nights." And that last part was completely true; slumped in the chair beside JD's bed in the ICU for two nights running is not especially a recipe for restful sleep.

"Mmm." He nodded his head and narrowed his eyes. "And does lack of sleep also explain the anxiety that's rolling off you in waves?"

Maggie took a deep breath and puffed it out in a long stream. *No way around it but through it. How to begin?* "There's been a problem," she said finally and over the next miles told him all that had occurred.

"So, he's still unconscious, medically sedated you said?" She nodded in answer. "For how much longer?"

"We don't know." Which was true, but she didn't yet want to add on the real possibilities of continued coma, kidney failure, and death, and she was unsure just how much to tell him. She settled on truthful but spare. "The course is quite variable. The toxicology report on his stomach contents finally arrived this morning and confirmed that what he ate was the toxic root of a plant called water hemlock. It has no known antidote other than time for the body to detoxify the poison, so all that can be done in the meantime is to keep him sedated and maintain all his vital functions." The look of worry on Papa's face made her wish she hadn't shared even that much yet. And she'd have to repeat it for Miz Hendri once they were back home.

"Hemlock," he said, nodding. "I know it well. Sometimes the cows or horses will get into it. Sickens them, too. Can cause them to abort a calf or foal. Can even kill them if they get enough."

The awful realization that hemlock could fell a half-ton animal struck Maggie like a punch in the gut. She'd read it, of course, but hearing it uttered aloud somehow made it scarier. She noticed she was gripping the steering wheel so tightly her knuckles blanched white. She loosened her grip and made a conscious effort to relax her shoulders.

"On the positive side," she said, aiming for an upbeat tone and trying to steer the conversation away from the dire downside possibilities, "Tommy O'Connor apparently ingested the same toxin, and he's come around and is off the ventilator now."

"That's good news. For JD, too, isn't it? I mean he's a lot bigger and stronger than little Tommy is."

"He is." *But not as big as a horse.* She signaled and pulled out to get around a slow-moving tractor. Papa waved amiably to the driver as they passed him.

"How's Molly?" he said. "She must be beside herself with worry. She does dote on that boy." He said softly. "Parents and grandparents aren't supposed to have favorites, you know. You adore them all, equally, of course. You'd step in front of a train for any one of them. But sometimes there's a special connection from birth with a child or a grandchild that goes beyond just the bonds of heart and blood. That's how it is with Tommy and Molly."

Having had no grandparents to dote on her—her father having been orphaned at a young age himself and her mother's parents having died before she could remember them—and being an only child, she couldn't say she really did know, but nodded in agreement anyway. "I haven't actually had a chance to speak to her myself; I haven't seen her at the café since Tommy got sick. But I talked to Velma—as you'd expect, she's been keeping close tabs on her—and you're right; Velma said Molly was pretty shaken up by it. I'm sure she's doing better now that Tommy's improving."

Maggie flicked on her left blinker and eased the SUV off the highway, over the railroad crossing, and down the steep incline to the low water bridge across the Caddo, then gunned the motor to climb the hill on the far side and head down the country road that led into Caddo Bend. Schools had let out for the Christmas break, and the tiny downtown, fully bedecked for the holidays, was bustling with traffic, or as bustling as such a small town ever got. Cars were parked in every spot around the square and others waiting with blinkers flashing. Traffic in so picturesque a setting seemed somehow more charming than the traffic they'd struggled through leaving Hot Springs.

She pulled into her usual spot behind the boarding house and hopped out to help Papa.

He waved her off amiably. "I'm not that decrepit," he said laughing, "not yet anyway." He was right, of course. Papa was a very fit septuagenarian, but he'd just suffered a serious head injury, and Maggie thought she could detect a tiny degree of hesitance in his step, a tiny bit of sluggishness when he swung the right leg forward. But it was critical to his full recovery that he use the weakened muscles as much as possible, at least within reason. So, she grabbed his bag from the back and followed behind him, close enough to help if needed, but far enough behind to let him make his own way.

Miz Hendri opened the kitchen door and held the screen wide for them. "Manny!" The joy at seeing her old friend back on his feet was inscribed clearly on her plump face. "Come in, come in. I have pound cake, still warm. And coffee."

"Told ya," Maggie leaned forward to whisper in Papa's ear. "It's going to be a holiday eat-a-thon. Starting in about 60 seconds."

The three of them sat around the big wooden farmhouse table in the warm kitchen enjoying the moist, buttery cake and coffee, as Maggie, between small pinches of pound cake, repeated what she'd told Papa in the car for Miz Hendri's benefit. Pound cake wasn't the sort of breakfast she usually indulged in, but she had to admit it was comforting, and Miz Hendri's was the best she'd ever tasted. Bar none. But beyond that, it was important for Miz Hendri to feel she was helping in some small way in a situation far out of her control.

"He will recover," Miz Hendri said with utter conviction, staring at her hands that fiddled idly with the tissue tucked under the expandable band of the old watch she always wore. "I know this."

Maggie reached across the table and squeezed her arm. "We're going to do everything possible to make sure of that." She affirmed her intent with a nod and stood. "If you two are good here, I'm going to grab a shower and pack a few things, then run a couple of errands and get back over to the hospital. Papa, I'll take your bag back to the guest room for you."

"You'll leave it right there and go do what you need to." He gave her a look that said he'd brook no argument about it. "As I said, I'm not decrepit. I'll get it back there just fine. Now you run on; get your errands done before the rain moves in."

***

Max Rosenthal laid the crystal pendant across the suede pad on the display counter and let Maggie pick it up. The fine links of silver chain were so light and delicate you could almost imagine them floating. The crystal and its silver setting were similar to her own pendant, just a touch smaller. She held the chain by its clasp and let the quartz needle dangle; it caught the light and threw a rainbow onto the jeweler's crisp white shirtfront.

"It's perfect," Maggie said. "She's going to love it."

"Would you wait and let me wrap it for you?"

"If it wouldn't be too much trouble, that would be a huge help. I'd like to drop it at the Davis's before I go back to..." she left the thought unfinished, not wanting to open that avenue of conversation right now.

"No trouble at all. Just between us," he lowered his voice and leaned forward, "I actually quite enjoy wrapping gifts, which I guess is a good thing if you own a jewelry store." Max disappeared into the back room of the tiny shop and reemerged in a few minutes with a long, slender gift box, crisply wrapped in embossed gold foil and a fluffy bow of deep red organza, finished with a silk holly sprig. As elegantly festive as any she'd ever seen in the shops on Fifth Avenue.

"It's so pretty she may not want to open it!"

"Ah, but when she does…" The knowing nod and smile that lit up his eyes told her his passion for jewelry lay as much in the joy a piece brought to both giver and receiver as in the artistry of the physical creation itself. Though his pride in the finished pendant was evident, too. "She'll treasure it, doctor."

"I can't thank you enough, Mr. Rosenthal." He looked the reminder over the rims of his glasses. "Max," she corrected herself. "It really is just perfect."

CHAPTER 23
A Christmas Gift

She'd taken the package over to give to Rose Ellen but found no one at home. Probably out among the bustling throng on the square, she assumed, everybody hoping to get the last of their shopping done before the front came in tonight. As she climbed back into her car, her cell buzzed.

"This is Dr. McKinley."

"Doctor," the high-pitched male voice immediately rang a bell. "This is Michael Pearcy calling from Mercy ICU."

"Michael. Is everything OK with Baby Sanchez… Milagro, I mean? The nurse I spoke to early this morning said he was much improved."

"Oh, uh, yes ma'am. I think he's fine, but I'm not in the NICU today. I'm in the adult unit, and I'm calling about your patient Mr. Langston."

The words struck like a blow; she was almost afraid to ask. "What's wrong?"

"The doctors decided to lighten the sedation a little while ago."

"What? I thought they were going to wait until this evening. At least that's what Dr. Jensen told me before I left this morning. I wanted to be there."

"I don't know what changed. I know his numbers looked good this morning, and it's been three days now. I think Dr. Jensen's heading out of town for the holidays tonight, and maybe she didn't want to delay it 'til this evening in case something…" he paused, leaving the rest of the thought unspoken. "Anyway, the deal is when they tried to bring him up, he became extremely agitated and combative. Pulled his tube out and everything.

"He extubated himself?" She felt a moment of panic at the damage pulling out an endotracheal tube with the cuff still inflated could do to the vocal cords and, she thought miserably, to the voice.

"Yeah. They had just deflated the cuff and were getting ready to pull the tube and he grabbed it." Maggie breathed a major sigh of relief that at least they'd deflated the cuff. Michael went on. "He's pretty strong, even sick as he's been, and Dr. Jensen and the nurse had a struggle restraining him and getting him back under. There was a note in the chart to call you with any change, so…"

That a former Army Ranger would become combative under such circumstances wasn't actually surprising to Maggie. Agitation and combativeness were not uncommon symptoms when bringing someone out of deep sedation. Concerning, but not surprising. It could even be a positive sign that his brain function was normal beneath the veil of the sedative and in that sense, it gave her reason to hope.

"I'm heading back right now," Maggie said. "I should be there within the hour."

As Maggie headed out of town, the skies behind her had gone from leaden to a darker gray, with that eerie greenish cast that she'd learned sometimes preceded a storm front's arrival. The wind had picked up and was rattling the bare tops of the trees, sending the few dry leaves that still clung to their branches swirling before it. She glanced at the dash and saw the outside temp had dropped to near freezing. The storm was coming in sooner than expected. And, indeed, as she waited at the intersection of the main highway toward Hot Springs a few fat drops splattered on the windshield. The clouds were rolling in from the west, and she was headed east; if luck was with her, perhaps she could outrun the storm. At least she was going to try. But the best laid plans, as the saying goes, and before she'd gone a dozen miles the rain had instead caught her. She cranked the wiper speed up and the car's speed down.

"I freaking hate driving in the rain," she muttered to herself. To be fair, she mused, she hated even riding in the rain. "Just go slow. Keep calm and go slow."

Even slowed to a crawl, the downpour was so heavy that she could scarcely make out the white lines demarcating the center of the road ahead. The right side of the county highway was a soft shoulder of dirt, rocks, and scrubby grass with a worrisome drainage ditch of varying depth beyond that. Maggie took a deep breath to calm herself and strained to see. Cranking the wipers to their highest speed helped visibility only minimally; despite it, heart racing, she pressed on.

After driving through it for what seemed to Maggie like a day and a half but was in fact only about ten or fifteen minutes the rain slacked off to a light *pitter patter*. However, its drumming was replaced by the ominous *tick tick tick* of sleet pellets now hitting the windshield, a sound that rattled her almost as much as the deluge. Though it was only mid-afternoon, it had already grown so dark that her car's lights had come on. She could see the sparkle of the falling pellets reflected in the beams, and the glistening accumulation of sleet at the edges of the road and in the low spots. She reflexively slowed her speed. It was going to take more than the hour she'd planned to get there, and she cursed the weather again. And sped up a little.

Music. The thought inserted itself into her brain unbidden. *That's what's missing. Something soft and soothing. Maybe a little Harry Connick, Jr.* She took her phone from its perch in the cup holder and thumbed it awake, then scrolled through her iTunes playlist for *Only You*, glancing intermittently at the road. She looked back down just a second to click on the album and set the phone back into the cup. When she looked up again, two glowing green circles shone directly in front of her, the reflected retinas of a large deer standing stock still in her lane. She swerved sharply toward the center of the road to miss it, but the animal wheeled and bolted back in the direction it had come, toward the opposite ditch, and directly into her path. It smashed into the front of the car with a shuddering thud that sent its body cartwheeling up over the hood and into her windshield, completely obscuring her view of the road and sending the car sliding sideways on the slick, icy pavement. She fought to regain control of the car, which responded by fishtailing back and forth. Her overcorrection and the unbalanced weight of the deer's carcass sent the SUV careening toward the shoulder where the soft dirt and grass slowed its progress, but not enough to keep it from nosing over into the ditch, where it now rested at a steep angle with its butt in the air. The deer's body slowly slipped off the hood, leaving a wide smear of mud, blood, and fur across the windshield. Harry's voice crooned *the very thought of you, and I forget to do the little ordinary things that everyone ought to do...*

Maggie was stunned and emotionally shaken, but after a quick inventory of body parts, she pronounced herself unhurt physically, though she knew she'd be sore tomorrow from the jolts. She was less certain of the condition of her car, and pretty sure the deer was dead. She turned off the engine and Harry, activated the emergency flashers, and climbed out to survey the damage. The spitting sleet and rain hit her in her in the face as soon as the door opened, and she reached into the back for her jacket, pulling it on and zipping it to the neck.

The embankment of the drainage ditch offered little in the way of good traction, and her boots slipped in the sleet and mud as she made her way to the front of the car. There appeared to be some minor damage to the front grill and the hood, otherwise everything seemed to be okay, but what did she know? Very little about assessing the travel worthiness of a car. The deer, however, was not okay. Of that she was pretty sure. It lay in the bottom of the ditch, its neck awkwardly bent, tongue lolling to one side, its big brown eyes staring blankly. She knelt beside it and lay her hand on its still-warm body. *What the hell was it doing out on the road in a sleet storm?*

"I'm so sorry," she whispered, repeating the words over and over as she gently stroked its neck. "I'm so very sorry." There was nothing she could have done to avoid hitting the deer, she knew that, but somehow that knowledge didn't quell the sorrow that filled her heart at its needless death. The icy wind whipped her long hair, which had come loose from its claw clip in the accident, and it lashed in stinging wet strokes across her face; she brushed it away, shivering already in the cold, and pulled up her hood.

She wasn't sure what she should do next, so lacking a better plan, she climbed back into the relative warmth of the car to think. The SUV had front wheel drive, but maybe she could just back it out and be on her way. She started the car and put it in reverse, but the embankment of the ditch was too steep, and the tires couldn't catch enough purchase to pull it up. They spun vigorously but didn't engage, and the car stayed put. How the hell was she going to get out of this ditch? She'd have to call AAA and get them to send a tow truck. And who knew how long that would take? *Won't be any sooner for waiting.* She grabbed up her phone and thumbed up the AAA app, watching the activation wheel whirl…and whirl…and whirl. A glance at the display told her why. *No service.* She fought down the impulse to throw the phone out the window. *Lotta good that would do!* She closed her eyes and leaned back against her seat. Now what?

She was cold. She cranked up the heater and let it blow on high until the inside of the car was toasty warm and her breath had fogged up all the windows. Then she turned it off and tried again to think. She cleared her mind and forced herself to take slow, deep breaths, in-two-three-four and out-two-three-four, over and over until she restored her calm. And yet no solution emerged. She appeared to be stuck, literally and figuratively. The car wouldn't budge. The rain and sleet continued to fall outside, so she couldn't very well walk to the next town. She'd freeze. Besides, in the dark with all her attention focused on driving in the downpour, she wasn't completely sure where she was or how far the next town might be, and no cell service meant no GPS clues to her whereabouts. Surely someone would come along the road before long late on a Friday afternoon. Her best course would be to stay put and wait it out. She cranked the engine back on to run the heater for a couple of minutes of added warmth and tried to relax again, taking deep breaths, rolling her tight shoulders backward and forward, consciously pulling them away from her ears and envisioning dropping the points of her shoulder blades into her back pockets. When she finally felt some of the tightness ease from her muscles, she checked her phone again. *Still no service.* And her battery was half down. She plugged it into the charging port, unsure whether that port worked if the engine was off. She decided to let the engine run for a bit longer just in case, thankful she'd filled up the tank at Eddie's on the way out of town. And, admittedly, she didn't mind the added warmth. She locked all the doors, pulled on her gloves, and closed her eyes to wait. After a few minutes she turned the motor off and sat in the silence, calling up images of JD smiling, laughing, the feel of his strong arms around her, his lips on hers.

She must have drifted off, because she was startled awake by a man's voice and a sharp rapping on the window beside her head. It had grown dark outside, truly dark, not storm dark, but the immediate area was awash in light from a big truck pulled up behind her on the shoulder. The blurry outline of a man's face was barely visible, peering at her through the condensation on the glass. Her heart was beating like a trip hammer, and she was pretty sure rolling down the window to a stranger on a desolate road at night was not a particularly smart idea. She wiped a porthole of visibility in the fogged-up glass and was immediately relieved to see the slimmer but still recognizable face of Boyce Dugan. She rolled down the glass.

"Boyce! Thank goodness it's you."

"Thank the Lord you're okay. When I saw your little silver ute in the ditch, I thought…" he stopped and just shook his head. "You *are* okay, aren't ya ma'am?"

"I am. I'm fine now."

"What the heck happened?"

"A deer." She pointed toward the front of the car. "I, uh… I hit a deer and lost control of the car. It skidded on the slick road, and I landed here and couldn't back out."

Boyce walked to the front of the car and saw the deer in question. "How long you been here?"

"I'm not sure. What time is it now?" She picked up her phone to check, but he answered the question immediately.

"About half past six."

"I guess about three hours then." From the temperature in the car, which was glacial, that seemed about right. She was stiff and sore and cold. At least the sleet and rain had stopped.

"Fuh…" he breathed out, arresting himself in mid word. "Oh, sorry, Doc. Didn't mean to…" he shrugged. "Shame I didn't get by sooner. We coulda salvaged that deer meat, but now it's not been bled out. It'd be real gamey. I'll call Game and Fish. First, let's see if we can get you out of here. I got a cable I can hook onto the back of your car, and then I think we can pull it out. Hang on here."

Boyce sprinted back to the tractor truck that was pulled up behind her. It wasn't pulling a trailer at present, and Maggie thought it looked something like just the head of a giant caterpillar without the body and all the legs. It was so close she could feel the deep rumble of its big diesel engine in her chest as he backed it out and turned it around. When Boyce had it eased into place at the canted-up rear end of her SUV, he hopped out again and flopped down on the wet shoulder to attach a large hook and cable to the undercarriage of the car. "Could you put it in neutral first and be sure the parking brake is off?"

Maggie did as instructed.

"You might oughta get out while we do this. If you don't mind, ma'am."

She nodded and climbed out into the cold night air, then walked well away from her car. He clambered back up into the cab of the big rig and put it in gear, slowly moving the powerful tractor forward and easily pulling her Toyota back up onto the road.

Once he had the SUV safe and securely up on the shoulder, he stopped and climbed back down. "Let me take a look at everything. Be sure it's all OK before you go."

Boyce took his flashlight out and looked under the hood, then crawled in the freezing mud up under the car, looked it all over, got into it and drove it up the road a half mile or so and back. "I think it'll get you there, ma'am," he said when he'd parked it again. "But if you don't mind, I'll just drive behind you 'til you get wherever it is you're goin'. Just in case."

Maggie was deeply moved by the kindness of his gesture. Unexpected and utterly welcome. "I'd be very grateful, Boyce. I need to get over to Hot Springs. To Mercy General."

"I know. I heard about JD. I'm so sorry. I hope he's gonna be OK."

"Me, too, Boyce. Me, too."

Boyce and his bobtail, as he'd told her the bodyless caterpillar truck configuration was called, shadowed her all the way to the Mercy parking lot, where at the lot entrance she stopped, got out, and walked back to his window. "Thank you again. You were a life saver tonight."

"Turn about's fair play, Doc. You saved mine." With a nod to her he put the big rig in reverse and backed out, leaving her standing in the chill, washed in the glare of his headlamps. She waved goodbye and stood for a moment longer watching him go until another car pulled into the entrance lane, and its driver gave her a 'move it' glower. She shrugged an apology, climbed back into her car, grabbed the ticket from the box, and found a place to park in the relative safety offered by the illumination from a light pole in the lot.

Maggie slipped into the dark quiet of JD's ICU cubicle. Nothing visually seemed to have changed since she'd left this morning to get Papa home. He lay still as before, but something was different. It took her a moment to realize what it was: no rhythmic *click whoosh sigh*. The ventilator was gone now. Michael Pearcy had told her JD had pulled out his endotracheal tube in his agitated state, and apparently the docs had found it unnecessary to re-intubate him—something Michael hadn't told her—but for which she was grateful as she realized that meant he was able to breath adequately on his own now, and that was something of a blessing in itself. She lifted the crystal pendant she wore to her lips and kissed the needle, murmuring a prayer of thanks, then pulled the chair up beside his bed and picked up his hand, her fingers automatically seeking the pulse point at his wrist, finding it strong and steady. Another comfort. She began to talk softly to him, not knowing if he could hear her, but the connection brought some comfort.

"I picked Papa up for you today," she began. "He's doing very well. Both he and Miz Hendri sent their good thoughts to you. As did just about everybody else I encountered today in Caddo Bend." She smiled as she stroked the ropey vein on the back of his hand, pressing the blood out of it and watching it immediately refill, further proof his heart was pumping and his blood was circulating; he was alive and for now that's all she could ask. "It's Friday night, in case you were wondering. Christmas is just four days away, and you promised we'd sing carols around the big tree on the square on Christmas eve. I'm going to hold you to that promise." She reached into her purse and got out her phone and earbuds, thumbing up her iTunes playlist. "I thought maybe you needed to practice up, so I brought along some favorites." She scooted the chair closer to the head of his bed so she could put one earbud into JD's ear and the other into her own. She laid her head on the mattress next to his pillow as Nat King Cole's mellow voice intoned *Chestnuts roasting on an open fire...* Over the next hour the playlist flipped through the selections: Bing Crosby's *White Christmas*, Kathleen Battle's ethereal *Ave Maria*, Kings College Cambridge boys' choir singing one her favorite old English carols, *Ding Dong Merrily on High*, and on and on through an eclectic cannon of choral Christmas music. Did he hear it? She couldn't know, but she hoped so. Music could mend a wounded heart, could soothe a battered soul; would it heal a poisoned body?

The playlist ended with Karen Carpenter's *I'll Be Home for Christmas*, which Maggie preferred to all other recordings of it; her voice was like a cup of Angelina's hot chocolate, deep and rich, warm and comforting. But hearing the words brought renewed tightness to her throat, and she swallowed to relieve the lump. *I'll be home for Christmas, if only in my dreams...* When the song ended, she removed the earbuds and wound up their cord, tucking them and her phone back into her purse.

She was utterly exhausted. She'd had little sleep for going on three days. She'd hit a deer in the driving rain and sleet and landed in a freezing ditch. She was bruised emotionally and physically. She just wanted to sleep, and her body was more than willing; it was in fact weary to the bone, but her brain still wouldn't let go. For some reason a medical article she'd once read with the title 'Therapeutic effects of intercessory prayer in the ICU' kept surfacing in her mind. One of the oldest therapies known to humankind, a prayer to a higher power for recovery. The phenomenon had been scientifically studied a number of times, and the results were equivocal: sometimes the data showed it seemed to help, others it didn't. But when science and medicine offered such limited options, her Catholic upbringing weighed on the side of appealing to the angels. She laid her forehead against the back of his hand and silently prayed for God's mercy.

She recited the rosary. She prayed to St. Raphael, patron saint of healing. She prayed to her parents in heaven to intercede if they could.

She felt his hand move, ever so slightly, just a twitch of movement that she at first thought she might have imagined. So, she squeezed his hand again more strongly, and there was another response. A flexion of his fingers. Slight but undeniable. She rose to her feet and brought her face close to his, so close she could feel the warmth of his breath on her cheek. She took his face in both her hands and spoke directly to him, praying her words would penetrate the sedative fog. "Don't you leave me, JD Langston. Now that I've found you, you cannot leave me. I cannot lose you. I will not." The corners of his lips, relaxed in drugged sleep, seemed to lift for an instant, an ephemeral suggestion of a smile. She wasn't sure she'd seen it, so she kissed him full on the lips, tenderly. And the corners of his lips lifted again. Then his left eye opened just a crack, and Maggie's heart leaped.

"JD," Maggie cried out, her heart now pounding in her chest. "JD! Can you hear me?"

The other eye opened, and he looked at her face, unfocused.

"JD! Do you know where you are? Do you know what happened to you?" She searched his face and saw his confusion as he struggled to answer. *Don't confuse him! One question at a time!*

"No," his voice a hoarse whisper, almost inaudible to her even so close. He scanned the room around him for a moment. "A hospital?"

Thank God he's conscious and oriented to place! Maggie took his hand in hers. Next step was to determine if he was oriented to person. "And do you know your name?"

"Langston," he breathed out. "JD… Langston." He closed his eyes again, and she thought he'd gone back under. Then he whispered, "You're so beautiful. What's your name?"

About the Author

Mary Dan Eades is a native Arkansan and a retired medical doctor, who trained at the University of Arkansas, and who, with her husband, developed and operated a chain of urgent care family medicine clinics for many years. She is a *New York Times* best-selling author, having authored or co-authored 14 non-fiction books on nutrition, health, and fitness, including the best-seller *Protein Power* (Bantam 1996) as well as multiple books on low-carb and sous vide cooking.

She is married to the physician, author, and blogger Michael Eades. The couple have three sons (all married to strong, smart women) and seven grandchildren. The Drs. Eades divide their time between Montecito, California and Dallas, Texas. Find out more about them at proteinpower.com.

Eye of the Storm is Dr. Eades' second book in the Caddo Bend series that follows the life, loves, and medical adventures of Dr. Maggie McKinley in the small rural Arkansas town. If you enjoyed meeting Maggie, Jeff, JD, and all the characters that populate Caddo Bend, you'll want to look for Caddo Bend Book 3 expected to be released in 2023. Visit caddobendbooks.com for publication updates and more. Follow and engage with other readers on the CaddoBendSeries Facebook page, on Twitter @ caddobend, and at Instagram.com/caddobendseries.

www.ingramcontent.com/pod-product-compliance
Lightning Source LLC
Chambersburg PA
CBHW020947260626
47169CB00006B/1857